ACCLAIM FOR

A GROWN-UP KIND OF PRETTY

"This is a quirky mystery that serves up a delicious blend of likeable characters, plot twists, and life as seen through the eyes of three remarkable women...The dialogue is authentic and the writing insightful and unexpectedly witty." —*Tucson Citizen*

"Liza, as the unreliable narrator, is used to perfection in this warm family story that teeters between emotional highs and lows, laughter and tears. Book groups will eat this up."

—*Library Journal*

"A GROWN-UP KIND OF PRETTY is a clever, hilarious, wild adventure of a mystery that immediately pulls you in. You'll be desperate [illegible] es beneath the willow tree—an[illegible] of Joshilyn Jackson's latest."

[illegible] of *Don't Breathe a Word* and *Promise Not to Tell*

"Funny, suspenseful, heartbreaking, and triumphant...a truly riveting read." —*Burlington Times-News* (NC)

"Joshilyn Jackson has done it again. Her Southern fiction style can't be perceived as anything but pure talent. Her entertaining, if not quirky, characters keep you caught up in a world that has mystery, love, and devotion."

—*Fredericksburg Free Lance-Star* (VA)

"Highly immersive...a compelling page turner."

—*Publishers Weekly*

"The story is Southern in vernacular but modernized in a way that other Southern stories often are not...Jackson's engrossing fifth novel is a mystery, comedy, and drama wrapped up in one."

—*BookPage*

"[A GROWN-UP KIND OF PRETTY] would leave you broken-hearted if you could stop laughing long enough. But in a Joshilyn Jackson book, that will never happen. If you're new to Jackson, you'll discover her knack for hitching misfortune to wicked humor within the first few pages." —*Atlanta Journal-Constitution*

"Jackson taunts us with clever prose and revealing chapters disguised as an all-in-one thriller, mystery, and love story...Jackson delivers more than a fresh story; she transports readers to a world of superb fiction decorated with spunky language and unforgettable characters." —Examiner.com

"Reading A GROWN-UP KIND OF PRETTY feels a lot like falling in love: giddy and enthralling and a little bit dangerous. It's a heart-thumping mystery, an edge-of-your-seat drama, and a fiercely sweet comedy all at once, with a fistful of crazy-brave characters who reach up from the wild pages and grip your heart. I loved this book about what it means to be a family for its big heart, its pitch-perfect dialogue, and the clever plot twists I've come to expect from Jackson. Book clubs take note: Here's your next pick!" —Sara Gruen, author of *Water for Elephants* and *Ape House*

"Snappy dialogue with a Southern twang, spiritual uplift, and undeniably likable characters." —*Kirkus Reviews*

"Compelling...Jackson introduces some truly appalling villains as well as a handful of affable supporting characters...The Slocumb women are easy to root for." —*Miami Herald-Tribune*

"An entertaining Southern whodunit." —*All You* Magazine

"Jackson's too clever to let her mystery be exactly the one you expect, and her heroines are too stubborn to be the victims their circumstances should dictate. Despite the heavy subject matter, Big and Mosey are delightfully sassy." —*Philadelphia City Paper*

"A GROWN-UP KIND OF PRETTY proves again that Joshilyn Jackson is one of the best writers of the new generation. This spellbinding novel unfolds through the voices of three women in one family: a grandmother, a mother, a young daughter. Jackson renders each of these women with vivid tenderness, ferocity, and great humor, so that the family itself becomes the fourth vital character in the story. You will find yourself rooting for them all, to the very last page." —Mark Childress, author of *Georgia Bottoms* and *Crazy in Alabama*

"Gripping." —*Times Picayune*

"In her latest Southern Gothic joyride, Joshilyn Jackson creates an unforgettable story of generational dysfunction and sloppily buried secrets." —*Atlanta Magazine*

"Madness! Mayhem! Laughter! Tears! Emotional roller coasters, old lies, and an unmarked grave propel the Slocumb women into action. Joshilyn Jackson's signature style explodes in A GROWN-UP KIND OF PRETTY. Buckle up and enjoy!"
—Adriana Trigiani, author of *Very Valentine*

"More than a Southern whodunit; it's a tale that probes deeper and asks the reader to consider universal themes of self-identity, family, and love...The novel moves quickly, and Jackson gives each character an interesting story line."

—*Charleston Post and Courier* (SC)

"Stepping into the worlds created by Joshilyn Jackson is a lot like enjoying a sumptuous summer day in the South, nestled on the front porch swing drinking a glass of sweet tea with your best friends. Except in Jackson's world, the tea is spiked, your friends are heart-warming, hilarious women, and there may very well be a body in the trunk of one of their cars...[A] captivating tale filled with plot twists and characters with, well, plenty of character."

—*Huntsville Times* (AL)

a grown-up kind *of* pretty

Also by Joshilyn Jackson

gods in Alabama

Between, Georgia

The Girl Who Stopped Swimming

Backseat Saints

a grown-up kind *of* pretty

JOSHILYN JACKSON

GRAND CENTRAL
PUBLISHING

NEW YORK BOSTON

Lydia Netzer's interview "The South Changes, The South Stays The Same: An Interview with Joshilyn Jackson" is printed here in modified form with kind permission of *The Chattahoochee Review*.

Grand Central Publishing
Hachette Book Group
237 Park Avenue
New York, NY 10017

www.HachetteBookGroup.com

Printed in the United States of America

RRD-C

Originally published in hardcover by Grand Central Publishing.

First trade edition: September 2012

10 9 8 7 6 5 4 3 2 1

Grand Central Publishing is a division of Hachette Book Group, Inc.

The Library of Congress has cataloged the hardcover edition as follows:

Jackson, Joshilyn.
A grown up kind of pretty / Joshilyn Jackson. -- 1st ed.
p. cm.
Summary: "A novel that follows a young woman's search for the truth about who her mother really is"--Provided by publisher.
ISBN 978-0-446-58235-3
1. Mothers and daughters--Fiction. I. Title.
PS3610.A3525G76 2012
813'.6--dc22

2011004744

ISBN 978-0-446-58236-0 (pbk.)

For Angela and Jenny, the girls at the end of the world

Acknowledgments

Glorious thanks to the brilliant Helen Atsma. She's an old-school, hands-on, invested editor—thank God—fearless and whip-smart. I see her fingerprints all through this book and, as Mosey might say, the book is hella better for them.

Thanks, as always, to my longtime friend and agent, Jacques de Spoelberch. He starts pushing me the second I look comfortable, and I love him for it. Caryn Karmatz Rudy is more than a friend and former editor; she's a voice I always trust.

Grand Central Publishing has consistently gone the extra mile (more like the extra width of a mighty nation) to back my work. I sing their names aloud, probably to the tune of some old-school, righteous Springsteen hit: Jamie Raab, Deb Futter, Martha "Inimitable" Otis, Karen "Incomparable" Torres (isn't it weird how they have the same middle initial?), Chris Barba, Cheryl Rozier, Evan Boorstyn, Elly Weisenberg, Nancy Wiese, Nicole Bond, Peggy Holm, Liz Connor, Thom Whatley, Toni Marotta, Carolyn J. Kurek, Emily Griffin, Celia Johnson, and Bernadette Murphy. I lift a glass and toast with a mighty STET/OK the work of Maureen Sugden. I will remember always the kindness and support of Les Pockell.

As I wrote this book, Lydia Netzer, Karen Abbott, and Sara Gruen acted as an odd, unholy trinity. Sara had her wise finger on the pulse of Mosey from the first word. Karen, my whoodie, insisted I not prudishly shy from Big's (absolutely necessary, sorry, Mom) sex scenes. Lydia was Liza's advocate, demanding that I find a way to give my lost girl a voice. All three holed up with me in various hidey-spots, armed with laptops and liquor. My best working times were side-by-silent-side with them, each of us buried in our own imaginary landscape. I can't imagine how people write books without friends like these. I bask in their collective radiance.

Thanks to Gray James, for her valuable anthropological expertise (the girl knows bones!) and her even more valuable friendship. My Atlanta writing group—Anna Schachner and Reid Jensen—are sexy, sexy beasts: relentless, honest, bold, and talented. Thanks to Mir Kamin for early reads and for being part of the full and plate-ly fellowship that is rounded out by Kira Martin. I am not the elephant plate.

Donna Baker, CTRS, the supervisor for therapeutic recreation services at the Emory University Hospital Center for Rehabilitation Medicine, and Dr. Ray G. Jones Jr. were wise and generous as I researched brain injury and recovery. Emergency room nurse Julie Oestriech was, as always, my go-to girl for information about the likely medical fallout from my characters' less savory ideas. Any mistakes are mine alone.

A secret decoder ring message to my Best Beloveds at *Faster than Kudzu*, and to the evangelical handsellers who are still singing out for books in this rapidly changing industry, and to my bonded set of dedicated monster-killers in the Vents: You are my very favorite one.

Long live Jack Reacher, who taught me-n-Mosey the difference between a SIG and a Glock.

I have two families who keep my heart safe: The first begins with Scott—of course and ever and only—and with Sam and Maisy Jane, our amazing collaborations. Also Bob and Betty Jackson, Bobby and Julie, Daniel and Erin Virginia, Jane and Auntie

Assilon. The second is my family at Macland Presbyterian, especially the odd, good eggs of smallgroup. They love me through my best and my worst, along with the wild bunch of Irish pub–churched Emergent Cohorts who stand shoulder to shoulder on the slanted sidewalk and try to make the world a warmer place.

Most of all, I thank you, if you are one of those sainted people who respond to my books, who like my redemption-infested stories and my weird, imaginary friends. You are the ones who spread the word; because of you, I get to keep this job I love. Thank you, thank you, thank you.

I'll keep writing as long as you keep reading.

a
grown-up
kind *of*
pretty

PROLOGUE

Big

My daughter, Liza, put her heart in a silver box and buried it under the willow tree in our backyard. Or as close to under that tree as she could anyway. The thick web of roots shunted her off to the side, to the place where the willow's long fingers trailed down. They swept back and forth across the troubled earth, helping Liza smooth away the dig marks.

It was foolish. There's no way to hide things underground in Mississippi. Our rich, wet soil turns every winter burial into a spring planting. Over the years Liza's heart, small and cold and broken as it was, grew into a host of secrets that could ruin us all and cost us Mosey, Liza's own little girl. I can't blame Liza, though. She was young and hurt, and she did the best she could.

And after all, I'm the damn fool who went and dug it up.

I should have known better; I was turning forty-five, and that meant it was a trouble year. Every fifteen years God flicks at us with one careless finger and we spin helplessly off into the darkness. I'd known that Old Testament–style plagues of Egypt would be stalking my family the second that December ticked over into January.

Now, I try not to be overly superstitious; I like black cats about as much as I like any other color cat, and I'll go straight under any number of ladders if you put the right kind of pie on the other side. But the hold the number fifteen has on my family, there's no natural explanation.

I was fifteen when I gave birth to Liza. Then, fifteen years later, Liza had her own girl. Not a hard pattern to catch on to. Liza and I had been prepping, in our separate ways, for this year ever since Mosey was four and kept holding hands with the same chubby blond boy at the park. I'd spent double for organic milk because I'd heard that the hormones in the regular stuff could make little girls bud early and jump-start their periods. Liza worked nights and I worked days, so one of us was always around to keep tabs on where Mosey was and who she was there with. Liza was vigilant for any hint that Mosey was walking in a bad direction, and Liza would know; when it came to mapping all the bad ways adolescent girls could go, Liza had been Magellan. And she was so strong-willed, I never could pull her back to some more reasonable path. . . .

I remember taking Liza down to the beach when she was two, young enough to have forgotten she'd seen waves the summer before. She came to the ocean like it was a mystery. She sat by my towel on her fat bottom, made fatter by her damp Huggies, and she patty-caked the sand and stared at the blue-green water, mesmerized. I'd never seen Liza sit so still, so long. After a couple hours, I packed up and told her it was time to go home. Her whole face went mulish. She stood up and braced her little legs against me, readying for a battle.

"Wannit," she said.

"What do you want, Little?" I asked, and she pointed her baby finger right at the waves.

I laughed. I couldn't help it. She responded by digging her toes into the sand, and I could read savage kickings and the wailings of the damned in her face. I didn't have anything inside me to match it.

I tried to misdirect, saying in cheery tones, "Aren't you ready for snack time, Liza-Little? I've got pizza-flavored Goldfish crackers at home."

She ignored the bribe and repeated "Wannit!"—demanding I pack up the water and the sand and the deep blue sky above with half a hundred seagulls and pelicans wheeling around and bring it home and put it in her room. I looked at the rigid set of her spine, her set jaw, and I was already so tired of the fight we were about to have. She was willing to die on this hill, on any old hill, and I wasn't.

I told her she could have it. I gave the child the Gulf of Mexico, just like that, and then I picked her up and we stood looking at her ocean. After a minute I turned my back, and she shifted in my arms so she could still see. She rested her cheek against my shoulder, and I swayed back and forth to the rhythm of the surf. I stood that way for at least a half an hour, until she fell asleep. All the while the waves crept closer, as if the very tide were trying to appease her by coming in and packing itself up into my beach bag.

I know that some folks think Liza was so wild and willful because she didn't have a daddy to speak of and her mother was a teenage dumb-ass. Maybe so. I admit she bent me like a weed to her wind, but I was a woman grown now, and no one could say I hadn't done a good job raising Mosey. Mosey was a peach, right up until the trouble year came.

I was caught off guard, even though from the first minute of January all the way to June I had my eyes on the horizon, trying to see whatever might be coming for us. It never occurred to me I might be looking in all the wrong directions. I never thought to look under, never suspected we'd been living on a fault line for years.

Then summer came, and Liza had her stroke. I thought that was it. Surely losing most of my own daughter was enough to feed and silence even God. How could that not be all the trouble we were due, and more?

So I went digging, and what I unearthed would pull Liza down into the black of her own past, would lead Mosey so astray I wasn't sure that I would ever find her, and would finally land me here: standing outside the glass wall of a fishbowl conference room full of lawyers and their legal books. Not a one of them was on my side. All I had was me, the truth, and an empty Dixie cup. I don't think the lawyers cared a fig about the truth, so it was pretty much me and the cup.

I'd never before thought of "custody" as an ugly word. To me it meant that the police had the bad guys, so the streets were peaceful and the dark corners of the garden were safe. But today that good word had turned on me, gone purely ugly. Today it meant this cold-eyed crew was coming after Mosey.

I could have put an ad up on the Craigslist and tried to get one of my own: "Desperately seeking lawyer. Must like long walks on the beach, not getting paid, and losing." I hear there's a whole mess of lawyers just like that; they keep an office between Mermaid Cove and the Unicorn Forest.

I wished for Lawrence beside me. He'd been on the job, as cops say, for twenty-some years now; he ought to be able to stare down a few lawyers. He could make it their silence to break instead of mine. If Lawrence was with me, if he even knew I was here, he'd have my hand in his. I knew what he would tell me. That I should trade anything, surrender anything, sacrifice anything, but not let go of Mosey.

I knew better than any person breathing how much he'd given up for his own little boys; I was one of the things he'd given up.

I imagined his low-set rumble of a whisper in my ear, tried to hear him telling me that I could fight for Mosey, now, because he knew how hard I'd fought for Liza. But I knew better. He hadn't been around when I fetched up pregnant. I never said boo. I was so scared I didn't even tell my folks I was knocked up until I was almost through my fourth month. One night my mother gave me the fish eye after dinner and told me to skip dessert. She said I'd been eating like a trucker recently and I had a new thickness round my middle that she found unbecoming in a girl. That's when my secret came blurting out.

The very next day, they carted me to a strange doctor a town away. They picked one with a Jewish name, thinking he would be pro-choice. After he examined me, with Momma in the room, Daddy joined us. They started asking him about "discreet options," and all four of us knew what that meant. I sat there, naked under my cotton gown, my arms wrapped tight around Liza inside me. I looked at my own bare feet, and I let them ask. I didn't say a word.

Lordy, but they had picked the wrong doctor. He asked them, in a deep, judgmental voice, if they had any idea just how far along I was. He showed them a picture of a five-month fetus, its kicky little feet, eyes squinched tight against the watery black around it. He added, in dark tones like a sorrowing Christ, "We're way past routing out a blastula here, you know. If she really wants to terminate, you'll have to take her to Louisiana. They do that sort of thing in New Orleans." His tone made it clear he thought New Orleans was a den of godless, baby-killing vipers. My folks must have felt spanked up one side of their thin Baptist skins and down the other.

So they took me back home, and I never had to fight. If I'd been in my first trimester, I'd have had the abortion with no idea whether I wanted it or not. But I was halfway through, and I'd fallen in love with her.

Liza had quickened, which was the perfect word for what she felt like, popping back and forth inside me like a sea monkey. That's how I pictured her, too. Not like the actual ones. I ordered the actual ones once, and they were only white, specky-size brine shrimp. One of mine got huge, like head-of-a-pin size. Then he ate all his brothers and swam around so swollen up and hateful that I finally flushed that fat old cannibal down the toilet. I pictured Liza more like the sea monkeys they showed in the ads, little smiley merpeople with crowns and friendly, waving hands. If I'd known her better then, I'd have pictured a sea monkey wielding a flaming sword.

But today my Liza wasn't in any physical shape to take on anyone. She was still trying like hell to fight her way back to using language and crossing the room without a walker. I was on my own.

The cool-eyed woman sitting in the center looked up and saw me through the glass wall. She was dressed in white and had a man on either side of her, both in sleek, dark suits. The three of them looked to me like an evil ice-cream sandwich, corpse-cold, waiting for me to walk in and begin. There was a cut-crystal pitcher of water on their side of the table and three matching tumblers sweating from the ice, each one set neat on a coaster to protect the dark cherry gloss on the table. My own cup was waxed paper, and it was sitting in my purse, bone-dry.

The woman's jacket was spotless. I can never wear white. I drip coffee down my boobs, first thing. She was older than me, but she looked my age, maybe younger. It wasn't like I was going gently into that good night either. I hid my strands of gray in highlights, moisturized like it was my religion, and I could still fit into my favorite Levi's. But she'd had a little work done, as they say. Good work. Not the obvious things like those actresses whose lips look like inflamed cat intestines, just her jawline was crepe-free and her eyes had that wide, lifted look. She had a couple of smile lines, but they were almost too shallow to mention; that may have been from a lifetime's underuse. The men on either side of her had set their foreheads into stern rumples, but hers looked like an egg. Nobody past fifty has a brow that smooth without Botox, especially not while saddling up to rough-ride and rule the law as if it were her own nasty-tempered pony.

I'd come here today to beg, to plead for them not to take Mosey. Fifteen was a hard year, and they'd be sending her to a place where no one knew she still woke up scared in thunderstorms. That she worried at her lower lip with her fingers when she was lying. That you couldn't make her talk by asking questions, but if you left her be and got real busy in the kitchen, she'd come boost herself up onto the counter and swing her feet and spill her guts. That her old one-eyed boo-bunny was hidden under her pillow and she slept with one hand stuffed under, clutching him.

If they took her from me, I didn't even know where she'd be going. I'd seen the worst-case scenario, though, and it was an apple gone wholly bad. There was no place to put your teeth where you wouldn't get a mouthful of a foul, grainy mash with worms in it. Pure poison. I wanted to ask them to leave Mosey be for her own sake, not mine, but I looked into those six cold eyes, now all staring me down through the glass wall, and I knew that it was fruitless. She was a pawn, here, not a person.

So the question was, would I let these corpse-cold bastards come after my granddaughter without a fight, without every bit of fight I ever had? I didn't see a way to win, so what did it matter if I kicked and flailed? You want the ocean? Have the ocean. You want my Mosey, this girl I helped Liza raise? Hell, I'd done most of the raising, truth be told and Liza being Liza. I'd taught Mosey the ABC song, tied her shoes a million times, been her Brownie troop leader. Last year I'd gotten up an hour early every day to try and figure out algebra with her. It was the worst grade she ever got, but we were both so proud of that C-plus we'd held hands and danced around the kitchen hooting and cheering when her report card came.

Standing outside that glass wall, I believed I had come to the awful end of everything. My family has long been familiar with that territory. Liza came across it at the Calvary High End-of-School Luau. Mosey, the day I hired Tyler Baines to take down the willow tree in our backyard.

But for me? It was standing at that window. I tried to preload my mouth with some fruitless begging, and the words stuck in my throat. I had this vision of Mosey in her best dress, the one with a thousand little flowers making up the print, standing on our front porch with all her things packed up in Liza's battered duffel. I saw it as she turned to me, felt it as she wrapped her skinny monkey arms around me, heard it as she whispered, "Bye, Big."

That's when I understood that what I did today was a message. Even if I lost, if Mosey was being driven away from the only home she remembered in a sleek official car, it would absolutely matter. She'd be alone, afraid, and with good reason; she had to know, know down to the bone, that I had fought like hell. That I would always stand with her and fight like hell. That the second after the sleek car pulled away, I'd be in my Malibu, seeing where she landed, sitting outside. Law or no law, she was mine.

I took a deep breath in, as painful and surprising as a baby's first. I straightened my spine and swallowed, though my mouth was paper-dry. I got the Dixie cup out of my bag, and I shoved my way through that door. I banged it down directly in front of them, like a flimsy barrier dividing the table. It made a scuffing noise against the wood, too soft to count as my first gunshot, but it was all I had.

I set it down between me and them, and I went to war.

CHAPTER ONE

Mosey

I NEVER WOULD have known about the other Mosey Slocumb if Tyler Baines hadn't brought his mullet head and a chain saw over to murder my mom's willow tree. I wouldn't have bet someone else's dollar that Tyler Baines, of all people, would be the one to discover her. Tyler Baines was not the discovery type. He was more the patchy-chin-pubes, tats, dirty-white-truck type. He was totally hooked on Red Man, too, so he spewed brown juice like a cricket everyplace he went. Last year my mom nicknamed him the Mighty Un–Butt Crack, because she said he was a single flash of ass plumage away from being the walking definition of redneck.

"It's like he wears mom jeans," she'd said, and I'd reached for a pencil. I'd been supposed to write down three examples of irony for freshman English, and Liza was barefoot in low-rise thrift-store Calvins that showed her silver belly ring, talking about Tyler Baines's mom jeans while he mowed our lawn. But I'd given it up before I dug out paper; I'd been exiled to Baptist school for more than half a year by then, long enough to know that Mrs. Rickett wouldn't like any irony example that involved thong underpants.

Tyler Baines was the last person on the planet my mom would have wanted laying hairy hands on her sacred willow. Before my mom had her brain event, I never even saw him have a conversation with her face. He talked lower, like he thought her boobs had microphones in them and if he aimed right he could order up a chili-dog combo.

For a couple of weeks after the brain event, my mom didn't talk at all. Now if she said one of her slurry words made mostly out of vowels when Tyler was around, he'd goggle at a spot past her good shoulder with his egg-size eyes, whites showing all the way around, and ask me or Big, "Liza says what, now?"

The morning he came to murder the willow seemed like any stupid Tuesday, with me at the breakfast table trying to eat civics facts and toast at the same time and Big scrambling eggs and stirring them into grits for my mom. Liza sat at our old butcher-block table staring at the faded pomegranates on the kitchen wallpaper like her mind was far, far away. So far that she couldn't quite get to it.

These days I liked to sit in Big's old chair, beside the half of Liza that looked like her, even though she sat too still. I felt guilty for picking to sit by the good half, like a magic monkey paw had read my wish for a more mommishy mom and it had broken Liza and left me this. Still, it was better than sitting by her right side, where her bottom lip hung a little slack and sometimes drooled and she kept her bad arm cuddled against her side like a hurt bird tucks his wing.

Big set the bowl of eggs and grits on the table, then picked up a spoon and wrapped my mom's good hand around it.

"Liza. Liza-Little? You see your breakfast?" Big said, and waited until Liza blinked and looked down, making her "yes" noise.

Big had fixed herself a plate, too, and she sat down still wearing Big-style flannel pj's that practically billowed around her teeny body. The clock said she ought to cram a slice of toast in her mouth and run to shimmy into her tweed skirt and bank blouse, which was the color of old mustard and had this vile, floppy bow at the neck.

I said, "You're not going in to work?"

"I took a half day off," Big said, not meeting my eyes, and I felt a nervous little serpent uncurling in my belly.

"Is this about the pool again?" Big'd had a pool guy out to the house last week, but he said that to fit a pool inside the backyard fence we had to take out Liza's willow. That should have ended it right there; the willow was sacred. All my mom's yearly pins from Narcotics Anonymous were pressed deep into its bark. She hung that tree with twinkle lights every year when she got a new one. Those pins were like a love carving that read "Liza + Sobriety" inside a puffy heart. Big should have been laughing at the very idea of taking it out, but instead her lips pursed up and she shushed at me, fast and quiet, darting a glance at Liza.

"Big, you can't—"

"Toast!" Big interrupted. "Put it in your gobhole, please."

Big took Mom's spoon and helped her eat another bite of grits and eggs, then wheeled her away into the den. That was wrong, too. Big always made Liza get in the walker after breakfast. I heard the TV go on, and then Big came back to get Liza's morning meds.

She talked soft while she opened each bottle and dropped the pills into a coffee cup. "Your mom didn't get any better until they started working with her in the water. That's when she started saying 'yes' and 'no,' and now she's got at least eight words I can make out. She hasn't added a word except for 'Mosey-baby' since she got home."

Math's my weakest subject, but even I could figure that Big plus a pool and WebMD didn't equal the team of physical therapists who worked with Liza while she was still in that aftercare place.

"It's almost fall. She'll hardly get to use it, even."

Big was heading into the den, but she paused long enough to grab Liza's juice cup and say, "We get a discount if we do it now. No one else is thinking about pools, and we'll get a good couple of weeks in before it's too cold. Don't fret. I got her NA pins out, and I put them in my jewelry box." Then she turned her back and left. Before the swinging doors had swooshed closed behind her, I'd whipped my cell phone out of my back pocket and was texting Roger.

911! Pool v/s willow. Big 4 pool.

I could hear the TV fellow with the poofy girl hair talking about weather, every word clear as the day he was promising. Big had the TV on twice as loud as normal. Almost immediately my phone vibrated in my hands.

Roger's text said, Tell Big tree = Jesus. I thought about that for a second. It was crap, but it was crap that might work. Big was way serious about respecting other people's religions, even Baptists'. Mostly because it gave her the right to not have one.

I put the cell phone under the table and tucked it between my leg and the chair. I waited there until Big came back in to put the coffee cup in the sink. Before she could say a word, I said, "You can't take out that tree. It's her *religion*, Big."

Big cocked her head like a robin to fix me with one bright black eye. She said, "A tree isn't a religion. It's an object."

"She's a druid," I said.

Big made a scoff noise, but it sounded like she had to force it. "Liza the Lorax, she speaks for the trees. Spare me. She's only a druid because it gives her an excuse to be mystical and wear a lot of white." Big was so flustered she said it like Liza was still my whole mom, the one who knew that white made her black eyes shine and her pale skin glow gold. It made me flinch, because that mom was gone, and Big swallowed hard, like her throat hurt her. She blinked it away and said, "You sure are suddenly pro-druid this convenient morning, Mosey."

I flushed, busted. When I was little, watching Liza prance off into the woods wrapped in a sheet with a bedroll and a foster dog, I'd always wanted to go, too. She never let me, and I was dumb enough to believe she was out there being deep and spiritual, sacrificing heaps of apples and grapes to the pine trees. I'd followed her one time, wanting to know how to be deep and spiritual, too. I'd learned hella more about druidism than Big needed to know. I never told anyone, not even Roger, what I saw that day. I wasn't about to start now, when I was trying to use it to save the willow.

I said, "Yeah, it's retarded. But you wouldn't let some godless heathen slap ham and mustard on some Catholic guy's Communion bread." Big cocked her eyebrow at "godless heathen," but she was the one who let my mom exile me to Calvary to save me from my own predestined high-school sluthood. Too bad on her if she didn't like me picking up the lingo.

All she said was, "Don't say 'retarded' like that. It's not nice."

"Big, you know that tree helped make her well before!" That was too true for Big to smack down. Liza had been a clean and sober druid since I was a toddler. Before druidism Liza was a speed-freak atheist who bundled me up and ran away with me when I was only a couple of weeks old. She'd hitchhiked across the country, reading palms and washing dishes for cash, all with me strapped to her back like a papoose. Before *that* she'd been a high-school free-love pothead who got knocked up at fourteen.

I knew because she told me. I couldn't stop her from telling me, because she thought I should learn from her and Big's mistakes. She was a wreck on *my* fourteenth birthday. While I blew out my candles, Liza sat, arms crossed, looking at me from head to toe. "You've outgrown that T-shirt. It's too tight. You don't need to look a grown-up kind of pretty."

I snorted. Maybe the shirt was old, but all it showed was that some merciful fellow flatty in the Sears lingerie department had sold me a trainer with a little padding.

Liza leaned across the table, pushing her face closer to mine. "Just so you know, sex at fourteen feels about as pleasant as a hard case of constipation. Don't you let a boy so much as round first base this year."

"Oh, my God, I'm not having sex," I said. I wished that my outgrown T-shirt had those words on the front. I'd wear it every day, so Big and my teachers and our neighbors and the kids at school would stop waiting for me to swell and pop into the shape of a porn star, new huge boobs ripping my top open, bleached-blond hair pouring off my skull in waves, slutting out like some whorey version of the Hulk.

Big picked up the knife and started slicing the cake, saying, "Hush it, Liza. It's her birthday dinner."

Liza passed me the first slice and said, "Yeah, and I lost my virginity less than a month after my fourteenth-birthday dinner, out on the track field at Pearl River High. I lay down in the long-jump trench with that asshole Carter Mac. He had a lubricated condom, which I cannot recommend putting on while kneeling in a sandpit, Mosey. That sand stuck to the—"

"Who wants ice cream?" Big interrupted, at about volume nine. I went ahead and started eating, because there was no stopping Liza when it was Story-with-a-Moral time. She'd even named me to keep my legs together: Mosey Slocumb, so I'd mosey real slow toward all the stuff you can't take back. Though sometimes I wondered if the real moral to her stories was that she was hella cooler than I'd ever be.

Liza said, "I went around for the next month thinking penises must be made out of emery board, and she needs to hear this, Big, if you want the girl to do any better than us. You had me when you were fifteen, too, so it's not like you spent *your* fourteenth year doing needlepoint and thinking about Jesus."

"Oh, my God, I'm not having any sex!" I hollered around a huge bite of cake.

Liza said, "Keep it that way," and Big said, "Time to open presents!"

It wasn't exactly a Very Brady Birthday, but it sucked a lot less than my fifteenth. That was almost three months ago, right after Liza came home from the stroke-rehab center. She slumped in her wheelchair at the kitchen table while Big sang the birthday song alone and off-key. Liza gummed at her cake like she didn't have teeth. Brown, suck-covered crumbs fell out of her mouth and stuck to her pajama top, until I wished I'd asked for anything but chocolate.

If Big really believed that a pool would get my mom back whole, she'd kill more than a tree to make it happen. She stepped toward me now, leaning down and talking low. "Medicaid is not going to pay for any more physical therapy, Mosey."

"Ask them again," I said. Under my thigh I felt my phone buzz as a text landed in it.

"I've spent two weeks' worth of lunch hours on hold, waiting so I can ask again and be told no again. I've filled out every form they've got. They won't pay." My mom was a bartender down at The Crow before her brain event, and bartenders don't get health insurance. Big'd taken a loan out on our house already, to pay some of the hospital bills and for Mrs. Lynch to come sit with Liza during the weekdays now that I was back in school.

The only good part of us being so broke was, Big couldn't pay my tuition at Calvary. I'd started my sophomore year taking the bus to Pearl River High, back with all the kids I'd gone to middle school with. I still had to leave the house in a knee-length skirt every day and change into jeans in the girls' room. Big worried there was enough of my mom left to catch wise. At Calvary they called Pearl River a "hive of vice," and that was the only thing a Baptist ever said that both Big and Liza believed wholeheartedly. Liza thought if I went to Pearl River High, I'd be stoned by the end of homeroom and pregnant before third period. Like she was. Homeschooling was out, because Big worked all day and Liza said all she could teach me was how to make a perfect dirty martini.

The second that Big grudgingly admitted Calvary gave me a better shot at college, my mom had pulled a total coup and prepaid a year of tuition.

Under my leg my phone buzzed again. Roger, the only good thing I got out of that year at Cal, was texting up a storm.

"Maybe we can borrow a pool? Just please don't take out the willow," I said.

Big drew herself up as high as she could, which was only about five foot three, but I could see how her narrow shoulder bones braced. "Tyler's coming to do it this morning. A willow tree can't give me your mom back whole, not even if she prays to it."

I thought it was more likely my mom would get so het up that a chunk of her brain would burst again and we'd lose the rest of her. But I didn't say so. It was pointless to fuss when Big's shoulders got all squared up like that.

"You're gonna do what you're gonna do," I said, "but killing the willow is wrong. And it sucks. And it's wrong." Big didn't unbend even an inch, so I pushed my breakfast away, and then I palmed my phone and stomped off to my room for my backpack. As soon as my door closed behind me, I flipped the phone open. Roger's first text said, Willow > Pool? And the second said, R U DED?

I texted back, Sorry, Big fite. I am full of lose. Pool > Willow.

Meet me in ur tree house.

I texted, School, fool.

He sent back one word: Skip.

I looked at that word. I was tempted, but skipping was a Liza thing. I didn't do Liza things. If I got caught, Big and probably half my teachers would go ahead and assume I was already failing out, smoking diet pills, and meeting senior boys in squads of ten behind the trailers. I thumbed in, Hellz 2 the no.

His reply came back so fast he must have had it pretyped in: I won't let u get caught.

He didn't understand, because skipping was super easy for

Roger. He looked younger than he was because he was so short, and he had a great big head and round eyes like a bush baby. He said "yes, ma'am" and "no, sir" and held open doors for old ladies and passed out *Are You Truly Saved?* tracts in the park during Youth Week. Plus, he was a Knotwood, and his mom ran the Calvary Booster bake sales, and his dad owned a car dealership in Pascagoula. Teachers never watched him hard enough to catch him perpetrating evil.

I flipped my phone shut without answering. I grabbed my heavy pack, slung it on my shoulders, and walked through to the living room. Liza was slumped in her chair, pointed at the super-loud TV. Big sat in the center of the ancient sofa, her slight weight pulling the saggy cushions into a smile-shaped curve. With the two big front windows right behind her like eyes, it looked as though the whole damn living room was giving me a vile, gloaty grin, watching me tuck my tail under and creep obediently away while Big killed the willow.

Big was barefoot but dressed now in her polyester-blend bankbot uniform. I guessed she planned to go to work after Tyler took the tree out, like it was a regular day.

I tried one last time, giving her my best pleady eyeballs. "Don't."

"You are going to miss your bus and end up with a tardy if you don't scoot," Big said. She was sure that would light a fire under me. I never got tardies. Just like I never hooked her beers or snuck out to meet boys or even turned in a paper late. Never.

My eyes went all narrow. "Oh, yeah. If I got a tardy, the earth would fall into the damn sun."

"Language!" Big said, but I was already stomping out the door. I paused for a tick on the stoop to let Big say, "Don't you slam the—" before I slammed the door and cut her off.

It felt really good. The sound rang in my ears, and my feet didn't seem to want to walk me to the bus stop. Instead, before I could think it through, I ran around the side of the house, through the wooden gate, and into the backyard. I sprinted as fast as I could, my heavy pack slamming me in the spine with every step, and got behind the big oak tree in the far corner.

I clambered up the wooden rails nailed to the oak tree's backside and poked my head through the hatch. Roger was already there, grinning because he'd heard me climbing up. He'd pulled the old pool-chair cushions out of the built-in toy trunk and made himself a nest. He spent a lot of his skip days tucked away high in my backyard, reading Ayn Rand and sending me smug texts about not having to dress out for gym.

"I didn't think you would do it," he said as I scrambled all the way in and shucked my pack.

My heart was pounding so hard I could feel it in my ears, and I thought I might puke. I tried to sound cool, though, as I said, "Rats. I was about to text you to bring chips." I yanked my Baptist-costume skirt down over my knees, prim like.

Roger rummaged in the cushions beside him and pulled out a Big Grab of Cheetos.

"Who's your daddy? Say, say, say it," he chanted, and waited till I had rolled my eyes and said in the flattest voice possible, "Roger is my chip daddy, oh, yeah, holler," before he passed them.

I opened the top, but then I couldn't eat even one. My throat felt like it had screwed itself closed.

"OMG, what am I doing?" I said.

Roger said, "The right thing. When your mom sees that tree is gone, you need to be here."

The oak was in the back left corner, so huge that Liza used to worry its roots would warp our fence and let one of her foster dogs out. The tree house had a big cutout window that gave me a good view of the willow, growing smack in the middle of our yard.

There was another window aimed back toward my house. The oak was so tall I could see a good piece of the road and a couple of our neighbors' houses. The oak's leaves were turning red and gold, but they were still on, and I didn't think anyone would see us peering out. Even so, my hands were shaking and my palms were leaking clammy sweat.

"I'm going to get caught. And then I will puke. And then I will be dead because Big will kill me," I told Roger.

"Don't think about it," he said, totally at ease. He reached for my backpack and unzipped it, pulling out my civics book. "Here, study while we wait."

I opened it and tried to concentrate. Most times I found it real soothey to put facts away in tidy bundles in my brain so I could unpack them all out onto a test and then get it back two days later with an A or at least a B on it, sometimes with a *"Good job, Mosey!"* note. I was a regular on the dean's list, but the exclamation point always looked surprised to me.

I heard a car coming, and I dropped the book and craned out the front window to see if it was the Mighty Un–Butt Crack's truck.

"Excellent studying," said Roger. "You should eat the relevant pages. Seems like you'd get more of the test material in you that way."

It was only the Wheatons' station wagon with those vile fake oak panels on the sides. If I left now and sprinted the woods track, I could catch the bus on Marlin Street, down farther on its route. Tyler might not show for hours, if he even came today. Big hired him because he worked cheap, he had his own tools, and he knew how to do all the stuff most families had husbands and dads to do. He'd snaked out our clogged toilet, built my tree house from a Home Depot kit, tarred our roof, and put a new battery in Big's old Malibu, but he came when he came.

"Chill," Roger said. "You are not going to get caught. I already made you this, in case you showed." He pulled a sheet of folded paper out of his back pocket. I opened it and read, *"Sorry, Jean, about Mosey's tardy, but she had a doc appointment and so please write her a pass."* He'd already signed it *"Virginia Slocumb,"* in blue pen. The handwriting was super close to Big's, but the best part was how it said things exactly like the real Big would.

I blinked at him. "I sometimes wonder what the world would be like if you ever decided to use your powers for good."

Roger shrugged, like real rueful. "It's a tragedy for Earth, I tell you."

That almost made me smile. If he hadn't been with me, I would have cracked and run for the bus by now. Roger had been my only friend at Calvary. He still was, even though I was at Pearl River High now. It was like that year in Baptist exile had made me lose my place. The girl who'd been my best friend since kindergarten, Briony Hutchins, had come back from her summer in Nevada twenty pounds lighter, except in the boobs. She'd also straightened her hair and found poisonously beautiful cheekbones. She sat between Kelli Gutton and Barbie Macloud now, the two of them turned in toward her like she was the Tome of Gorgeous and they were the prettiest pair of bookends available, whispering about hair-tossing techniques and being way too good for me.

"Keep studying," he said. "I'll watch."

I shook my head. I put the book and Roger's note in my backpack and then hesitated. I felt like my lungs were slowly filling up with beach sand, so I could only get oxygen in smaller and smaller sips. My palms leaked sweat. I gave in and rummaged down to the bottom until my hand found the two-pack of dollar-store pregnancy tests tucked under my pink Trapper Keeper. I pulled them out and waved the box at him. "I need to go pee."

"Love a duck," he said. "Again? Really?"

"I need to," I said, and he rolled his eyes. He knew that the hawtest sex action I'd ever seen was when Dougie Breck and I touched tongues on a dare in sixth grade. "Whistle if you see Tyler's truck?"

"You're such a 'tard," he said, but that meant he would.

I got one of the tests out and tucked it down into my bra. Lord knows my bra didn't have much else in it to speak of, so it might as well make itself useful. I peered through the foliage, but I didn't see any of our neighbors out, and Big and Liza were likely still in the den, where the windows pointed at the street. I shimmied down the back of the oak and skimmed over the fence to the woods behind our house as fast as I could. Big took me to Girl Scouts when I was little, so I knew to watch for poison oak and ivy when I left the trail. I found a good spot behind some bushes. I got the test out and said a quick thanks heavenward that Roger had beat me to the tree house, so I hadn't changed into my jeans. The skirt made it so much easier.

I squatted down over the stick, and even before I started peeing on it, I felt more air getting down into me, like my squeezed-shut insides were untwisting, even though I already knew the test would come out negative. That was kind of the point, to hold this solid piece of plastic proof that I wasn't going to turn out like Liza and kill Big in the heart. I yanked my underpants back up and sat on a log with the stick beside me. A minute passed, two, three, and I sat watching while the pink line that told me the test was working properly formed, real bright and obvious. Beside it, the window that would get a pink line if I was pregnant stayed blank and white, the way it always did. It was perfect and clear, and the leaves and dirt and trees around me got fuzzy and out of focus, and I looked only at that pure white window.

I don't know how long I sat staring at the test stick with the morning air tasting real clean and sweet to me. I sat until I heard a quick, sharp whistle, and then my heart leaped up and started trying to jam itself into my throat, undoing every bit of good the pee had done. Roger's whistle came again, but I still took thirty seconds and dug a hole and dropped the test down it and covered it. Big didn't come out to the woods hardly ever, but if she caught me with a preggo test, she'd crap herself. Then she'd murder me before she even paused to change her pants.

I hightailed it back to the fence, popped quick as I could over it again, and scrambled up the tree.

Roger said, "There."

I turned to crane out the window. Sure enough, Tyler's filthy white truck had already pulled up and parked on the street, parallel with the back gate.

"Crap, crap, crap!" I said.

Tyler got out in his mom jeans and a green tee with the sleeves rolled up to show off his fifty million arm tats. He did his Tyler Baines slouch walk around to the truck bed and pulled out this enormous chain saw.

"Should we at least try to stop him?" I whispered.

Roger shook his head. "That guy looks like he would eat his own children."

We shut up then as Tyler passed by us on the way to the willow. He yanked at the chain saw's cord, and it roared to life.

I should have run down right then and handcuffed my arms around the willow. I should have sent Roger to set Tyler's truck on fire to distract him. But I didn't think of any of those things. I sat, dumb and unmoving, and watched while Tyler swung the saw forward. It bit into the willow's trunk with this vile, harsh grinding, and I sat there, like I couldn't quite believe it. The saw roared so loud I felt the buzz of it in my teeth. I knew I should do something, but I kept looking at the back door. Part of me thought Liza would rise up and come roaring out herself again, all smitey and alive, magically cured to save this tree. The back door stayed closed, though. The TV was on so loud that Liza might not realize for days that her willow was gone, if her brain wasn't too effed up to even notice, and I was missing my civics test.

Tyler's saw bit at it from one side, then the other, rattling my eyes in my sockets. The old Liza would have known how to make him stop, but I wasn't like her. I sat there and let it happen. Finally the tree tipped slowly and went over with a crash, and the chain saw stopped.

It was so quiet then, it felt like the whole world was holding its breath. I blinked, shaking my head in a little "no" shake, back and forth, so small it was like trembling. Tyler began hacking the willow up and carting off the chunks of it, businesslike and fast. It took a couple of hours, and we sat and watched, and Liza didn't come. Finally Tyler opened the fence gate wide and backed his truck up into the yard to winch out the stump.

He attached the chains and revved his engines and yoinked the very heart of the willow right out of the ground. The sound of those old roots ripping as it pulled loose was a tinfoil bite of a noise. It made me and Roger both clap our hands over our ears. The stump came out and got dragged, trailing its torn roots like guts as the truck lurched forward.

Tyler stopped then and got out and came back to look at the jaggedy hole. The willow's stump lay on the grass like a dead sea creature, wrenched out of its proper home and flopped up on the shore. He started to turn away, then paused and scratched at his head, staring down into the tangly mess of dirt and thready roots. He took two steps closer, then squatted like a caveman. From my perch up high, I could see something gleaming silver from the side wall of the hole, almost at the bottom. Tyler let himself down into the hole and dug at the earth around whatever was lodged there. He pulled and worked at it until he got it out.

It was a dirty silver box, like a miniature treasure chest. Some of the dirt fell away as he clambered out with it, and I could see that the back of the box had pink metal hinges shaped like daisies.

Roger pointed at me, eyebrows lifting, like asking if the little trunk was mine. I shook my head no. He whipped out his iPhone and texted to me, Backyard pirates?

I texted back, MayB. Weird.

We both leaned forward, peering down, hoping Tyler would open the box.

Tyler set it down on the ground, and then he squatted and pried it open. He had to work at it, like the box was latched or stuck shut. He got it, though, and then he pulled out what looked like a rotty stuffed duck, tiny and deflated, so old that the yellow of his cloth body had browned out in big patches.

Tyler gave the duck a shake, and even from all the way up in the tree I heard it chime. The old bell sounded off-key and weirdly sad, like a noise in a movie that tells you something bad is coming.

Roger made a bored, blowing noise and whispered, "Some kid's box," but I wasn't bored. I felt all at once hyper and alert, like under my skull a pair of inside ears had pricked up.

I found myself reaching for Roger's hand and grabbing it, tight. Roger gave me a WTF look. He had this unspoken rule that I didn't stuff myself into his same beanbag chair or sling my arms around him and be all snuggy-touchy like I used to with Briony. He didn't want me that close to him. Not unless I meant it in a way I didn't feel about him.

When he saw my face, he left his hand in mine, mouthing, *What?* at me. I was like a dog on point, leaning forward, and Roger craned to look out the window, too, puzzled enough to be interested again.

Tyler set the duck aside and picked something else out of the box. Something small and strangely curved, cream-colored under the dirt. He turned it around and around like a raccoon washing something, and as he spun it, the dirt fell away. He reached down and picked up another one just like it. I couldn't make out what they were, not at all, not until he held the two pieces together. When I saw the way they fit, saw the shape and how they hooked on the ends, I gasped. Roger did, too. Then he clutched my hand back, very hard. We looked at each other, and his big eyes were as round and green as crab apples.

We looked back down, and Tyler's mouth had gaped open wide enough to let drool fall out. We knew what he was holding. It was small, too small to be a grown-up's, but I've watched about fifty million *CSI* and *Bones* reruns with Big. It was a teeny jawbone.

Roger breathed out, "Is that from a person?"

Tyler bent down again and picked out a piece of faded pink fabric, streaked with slimy brown. It hung like a rag in his hands, and I saw that it was a ruffly baby dress, and that's when Roger and I heard the sound, this horrible moaning wail. Tyler dropped the dress, and Roger and I both jumped. It sounded like someone tiny and damned had been in the darkness under Liza's tree, and Tyler had yanked its sleeping ghost into the sun. I screamed a short sound like a bark and clutched at Roger's hand so hard I felt his own bones grind.

But the noise wasn't coming from a ghost. It was coming from my house. The back door slammed open, and my mom came stumping and wailing into the yard on her walker. Big was right with her, saying urgent things no one could hear. My mom unleashed a noise that held every bit of hell she had left in her, and I squeezed Roger's hand so, so tight, so tight. My mom sucked in a desperate whoop of air, and then a new wail came. I thought it was because of the tree, but she wasn't looking at the tree.

The wail changed and became shaped, words made mostly from vowels. My mom was screaming words at Tyler. He stood there staring with that tiny, awful jawbone still in his hand. My mother said a thing over and over, a thing no one but me and Big, who'd listened to Liza for almost four months now since the stroke, could possibly understand. It was a garble, but after the third time I could make it out, what she was screaming, and it made no sense.

My mom let go of the walker, like she was trying to run at him, and her bad leg gave out, and she went down still screaming those crazy words with poor Big trying to catch her.

"What the what?" Roger asked.

"She says that it's her baby. She says the bones are her baby." I ground Roger's fingers to paste, and he clamped down, grinding mine right back, because it sounded so unpossible.

My mom's good leg kicked at the ground, like she was trying to swim to Tyler and take the little curve of bone away from him. Big fell to her knees, reaching for Liza, white and shocked and weeping. Liza kicked and stretched her arm toward Tyler, straining toward the dress and the bone, demanding her baby, over and over, and it made no sense, no sense at all, because my mom had only ever had one baby, and that baby was me.

CHAPTER TWO

Big

WHEN LIZA DREW her first breath and screamed her first mad scream, it was so loud I could hear her through my headphones. She pierced the cheery pop drumbeat of "Walking on Sunshine" to make herself known. I'd hit the Rewind and Play buttons on my Walkman at least a hundred times by then, letting Katrina and the Waves wail away six hours' worth of hard, induced labor. Katrina sang, and I pushed and heaved out the baby they told me had already died inside me, probably days ago. I went to live inside that song, disconnected from the body that was busy doing strange and painful things. "And don't it feel good?" Katrina asked me, over and over, until the words didn't mean anything.

I went with Katrina because otherwise I might've thought about how the sharp-nosed asshole doctor at the emergency room said it would be easier to slip wires up inside of me and cut it up and take it out in pieces. He was talking to a nurse, but he had that bossy kind of bored, rich-fellow voice that carried. Then the nurse came and said it to me, but she used nicer words. They both called Liza "it" because it's easier to cut up an it.

I said, "No, no, please, God, no," because back then I was still praying. I said, "I want to hold my baby even if it's only one time. I want to see my baby." I called Liza "my baby" because I didn't know her sex. I only knew that, dead or living, my baby was not anybody's it.

Then I pulled on my headset and hit Play, cranking up the volume on my Walkman while they wheeled me out of emergency to a different place upstairs. A new nurse shaved my privates and put a drip in my arm that started up labor. Hours later, when I heard Liza's first enraged miracle shriek, so loud and fierce it reached me through my headphones, I opened my eyes. They were lifting her up, the new doc's eyes wide with pleasure over his mask. Her squanchy face was all screwed up into a wad with mad, and her round head was sticky-tacky with gore. She kicked her springy frog legs, beautifully alive and righteously pissed off, but they had told me my baby was dead, so this couldn't be my baby. And yet a slick cord trailed from her belly back into me. We were attached.

I stared at her, unbelieving, while Katrina sang all cheerful about love and sunshine. I looked at Liza: shrieking, tiny, red-faced, enraged, willful. The first thing I thought was, *Beautiful.* Then I thought, *Mine.*

That entry was a harbinger; Liza was a dreadful baby. Seemed like I spent the better part of her first year walking her up and down and up and down my parents' hall through her endless colic. I'd walk her, and she'd scream, and both my parents would come out of their bedroom, dull-eyed from no sleep and still seeping that gray disappointment that had been oozing out from all their pores since I set my dinner fork down and told them I had, as Daddy decided to call it, "gotten myself knocked up." I would have thought it was grammatically more proper to say Lance Weston had done the knocking, but my parents didn't see it that way. No one did; Lance Weston didn't have to leave school.

One night, after I'd been walking Liza more than four hours, each minute ticking me closer to my breakfast shift at Pancake Castle, my mother came out alone and stood in the hall watching me pace up and down joggling my wad of unhappy baby. Liza made a thin, high, endless noise like a miserable teakettle. In ninety minutes I'd have to bike to work. I'd spend six hours on my feet slinging coffee and corned beef hash, hoping breast milk wouldn't gush out and wreck another uniform and make me have to do laundry during Liza's afternoon nap, the only time each day I had to study for my GED.

My mother looked at me, so sorrowful, and I said, "What, Momma? What?"

I don't know what I expected her to say. I'd always been her good girl, a decent student, second chair for flute in band. Something to be moderately proud of. Until I went to the first party anyone had ever invited me to and Lance Weston, a junior from a rich family and co-captain of the baseball team, paid me some attention. I was so blushed and flustered that I took a sip of the zombie punch I'd been holding to be polite, and one sip led to the rest of the cup, which buzzed and heated up inside me and called out for another cup and another and then another to join it in my belly.

Next thing I knew, me and Lance Weston were slipping off together. I was pretty sure we were falling in love, and he was pretty sure that freshman girls with that much zombie punch in 'em put out. Only one of us was right.

So there I was walking Liza, four o'clock on a Wednesday morning, and my mother looked at me with such sad eyes that I thought I recognized pity there. I was too tired to be proud about wanting it. I was plain starved for a little mercy. Liza wailed unending on my shoulder, and I said, again, "What, Momma?"

She shrugged and blinked and sighed at me. She folded her arms around herself, and I could see she was as tired as me. Her gaze settled on my howling baby, and finally she spoke.

"We're going to need to charge you rent."

Then she went in her bedroom and closed the door. That was when I'd finally understood that she'd never forgive me for making it so the ladies in the Mary-Martha Club at Faith First Baptist could cut their eyes at her and tut. Those women I'd known all my life hadn't even given me a shower, as if shameful babies didn't need teethers or warm blankets. The pastor made my daddy step down as deacon, telling him a man who couldn't run his own family couldn't be trusted to run the church. I looked at Liza, so beautiful and loud, so fierce, and I thought that word again. *Mine.* I wasn't one to make a fuss, but Liza deserved one. No one was going to help me. Not my family, not God, and not my church.

That morning I called in sick for my shift and went instead to the office of a lady lawyer, new in town, who wasn't getting a lot of business. My daddy said it was because she had "hair like a lesbian." Turned out she had a girlfriend like a lesbian, too. She took me on, pro bono, and within six months me and Liza were camping in her guest room, emancipated. Three weeks after that, she poured out plastic cups of sparkling cider and we toasted the Westons. Then we cashed the big-ass check I'd gotten in return for not demanding a paternity test, shutting up like a good little girl, and moving at least a hundred miles away.

I'd have gone farther, except I ran out of Mississippi. I dropped most of the Weston cash on my little house in Immita, five miles from the Gulf. I spent the rest on tuition to Clayton Career Training Center in Pascagoula, learning to be a bank teller. It was just me and Liza, who never for a breathless second got a single speck easier to live with. I spent her toddler days with my heart lodged in my esophagus, because all she wanted to do was lick the electrical outlets and then wander into traffic. By the time she was school age and took to scrapping with any boy who said he could whoop her, there hadn't been a day got by me where I hadn't wanted at some point to sell her to Gypsies.

On the darkest days, when I was so tired I thought it might be better to go lie in the road and pray for heavy traffic, I could forget for a minute that this willful child was mine. In the bottom blackest corner of my sorry heart, where I was still scared of snakes and what might be under the bed, I sometimes felt a pinprick of belief that the pointy-nosed asshole doctor who couldn't find Liza's heartbeat had been right: My good and reasonable baby must have died. Maybe fairies stole out a Little Dead It right from my belly. In return they loaned me something magical and half cussed. Something beautiful but flawed, whose brain broke in half when she was barely thirty. A changeling with an early expiration date, my Liza-Little, and I'd been wrestling her for two-thirds of my life.

I was wrestling her for real today, sliding across my lawn, my skirt rucking up over my thighs while she thrashed like a mad pony, doing her best to throw me off her. "Liza, Liza, Liza," I crooned, trying to calm her down and make her listen, all to no avail. *So this is nothing new*, I thought. But inside I was soaring, because maybe it wasn't new, but this wild thing that bucked, willful and mighty, had been blankly, blackly absent from Liza's body since the stroke. This was my real Liza trying to throw off my hands, half girl, half hurricane. She might still be in there.

All the hope I'd banked flooded me, sweet enough to mute even the roared thunder of mother guilt, saying I had done this to her for a swimming pool. I'd eat this guilt and kill a thousand more willows, twice each, for a speck of hope that Liza was still alive inside this broken body.

"Liza," I said, too loud to be soothing, "Liza, you need to breathe."

She writhed like half a bag of snakes, kicking and one-hand-clawing her inchy way across the yard on her belly, her voice cutting into my ears like an air-raid siren.

"Be still," I said in hard, commanding tones, which had never worked on my old Liza. It did not work now. I tried it softer—"Shush, baby"—but she only shrieked again, a desperate cawing noise. I grabbed her arms and felt her heartbeat in her skin. It was like a reverb pounding through every inch of her. That scared me, the thought of all that racing blood moving thick and fast, launching an assault on her broken brains. Liza hollered something that sounded like words, too garbled to understand over my own shushing and my rising fear as I felt the machine-gun desperation of her pulse.

It was too much even for the old Liza, even over this tree. This wasn't temper or brass, this was crazy-desperate, pressing toward suicide. She squirmed and shrieked like I wasn't there, her good eye fixed on Tyler Baines. She scrambled toward him like he was a finish line. I lurched after her, rearing up on my knees and grabbing her around the waist.

Tyler was holding what looked like curly bits of old ivory in his hands. Liza shoved herself forward again, repeating those wordlike sounds, pulling me with her. As I toppled forward across her back, sunlight flashed off a silver box at Tyler's feet. I took my weight off Liza but then froze like I was about to knock out ten pushups, because the shape of that box was so damn familiar. It was filthy, clearly dragged up out of the earth under the downed tree, but there was something about the domed top and the splotches of hot pink on it that struck me as haunting and familiar. Liza was writhing her way out from under me, and I let her go, staring.

There was a scrap of fabric on the ground by Tyler's boot, and in the same buried way I knew that shade of pink. It was like that French word where you wake up in a strange house but you somehow know exactly where they keep the coffee filters. That splotch of pink flared and went blue-hot, becoming a bright, bad thing that would take my eyes if I looked at it directly. I made myself look away, fast, and I saw Mosey at the back of the yard, scrambling down out of her tree house. At once the mother in me took dry, distant note that Miss Mosey was skipping school.

I was almost glad to notice. Skipping school was regular. I had this unaccountable longing to get up and take Mosey's arm and go inside and have an After School Special–style talk about responsibility. I wanted to let this whole nightmare backyard landscape sink into hell, to no longer hear Liza howling like the damned, to never again look at that silver box, to never, never study on the little heap of pink cloth at Tyler's feet. Mosey stared at me with her eyes and mouth all gone into big, round O shapes, and now I could understand the words that Liza was saying over and over as she kicked and shoved her way toward Tyler.

"Umbay! Umbay! Geem, gee!" Liza wailed. *My baby! My baby! Give me, give!*

I looked again at the box, lying open in the churned earth, and could no longer stop myself from recognizing it. It was Liza's old silver footlocker. The splotches were its pink daisy hinges. I sat up on my knees, my hands slack by my sides, palms pressing the grass as if to make sure the world was still spinning underneath me. When she was fifteen and took baby Mosey and disappeared for two years, four months, and eleven god-awful endless days, I'd thought the box had gone with her.

Liza screamed again. *My baby! Give! Give!* Her words clanged and rattled in my head, and there was our Mosey, standing white with shock under the oak tree. Mosey's pretty hands were holding each other, twisting hard at her own fingers, and so I flat refused to wonder what the treasure box was doing here, buried under Liza's willow tree. I snapped back into movement, dropping onto all fours, crawling fast after Liza. I scrambled right up over her and wrapped my arm around her front, pressing my palm over her mouth to make her quiet. I bent close to Liza's ear to hiss, "Liza? Liza-Little? Mosey is here. Shut the fucking fuck up."

She kept yelling through my hand. I could feel the flat fronts of her teeth pressing my palm as her lips snarled. My hands were weak. They shook and couldn't hold back even her words. My gaze darted to Mosey, my little pitcher, big-earing another step toward us across the lawn.

Tyler called, "Ginny? Ginny?" and now I understood the little pieces in his hands, and they were not old ivory at all. He held them up, fitting them together, and a thought was bouncing about in all the nerve endings in his hands, hopping finger to finger. He looked at the pieces, puzzling, then down to the open footlocker. I looked, too.

I saw a ruined yellow baby blanket with more little ivory-colored bits of bone resting in its folds. Some of the bits were like sticks, some like dice. No skull, just some curved pieces like little dishes, and I thought, *She was so young her skull bones hadn't fused yet*, calm and cool and distant. On the ground by his boot lay that heap of disturbingly familiar pink cloth and the rotted-out remains of a rattle-bellied duck.

The thought found its way up Tyler's arms to his spine, where I watched it rise as slow as a bubble trapped in gel shampoo, until he came to know what I already understood: He was holding the pieces of a tiny, tiny dead person. His fingers twitched open, and he dropped those frail bones down into the dirt, and it was a mercy, a mercy, that my hands were busy trying to still Liza's flailing, or I'd have stepped calmly to him and ripped him clean in half.

My dead voice said, "You pick that up, Tyler. Respectful like." He only blinked, then shook his head at me and used his empty hands to touch his ears. He hadn't heard me clearly over Liza's howls.

"Big?" Mosey called. She was chalk-colored. She took another step toward me, and I saw from her face she'd understood Liza's words. Her lips pursed to form a word, the first word in a question I did not want asked, because all at once I was scared that I might know the answer.

Then I couldn't stop looking from the box of bones to Mosey, couldn't help seeing all the ways I'd pegged her as her mystery daddy's girl. She was tall and had a lanky string-bean body, while Liza and I were built small and as curvy as that famous road in San Francisco. We had fat, round mouths like plums, while Mosey had a wide smile; Liza used to call her "Hot Lips Houlihan." Now that mouth was making words, asking things I could not or would not hear over Liza, and my body regained its strength.

I tore my gaze away and put my hands on Liza's good side and turned her, turned her whole body, pushing so her weak arm and leg rolled under her and then she was on her back, helpless as a turtle. I straddled her body with one knee pinning her good arm and the other pressing into the grass by her bad arm, my palms touching down on either side of her head.

I leaned in close and called, "Liza! Liza!" But her eyes were loose in their sockets, unfocused now.

"Umbay," she said. *My baby.* "My" was a new word. Right after the stroke, Liza didn't say much more than yes and no. Mostly no. Now she said "Big" and "Mosey-baby" and a few more things, like "gimme" and "potty" and "hungry" and "help." The doctors couldn't tell me how much of Liza was left inside, and Liza couldn't tell me either. Now this. *My* baby. It was the first time since the stroke I longed to take a word away from her.

I reared back and grabbed her chin in one hand, forcing her head to turn toward Mosey. Mosey was running toward us now, and my mean hands made Liza see our long-legged child with all her grace gone. Her usual gazelle-style leaping had been reduced to a stagger.

"There is your baby. There is Mosey. Look at Mosey," I hissed in Liza's ear, and I was looking, too, unable to stop cataloging all the thousand ways that Mosey wasn't one of us. I took her in, from her long, skinny feet, toes like fingers where we had toes like peas, up to her wide milk-chocolate eyes. Liza had my eyes, tilted at the corners like a cat's, so black I could barely see where her pupils started.

Liza finally focused on our girl, and her voice turned off like a wire had been cut. She went flat and limp under me. Her bad eye drooped all but shut, and her good one blinked. Both were streaming tears, and her nose was running.

It was enough to have her quiet. I was still seeing only the edges of it. I couldn't get anywhere from the hellish here except into the next second of the hellish, hellish now. The silver footlocker was Pandora's box, full of a living darkness, and I would not look directly there. It was more important to take care of Mosey. Shutting up Liza and taking care of Mosey was as far as I could get.

I said to Mosey, "Help me get your mom inside?"—and I was proud at how calm I sounded.

"Is she okay?" Mosey asked.

Behind me, like a deep echo, Tyler said, "Ginny, what the hell?"

"Language!" I said to Tyler.

"What should I do?" he called.

Before I could even think, I'd snapped back, "Don't you do a single, fucking thing," like he'd played the word "hell" in cussing poker and I was upping him, going all in by laying down the ugliest cuss there was. Mosey's wide eyes went even wider to hear that word come out of my mouth. I made myself take a deep breath. My heart was pounding so hard I could feel it pulsing in my eyes. The heap of pink fabric at Tyler's feet pulled at my attention. I had to force myself to look away.

Mosey and I tried to get Liza on her feet, but she'd gone floppy and unwieldy. Tyler took over, grabbing hold of the side of my daughter that was close to deadweight and pulling her upright.

"Get the walker," I told Mosey. It was lying tipped over in the yard on its side.

"Is this because of I cut down her tree?" Tyler asked as we started shuffling Liza forward. Mosey trailed along beside us, toting the walker and chewing her lower lip so hard I was worried she might nip a piece clean off.

I answered in a voice so fake cheery-ghastly that I sounded like the zombie version of June Cleaver. "Yeah. Liza surely does know how to throw a fit. She loved that willow like it was her own baby." Mosey gave a little startle when I said the word "baby." She'd understood Liza's mangled shouts, all right. Tyler blinked at me, dumb as a sweet-faced cow; he hadn't understood a word.

We walked her slow across the concrete patio. She was tractable now, faded once more to the Liza-less creature the stroke had made her. Her eyes were unfocused, and her feet shuffled in the direction we pointed her.

"Big," Mosey whispered, while I pushed the back door open and let Tyler drag the heavy half of Liza in. "Big, those were bones!"

"Oh, yeah," Tyler said, loud and excited.

"You may be right," I said. I still sounded ghastly. We walked Liza through the den and down the hall, and my mouth felt stretched into the Joker's smile.

Tyler said, "There were all kinds of baby things in the box. Do you think someone killed a—"

I interrupted him with a loud *pish* noise. Liza echoed it with a sleepy, bubbling sound. I kicked Liza's cracked bedroom door the rest of the way open. "For all we know, those bones could be hundreds of years old. Maybe the whole neighborhood is built over an old cemetery."

"Like in *Poltergeist*!" Now Tyler sounded excited. He was easy to distract, but Mosey had her thinking face on.

We eased Liza down onto the side of the bed. She looked tired enough to tip over, and she was filthy and covered in grass stains. "Tyler, step out, if you don't mind? We're going to get Liza changed. Mosey, help me get your mother's shoes off. Her socks are full of yard dirt."

I heard the click of the door closing behind Tyler as he skedaddled. Yet another thing that had changed; before the stroke he'd have stood on his head with his feet on fire for a glimpse of Liza with her clothes off.

Mosey knelt down to slip off her mother's Keds, and I took Liza's frail wrist, the good one, and looked at my watch. She slumped, staring at nothing, but her pulse told me that inside she was running like hot lava. Mosey went to the closet to put the shoes away, and I quickly leaned down so my face was close to Liza's face and whispered, "Liza? Liza, is that you?" She didn't so much as blink.

"Is her pulse bad high?" Mosey asked, and I made myself turn and smile at her.

"Don't you worry. It's down some already. We'll wait three minutes and take it again. If it doesn't keep coming down, we'll go right to the hospital and figure all this mess out later."

Mosey said, "Those bones can't be *that* old. Unless the pioneers made terry-cloth rattle ducks."

"People have been sewing since the caveman," I said, sharp, but truthfully, I was relieved to see her rallied enough to give me some sass mouth and her "get real" gaze.

I got a fresh pair of sweatpants and a soft cotton T-shirt out of Liza's dresser, and together Mosey and I got her peeled out of her grass-stained clothes. I didn't like to see how her bad leg looked withered, thinner than her right leg. She was so skinny her hipbones pressed at her skin.

Liza let us change her, drooping and limp as a home-sewn doll. By the time we got her new socks on and brushed her hair to get the dirt out, her pulse was down. Her head was nodding, and the willful, writhing flash of my missing daughter I had seen as we fought on the lawn was gone altogether. I couldn't even be positive it had been there as Mosey and I muscled a hundred pounds of floppy Liza into the bed.

I said, "You sleep now, Little," and I lowered her to her pillow and tucked her in. Then I said quiet to Mosey, "Call Mrs. Lynch. See if she can't come on over now instead of after lunch."

"Okay."

Mosey still looked in terrible danger of thinking, so I said, "Don't imagine that just because your momma blew a gasket over that tree, I didn't notice you were skipping school. That *will* be discussed."

That gave her something more immediate to fret on, and she turned and walked out double-time to make the call. Teenagers are like that. In a cave post–nuclear war, I bet I could distract any high-school kid still living by peering at her chin and asking if she was getting a pimple.

I went back up the hall, hunting for Tyler. He wasn't in the den. I went through the swinging doors into the kitchen and saw him standing framed in the open door to the backyard. He turned toward me, and I saw he had his cell phone clutched in his hand.

"Who did you call?" I asked, my voice too harsh, accusing.

"Rick Warfield?" he said, and in that moment I could have cheerfully shot Tyler and dumped his body directly into the hole the willow had left. I could not tell Rick Warfield a story about *Poltergeist* and archaeology. He was a brighter bulb than Tyler, by several thousand watts.

I heard my voice, at top volume, asking him, "On what planet does, 'Don't do an effing thing,' mean, 'Please call the chief of police'?"

Tyler shook his head at me. "Aw, man, Ginny, we had to call someone. He's coming right over. Maybe we should back off and put up tape around that spot?"

"We don't know it's a crime scene, good Lord," I said. "And it's not like you travel with yellow cop tape in your toolbox."

"I got duct tape," Tyler said, and now he sounded almost hopeful.

"We are not on *CSI: Miami*, Horatio," I snapped, and his crest fell a little. The meanest piece of me thought, *Good.*

I pushed past Tyler onto the concrete slab that passed for a patio. I stopped there and stared across the yard toward the open silver keepsake chest. Rick Warfield was coming, to lay his rough hands on the bones wound up inside that yellow blanket. I could not stop him. My gaze moved to the heap of streaked and faded knit cloth lying beside it.

My feet walked me toward the box like they'd had their own terrible idea and they didn't feel like checking with my brain parts before putting it into action. I bent down and picked it up in both hands. It unfurled into a shape I recognized. A baby dress. I turned the dress in my hands until I had it by the shoulders and could see the tag. Kidworks. I found myself pinching the cloth so tight that my fingers cramped, but I could not let go.

I knew this dress. I knew it. I had bought it myself, for Mosey. For Liza's little girl, along with a host of blankets and fuzzy socks and sleepers. That was fifteen years ago, and the dress was faded and striped with mud and some kind of green-gray moldy slime I didn't want to think about, but I recognized the ruffles at the hem. I could not help remembering it. It was the last thing I saw my grandbaby wearing before she and Liza had disappeared.

I remembered putting Liza's baby in that dress when she was only a couple of weeks old, bald as an egg with foldy legs she kept frogged up against her belly. Liza sat in a heap on the sofa, plumb wore out. The baby was fretting, but this baby's brand of fret was nothing. I'd gotten through Liza Slocumb's screamfest of a babyhood without ever once throwing her off a train trestle or eating her like a hamster momma would have. I could handle a little gritching. The baby seemed mellow to me. That's how I thought of her then: sweet, not weak.

I said, "Liza-Little, I got this. You can take the second shift."

Liza said, "You got work tomorrow, Big."

"Well, so do you. You have to momma all day and get enough brainpower to finally give this child a name. We keep calling her The Baby like no one ever made one before. If you don't decide soon, I'm going to saddle this poor child with Gretchen, just to spite you."

When the baby fell asleep, I moved her to her bassinet in Liza's room without bothering to change her into pajamas, because the pink knit dress was so soft. Liza was sleeping more deeply than the baby, flat on her back with arms thrown up over her head like a child herself. The skin around her eyes was peachy-colored, smooth and tight.

Hours later I stirred, hearing Liza up in the night, rattling around. I didn't hear the baby, but her gritchy cry was always so quiet that this didn't set off any worry bells. I rolled over and closed my eyes.

The next morning the door to Liza's room was shut and the house was quiet. I figured they were sleeping in. I knew how it could be with babies, day and night mixed up. I crept around dressing, eating oatmeal and a banana on the quiet.

When I got home from the bank that evening, the house had a dead-aired, empty feeling. I went to Liza's room and saw the closet standing open. There were a few empty hangers in the center. Both pairs of her favorite jeans were gone. The big red backpack she'd planned to use as a diaper bag was gone, too. I opened her drawers and saw gaps in the stacks of socks and underpants and T-shirts. The baby's yellow blankie was no longer in the bassinet, and neither was her stuffed duck with the bell in his gut that slept beside her teeny feet.

I dropped to my knees by the square of carpet that used to hold Liza's silver footlocker. All her keepsakes had been dumped out of it and left in a heap on the floor: notes from school friends, pressed flowers, the birth certificate that said "Baby Girl Slocumb," with "Liza Slocumb" typed in the space for the momma's name and nothing at all typed in the space for the daddy. Liza'd said it was a tall, pretty boy who'd run the Ferris wheel at a weekend carnival she'd gone to with her so-called friend Melissa Richardson. Liza said she couldn't remember his name, but I found I slept easier if I pretended that only meant she wasn't telling it.

I didn't know Baby Girl Slocumb's name for more than two years, not until Liza showed back up, her red-gold hair dulled down and flat with filth and her tilty eyes so tired. She had a long, skinny-legged girl child with a round belly and an earnest gaze slung up on her hip. That little critter clung tight to Liza like a solemn monkey baby. Liza looked like she'd already dialed herself to four past desperate. She had meth sores all around her mouth, her cheekbones so sharp I thought any second they would split and let her tired skull peek through. But the baby—a toddler now—was relatively clean and didn't look underfed. She had one hand fisted up in Liza's hair and was resting easy in her arms.

Liza said, "Big, can I please come home?"

I stared, hope and sick warring at the heart of me, while my angry brain was yelling that before they crossed my threshold, there would have to be a deal. If Liza wanted home, there would be rules, and there would sure as hell be rehab, and I would have to have a legal stake in this child's life, because if rehab didn't work and Liza fell back off the world, I could not lose this child again. She wasn't safe with Liza; I could read more than two years of a hard-road life with drugs and men and God-knew-what-all in the defeated downtilt of Liza's once-mighty mouth and the paper frailty of her skin.

I said, "I don't even know her name. You left here, and her birth certificate still says Baby Girl."

Liza said, "This here is Mosey Willow Jane Grace Slocumb, and, Big, I'm so tired. We are both so tired. Can I please, Momma, please, please come home?"

Mosey Willow Jane Grace Slocumb stuffed a thumb into her mouth, and her lids dropped in a sleepy blink. I was lost in such a rush of pent-up love that my vision pinholed and all the rest of the world grew dark around her. Deals and details could come later. I swung the door wide open for them, right then, because it was all that I could do.

Now I was looking at the keepsake box, full of bones. The baby dress. The old stuffed duck. I knelt down and laid the dress down over the bones like they were cold and it was their small blanket. I couldn't keep myself from understanding. I tried to stand up, but my legs were all atremble. I rocked back on my heels.

"You okay?" Tyler asked. He'd come up behind me with Rick Warfield. I looked over my shoulder. Officer Joel, Immita's only other cop, was with them. Rick was taking this serious, and I had no idea how long I'd been kneeling in the churned earth where the willow used to stand, clutching the sad rag of dress. Warfield squatted down beside me and made a thoughtful *hmm* noise.

"I'm fine, Tyler," I said. I was watching Rick's hands. He kept his nails short and plain, very masculine. I hoped they could be kind hands, as they reached toward the dress. I let him take it and stood up abruptly, turned my face away. I didn't want to watch Rick Warfield touch the bones.

"Uh-oh," Rick said behind me. "See the tag? The Kidworks in Moss Point opened less than twenty years ago, and this dress is still in decent shape. This isn't some old cemetery, Tyler."

But I knew that already.

This was the remains of Baby Girl Slocumb, wrapped tenderly in her yellow blanket and buried with her crib duck for company. Had to be.

I knew, and Liza knew, too. *My baby!* Liza had screamed, over and over as she'd wormed her desperate way across the back lawn. Well, of course she knew. Liza was the one who had buried her. I recoiled a step. Couldn't help but.

Joel and Rick were talking, but none of the words they said made any sense to me. I kept backing up.

"Ginny?" Rick said, and I wondered what dreadful shape my

face must be making to have him sound so worried. My arms went to gooseflesh; he could be acting worried to cover up suspicious.

I said, "I'm fine. It's just so sad and strange." I tried to imagine a huge, cold stone rolling across me and flattening my grimace back into a plain, closed mouth, cool-ironing away the lines that wanted to map grief around my eyes. I turned and walked as straight as I could with the world tilting and rocking and whirling under me to the concrete slab we called a patio. I sank down into one of my stripy plastic lawn chairs.

A word came into my head then, and it was a fairy-tale word, Grimm variety, like "bad wolf" or "wicked witch." Those kinds of words don't hold power over adults. A wolf for a grown woman is just a date who has the grab hands. A witch is the nicest word you call the snappy lady who needs two hundred in cash back, all in fives. The one who rolls her eyes and taps her foot at your careful counting, then says she wants twenties after all while the line rustles angrily behind her in the bright noon rush of lunch hour at the bank on a paycheck Friday. The word was "changeling," and this word had been dug up, ivory-colored and frail, from my own backyard.

I was teetering on the brink of something, and any push could tip me over. I held myself still in the chair, so still, as Officer Joel called in a scientist from the junior college. I didn't even offer coffee, barely breathing. I watched the first scientist call in someone smarter. Tyler spit brown juice on my grass, and Rick made him back away from the hole and the box. It all seemed far and silly and nothing to do with me as I held my balance, a breath away from tipping. I'd have teetered there till the sun winked out, if Mosey hadn't pushed me over. I heard her voice behind me saying, "Big?"

She came and squatted by my chair, her arms looped around her own self in a comfortless hug. I stared at her, blinking. *Changeling.*

"Mrs. Lynch is with Mom. Big, are you okay?" Mosey asked.

I looked at her and I fell, sliding over the lip, down to find what was waiting for me in the dark-lined box they'd dug up from my yard.

Liza's baby had not been given back to her, like mine was when Katrina and the Waves had asked and asked if it felt good; and oh, but it had. It had felt so good to hold my magic, living baby that I hardly remembered labor.

But Liza's baby had really died. I didn't know how. I couldn't even consider that yet. All I knew was that Mosey was the stolen child and Liza was the nixie, trading a loss for something lovely and alive. She'd found Mosey somewhere out in the black span of two and a half lost years, when she was grieving and strung out on every drug she could find to gobble, crazy on the road.

My first thought was that Mosey couldn't know. It would break her heart and could derail her at this crucial time. This was our trouble year. A thing like this could send her careening for comfort into the arms of some boy. Then my vision widened, and I realized that nobody could know. Mosey wasn't ours, and if Rick Warfield figured that out, the state would take her. No one is allowed to keep a child they kidnapped, no matter how many years have passed. They would come and take Mosey.

With that thought, two louder words came in, burying every other living thought. *Beautiful* came first, as I looked at Mosey's damp, dark lashes. She'd been crying, and her mouth had scrunched into a worried wad. Then I thought, *Mine.*

They were the only two words that mattered.

CHAPTER THREE

Liza

THERE IS A true thing that Liza never let go, even in the black, when there was no hum, no breath, no light, no self. This is what she knew: The baby is under the ground, the baby is safe, the baby is safe underground.

It's changed, though. Big is calling for her to come and fight and fix it. "Liza? Liza, is that you?" Big sounds desperate.

The tide rolls Liza back and forth, trying to take her anywhere but now. She spins, so caught in her past that she can't tell where Big's voice is coming from. There is no sandy bed defining the bottom, and she's too deep for light to get down. There is no up. There is nothing but the tide that turns and spins her through the dark. Sometimes in her sleep she sees pale white fish go by, sleek and muscular. They make their own glow, and they have mouths full of needle teeth and bumps where their eyes should be. She isn't afraid of them. Why should she be? She is like them; she belongs here. She deserves it.

She feels a hand that is Big's hand petting her hair. She wishes she could send a message in a bottle, float it up. Liza can imagine herself writing the message with a yellow thing, black point on one tip, the other end squared off and rubbery pink. She has no word for it. She has no word for paper or bottle or message either, no word for under, no word for ocean or fishes or up. Liza knows things and needs things anyway, without the words. Most of all she knows that the baby is no longer safe and she needs to get a message out.

"...the pioneers made terry-cloth rattle ducks," Mosey says, from very far away, and Liza tries to ask Mosey what the ever-lovin' fuck they are teaching her at that Baptist school. She can't find the words for this either, but Mosey's voice is up. Mosey is the real true now; Liza struggles and heaves herself toward Mosey, but when she surfaces, the only face she sees is Big's.

"You sleep now, Little," Big says, hands on Liza's shoulders, lowering her backward into the water. The water closes over her, and the tides catch her, rolling her backward through time, tumbling her through her own memories. Hands are pulling her up now, and they belong to Pastor John at Calvary. She knows these hands, this place, this time; she is thirteen years old, and this is the day she pretended to get saved.

Liza comes up sputtering, waist-deep in pale blue water that smells of chlorine. Pastor John turns her to face forward and drapes one arm across her shoulder, grinning down from the baptismal pool to the church below. Liza scrubs at her eyes. Most of the pews are empty, but the middle rows are full of Calvary Baptist youth-group kids and their chaperones. The kids are hooting, and everyone is clapping for her.

Liza aims a wide smile at Melissa's mother, the only person frowning, the only one whose hands are resting quietly in her lap. *A shame she's not enjoying this more*, Liza thinks. *It's for her, after all.* Mrs. Richardson told Melissa no more hanging out with Liza. There's a Scripture, something about not being yoked up with non-Baptists. So here is Liza, getting dunked at Youth Rally Weekend, and Melissa gets points for the save. Liza's only prayer is that Big won't find out. She doesn't know what would make Big madder, the thought of Liza going Baptist for real or Liza being dishonest enough to go Baptist in name only.

Melissa stands by her mother, her electric blue eyeliner drawn so thick that Liza sees it flash as Melissa tips her a wink. She glances down to see if the red bra Melissa loaned her is showing through the white, and yes, it looks like she has a pair of Claymation Rudolphs pressing their noses through the wet cotton. The bra belongs to Melissa's mother, because Liza couldn't fit in Melissa's A+ cups, even if Melissa owned a red bra. Liza wonders if Mrs. Richardson will recognize by color or cup shape the crimson glow of Liza's boobies, shining through the white.

Liza presses her lips together, trying to look solemn. If she meets Melissa's eyes now, they will both bust out laughing and the whole thing will be ruined.

Pastor John hasn't noticed the bra. He stands sideways to her, talking to the youth about the angels rejoicing at a single lost lamb coming home. He has no idea that as he turned her profile to the audience and began to lower her, she snaked one hand beneath his armpit and held it up behind his back. As her head went under, Liza made sure to keep her fingertips above the surface of the water. Melissa said it doesn't really count if you don't go all the way under, and Liza doesn't want it to count.

She doesn't want to be fresh and sinless this afternoon, when she meets Melissa and Danny Deerfield and Carter Mac up in the tree house. Danny will bring warm beers and some applejack, and she will make out with him. Carter will bring nothing and make out with Melissa, but he'll peek at Liza even as he tries to worm his hand up under Melissa's shirt. If she had let it all be washed away, if she'd let herself be scrubbed clean, returned to the girl she was in middle school—that girl would not do any of the things Liza will do this afternoon. Back in eighth grade, guys like Danny and Carter wouldn't have noticed she was breathing, and she wouldn't have cared. Last year she was a baby who had never been in love.

Now? She's so in love it eats away her oxygen. It's the one thing she doesn't share with Melissa; loving him is something that's only hers. He kissed her once, pulling her into the AV closet after fourth period, but he isn't taking her seriously. He's too cool and beautiful to screw around with fumbling virgins, so she's learning off of throwaways like Danny and Carter Mac. She needs to know everything, so she keeps two fingers in the air behind the pastor's back, curled in a hook to hold her hard-won sins.

Pastor John is still droning on about redemption, and Liza knows what will happen next. She has lived this before, and though she can't make her own body obey or find words or stay grounded in the present, her memories are still her own. She is alive when she can get herself inside them. Next she will change and go downstairs to take her First Communion, lined up with all the other youth. When her turn comes, Pastor John will let her break off a piece of a wide, flat cracker. Melissa's mom will hand her a plastic shot glass, and she'll toss back a dribble of sour grape juice.

But she can't move. She's stuck in this moment, and now the concrete of the baptismal font under her feet is softening. She is sinking, falling below her memories, down into the black depths of dreaming.

Liza turns to wade up out of the pool, to go to the next part of the memory. Communion, the bread, the cup, but the preacher's arm on her shoulder has become an iron bar.

The disapproving face of Mrs. Richardson wavers, and as she sinks, the smiling, wide mouths of the youth-group kids yawp impossibly wider, their faces hinging almost in half to show rows and rows of teeth. They look carnivorous, as though they want to climb up the walls of the font like sticky-fingered tree frogs, join her in the water, maybe get a piece. She's sinking, losing her place, going back under.

Liza strains up, trying to stay in this moment. Trying to keep herself in this small piece of her past. She should be dressed by now, standing in her jeans in the sanctuary to eat that bit of dry, unsalted cracker. She must take the cup from Melissa's mother and drink. The memory holds a message that she has to get to Big.

But there is no floor under her feet, and she sinks deeper and deeper into the darkening water, the smell of chlorine shifting into salt. She is all the way under now, learning what Melissa has known all along: If you don't go all the way, it doesn't count.

Melissa is gone, and her mother is gone, and the youth-group kids. The preacher's hands are gone. There is only Liza, drifting asleep, alone in the black, deeper than anyplace light can touch, no shore in sight.

CHAPTER FOUR

Mosey

I SAT BY LIZA for I don't know how long, waiting for Mrs. Lynch to come. Every now and again, I'd hear the front door open and then someone else tromping through the house and out to the backyard. I stayed put, whispering, "Liza? Liza?"—but my mom lay limp. She'd curled on her bad side in the cold metal hospital bed that looked like something from space. It didn't belong by her moss green wall with all her feather dream catchers hanging over it. Finally I tried, "Mom?" even though I never called my mom Mom. I always called her Liza. Still nothing. "You tell me how is that box of bones out in the yard your baby? Liza?"

I finally heard Mrs. Lynch coming down the hall, talking. I couldn't make out the words, but I knew that nostril-honky voice, all right. My fist snaked out toward Liza like it had its own idea clutched tight inside. When it reached her good side, where all her nerves were working, my thumb and my finger unfolded and got themselves a piece of the skin over her ribs. I pinched her as hard as I could.

She didn't move, not a squawk or a shiver. I twisted my pinchy fingers, like she used to, back when she'd tweak my ear and say, "Cool it, Mosey," if I was showing out. She didn't even twitch, and I let go, panting. She was someplace deeper than sleep, and I couldn't get to her.

I wanted to grab her arms and make her sit up and look at me and relearn how to talk and tell me something that made sense, but Mrs. Lynch was paused right outside the bedroom door. Now I could understand her.

"...hide the dead baby is exactly what a kid would do. Remember that Yankee girl who tried to flush hers down the toilet at her senior prom? That child went right back out to dancing." I found myself standing up and crossing the room fast, while outside the door Mrs. Lynch said, "That was my first thought, too. Apples and trees, but Mosey's skinnier than a ribbon fish, and where would she hide a pregnancy? In her ear? In her little back pocket? Maybe she..."

I yanked the door open, my breath coming so hard it felt like I'd sprinted a mile. Mrs. Lynch jumped and whirled around, clutching her cupped hands to her chest like she was sheltering a teeny, secret rabbit in them, but I knew it was a cell phone.

"Mosey!" she said, her eyes all shifty. "I thought you must be out back with the rest of them."

My voice came out louder than I planned. "It's not a dead baby. It's old, old bones, older than me, even, so you shut the hell up."

Her caught look disappeared, and Mrs. Lynch drew herself up tall, shaking her head at me so the front frizzes of her grayed-out hair trembled. "Young lady, you had best watch how you speak to me." My eyes blazed so hot it seemed weird to me her face didn't melt and drip away like mean wax. Her mouth set, and she said, "Do you hear me? Because I can turn around and go right home. You best apologize."

I blinked, twice, a thousand ugly words rising up all at once and jamming in my throat so hard it hurt. But I worked every word of them down and swallowed. Mrs. Lynch charged Big three dollars an hour to sit with Liza and watch soaps, while a real home nurse cost more an hour than Big made. Anyway, what could my mom tell me with her few words that she hadn't already said in the yard?

"Sorry," I made myself say, and I pushed out past Mrs. Lynch and ran into our tiny cube of a bathroom and slammed the door loud as I dared. I yanked off my stupid skirt and left it on the floor. I stomped on it for good measure. I dug in the hamper for my favorite jeans, and under them I found a T-shirt of Liza's from her job's last Halloween party. It had a leering, pervy skeleton on it, and it said, I GOT BONED AT THE CROW. It was a girl tee, cut curvy with room for boobs I didn't have, but I put it on anyway. It smelled like my mom's fig-leaf body lotion, and for some reason I busted out crying. Only for like thirty seconds, four big whooping sobs, and all these hot tears spilled out so fast it was like both my eyes streamed. I gulped in a big breath, and then, snap, it stopped.

I went looking for Big and found her flopped into one of the patio chairs. She had her back to me and her head hung down. She didn't so much as twitch when I pushed the door open. The yard looked crazy-wrong, with a chunk of blue sky and some slats of the fence where the willow should have blocked my view. The side gate was open, with Tyler's truck stopped halfway through. It was still trailing the chained-up tree trunk with all its twisty roots dragged out behind it. Tyler stood in his truck's bed, leaning with his legs crossed and his butt perched on the roof. Our chief of police, Rick Warfield, was standing by the hole and the open silver box, glaring at two men I didn't know, one an old guy in saggy-butt khakis and a younger fellow with a scraggly beard and those kind of round black glasses like the Santa at the Moss Point Mall wore. Officer Joel was there, too, and it was so weird to have him in our yard. He'd come to school and done the Drugs Are Bad talk every year since I was in the second grade.

I saw I'd left my cell phone on the patio table behind Big. I grabbed it and was about to stuff it into my pocket when it buzzed in my hands. I flipped it open and saw I had about fifty million texts from Roger piled up. The first one said, What did ur mom mean, her baby?

I flipped through the rest of his texts fast, skimming, and they were either asking if I was dedded or trying to puzzle out when my mom could have made another baby without the overinterested folks of the nosiest damn town in Mississippi noticing.

I had no idea. Liza'd told me a thousand times how she'd lost her virginity in the sandpit with Carter Mac. Only six months later, she'd met my nameless sperm donor at a carnival, so she couldn't have had another baby before me. A few weeks after I was born, we hit the road. No way a baby she'd had in Texas or Arkansas would end up buried here, in Big's backyard. Then once we came back home, people would have noticed her being pregnant again. I texted back, Dear U, hi, I am not ded and the bones can't be mom's baby. Unpossible.

His answer came back thirty seconds later:

Dear U, Also unpossible: I am treed by cops in ur yard. 0.o

I texted back, quick as I could, Y R U still here anywai?

Thirty seconds later he came back with, Duh, I had 2 c what happened. Stuck now. HA!

All I needed, on top of baby bones in my yard, was for Big to find out I was skipping to hole up with a boy in the tree house. I could tell her all day long I didn't think like that about Roger, but technically speaking, Roger had a wiener. Big didn't like me to be alone with those things. She acted like I could get pregnant if I so much as stood downwind of one.

I had to move everyone long enough to get Roger down and away. Looking at Big, though, she didn't seem like she had any plans to go inside anytime soon, or even stand up. Her legs looked like noodles.

"Big," I said. Big's head lifted, and she turned it toward me real slow. I didn't know what to say after that to keep her attention away from the tree house. All I could think was, *Hide and seek, Big? Close your eyes and count to a hundred.* That would work perfect if I was five. And if Big had been born stupid. So all I said was, "Mrs. Lynch is with Liza. Big, are you okay?"

She didn't answer or blink. It was like talking to my mom, how she was now. Big's lips sagged open, and her eyes looked like no one was home behind them, and that scared me more than anything that had happened yet today.

I crouched down on my haunches by her and whispered, urgent, "Big? Big? Did you hear what Liza was say—"

She stayed flopped, but she shushed me with a noise so hard it didn't seem made of *sh* sounds—more like a hard *t* had gotten at the front. She stared at me like she was only just now really seeing I was there. She flicked her gaze back and forth, like the good blond girls on *Days of Our Lives* always do when they're being all sincere and desperate. I tried again, lowering my voice and saying, "Liza was saying, 'Give—' "

Big sat up so straight, so fast, it was like God had shot her spine back into her body from space. Her hand darted out, and she pressed it over my lips, her middle finger almost going up my nose.

"We'll talk about it later. Hush now," she said, and she was Big again.

She stood up, moving in her normal quick way, staring all intent across the lawn with her brow furrowing up and her eyes gone squinchy at the corners. Officer Joel was looking at the silver box, one hand rubbing at his mouth. The two guys I didn't know had their heads bent in toward each other and were talking, while Chief Warfield still glared at them all toad-throated and indignant.

I stood up, too, and followed Big to the edge of the patio, nervous. "Who are those two guys that Chief Warfield hates?"

She made angry, thin lips. "Oh, it's too stupid. That one in the glasses is from that junior college over in Barth. He teaches about dinosaurs, and apparently Joel brought him along to say how old the bones were. Which he did not know. However, he was able to confirm that they are not the bones of any kind of dinosaur, so that's a load off, eh, Mosey? I might have guessed all on my own that brontosauruses weren't sleeping all snuggled up to stuffed ducks in the Plesiolistic era, but what do I know? I never went to college."

It seemed to me from her tone that this would be a bad time to point out that she'd kinda melded Pleistocene and Paleolithic and was letting dinos into both to eat up cavemen, but at least it made sense now. Chief Warfield was a deacon at Calvary, where believing in dinosaurs was a sin, but Officer Joel was a Methodist. That was good, because Big got antsy anyplace where, as she put it, there were more Baptists than people.

Big added, her voice only a jot milder, "The dinosaur guy called in that older one, who is some kind of bone teacher, too. So pretty soon we'll have most of Mississippi's masters of higher education in our yard to tell us the sky is blue and water's wet and that is not a T. rex."

Chief Warfield headed across the yard toward us. Big watched him coming, her hands flexing into fists and then opening without her knowing. Past Chief Warfield I saw two heads pop up, peering over our tall wooden fence. It was Jim Place and his basketball son, Irvin. They must have cut through the Baxters' side yard and come up through the woods.

"The Places are peering over our fence," I called to the chief, and it came out sounding real whiny. When I was little and complained about another kid in that voice, Big would turn me around and pretend she was searching my heinie for a tattletail.

The chief glanced over and saw them. "Y'all move along," he called, but real mild. He didn't even wait to see if they obeyed, just came straight up to us, so they stayed right where they were.

"Olive says there's a dead body in here?" Mr. Place hollered at his back.

That made Chief Warfield throw them an irky look over his

shoulder. He called, "Go on, then," instead of answering, but they didn't.

"Olive? Mrs. Lynch's daughter?" Big asked me. "Is she here?"

I shrugged. "She didn't come in with Mrs. Lynch."

Big wheeled toward the chief, but right then his phone started playing calypso music. He held up one finger and said, "My wife," and answered it.

Big stared at him, this WTF look on her face. He turned away and hunched his shoulder up at us. After a minute Big turned her glare at the Places and yelled, "Jim and Irvin! You get your sorry selves out of my woods before I fetch the shotgun and load it up with salt and shoot your looky eyes out!"

Jim's and Irvin's mouths went all unhinged, and they moved away and then disappeared.

"And *that's* how you do *that*," Big muttered at Chief Warfield's back.

I said, "How much longer are these people going to be here?"

She shrugged. "They're waiting on the state medical examiner."

"Why is he taking so long?" I asked.

"I don't know," Big said. "Probably he's held up at a *real* crime instead of whatever mess this is?"

She said it real dark like, and all at once I got that Chief Warfield and Officer Joel and the two professors were standing around nodding and whispering to each other because they thought the bones meant there had been a crime. Big was worried that they were right, that there was a crime. Maybe even that my mom had done a crime; that's why she was shushing me. She didn't want anyone to know what Liza had said about the bones being her baby, and she was so het up over it she was threatening to salt-shoot our neighbors, which was so un-Big-ly that I couldn't hardly believe I'd heard her say it. Her skin was pale and creased, like she'd been heavily asleep for hours and hours with her face pressed into crisp sheets, dreaming bad things.

The chief got off the phone, and Big stalked over to him with her legs gone all stiff.

I knew that Roger had a pretty good view of the back woods from the tree house, so I flipped my phone open and texted him, R the Places still behind there?

He answered, Nah, out in front with others.

That got my attention. Others?

Dood, 1/2 of Immita is in your front yard.

The chief was talking to Big now, pointing this way and that, from the willow's remains to the truck to the box, so I slipped inside the house. I hurried through the kitchen to our den. I jumped up on Big's saggy sofa, and my feet sank up to the ankles into the cushions.

I lifted one of the blind slats an inch so I could peek through on the sly, and all my breath came whooshing out of me. More than twenty people were standing in clots of three and four on our personal grass, whispering and shrugging and watching our closed front door like any second they expected Oprah to pop out and make concerned eyebrows and narrate.

Most were from our neighborhood—some Perkinses and Places and Baxters, all the Daughtrys, and even Emily Beaumont with her brand-new baby in a stroller. They must have seen both of Immita's cop cars parked in front of our house and come down to eyeball us. But I also saw Margee Beechum, who used to work with Big, and the Beechums lived all the way over past Chester Street. I blinked, unsure how the news could have gotten so far already.

That's when I saw Mrs. Lynch's skinny-skank daughter, Olive, wearing a jean skirt cut off so short that if she sat down, I'd have been able to read it was Thursday off her days-of-the-week panties. She was stomping it out from one group to another like a rexed-up Bond girl, face lit up in a vile grin. No doubt she was spilling those make-believe gory details I'd heard Mrs. Lynch saying into her cell, about how I'd hid a pregnancy and the bones were my secret murdered baby. And why not? I was Liza's daughter, just like Liza was Big's. A baby at fifteen was practically my destiny. I felt my stomach seizing up, heating and curling, going harder and smaller like a Shrinky Dink.

I forced my gaze away from Olive and saw we'd even attracted some of the Duckins family: two skinny young-man Duckins with only one shirt between 'em and a haggedy old-woman Duckins, who peeked out like some kind of wild animal between the curtains of her long fuzzy hair. A whole slew of them lived outside Immita on a big piece of trailer-dotted land everyone called Ducktown, and they were all cousins and brothers and aunts with one another so many times over that it was hard to tell who was exactly related and how. Growing up, I'd had six or so in school right around my grade, but I was a sophomore now, and only one was left. Either the rest had failed so many times I'd left them behind by middle school or they had plain dropped out.

OMG I spy Duckins!!!!11111one!!eleventy, I texted to Roger.

He texted back, IKR How did they hear?

I had no idea. It must have been drums or some kind of disaster osmosis, because their phones and power were always getting shut off for not paying and they were so clannish that no one I knew even had a Duckins's number.

I texted, They smelled our blood in the water?

Next a yeti will come then, Roger shot back.

But it was weirder than a Yeti. It was an ice-white Mercedes convertible, and the top was down, so I could see Claire Richardson with a silk scarf over her white-blond pouf of hair. I would have known it was her with the top up; there was only one car like that in Immita. Roger called the whole family the Rich-as-shits, but everyone knew it was *her* family money; her creeper husband was the football coach at Pearl River High, and on that money he couldn't even pay her shoe bill. They had three boys, and two of them had gone to Pearl River to play for him. Everyone called him Coach and made a big deal because we won all the time, even though we were division two and football is stupid anyway.

They had another boy who had asthma and a huge brain, so he went to Calvary. He was a junior the year I was there, so Mrs. Richardson had been around a lot, running boosters and the science fair. Every time she saw me, she looked at me with her thin, pale lip curled up like she was smelling poo. She'd always made it a point to come over to me to say hello, but not to be nice. It was so she could lean in too close, sniff-checking my breath for booze and peering really hard at my pupils. Liza said it was because she'd been tight with Mrs. Richardson's oldest daughter, Melissa, back in the day, and Mrs. Richardson still part-blamed my mom for getting Melissa into drugs and all the bad stuff that happened with Melissa later.

The Mercedes slowed to a turtle creep, and for a second I thought she might actually stop and get out, let her pink-frosted toenails touch Slocumb soil, but a state highway patrol car turned on our street and came along behind her. Mrs. Richardson sped up and cruised on by. I guess three cop cars was one too tacky for her.

I dropped the blind slat into place and turned around and sat on the sofa back. I couldn't stand to see who would come gawk at us next. My phone vibrated again, Roger texting, Starving. Pls put in a fridge. Also a toilet.

He wasn't the only one wanting a safe place to take a pee. I had one more pee stick in my backpack, and I would so literally have killed for three minutes alone in a gas-station ladies' room watching the white window stay blank and pure and tell me this was going to somehow, somehow be okay.

I texted back, O wah, suckitup. U have that Coke bottle. Boys can P anyplace.

Just then I heard Chief Warfield's voice, coming from the kitchen. Big answered him. I couldn't make out the words, but it sounded like they were heading my way. I knew that Big would crap if she caught me standing on the cushions—*My furniture is not a jungle gym, Mosey*—but I paused. If they saw me, they would only send me away. I was flat done trying to pinch Liza awake and getting shushed by Big before I could even ask a question. I stuffed my phone in my hip pocket and clambered over the back of the sofa. I lay across it, then tipped and slid down the wall and landed behind it. There was a narrow crack of space there, just big enough for me to lie sideways with my nose smelling under-the-sofa dust bunnies and my butt pressed hard against the wall.

As the swinging door opened, Chief Warfield was saying, "...lived in this house how long? Thirty years, about?"

"A little less. Since Liza was a baby," Big said.

He said, "That bone doc out there guesstimates the box has been down there more than ten years and less than twenty-five. So you would have had the house then."

There was silence, and it stretched and kept right on stretching. I found myself smiling, proud. Big and me, we watch a lot of *The Closer* and *Law & Order* reruns, and she knew he was fishing. She wasn't going to say an answer until he asked a question.

So he did. "You have any idea who buried that box in your yard?"

"No," Big said. She sounded near.

"No?" he said back, fast. "It's your yard. You must have a thought on the topic."

Big landed on the sofa right in front of my face. It creaked as she settled. "The yard wasn't fenced when I got the house, and we didn't have the patio. It was all woods. Anyone could have come up through the trees."

I breathed through my mouth, trying to be super quiet.

"When did you fence it?"

"Soon after Mosey and Liza came home. So maybe ten or twelve years ago?"

She wasn't giving him a thing he didn't ask for. After another waiting pause, he said, "Why?"

Right then stupid Roger texted me. My butt was pressed hard into the wall, and the vibration made a little buzz of sound against it. I sucked in my stomach and tried to press my hips forward. There was a pause, and then Big cleared her throat in this careful way that usually meant I was about to get grounded. All she said, though, was, "Liza started working with the dog rescue, fostering. She needed a fenced yard."

"So you don't know anything about the remains?" Warfield asked.

Big answered, calm and sure, "I told you, no."

I blinked. I never thought she would tell him what my mom had said, about it being her baby, but I also never had a clue that Big was such a super liar.

Warfield said, "All right, then. I need a minute now to talk to Mosey."

My heart stuttered. When I try to lie, I can feel my eyes opening too wide, and my mouth goes funny. Big busts me out every time. But I would have to lie, and at least as good as Big. Right now my mom didn't have enough consonants to defend herself if Chief Warfield took it in his head that she'd snuck-pregnanted a baby and somehow hurt it. That was so unpossible, though. I knew it wasn't true all through my whole body before my head even realized that the police or even Big might think it. My mom would never, and that was all.

But Chief Warfield didn't know Liza like I did. To him she was some ex-druggie bartender with a crazy, made-up religion. He hadn't seen her spend months slow-coaxing brokenhearted dogs back to trust, some of them so cagey and bad-habited that anyone else would have put them to sleep. He didn't know that if a person had hurt Liza's little helpless baby, we would have dug up that person's bones from under the willow, too, and most of them would have been busted.

Big wasn't having it anyway. "You leave that child be. Mosey's home from school ill today, and she does not need any kind of stress while trying to fight off a flu." She knew I was skipping and not any kind of sick, but she'd already told such a pile of big fat lies that I guess she felt she might as well be damned for a hundred as for one. "And what can she tell you anyway? If that box is at least ten years old, Mosey would have been a kindergartner at most when it was buried."

"All righty. It can wait. I'll go ahead and talk to Liza, then."

Big snorted. "I wish you luck with that."

He said, "Tyler says she seems to understand most of what people say?"

Big said, "Seems to, yeah. But it doesn't mean that she can answer you. She'll say yes or no if you ask her whether she wants to watch TV. She can point to the kind of fruit juice she wants."

Warfield said, "Still."

"Fine. You'll have to come back, though. She was so upset over her willow, and she hasn't got a lot of reserves these days. She's sleeping hard."

I heard Chief Warfield stand up, and he said, "All righty. When?"

There was a thinking pause, and I guess Big didn't see a way to stop him.

"I'm free most evenings," Big said. "Call first."

His voice was going away, like he was walking back toward the kitchen as he said, "Let the ME through when he comes."

I heard the swinging door swoosh open and closed. A bare second after it stopped swinging, Big said, "Mosey," so soft that it was plain she knew I was there somewhere. I poked my head up over the sofa behind her.

"Big," I said, and she jumped and craned herself around to look at me.

"I thought you were in the foyer," she said. That's what she called the teeny cube of hallway that hooked so people at the front door couldn't see right into our den.

I said, real quiet, because I didn't want her to shush me again, "When did Liza have another baby?"

Big looked genuinely surprised, and then she said, "Do what, now?"

I scrambled back over the sofa and hopped down and sat in the chair closest to her. The second I did, the phone in my pocket vibrated; Roger was sending another text, silent this time, because my butt was pressing on a cop-warmed cushion instead of a wall.

I said, "She said those bones were her baby. You heard her."

Big shook her head. Her eyebrows came together, and she said, "Mosey, honey, I know she was saying something, but I'm not sure you understood her right."

I shook my head. "I understood her fine. You did, too."

Big said, "Okay. But, Mosey, I would have known if she'd ever had another baby. She didn't. You know her brain is very, very hurt. My best guess is, somewhere in her memories she knows something about whose baby that is. You know how your mother is about strays. Maybe she helped some girl along the way, some girl whose baby died, who didn't have anyone." Big seemed so sure and calm, and I could totally see my mom helping out some runaway. She had a thing for strays that would surely stretch to a sad, lost stranger girl whose baby'd died. I felt the weirdest feeling of unpinching then. It was like I'd had a hundred awful crab claws clutched onto my spine without me knowing, and all at once a good half of them had let me go.

I said, "Did you know our whole front yard is full of rubberneckers? Not like just our neighbors, but Olive and some others who live all the way across town."

"Good Lord, how did they— Oh. Mrs. Lynch." I nodded, and Big turned to look toward the bedrooms, where Mrs. Lynch was pretending to watch my mother while burning through her phone minutes. Big turned back to me and blew exhausted air out her nose. "Okay, Mosey. I am going to go sweetly as I can tell Mrs. Lynch everything I know so she is at least spreading the truth. Then I am sending her right home, and I'll tell her daughter and any other yahoos on our lawn to move it on along. Don't fret."

She went down the hall to talk to Mrs. Lynch, and I got up, too, and went to the kitchen, needing to move. On the way I checked my phone and saw I had two more texts from Roger.

The first one said, Time for Occam's razor.

I felt my heart speed up a bump as the swinging door flapped like a wing behind me. I sat down in one of the kitchen chairs and braced my elbows on the table. Occam was one of Roger's heroes, although who beyond Roger has a medieval friar as a hero, I do not know. Occam's razor was a theory that said to find the simplest explanation, because it is almost always true.

His next text said, If the baby is yer moms, but she was only pregnant once, what's the simplest explanation? I knew he wouldn't be asking me Occam-style if he hadn't already applied it and had what he thought was the answer. The way Roger liked to use the razor was to call his explanation for anything the simplest and insist that Occam proved he was right.

I chewed my lip, thinking, and then, finally, I got it. I texted back, Holy shit!

He texted, I no rite? So who are you, then?

I thumbed in, A twin? I'm a twin and she buried another twin.

I waited. After a minute he texted, Secret dead twin is not simple, U tard. Still, I could kinda see it. Somehow my twin wasn't alive, and my mom maybe had crazy-bad postpartum and buried him in the yard and then grabbed me and took off hitchhiking to not think about him all dead and buried there. Still, Roger wasn't texting anything, and that sounded more *Days of Our Lives* than simple. Anyway, there was a picture of my sonogram on the mantel, and I sure looked to be floating around all by myself in there.

I prodded him. OK I am not a twin. WTH then.

There was a long pause again, like more than a minute, and then finally a message came: I need 2 do some research. Distract the backyard people?

How???

Just make them look @ U for a sec.

I can't.

Yes U can. You will. I am coming down.

He would do it, because he was Roger and he never got caught. So I jumped up and slammed open the back door and dumped myself out into the yard yelling, "Hey! Hey! Everyone, lookit! Look here at me!"

I must have sounded genuinely desperate, because they all looked: Chief Warfield and Officer Joel and Tyler and both bone professors, the dinosaur one and the real one. I didn't have a single durn thing to tell them. Worse, Chief Warfield was standing toward the rear of the yard; he'd still see if Roger came down.

So I kept on hollering. "I need you all to come here to the patio! Now!"

Tyler hopped down from his truck bed, saying, "Mosey? Is Liza okay?"

That got them moving toward me, and immediately I saw Roger's feet come out of the hole in the floor of the tree house. I yelled even louder, "My mom is okay, but *I* am not okay! I am *not* okay!"

It sounded very, very true when I heard me say it, and Roger had said that the simplest explanation would be true. I could see Occam, with that weird shaved ring of hair like friars have and a brown robe, standing stern and barefoot in my mind's eye, asking me, *If the bones are your mom's baby and she only had one baby... then who the hell are you?*

"What do you mean, you aren't okay?" Tyler said, trotting toward me with worry lines mapping across his forehead.

The look on his face made me realize that he'd been around my whole life, practically, cleaning our gutters and changing the filters in our furnace; he must by now really like me to look so worried. You have a person around for years, maybe you get fond of them even if they aren't really anything to you, and that struck me as huge and important in some way I couldn't get a good hold on. Everyone else sped up, too, coming toward me, and behind them I saw Roger drop the last two feet, stumble, and then he righted himself and swarmed straight up the fence and across like a big-head monkey. He dropped over the top and was gone.

I guess I should have stopped then and said never mind, but I found myself still yelling anyway, desperate like. "I want you all to get out of my yard, is what. Y'all need to go away now, please." My voice was rising and getting louder and louder, and I couldn't make it stop getting louder even though Roger was already gone. My voice yelled, "I am so tired of this, and it is time for you to go away! I want you out, and plus, you are all bastards! You are all all all all bastards!"

The back door had opened behind me while I was yelling, and Big came up beside me. Her cheeks were bright red, and her eyes looked red, too, almost swollen. Her mouth dropped open in surprise. She gaped at me and didn't even say, "Mosey! Language!" so I knew then I must look like a total freak. I started up crying, and Big turned to all the adults who were looking at me, some worried and some just surprised.

Big said, "Okay, you are done here."

Chief Warfield said, "But the medical examin—"

"Rick, please," Big said. "All you people are making my kid a dead mess."

"I can't leave," Chief Warfield said. "The medical ex—"

Big interrupted, almost yelling, "Fine! You stay, but you don't need this whole herd of mammals milling on my grass."

She sounded close to going as hysterical as I was, and Chief

Warfield took over, saying, "You heard the lady. Let's move it out, everybody. No, Joel, don't troop through the house, use the side gate. Tyler, move that truck."

While Chief Warfield rounded them all up, Big put one arm around me and turned me away and pulled me into our own kitchen. She kicked the door shut behind us with a great whamming slap of sound. I couldn't stop crying, because I'd gotten it by then, what Occam and Roger thought was the simplest explanation.

That baby in the yard. My mother said that was her baby, and so I was what? A little something picked wild in Nevada or California, unwanted or stolen or maybe abandoned someplace and rescued like a foster dog? I wasn't Liza's. That meant I wasn't anything to Big either, and Big didn't know. Big's real grandbaby was the baby in the yard. I couldn't hardly be still thinking this, and my arms started flailing and my head went whipping back and forth and my whole middle churned.

Big stayed so calm, gathering all my flailing pieces one by one and tucking them into herself, like my body was made up of fifty different upset ducklings. Once she got me still, she held me while I wailed it out. It seemed like it took a long time. But finally I couldn't keep listening to myself, and I stopped. I snuffled against her shoulder, soaked with all my gross snot and tears. I stayed anyway. When I'd been still for what seemed like a long time again, she sat me down in the kitchen chair and said, "I think we need hot chocolate."

I sat like a tumor while Big got out the milk and a saucepan and the powdered cocoa and the sugar bowl, making me cocoa the same way she had the day I realized Briony Hutchins had ditched me, or when I got that D on the algebra midterm I'd studied so hard for. Big didn't have a Roger. She didn't know Occam. She didn't know. I part wanted to tell her, but I couldn't stand for her to know I wasn't really hers. I pulled my phone out and texted Roger instead.

That's Mosey Slocumb, buried in that box.

I waited for him to say that I was crazy. I waited for him to say anything.

Finally his answer came: Occam? Is that you?

Maybe. I could be Occam. I could be NE1, since the real Mosey is bones.

Big said, "Who is texting you? I thought you kids couldn't text from school."

"Roger must have study hall," I said. "He can text from there."

"Mm-hm," said Big in a skeptical voice, stirring.

I sat there holding my phone, waiting for it to buzz. Waiting for Roger to give me any kind of answer. It was weird, though. Now that I'd decided not to tell Big, I felt clear and light, and I felt little bubbles forming everywhere inside of me, just under my skin. Like when you pour a Sprite and forget about it and all the carbonation sticks to the inside of the glass.

When he finally did, I lifted the phone and read five words: Yes. You could be anybody.

I nodded like he was there to see me, and I felt a couple of the little bubbles launch off the sides of me and rise.

There was another Mosey Slocumb. If she had lived, no doubt she would be scared to move, because every step took her closer to what everyone already knew she would become. Mosey Slocumb would have to be perfect every second, or else she'd slip and land on her back only to stand up pregnant, or she'd gobble drugs and worship trees like a freak, or she'd end up a bank teller in ugly uniforms so no one noticed she was still cute and she'd live for her kid and her kid's kids and probably their kids, and she'd never so much as have a date. But I wasn't that girl.

I was something stolen from someplace so foreign it sounded made up: Miss No One from Nevada. Anonymous from Arizona. My phone buzzed again, but I ignored it. Outside, I held my body still, and the lady who had raised me stirred my cocoa, and the big world turned. But inside, the bubbles went running up through me, more and more, until I was fairly popping with them.

I wasn't me. I wasn't Mosey Slocumb. It was like weights falling off. I could be anyone, and that meant I might do anything. Any damn thing I felt like. Anything at all.

CHAPTER FIVE

Big

We lost Liza almost four months ago, on the night of Calvary High's End-of-School Luau. That night she seemed altogether too pleased to be going to an event that seemed about as much fun as dental surgery to me. Too pleased, and way the hell too pretty. She sauntered out to the car with her eyes striped in black liner and her fat mouth painted a deep plum. She wore a pair of her regular tight Levi's, the ones she called her tip-getters, but she'd paired them with a dressy white silk blouse. It was buttoned to the top, but sheer enough to tell me plain she'd put on a black bra.

"Shotgun!" she called over her shoulder; Mosey was dragging out the front door in her wake.

I was sitting in the driver's seat already, engine running. I narrowed my eyes as Liza climbed in, and she widened hers at me in response, feckless and overinnocent as a kitten who's been off in the kitchen licking the butter.

"You're a little too cute for the room," I said, but she only flirted one shoulder up at me and climbed into the passenger seat. I added, "Would you let Mosey out of the house in a top like that? Monkey see, monkey do."

"Lucky we're not raising any monkeys, then." She tipped her seat forward to make a crack for Mosey, who had finally trudged across the yard to the car. Mosey slipped in, sighing a loud, martyred sigh.

I said, "Oh, stop it. It's not like anyone in this car wants to go."

"I do," Liza said, slamming the door. "I like a luau."

"A Baptist luau? Since when?" I said.

Liza smiled all smug and creamy to herself, facing out the front windshield. Right then I should have sent Mosey back inside and pinned Liza down and tussled it out of her, exactly who she was all dressed up for. Almost every man there would be married and either a teacher or the devout daddy of one of Mosey's classmates. That read to me like three different kinds of hands off, but when it came to men, Liza could miss the nuances.

It was already pushing six, and the luau only went to seven. I backed out of the drive and pointed the car toward Calvary. I'd keep a hard eye on Liza tonight, but I figured I could tell her later on that she ought not to crap where Mosey had to eat. I was certain that all the later on I needed was waiting right around the corner.

Once we were out of our neighborhood, I sped up and said to Liza, "Don't run off. The new science teacher will be there, and we need to meet him. See exactly who is going to be screwing up Mosey's worldview next year."

"Oh, my God," Mosey said to no one, in the back.

"She's not five, Big," Liza said. She was making hula-girl arms, first toward the window, then toward me.

"How else will we know if she only needs to watch Discovery Channel for five hours a week or if I'm going to need to hire one of the fellows who kidnaps cult members to do an un-Baptisting detox?"

"Please don't embarrass me," Mosey said.

Liza was still dancing her top half around in her seat, but she shot me a sideline grin and then said, "Sucks to be a teenager, Mosey-baby. Big has the power to embarrass you just by breathing in public."

Mosey said, real pointed, "I mostly wasn't talking to Big."

Liza laughed outright at that. "I'm the only one looking forward to this, and you want me to sit it out? Fat chance." She was getting used to this new tone Mosey took with her now. A few months ago, Liza had left her little girl to go on an overnight druid campout, and she'd come home to a full-fledged teenager who eye-rolled and flounced and sighed at everything her mother did.

I said to Liza, "Durn right you're going. The first half of Mosey's tuition is due this week if we want to hold her place. Mrs. Doats has left me four messages saying you have not returned her calls." I wasn't about to shell out almost a third of my yearly salary so that Mosey's civics teacher could tell her who was going to hell (Democrats, loose girls, and most medical professionals) and those who weren't (Baptists). "Can you write her a check tonight?" I pressed. Last year Liza had paid every scrap up front, out of her "savings," an animal I would have thought was off playing cards with Pegasus when the ark filled up.

"Tell her I got it covered," Liza said, unconcerned. I felt the little row of suspicion hairs that grow on the back of my neck rising up even higher, because having it covered wasn't the same thing as saying plain she had the money.

I turned in to the Calvary lot and parked, and all I said was, "Mm-hmm. After you write the check, take Mosey around to the booths and take a look at next year's extracurriculars."

"Oh, my God," said Mosey and Liza, same time, same exasperated inflection.

"I'm sorry, but if the child is going to stay at Cal, she needs to have more friends than the Evil Fetus."

"She's staying at Cal, all right," Liza said, firm, at the same moment Mosey said, "His name is *Roger*."

"His name is Raymond," I told her, and Mosey sat up straight so I could get a good view of her rolling eyes in my rearview.

Liza was already slipping out of the car and speeding away ahead of us across the parking lot, getting the jump on me, no doubt running straight into man trouble. Or money trouble. Or both. I tilted my seat back open so Mosey could scramble out, and she stomped along slowly right in my way with her arms crossed and her shoulders in an angry hunch. Liza had disappeared inside before I could hustle our mud-foot kid even halfway across the lot.

Inside, the gym looked as though a discount-vacation brochure had thrown up all over the auditorium. Inflatable pink-and-green plastic palm trees hung down from the ceiling, and a long sheet of butcher paper with a wobbly ocean view painted on it lined the wall behind the stage. Way too many of those seagulls that look like M's had been drawn on, as if it were the backdrop for the high-school musical version of that Hitchcock film. Parents and kids who had come on time were standing in chatty bunches, eating store-bought cookies and drinking what looked like foamy white slushies.

I went with Mosey to get a cookie and said hey to a couple of her teachers, all the while scanning the huge room trying to find Liza and see who she'd been so all-fired eager to talk to. I eventually spotted her up on the stage. She was faced forward, scanning the crowd herself, side by awkward side with Claire Richardson, of all people. They each held a paper cup full of those foamy white drinks, and Claire was facing the crowd as well, unwilling to waste her minty-fresh moneyed breath on small talk with my daughter. Liza sucked at her straw and ignored Claire right back.

I saw Mrs. Doats wending her way toward us through the crowd at the snack table, so I got a good hold on Mosey's arm and steered her the other way. We fetched up by some decorated folding tables where kids were recruiting for chorus and soccer and track and chess. I waved a hand at them and told Mosey, "Pick something, and which one is Mr. Lambert?"

She pointed at a stocky, bearded fellow, and then her expression brightened and she said, "Hey, there's Roger!" before she darted right and wriggled off through the crowd, gone as fast as a skinny minnow. I went over to meet the new teacher. After ten minutes with him, I was confident the fellow knew his way around a microscope and also that he wasn't a pedophile; he told me how the sophomores would be making their own plant-cell slides while sneaking a subtle peek at my age-appropriate breasts. He was cute, and he made a point of saying something about his "late wife," but I'd never date one of Mosey's teachers.

I left him and started looking for Liza again. I was back up near the stage when I felt a light touch on my arm. I turned to see one of the cheerleaders standing there with a tray full of those white drinks.

"Virgin colada?" she asked.

"Good Lord, child, what are you wearing?" It just popped out.

She bridled up and said, "I'm a hula girl. Mrs. Richardson got us these costumes." She had on a grass skirt and a coconut-bra top over a flesh-colored leotard that made her body look naked but strangely wrinkled, like she was a slim, peachy-pink elephant.

Sharla Dartner, another cheerleader, came up on my other side and handed me a large wicker tote bag full of papers and sample-size fruit snacks and hand sanitizer, saying, "Here's your gift pack!" Claire Richardson had put Sharla in a peach-colored leotard, too, as if getting her one that actually matched her flesh might lead folks to realize she was black.

I thanked Sharla, and as I turned away, I found Mrs. Doats blocking my path, staring at me down her knife-thin nose. She bobbled her plastic hump of hair at me and said, "I checked my log, Ms. Slocumb, and I see I have yet to get that installment on Mosey's tuition?"

I busied myself tucking my clutch purse down in the big wicker tote so I'd only have one thing to carry, saying, "I told you, Mrs. Doats, you're going to have to take that up with Liza."

"She seems a little busy just this now," Mrs. Doats said in a prim voice, and she cut her eyes in a telling glance to my right.

I followed her gaze and saw Liza near the wall talking with Steve Mason, a big barrel-chested fellow with a sweep of brown hair and two kids at Cal. I frowned. Steve certainly had enough money to pay a few extra tuitions. He also had a wife. Liza was leaning toward him, very close. Too close. She put one hand on his chest, and her shiny lips parted. She still held her cup with the last sips of her slushy colada in her other hand, and it was like she'd forgotten that it existed. The cup tipped sideways as she leaned in. She looked as if she was about to take a lick off Steve's neck, see if he tasted like ice cream. Steve craned his head away from her and twitched his eyes back and forth, seeking help.

Something was very wrong. Liza, who could read men easier than the morning paper, didn't seem to realize how uncomfortable he was. I left Mrs. Doats without a single word and hurried toward them.

Steve stepped back, and Liza followed, letting her cup fall out of her hand so that the remains of her white drink splashed onto some woman's metallic sandals and up the backs of her bare legs. The woman wheeled around, gasping, and more people turned to see what was going on. Liza cackled like a drunk hyena and splayed both her hands across Steve's broad chest. I caught sight of Steve's wife, off to port. Her eyebrows were up so high they'd nearly hit scalp territory, and she began fast-winding her way through the crowd. I sped up, pushing through and saying excuse me, hurrying to beat her to my daughter.

Claire Richardson was handing a wad of Kleenex to the woman with the splashed shoes, her mouth pursed up tight as a cat's butt, pushing her lipstick into humps. She started to kneel down, more Kleenex in her hand, but I bent and snatched the cup before she could. I sniffed at it, trying to tell if Liza had brought a flask and turned those virgin drinks into something right sluttier. I smelled nothing but that suntan-oil smell, and anyway, Liza didn't drink; in January she'd pressed her twelve-year pin from NA into the trunk of her willow. As I came up beside her, she pushed her thick coils of hair back over her shoulder. I saw how hard her hand was shaking, and I thought, *It's worse than that. It's drugs again. Dear God, she's jacked up.*

Liza vibrated from head to foot, and the years melted away, and it was as though no time at all had passed since she'd shown up on my doorstep with meth sores around her mouth, poor Mosey riding her bony hip. I started shaking, too, with rage, though, a red wave of pure angry that Liza could decide to shit-can her life like this, now, here, at Mosey's school. How could she? How could she?

I grabbed her arm and turned her toward me. She was cackling again, this high, weird pitch of sound, and she kept making it as I spun her. I pulled her away from Steve, everyone staring at us, and I knew what I would see if I got her face pointed up into the light: her dark irises whittled down to rims around huge pupils.

I tilted her face up toward the ceiling, and as the light hit her eyes, I saw one pupil blow open like one of those roses they film blooming fast in stop-motion. Her other pupil spiraled closed, becoming no more than a speck, and she frowned at me, one side of her mouth pulling down as if someone had run a needle and thread through a corner of her bottom lip and yanked.

I took hold of both her shoulders, my anger flat gone and fright rising up behind. This wasn't drugs. Behind her eyes something else, something very bad, was happening. "Liza? Liza?"

She stared at me and said, "The drums gave me a headache," and then I saw it happen. I saw Liza go away. Everything Liza drained out of her twisting face. Half her mouth yawped downward, and she jerked like a puppet with its strings cut and tumbled straight to the floor so fast, no sway, no warning, nothing theatrical about it. I fell to my knees by her and grabbed her, hollering, "Help us! Help!" Conversation died around me, leaving the awful tinny sound of the surfer music coming out of a boom box that was too small for this cavern of a room. I flipped Liza over, and her head lolled back, and both her pupils were blown now. She started jerking in my arms, and her tip-getter jeans darkened as her bladder let go.

I heard a man say, "We need to get a spoon in her mouth," and I yelled up at Claire Richardson, "Call 911, call 911!" Her lips fell open out of their little pursed-up wad, and she stood there, teetering on her high, expensive shoes like a stupid giraffe with her lipstick all in stripes. "Help us, oh, God, help her!" I yelled, but it was like I wasn't speaking English. She stared at me and Liza on the ground, her nose wrinkling as the sharp tang of Liza's urine rose to meet it. Steve Mason stepped around her, and he already had his cell phone out, dialing, so I turned back to Liza.

I heard Mosey wailing "Big? Big?" in a scared, shrill voice, but I was grabbing Liza's head and making her face point at my face and calling her. Her body stilled into deadweight, and she wasn't in her eyes anymore. I started screaming, and strong male hands lifted me and shoved me to Mosey.

The school nurse was by Liza now, saying, "Get that spoon away! Step back, give her air."

I pulled Mosey to me, and we held on to each other in the endless minutes before we heard the sirens in the distance. Liza kept breathing with her head lolled back and her eyelids at half-mast, but she wasn't Liza anymore. She was just a body, taking in oxygen, sending out carbon dioxide for the plastic palm trees.

She never came back. Not until today anyway. I had not seen my daughter for a red second, not until Tyler Baines dug that box up and she'd fought me so fierce in the yard. That had been Liza.

I hoped so anyway, as afternoon faded into evening and I realized that none of us had even eaten lunch. I called Mosey. She came out of her room and sat at the kitchen table like I was paying her to do it, but she didn't much enjoy the work. She stared at the wall with her eyes bright and a feverish splotch in each cheek. Looking at her, I hoped to God I had seen Liza, pulled back into her body in the yard. I couldn't do this on my own.

I stepped to the table and put my palm to Mosey's forehead. She felt cool, almost clammy. She got very still under my hand, waiting it out the same as a cat who likes you but who doesn't much want to be petted will do. I took my hand away.

I couldn't imagine eating, but I went ahead and opened a can of tomato soup and started making grilled cheese sandwiches. I leaned on the counter by the stove, waiting for the soup to heat.

Mosey asked, "Are they all gone?"

I said, careful like, "Everyone except Chief Warfield. He's still waiting on the medical examiner."

"I meant Olive and them, all those people in the front yard."

I turned fast to the stove and flipped sandwiches that didn't need flipping yet, hiding the flush that rose up, hot and hopeful in my cheeks. When I'd gone to roust the looky-loos, our yard had been empty. It didn't make sense. Mosey had said half the town was there.

Then I saw we had a state trooper's car parked on our corner, and I thought his name. *Lawrence.* My heart jammed itself into my throat, pulsing there all red-hot and stupid, and my gaze darted all around, seeking him.

He was in the street facing away from me, but of course I knew it was him. He was ushering our across-the-street neighbors back to their own property.

Lawrence lived clear on the other side of Moss Point, but his territory stretched from the edge of Immita all the way to Pascagoula; he kept his radio tuned to the same station as the local cops. He must have heard Rick Warfield calling Joel to my home address, saying that human remains had been found in my yard.

And he had come. He'd come immediately to do me a kindness

on the sly. I hadn't seen Lawrence in more than twelve years, but it didn't matter. Looking at his straight spine, the shape of his broad shoulders in his trooper's uniform, it could have been a day ago. It could have been this morning. I was already stepping through the open door, as if my body had been called to his.

I only stopped myself by asking, when he got home tonight, would he confess to his damn wife that he'd been on my lawn today?

"The police sent them all home," I told Mosey now, and I was proud to hear my voice came out hardly trembling. I flipped the sandwiches onto the undone side. Not three seconds after I'd seen Lawrence, Mosey had started screaming in the backyard, telling the cops and the professors and even poor Tyler Baines to get out, calling them all bastards. I'd closed my front door and run to find her. Lawrence must have gone home to Sandy and his boys without so much as knocking on my door.

Perhaps he thought seeing me, even after a dozen years, was too powerful a thing to play with. The heat washing even now through my face, down into my chest, landing lower, told me he might've made the right call. He had simply come and done what he could for me, not making any kind of scene. Very like him. I blinked hard and willed my cheeks to cool while I ladled out the soup.

When I brought Mosey's dinner to her, she said, "Thanks. Gramma."

She made the last word into its own sentence, then cocked her head sideways. She sounded curious but a little distant, like a scientist on Discovery Channel waiting to see what the things in his test tube might do.

"You're welcome. You want milk?" I said, puzzled.

"No thanks," she said. And then she added that word again, all alone. "Gramma."

Her bright gaze was fixed on her food, but she was watching me in her side eyes. I found myself going still, not sure what reaction she was looking for. I'd always been Big to her.

"What's with the Gramma?" I asked, careful to keep my tone light.

Mosey shrugged. "I think it's weird I call you Big. And it's super weird that I call my mom Liza."

I went back to the counter to load Liza's dinner onto a tray. "You were already calling her Liza when you came to live here."

I hefted the tray, and Mosey leveled a gaze on me so intense it felt like a glare. "Didn't you want me to call you Gramma? Or Mee-Maw or something?"

That question seemed as loaded as a pistol. I met her gaze and said, "Well, Liza named me Big, back when I used to call her my Little. When you came home, you picked it up from her. Maybe I still felt too young to be a mee-maw."

"What about now?"

I felt my lips thinning because, truth told, I thought forty-five was still young to be already a mee-maw. Mee-maws traded their skinny jeans for those Christmas sweaters with the three-dimensional sequined appliqués of reindeers with jingle-bell harnesses. They knitted and never learned the tango or went to France or had sex again in their whole lives. I wasn't there yet, please God, but I also wasn't sure exactly what Mosey was asking. "I am your gramma, doodle, so you can call me what you like. Let me get this to your mom while it's still reasonable hot."

Mosey's overbright gaze followed me out. The second the swinging door stopped slapping back and forth between us, a whole-body blush heated all my skin, and I felt a thousand miles away from being any kind of mee-maw. Lawrence had been here.

I walked back to Liza's room fast as I could with a bowl of hot soup sloshing around on the tray. Lawrence had come, and that meant he still remembered. Maybe too vividly, like me, maybe only in guilty flashes on the side. But he remembered. I pushed down the foolish curl of something almost happy that I felt rising in my belly and nudged Liza's door open with my foot. I would think of Lawrence later. If I truly meant to keep Liza's secret, there were things I needed to know that only she could tell me. Assuming I had truly seen a flash of Liza in the yard. Assuming Liza was alive, way down inside her body.

I went into her quiet room. She was lying down where I had put her, turned onto her good side with her weak arm tucked in close facing the wall. The last of the day's sunlight was coming in through the sheers to touch her face. I set the tray down on the wicker dresser that she'd painted up with vines and flowers, and then I crawled over the foot of the hospital bed and crept up into the crack between her and the wall, pressing my back against the cool green plaster.

The sun was close to setting, and I hadn't turned the lamp on, but I could see that Liza was awake now. Her eyes glittered at me, pitch-black in the dim room, floating a thousand colors like an oil slick. My heart leaped again at the fierceness of her gaze. This was Liza. She was here.

"I need help. You understand me, Liza-Little? You play your cards close. You always have, but you have to help me understand now, for Mosey."

Liza's gaze stayed fixed on me. I thought she would keep silent, but she made her "yes" noise. It came quiet, but not faint. A strong whisper of affirmation.

"Oh, God, I wish that you could tell me what happened, Little. I have to ask—only so I can protect you—did you do something? I forgive you already if you did, you understand? You were so young. I need to know about your poor little girl in the backyard, Baby Girl Slocumb. Did you do anything, anything at all that might have hurt her?"

Liza's good eye blazed up bright, and suddenly I felt a hot pain on the side of my breast, as if a bee had been hiding in the sheets and it had stung me. I jerked and slapped at it and found Liza's hand. She had reached forward and pinched the first piece of me she came to with every bit of fury she owned.

I felt my eyes well up. "Of course not. I knew that. I knew you couldn't."

Liza met my gaze, steady, waiting for the only question I could ask next. I had to know, and crib death was the only thing I could think of that made any kind of sense. "That night. The night you ran away. Are you saying you woke up and she was already gone?"

Liza made her "yes" noise, a heartbroken, small sound that seemed to echo in the dim room.

I nodded, and I wished we could stop here. I wanted time for us to lie quietly together and mourn. I wanted to hold my child. Liza had been carrying that silver box, so tiny, but so very heavy, alone, for years and years. But I couldn't pause just yet. There was more at stake here, more hard questions that had to be asked. My chest felt like it was screwing itself closed. I trusted Liza's heart, but I'd never had a single skinny reason to trust her judgment.

I said, "Was it bad, the place where you got Mosey?"

Liza didn't look away or even blink. She hissed out a long, serious "yes" noise.

"Very bad?"

Again her quiet yes.

"Should I go looking for her folks, to let them know that Mosey's okay?"

Liza made a fierce, unrecognizable noise, hard, pushing it out with all her breath, and this time I felt her good hand coming at me to pinch me. I caught it on my own and held it tight between us. I knew my Liza. She was wild, but I'd never seen her cruel. Look at how she'd buried her own lost child, wrapped warm in a blanket with a stuffed duck for comfort, resting in her special silver box. If Liza stole Mosey, she was making it plain now that Mosey must have needed stealing.

"Don't you get me wrong," I whispered. "I am not looking to return her. She's ours. No question, that's our girl."

Another pause, and Liza made a noise, soft and segmented, like a bleat from a baby goat. I shook my head, puzzled, and she repeated it, a jumble of *n*'s and *b*'s and vowels.

I shook my head, as frustrated as she was. I was thinking of my lost grandchild and my half-lost girl, who was too broken to tell the police that her own baby had stopped breathing in the night. She couldn't explain or defend herself. No statute of limitations would apply if they thought the unthinkable, that Liza had killed her baby. And even though she'd been blameless there, stealing Mosey was big-time felony bad. It had been Liza's crime until this moment, but it was mine now, too. Accessory after the fact, they called it on *Law & Order*. We still had Mosey, which meant we'd been actively kidnapping her for about thirteen years now. It was all kinds of wrong, and I knew it, but I couldn't see an open path that led me someplace righter. The law doesn't let baby stealers keep the kid, no matter how many years have passed, no matter how fond of the thieves the kid has grown.

I realized there was no decision to make. Mosey was mine, and I was hers. Liza hadn't had the legal right to give us to each other, but it was done. I could no more undo it now than I could stop my own heart beating.

That meant no one else could know that the baby in the yard was Liza's. No matter what. I needed to find out what Rick Warfield was thinking, if he was sniffing any territory near the truth.

That led me back to Lawrence. He was a statie, but Immita was a big chunk of his territory. He was in thick with our cops. Poker-buddies thick. He'd know every turn the investigation took.

He was home with his wife by now, but he'd come riding up like a white knight in his black-and-green cop car to kick everyone off my lawn the second he knew I needed him. He must have buried a secret box inside of himself where he still cared about me. That could be right helpful, if I was willing to use him. I asked myself if I was, and instantly this image rose in my mind: Rick Warfield reaching for the silent bones of Liza's baby. I thought of rough hands like that reaching for Mosey, taking her as if she had no more say in it than those poor little bones.

I felt pretty willing, then.

I said, "It seems to me the best thing I can do is keep a lid on this. At least until Mosey's eighteen."

Liza made her "yes" noise three times, emphatic.

I started to squirm backward to get up, but Liza's good hand caught me again, and she would not let me go. She made a new noise at me, like the caw of a crow. She made it again, her black eyes glittering in the last rays of sun. Since the stroke I'd wondered how much thinking was going on. At the emergency room, they'd stabilized her, but they hadn't done much else. During the little bit of rehab she had gotten, the main doc told me it was likely she'd been born with a flaw in her brain. All the drugs she'd done, especially the meth, could have made it weaker, but the stroke could have happened any minute, all her life. He said her speech center was hurt, but it was possible that inside she was thinking fine. She might talk again. Sometimes the brain could find another way, especially since she was so young and strong.

She was thinking something now. That was plain. Liza was seeking another way, desperate to tell me something. "I don't understand."

She made her noise that meant Mosey-baby, soft. Then she made it again, so desperate that it flat broke my heart in fifteen pieces.

I said, "I'm going to get you out of there." It came out quiet but so fierce. "I'm going to come down where you are and find you and dig you out and pull you up so you can tell me."

She exhaled, long and frustrated, then made her "yes" noise. We lay there in the last of the dying light looking at each other, and in that silence I heard the back door open and the buzz of conversation as Rick Warfield and the ME said good night to Mosey. I heard the heavy fall of their booted feet, and my hand reached under the covers for Liza's hand and found it coming to meet mine. We lay together in the white sheets, clutching each other, listening to the unstoppable sounds of busy men slow-stamping, overburdened, through our house.

They carried the bones of Liza's baby with them, and their solemn footfalls were the closest thing to a funeral procession our lost girl would ever likely get. In the echoes of that walk, I found myself whispering, "Peace, peace, peace." I didn't know if I said it to Liza and me, to soothe us, or if I was saying a funeral prayer, the first unangry words I'd said to God in almost thirty years. But either way, the footfalls passed through and our little girl was gone.

In the silence we heard Mosey digging around in the kitchen, probably hunting my stash of good chocolate.

"I need you back, Liza. We can't let them take *her*," I said.

I stared at Liza, and "dread" was the only word for what was filling me up. I clutched her good hand, and an answering word rose up in Liza's oil-black eyes, so clear she didn't have to say it.

War.

CHAPTER SIX

Liza

WHEN BIG LEAVES Liza alone in her room, her eyes stay wide, staring down the darkness; she is seeking the right word to give to Big. The bed pitches and rolls underneath her, trying to suck her down into the black of her own past, but she fists the fingers of her strong hand deep in the sheets. She stays, straining toward it.

She can see the word she wants to say shining in her head, clear and hard and empty and sparkling. She can imagine Mosey taking it down from the cabinet, setting it on the kitchen counter. She can see Big filling it with water from the tap. She knows exactly how its cool rim would feel against her lip if she lifted it to her mouth and drank, but her mouth can't find the shape of the word that is this thing. She's choking on it.

She feels the blood pounding through her, liquid and angry, and her head aches as she struggles toward the way that word used to taste, the way that word used to form itself so simply and spill out with a hundred other words, effortless.

Her head hurts, and it shouldn't be this hard. She's done this before. Every person has to learn these mouth shapes, word by word, starting with "Momma" and "bye-bye" and "uh-oh." But the first time Liza learned to speak is too far down in the black waters, in a place too deep to ever go.

There is another way to make this word, though. She does remember learning how to write. First grade. At Loblolly Elementary.

She closes her eyes, unfists her hand. Stops fighting it. The bed pitches and tips beneath her, a raft on the waters of memory, and she lets herself roll off it and go under. She tries to move with the tides now, knifing through the roiling black with purpose as she is pulled and washed and spun through all the Lizas that she used to be. Liza under the willow, pressing her nine-year pin into the bark, an offering and a promise to the baby who slipped away in the night. Liza in the middle of the meth year, her blood roaring through her, foamed and violent as white water, riding a nameless man toward unmanageable pleasure while Mosey sleeps in a closet in the room next door. Liza with her arm over Melissa's shoulder, holding a joint to Melissa's lips as Melissa sucks in, holds, and chooses the boy she's going to own tonight.

Liza goes deeper; past all this, looking for fat pencils and composition books. Mrs. Mackey. A class turtle in a terrarium. The mysteries of ABC plastered in bright colors on the walls.

She washes up close, very close. It is the tail end of summertime, the week of the double Vacation Bible Schools. First grade and Mrs. Mackey will come Monday.

Every morning she goes to what Big calls Hippie VBS at tiny River Bend Baptist. There Miss June has an acoustic guitar and a white rabbit named Angel in a hutch. They don't do a lot of crafts there. They run outside, Miss June tells stories, they sing. Mostly about Jesus, but they begin every day with a song that Big has on a record at home. On Tuesday, Liza asks Miss June why they sing a radio song at VBS, and Miss June gets her Bible out and shows Liza that the song is in there, hiding in Ecclesiastes.

"'To every thing there is a season, and a time to every purpose under the heaven,'" Miss June reads, her finger pointing to each word as she says it aloud. To Liza the letters are spindly black lines, as random as bug legs picked off and scattered on the page.

"'A time to keep silence, and a time to speak; a time to love, and a time to hate; a time of war, and a time of peace.'" Liza watches Miss June's finger, staring so hard she's surprised that the onion-paper page doesn't smoke and curl into ashes, but it's meaningless. All Liza knows is that Big would be mad if she knew the Byrds had snuck a Baptist song into the house.

Hippie VBS is over at noon. On her lunch hour, Big picks her up and dashes her to Rich People VBS at Calvary Baptist. They start at one. Liza sits by Melissa, gluing elbow macaroni to construction paper. Melissa is her new best friend, but after VBS, Liza will go to public school and Melissa will be here at Calvary Christian. Calvary has not expanded the school past fifth grade yet, so middle school will bring Melissa back to her.

Rich People VBS has lots of crafts and store-bought snacks, thirty-six-count boxes of brand-new Crayolas that each kid gets to keep, and a basket of shiny blunt-ended scissors with colored handles. There are only two pink pairs, and she and Melissa get them every time. Melissa makes sure, and she gets them the biggest cake at snack and first go on the swings.

Here you don't call the teachers Miss or by their first name like at Hippie VBS. She has to call Melissa's mom Mrs. Richardson. Story time isn't like at Hippie VBS either, where it's only Miss June and a picture book. At Calvary they have a felt board and a ton of people-shaped felties in Bible-times dress to act it out. They have puppets, too, and on Friday the youth group comes and does the Bible story like a play.

Liza likes the stories here. They remind her of the Grimm brothers' fairy tales that Big says are too bloody, that she begs for anyway. Little Snow-white, making her stepmother dance herself to death in red-hot iron shoes at the wedding, has got nothing on the Bible. Here King Solomon calls guards to cut a toddler in half, a man named Samson kills a thousand people with a bone, and God drowns everyone. Pharaoh murders babies, so one mom floats hers down the Nile, and—Liza knows from her *Big Book of World Reptiles*—that river is full of crocodiles. An especially big and person-eaty kind that only lives in Egypt.

Melissa and the other Calvary kids have heard these stories every week since they were too little to follow. They yawn and pick at their shoes and whisper all through story time, but Liza is silent, big-eyed; the tales thrill her no end. At the end of story time, she's the kid leaning forward, eyes bright, calling for the puppets to come back and show the awful thing that happens next.

It's Friday, her last day with Melissa. At the head of the table, Melissa's mom sits chatting with the other two moms who run the craft room, her hands cupping her potbelly.

Melissa says to her mother, "Can Liza and me have a play date tomorrow?"

Melissa's mom looks to Liza, surprised, then says, "I don't think so, Melissa. She lives very far away."

"So what?" says Melissa, getting whiny. "She's my best friend."

Melissa's mother says, "We'll see."

Liza shoots Melissa an agonized glance; when Liza's mom says that, it means yes, but she can tell that Melissa's mom means no. Melissa's eyes narrow. She doesn't like to be told no. Melissa's mom keeps on looking at Liza, mouth bent funny and her nose in a crinkle. Both her hands rest lightly on her belly pooch.

Liza says to her, "Melissa says she's getting a baby sister."

Mrs. Richardson starts, as if she didn't realize she was still looking at Liza in the same way she looked at the bug corpse she had to pick up with a tissue. She speaks too sweet, as if Liza is a baby. "Does she, now? Maybe she is. But she might be getting another little brother."

Melissa makes a gagging sound in Liza's ear, whispers, "Brothers have a weenus."

Liza says, out loud, "I wish I had a little sister."

The mother next to Mrs. Richardson says, "Oh, I bet you will soon enough," and for some reason this makes the mother in the middle laugh, but not nice. It's a nasty sound.

The nasty laugher says, "I'm surprised you don't have two or three already."

Even Melissa's mother smiles a sour smile at that, but she says, "Hush, now. Little pitchers."

Later, Big won't explain why it was funny. She gets choky-sounding and says, "Do you know what a week of day care costs? And you are starting real school next week."

All Liza understands is, it's the last day of double VBS, and she clings to Melissa, who bares her teeth like a mean dog when Big reaches to peel Liza away. Big says to Melissa's mom, "The girls are so attached.... Maybe we could..."

Liza—legs braced, hands fisted in Melissa's sparkly T-shirt—sees for the first time how her Big doesn't look like the other mothers. She looks like Miss June or one of the Calvary youth-group kids who did the Bible play. It is Melissa's mother who at last puts firm hands on their shoulders and peels them apart, saying in a stern motherful voice, "Now, stop being so dramatic. Good grief." Her hands pinch just short of hard enough to hurt. Liza is helpless against her firm hands, her grown-lady tone. She turns Liza and bundles her into the back of the car.

"We'll always be best friends!" Melissa yells after her as Big drives away.

Then Big gets choky and won't explain anything. Liza cries in huge gulping cries, aimed at her unfair mother's cruel back, all the way home.

By the time they pull in to their driveway, Liza is bored of crying, and when Big speaks, the choky voice is gone. She sounds like Big again. "If you can dry it on up, I have a surprise for you."

Liza sniffs and swallows. "What is it?"

Big will only say, mysterious, "It's a week of double VBS instead of day care, is what it is."

Inside, on Liza's bed, is a brand-new backpack, hot pink and splashed with Muppet Babies. There is a new Muppet Babies lunch box, too, and a little heap of brightly colored clothes with tags still on. There's a pair of Keds so white she knows they came from Penney's, not New to You or Hand Me Ups. The backpack is stuffed with school supplies: fat wax crayons, pink erasers, composition books.

She flips open one of the notebooks, but the pages are blank. The word she is looking for isn't here. There are no words here, and Liza rolls in the water, rolls away, leaves her little self trying on a first-day-of-school dress.

She is still seeking this word to send to Big, so intent on finding it that she almost misses the message she is sending to herself: As she spins through her memory, she wordlessly skims past Melissa-less moments, sticking in the places where she finds Melissa waiting.

The taste of salt on her lips. Melissa at the beach. That last day.

"It's you," Liza says. "You're the key."

Melissa smiles, agreeing, smug.

Bitch always did have to be the center of attention.

CHAPTER SEVEN

Mosey

NEXT MORNING, BY the time Big tapped at my door and called, "Mosey? You up?" I had my school stuff ready to go and I was dressed all the way to my shoes.

"I'm up," I called back, trying to sound sleepy even while I was beaming laser-hot "Do not even peek in here" rays at her through the wood. I heard her walk away, and I slunk across the room and pressed my ear against the door. I listened to Big help my mom into her walker and take her up the hall. As soon as the swinging door to the kitchen started flapping, I darted out of my room and into Liza's.

I started with the dresser, sifting through her underthings in the top two drawers, but I didn't find any convenient secret diaries buried in her bras. I opened the deep bottom drawer and felt my way through the stacks of clean T-shirts that had been folded the way Big did them, into threes. I found a big fat bunch of nothing there, too.

Most of Liza's books were on the hall shelves, but one was on the bedside table, open in a tent, like any day now she would remember how to read and pick it up and finish it. I grabbed it by the covers and shook it, pages down, but no letters from old friends fluttered out to say, "Congrats on stealing that baby in this specific town on that specific date." Not that I wanted it to, much. I wasn't really looking for anything about me or where I might have come from. I was looking for her, trying to meet the secret baby-stealing person she'd been all this time.

In the closet Liza's clothes hung in neat Big-sorted rows, all her jeans and leggings together, then her tops, then a couple of emergency dresses for when she had to get her taxes done or Big made her come to a parent-teacher conference. Her pretty shoes used to be all in a tumble in the bottom, but Big had them standing in neat pairs, toes pointed toward the bedroom door like they were waiting in line to leave. These days all Liza ever wore was Keds. The top shelf held only clean sheets and towels and an old stuffed bear of mine crammed in the corner. She stared at me all accusing with the one button eye she had left.

"Oh, shut up, Pauline," I whispered to her. "Like you wouldn't do the same thing."

It wasn't as if Liza *could* tell me anything even if she wanted to, and I didn't think she wanted to. I felt like I ought to hate her over it, or at least be mad enough to spit at her, but it was the opposite. While I pressed down the toe of each shoe, checking for secrets, my insides were bubbling up all through me like a brook with a bad case of happy.

From the kitchen I heard Big holler, "Mosey, are you really up?"

I froze. Big was making breakfast, thinking I had the right to call her Gramma, if I wanted. Liza and me, we knew better. Even though Liza was all brain-hurt and didn't know that I had figured out her secret, in some weird way it made me closer to her. Big was the only one in the house who was clueless that I did not belong here, and the way she kept treating me so regular and ignorant was making me crazy.

"I said I was, oh, my God!" I hoped she couldn't tell I was yelling from the bedroom next door to mine. My voice sounded shaky, even to me.

My mom kept her flat plastic picture bins under her bed. I slid all three out, then popped open the first one. It held a buttload of her weird photos in a loose stir. I dug my hands in and sifted through them. Nothing. In the middle box, I found the digicam she'd gotten at the flea market, more photos, and a ziplock bag with all her old, full memory cards; we didn't have a computer at home where she could store the files.

The only personal thing I found was a picture of Bunnies, one of my mom's old foster dogs, tucked all by itself into a white envelope. Liza still had a scar on her arm from the day she stole Bunnies. She'd had to shimmy through barbed wire to untie him from a tree. Bunnies had been bald from mange, so skinny I could have run my hand along his sides and counted his ribs if he hadn't been too gross with sores for me to stand to touch him.

We had Bunnies for almost thirteen months, longer than my mom had ever kept a dog. Big still called that time the Year of Whispers, because Bunnies was so trauma'd up that if anyone raised their voice at all, Bunnies would cut loose and pee a bucket. He was some little kind of terrier, but his bladder must have taken up 90 percent of his inside space.

I'd never known my mom to shoot pics of any her fosters, or of Big and me either. She liked to snap tea sets and garden lizards and stranger babies in hats and interesting shapes in the sidewalk cracks, not stuff from her life. In this picture Bunnies was a silky ball of toast-colored fur with a laughing face, standing all confident in the grass. My mom must have taken it right before she gave Bunnies away. I stuffed it in my back pocket.

I pulled the last box toward me, ticked that all I'd found so far was a picture of a foster dog she'd ditched three years ago. If some TV detective went through all the crap tucked away in my room, he'd be able to tell my age and who my best friend was and that I hate math but like science and that I have a bad Strawberry Bubble Tape habit that Big said was going to rot my teeth. A really good detective would find the stash of unused preggo tests under the loose floorboard in my room and assume all kinds of exciting things about my nonexistent sex life. In Liza's room there was nothing more personal than her underpants, and all they told me was that my mom sure liked thongs.

The last box only held the molding photo albums that Big had bought from a sale bin at Dollar General a few years back. Liza had named them the Old Maids because they had fussy floral covers like for a spring wedding, and she'd added, "And no one I know is ever going to slip a single picture between their pure white pages."

I sat back on my heels and peered around the room. There wasn't anyplace else to look. I blew the air out of my lips in a flappy raspberry, then started pulling the Old Maids out of the box, one by one, just to be sure.

The velvet pouch fell out of the third one.

It was a rich purple, almost as wide and long as the cover of the Old Maid. I flipped the album open and saw that Liza had removed a bunch of the empty pages. Then she'd slid this in between the covers. It looked like the kind of pouch Crown Royal came in, but my mom didn't drink. Plus, the pouch was pushed into a rectangle, like it had a box inside shaping it instead of a bottle.

"Breakfast!" Big yelled from the kitchen at the worst possible second ever in the history of interruptions.

"Just a minute!"

I picked open the strings of the pouch and pulled the mouth wide. I tipped it, and a sleek wooden box came sliding out. It had a gold clasp that latched it shut at the front, but no lock. I took a deep breath to steady myself, then thumbed back the clasp and opened the lid.

For a second I wasn't sure what all I was looking at. The box was lined in more velvet that was spread over a frame shaped to hold the objects inside: a couple of pink tubes, one large and one small, a string of smooth stone beads, each the size of a rubber bouncy ball, and a small, ivory-colored hooky thing. I picked up the bigger tube. It was blunt at one end and tapered at the other. It felt cool and too heavy to be solid plastic. I shook it, and it rattled; something was inside, all right. On the flat end, the bottom had a seam. I thought it must be a lid. My heart was thumping so hard. I twisted at the lid, and the tube came alive and started vibrating in my hands. I dropped it and let out a little scream.

"Your eggs are getting cold!" Big yelled.

"Oh, my God, can you ever leave me alone for one second?" I hollered back, and it came out just raging. No answer. I was suddenly horrified. What if I'd been snotty enough to call Big back to lecture me and she found me in my mother's room playing with a box of creepy sex things?

I picked up the one I'd dropped like it was a mouse corpse, barely touching it with a thumb and finger, but then I realized I had to turn it off or it would buzz and rumble in the bottom of the box until Big tracked it down by sound. I grabbed it around the base and shut it off, saying, "Ew, ew, ew," the whole time. I got it all put back the way I'd found it, box in pouch, pouch in album, albums in bin, and then shoved the whole mess as far under the hospital bed as it would go. I stood up and backed up all the way across the room.

I peeked out Liza's door. The hall was clear, so I ran to the bathroom and washed my hands with water so hot it turned my skin pink, wishing I had Clorox and freaking out. I couldn't stop myself from wondering if she'd ever taken this box into the woods, when she was druiding, and that made me have to wash my hands again.

"Grow up," I said to the Mosey in the mirror. My mom hadn't brought a boyfriend home to meet me in my whole memory, but different men used to call the house a lot, asking for her and not leaving messages. Sometimes I heard her coming home three hours after The Crow had closed. It wasn't as if the idea that Liza liked men and men liked her back was new or shocking to me. Besides, I knew Liza's biggest secret now, and it bound us in a way that was fifty million times bigger than her box of buzzing yuck, bigger even than the fact that her religion wasn't about any kind of god I'd ever heard of.

I went to the kitchen and found Big at the sink, washing her dishes. She glanced at me and said, "Hey, sugar-doodle, your breakfast is on the table," like everything was regular. I glared red needles into her head, but she didn't feel it. My plate was sitting in front of the chair by Liza's good side, the place I'd gotten used to sitting. I didn't feel like sitting there now. I sat down across the table from her instead, my back to Big, and pulled my plate across.

I said, "Hey, Liza."

She was looking right at me, and she made her Mosey-baby noise. I felt it again, that weird burble of happy feeling, like I wanted to lean across and kiss her on the hurt side of her face. I sat there swinging my feet and looking at her until Big said, "Eat your breakfast."

"Not hungry."

"You need the protein." I rolled my eyes for Liza, and the good side of her mouth twitched up, like she was laughing with me at this dumb-ass nutrition stuff when she knew and I knew that Big didn't have the right to make me eat any damn thing. Big asked, "You want to stay home, Mosey? I could take the day off if you want."

The very idea of sitting at home with her being Biggish and talky and helpy made my skin want to all come off and crawl away. I was glad I had my back to her. If Big knew I was some sort of squawky cowbird that Liza had slipped into her nest, would she be looking at me all worried, wanting me to eat her cooling eggs? They stared up at me with their yolks shining like glazy yellow eyes. Vile.

"Makeup civics quiz. I gotta jet." I gave my mom a fast conspirator's grin and then grabbed the toast and shoved my chair back, almost running to bang my way out the front door and get fast as I could away from Big's looky eyes.

I made the bus with time to spare. As I dragged my backpack to my usual seat near the middle, Beautiful Jack Owens looked up, pushing his floppy blond hair off his forehead.

"Hey, Mosey," he said.

I stopped dead and said, "Hey."

I guess I would have stood there goggling at him with my mouth swinging open till drool fell out, but the bus jerked forward and sent me staggering past him. I hustled to my usual place and plopped down. But after I sat, BJO turned and flashed me a smile over his shoulder, that lopsided one that could make a thousand pairs of cheerleader panties fall down on the floor in a pattery avalanche.

I ducked my head down fast and powered up my phone. My thumbs were already tapping out, ZOMG BJackO knows my name, when I saw I already had a couple of texts from Roger. The first one was from yesterday, and it said, # of missing babies = none babies.

I rolled my eyes. Roger had this bee completely up his butt that he was going to trace my mom's route and find out who I was. He'd sent me fifty million texts about it last night, using so many abbreviations I felt like I was being told his whole lunatic plan by lolcats. I'd finally turned my phone off when he'd said he was searching news archives to see if any babies between here and Pascagoula had mysteriously gone missing the same week my mom ran away. Apparently he'd come up empty, which of course he would. The whole idea of using Google Maps to trace my mom's drugged-up, hitchhiky route across America, fifteen years later and with her unable to help, was so wildly unpossible.

He had not downloaded any wisdom in his sleep, because his text from this morning said, What was L's first road job?

I sent him back one that said, U can b replaced, u no. BJackO just smiled at me w/ all his teeth. I am Bones in the Yard Girl now & totally superfamous.

His answer came back, Superfamous = ur destiny. If u were here @ Cal? You'd be Luau Stroke Mom Girl. So.

I texted, Way to brightside, giggling loud enough that the bug-eyed freshman girl on the seat across from me stared at me harder than she'd already been staring.

His next text said, I need u to sho me her route on map. Meet on roof of TRP?

He meant Charlie's Real Pit BBQ, which he called The Real Pit. It was this craphole right by my school that had this huge billboard with a picture of a vile person-style pig on top, like ten feet high, very fat with all his chunks lumping out of overalls. Roger'd once planned to spray-paint a talk bubble over that pig's head that said, COME ON IN AND EAT MY KIN! But once he found a way to use the back Dumpster to get up on the roof, he liked the shady spot behind the sign too much to call attention to it.

No. U must Stopppppit. For realz. Stop. I wasn't laughing anymore. I clicked my phone all the way off, done hearing about him snuffing around to find me like a lunatic bloodhound, not asking if I wanted for a single sorry second to be found.

At school the sudden friendliness of Beautiful Jack Owens had caught and spread. As I walked from homeroom to bio to lab, stoners and jocks, cheerleaders and mathletes all smiled at me or waved or said hello. I wasn't so stupid as to think I'd woken up hot enough for Jack, or cool enough for the wild kids, or that my 3.5 GPA was suddenly good enough to get me frenemied into the cutthroat Valedictorian-or-Die smarty set. This was like when a drunk driver killed a senior who went to Moss Point High, and all of a sudden everyone who ever met her (and some who totally hadn't) had these memories of her, and they stood around talking in soft voices about The Time They Shared a Coke with Her, like she'd so mattered to them. Now I mattered, too.

On my way to study hall, I stopped short when my ex-BFF, Briony Hutchins, came bouncing out of Coach Richardson's classroom door right in my path without ever noticing me. She paused right in my way to hump her amazing boobage up out of her shirt.

"See you fifth period," she chirped at him. He was such a creeper that fluffing her C cups was getting her an easy A in his Life Skills class. But when she turned and saw she'd almost run me down, she actually paused her grade whoring long enough to flash her teeth and say, "Mosey! What's the haps?"

I shrugged and tried to look through her.

"Well, text me," she said, and twirled away. I stood there for a sec, dying to tell Roger, even though it meant hearing more about his Mom-Mission Unpossible. Unfortunately my craptastic cell could only get a signal near the fire door, because the walls were super-thick concrete. There were hardly any windows, too, so they'd painted everything a putty-pink color that Roger called Mental Institution Blush because it was supposed to make us feel cheerful.

But I hadn't gone two steps before I saw Roger, real Roger in the actual flesh, standing ten feet ahead of me by the library. He was hard to miss, glowing white in his Calvary uniform shirt with the button-down collar and monogrammed logo. He peered back and forth, searching for me in the crowd.

My arm was lifting in a wave when this junior named Charlie who went to church at Calvary spotted Roger, too. He threw back his head and hollered, "Gay Ray Got-Wood, in da house!" He made the last word into a hoot that carried all the way to space. Even down the hall, I saw Roger flush a mad, dark red clear to the roots of his hair.

Roger's real name was Raymond Knotwood, but he was short

and pale and had a huge vocabulary and sucked at sports, so of course the guys at Cal all called him Gay Ray, which was retarded because the last guy caught being gay was a baseball god who shot deer on the weekends; it was a huge scandal, and now he went to school in Pascagoula. The Cal guys didn't like to think a guy like that would turn out to be gay. He'd been too much like them. Gay Ray Got-Wood's initials would be GRG, but everyone had my friend pegged so wrong that I called him those initials backward. RGR. Roger.

Roger stepped toward Charlie with his hands coming up and his eyebrows coming together, just as Charlie licked his hand and gave Roger a massive cathead. He whanged Roger's forehead so hard with his wet palm that I heard the smack all the way down the hall.

Roger'd completely hate for me knowing he got catheaded, like somehow me seeing it with my girl eyes would make it sting for so much longer. I ducked sideways out of sight, jumping right through Coach's classroom door. I fisted my hands and pressed them up against my eyes.

"Mosey?"

I whirled around.

Across the mostly empty room, Coach Richardson was looking at me like I actually existed. I don't think he'd ever said my name before, except at roll call. I hadn't ever rated even the uncancerous lesser leer he saved for flatties. Now he was actually smiling, his teeth so perfect they looked like they had been made up totally out of spackle.

I burbled, "Oh, I...um, I don't actually have Life Skills now," which was insane, because of course he knew that. Some kids pushed in behind me, heading to their desks.

He didn't give me any flak, though, just said, real serious, "I've been meaning to ask you, how's your mom doing?"

My eyes narrowed. This was maybe the first time he'd ever

asked me a direct question. A personal one anyway. He was Claire Richardson's husband, after all, and Slocumbs plain did not exist to him.

When I didn't answer, he added, "We've all been so concerned, since we heard about the stroke."

I walked over to his desk because I didn't want to yell back and forth across the room about Liza now that the kids in his next class were filing in.

"She's doing okay," I said.

He nodded, encouraging, like we were having some kind of conversation and he wanted me to say more, which was super weird. He'd taught my mom Life Skills, too, when it was plain driver's ed and home ec existed and sex ed didn't. A lot of my teachers had had my mom, because they'd all been teaching at PRH for about a hundred years, which proved Roger's hypothesis that death was the only sure way out of Immita. I'd gotten a lot of stink-eye when they'd read my last name off the roll at the start of the year, most of all from Coach. He'd paused after my name, looking me up and down with a gaze so cold it was like he had lizard eyes, then never bothered looking at me again. Every roll call after that, he rushed past me, calling the next name on the list while I was still saying "Here."

Well, he was a busy guy; he had tons of blouses that needed to be looked down, and every day he had to come up with a fresh new excuse to hug cheerleaders. It was time-consuming, being supercool, joking around with the sports guys and letting them pick on the scrubs. My mom, though, back in the day, she was friends with his daughter before she got pregnant and all the bad crap went down. Back then Liza would have rated his attention. He'd probably liked her the same as he liked Briony.

The last kids were wandering in and flopping into their seats. Janie Pestre and her friend Deb were already sitting on the far end of the front row. I could see them in my side vision, looking at me. Deb poked Janie with her elbow and then said, "Hey, Mosey," like we talked every day.

I gave them a little nod.

Deb poked Janie again, like egging at her, and Janie gave me a smile that was all pointy teeth, sharp and overfriendly. "We heard about your yard. What did the cops say? Was it a murder?"

"I'm not sure that's appropriate," Coach said, but he leaned in, and as he said it, his face flashed a look that was like hunger. Just for a second, but I got it: He hadn't really cared how Liza was. This was what he'd wanted to ask me. The room was full now, and as I glanced around, I saw he wasn't alone. Everyone had hushed to hear what I would say, staring at me like I was cake and they deserved a piece.

I looked down at the big zoo of crap on Coach's desk, stacks of health pamphlets and report binders and a collection of bobblehead guys in football helmets. Near the front was this hinged picture frame that opened like a book. Fifty million years ago, he'd caught some impossible pass to win a college game. He'd cut the story and picture out of the paper and framed them, and it still sat on his desk. It was a little sad. He looked like the Stay Puft Marshmallow Man version of the boy in the picture, still trying to be cool in button-fly Levi's with his belly pooching over the top. Him having that pic was like if I was forty and still had some old A-plus paper stuck on the fridge, all brown and curled up at the edges.

Staring at that picture, with everyone in the room craning toward me, I had this weird déjà vu feeling, like way back before this frame was all dusty, fifteen years ago, my mom had stood here, in this spot, twirling a strand of her hair and using her pretty to wheedle Coach into giving her the one practice car with an A/C that worked. I felt like my mother's teenage ghost owned the room, and standing in her footprints, I owned it, too, now. Like it was something Liza had bought for us.

I made a hard, mysterious face and dredged up some *CSI* memories to get the right vocab and the Horatio tone. I tossed my hair back and said, "I can't talk about it while it's... an ongoing investigation." I really needed some sunglasses to whip off, but it was good enough for them. Four or five conversations started buzzing in the room behind me, everybody wondering how much I knew, and me not giving any of them, especially Coach, a damn thing.

Coach leaned in a little closer. Too close. His breath smelled like peppermints. He dropped his voice so only I could hear and started to ask me another question.

But I didn't have any real information, and anyway, even if I did, he'd never once been nice to me. I started talking really loud and perky over him. "So, Coach, I was hoping you would write me a pass to spend study hall in the library. I want to work on my *Scarlet Letter* report for English." It was really a two-page reader response that any person with nine working brain cells and Wikipedia could do without cracking a single book, including the actual *Scarlet Letter*. It was already finished, stuffed in my pink Trapper Keeper, waiting for its due day, the way my homework always was.

But I wasn't that girl anymore. I was someone new, shutting Coach down in the middle of a question, lying to get a pass I didn't need, standing in this spot where Liza used to stand.

"Sure, let me get my pad," he said, subsiding, and the interested light was gone from his eyes. He was once again looking through me, like I was the same old Mosey Slocumb, the one girl at Pearl River who was too plain to perv on. He turned his back on me to open a battered-up briefcase on the stool behind him.

The kids were mostly talking to one another now, leaning across the aisles to whisper. Only Deb was still watching me, wide-eyed and interested, like Mosey Slocumb getting a hall pass was newsworthy. Yesterday, with Olive and that pack of assholes stomping around our grass, I'd purely hated it, but I'd been me then. Now that I actually *was* just The Girl with Human Bones in

Her Yard, I kinda liked it. All at once I wanted for her to see I'd changed. I wanted someone to witness me doing a thing Mosey Slocumb wouldn't ever, ever do.

I stepped up close to the desk so my belly was almost pressed against that newspaper story in its special frame. I waggled my eyebrows at Deb and put my hand on it. She raised her eyebrows, like to say, *What?* My hand clicked the frame closed into a book, and I slid it to the edge of the desk and stuffed it right down the front of my pants. I almost yipped out loud and had to turn the noise into a cough to cover; the back of the frame was metal and ice-cold.

It had happened so fast. Deb stared at me with her mouth dropped wide open. I stared back, shocked, too, but I told myself that I hadn't really stolen it yet. The frame was still in his room, after all. Just accidentally down my pants. I put a "shhh" finger against my lips. Deb snapped her mouth shut, choking back the giggles, and gave me a big thumbs-up.

Coach found his passes. He scribbled on one and then turned and held it out to me without even looking at me, saying, "Bell in one minute." I took it. Now I didn't see how I could get the frame back, and anyway, served him right.

I walked careful out the door with his football memento pressed cold against my belly, completely stealing it, as easy as if Liza really was my mom. Hell, she'd stolen a whole baby. Thinking that put my little teeny thieving in perspective, and I realized I was more excited than scared anyway, and dying to show Roger.

He was still in the library doorway, craning around for me. I kept my eyes forward and marched toward the end of the hall like I wasn't seeing him there. That gave him time to find me and arrange himself all leaned and cool in the doorway and be the one to say, "Yo."

I turned all surprised and then grinned at him and said, "How on earth?"

He shrugged. I could see that his forehead was red from where Charlie gave him the cathead, but he'd wiped the suck away. "Simple. I told Mr. Lex I needed to go the library to do research for debate. He wrote me an off-campus pass, and I told the secretary here it meant this one, not the branch."

"Pretty slick," I said. "Come in here, I have to show you something."

His eyes got bright behind his glasses, and we ducked into the library.

I paused to drop off my pass at the front desk, and then we hustled back to this dark hole of a room behind the biographies. It had a small round table in the middle, and against the wall was a thousand-year-old microfiche machine that looked like a headless R2-D2.

"So what'd you find?" Roger said, library-quiet, but real intense.

I pulled the frame out of my pants, Roger's eyes widening as I did it, and I opened it up on the small table. "I stole this."

He bent his head over and started to read the actual newspaper story, interested. "Is it about your mom?"

"No, it's about football. Why are you even reading it? Roger, listen: I totally stole this."

He looked down at the picture. "Why?"

I said, "I don't know. Isn't that so not like me, though?"

"Yeah," he said. "But, like, you stole it from your mom or—"

"Oh, my God, can you stop with my mom?" I said, exasperated. "Forget my mom. This is Coach Richardson's framed thingy, and I stuck it down my *pants*."

He waved that away. "Okay. Well, next time put something useful down your pants. Like a pizza. Mosey, I need you to focus." He made a peace sign with his fingers, then pointed it at my eyes and then his own. "We've got to find somehow to trace your mom's route. It's the only way we're going to find out who you are."

"Unpossible, Roger." My voice had gone all sharp. I took the frame from him and put it in my backpack, saying, "She was out there for almost two and a half fricken years."

He shook his head. "Yeah, but she had to get you pretty early on, when you were little. Because by the time she came home, the two of you were bonded and crap."

I shrugged, but it was mad, like my shoulders jerked up and then dropped. I'd only just stopped being me, and he was all hot to make me someone else before I'd even caught my breath.

"It was fifteen years ago, and they had only just invented e-mail. It's not like they had blogging back then or she had a GPS app and could tweet her location from her iPhone every fifteen minutes. She hitchhiked around in loop-de-loops, righteously effed up on fifty kinds of drugs. If we were serious, we'd have to try and go in her path. You think your mom is going to be all cool with that? If you and me blow town in the Volvo, you be Sherlock, I'll be Hot Watson, and we'll sleep by the side of the road and live on chips and gas-station-brand Cokes until we find my real mom, baking cookies in, like, Iowa and pining for me?"

His face flushed a dark, dull red, and he cut his eyes away and mumbled, "We could maybe fake a school trip or..."

He petered out, and I felt like Lowly Worm. He was always so careful to keep that I'm-a-boy-and-you're-a-girl distance in between us. He never let me get all huggy or treat him like my stuffed rabbit, and now I'd seen all the way back into his head, to where he kept his secret reasons why. This whole investigation, it wasn't really about finding where I came from. It was about me and him, maybe on the road, sharing all kinds of secrets and a sleeping bag, and I had just peed on it.

"Not that that wouldn't be super great," I said, lame like.

"Whatev," he said, trying for cool but with his cool gone. There was this awful teetering moment, and I felt like I'd busted something up, bad. He wouldn't meet my eyes, and I felt exactly like when I'd found my mom's secret sex vibrators all over again, except with Roger, so it was worse.

I had this lump coming up in my throat, and he started to stand. I knew if I let him walk away now, we might still be friends, but this thing where we were a team, him and me versus everybody, that would be over. I grabbed his arm, because I couldn't stand it, and he stopped and went into that kind of stillness he always got when I touched him.

I took my hand away and said, fast and quiet, "I searched Liza's room." That paused him. I spoke again, like the last six seconds had been some weird, unaccountable blink of nothing. "I'm being all hateful and acting like you are Detective Suck, but it's me, Roger. I'm the suck. I mean, I've been trying to make you quit it, and I keep saying I don't want to know anything. But then, this morning, I snuck into her room and tore through all her things."

He stuffed his hands in his pockets, leaning toward me from the waist, more like his usual Spocked-out self. "What did you find?"

I shook my head. "Nothing," I said, but I said it too quick, and I felt my own cheeks pinking, because of course what I'd found was a totally unrelevant pouch of perv toys. Maybe I would tell him that at any other time, but not right now. Not while he still had a little of the secretest piece of him showing on his cheeks as two red spots.

He said, "Nah, you found something."

I pulled the picture of Bunnies out of my back pocket. "This was the most personal thing I found in her whole room. Don't you think that's weird?"

"Mmm," he said, like real thinky.

I went on. "She lived in that same room almost for her whole life, but there's nothing there even from when she was a kid. I think I know all about her life, because she way overshares, but most of the time her stories have these big fat morals tacked on.

Drugs Are Bad. Keep It in Your Pants. Skipping Causes Cancer. Those kinds of stories. Nothing really... you know, personal."

He was looking at me now with his eyebrows raised and a crafty smile growing. "Come on." He got up and walked away, fast, leaving his stuff in the little room. I got up and followed as he race-walked through the stacks on a mission. He stopped in the nonfiction, dropping to sit on his butt on the floor between two tall shelves.

He ran his fingers along the spines of a long row of books that were all the same height—tall, thin spines, but in different colors. He pulled out two of them that were side by side and held them up, one in each hand, covers facing me. They were yearbooks from fifteen and sixteen years back. The years my mom was in school here at PRH.

He said, "Here's the thing. Your mom had to have friends in Immita. It was before texting, so what if she sent them snail mail, maybe postcards, from the road? She could have told some local chick all about you."

I stared at him. It seemed really long-shotty to me, but I didn't want to bust his happy when he was looking at me like we were in on this together, me and him, a team, and that weird moment in the microfiche room hadn't happened.

I fingered the picture of Bunnies. My mom never kept anything, not even a picture of Big and me on her nightstand. No souvenirs from the years she was on the road. No bring-home-to-meet-the-fam-style boyfriends. She gave away every foster dog as soon as it was well and ready, even Bunnies.

The only thing she'd ever kept was me.

I didn't think Roger's plan to investigate my mom's high-school years would tell us who I was, not in a trillion years, but I didn't care about that anyway. What I wanted now was to know who *she* was.

I plopped down on my butt beside him. "So we use the yearbook to figure out who her friends were back in the way back back, and then we talk to them."

Roger grinned and said, "And search their houses."

I ignored that and grabbed the book from her freshman year.

Roger started flipping through the other one. "Was she in any clubs?"

I snorted. "Just the kind where you need a fake ID. Can you imagine my mom in Junior Boosters?" I turned the pages, scanning for mom pics while I talked.

"Not really. But on the other hand, and sorry to say it, she was smokin' hot."

"Ew," I said. "Unrelevant."

"Not at all. If any of the yearbook-club photo geeks were guys that year, there should be plenty of pictures of her. Do you know who any of her friends were?"

"Just one, but only because she's such a major player in Liza's Just Say No stories. And *she* can't help us." I flipped a few more pages and came to a photo spread called "Best Friends Forever," with all these pics of girls posing in pairs. Right at the top, there was my mom, grinning up at me from the top of the page, her bright hair really long and crazy with curls. She had one arm slung over the shoulder of a blond, fox-faced girl who was rockin' that skeevy Seattle grunge look and wearing way too much electric-blue eyeliner. I leaned over and showed the photo to Roger. "You know who that is, right?" He looked at the picture and shook his head. "Melissa Richardson?" He still looked blank. "Claire Richardson and Coach Creeper's oldest daughter?"

His eyes widened. "Holy shit! The one that ate the bad X and thought her baby sister was a roast or something? I heard she baked her." He did an elaborate shudder.

I said, "I heard it was acid, and she drowned her baby sister."

"Either way, your mom was besties with the Beast of Immita. How cool is that?"

I said, "It's not going to help us. The way Liza tells it, Melissa ditched her sophomore year because Liza got pregnant and couldn't party anymore. Liza's moral was 'Druggie friends aren't real friends,' but I bet Melissa was just a typical asshole Richardson."

Roger's brow furrowed. "It's a chicken-egg thing. Like, was Melissa Richardson a baby baker because her parents are assholes, or did they become assholes because she baked their baby?"

"Drowned their baby. But still, if my mom sent any postcards from the road, they totally did not go to that house."

"I'm pretty sure she baked her," Roger said, studying the photo. "They look really tight. Maybe they made up."

"I doubt it, and anyhow, there's no way we can find out." After Melissa drowned the baby sister, she got charged with fifty million different kinds of crime. Claire Richardson and Coach Creeper bailed her out and took her home, but she never showed up for court. Either she ran away or maybe her parents sent Melissa off to rehab in Switzerland or someplace, because Richardsons don't go to tacky places like prison. Now people acted to their faces like Claire-n-Coach had only ever had their herd of boys, like the oldest and youngest girl kids had never happened.

"I bet her parents still have a bunch of Melissa's shit tucked away in the attic," Roger said, speculative.

I snorted. "You want to break into the Richardsons' house? You are going to so end up expelled, you moron."

But Roger wasn't listening. He'd kept flipping through my mom's sophomore year and said, "So after Melissa dumped her, who did your mom hang with?"

"How would I know?" I said. "Who did your mom hang with in high school? I bet unless one of her friends turned out to be an infamous baby *drowner*, you can't list a one."

"True fact," Roger said, and then he froze. He let a whistle out between his teeth.

"What?" I said, but he stared down for a good long thirty seconds before finally flipping his book around so I could see, too. It was open to a big spread of pictures from Fall Formal. I did some quick math. My mom would have been pregnant by then, but not very. I found her in a photo on the edge of the right page. She was leaning back-to-back on a bushy-haired girl, who was pretty in a wiry, slouchy way.

"Holy shit, is that . . . a Duckins?"

Roger pointed at the bottom of the page, where the names of everyone in the pictures was listed. He ran his finger across the line and stopped when it hit "*Liza Slocumb, Noveen Duckins.*"

"Ew. On what planet is anyone tight with a Duckins?" I said. "They all seem part retarded and practically feral."

Roger's eyes were totally, suspiciously overbright. He said, "Look really close, though, Mosey. I mean really close."

He ran his finger down the length of Noveen Duckins. She was super skinny, but under her crossed arms I could see how her belly pooched out as Roger's finger ran along the curve of it.

I exhaled. "Is she knocked up? My mom bonded with a Duckins because they were both knocked up?"

"Right," Roger said. "And if a Duckins baby went missing, maybe it never got reported. . . ."

All at once I saw where he was going. "You think I'm a *Duckins*?" I said. "Zomgah, how inbred do I seem to you, exactly?"

Roger shrugged. "Maybe Noveen did it with a physicist or something and his genes evened you out?"

"I am *so* not a Duckins," I said. "Anyway, it's the angle of the picture. She probably isn't even pregnant. Maybe she just has that Third World bloat."

"But we have to go find out," Roger said.

"Yeah, right. Let's head over there and get shot by some shirtless, old, fat, scraggle-bearded man Duckins who has *Deliverance* coveralls and bigger boobs than me," I said darkly.

"And the worst part is, he'll turn out to be your uncle."

"Gah!" I said, and punched him in the arm. I didn't think I was a Duckins for a single red second, because even a Duckins would notice a whole baby going missing, probably. But in the picture my mom peeked slyly over her shoulder at Noveen, who was peeking right back. They grinned at each other like girls who shared a secret. I super wanted to talk to Noveen Duckins if she still was around.

I said, "I'm in."

Roger grinned. "I'll pick you up at The Real Pit tomorrow after school. You and me? We're busting into Ducktown."

CHAPTER EIGHT

Big

I MET LAWRENCE ON my granddaughter's birthday, a couple of weeks before the second anniversary of the day Liza and her baby disappeared. I was speeding down I-10, weeping my guts out, thinking that somewhere out in the bigness of America my grandchild had learned to walk and was stumping around in that stiff-legged toddler way. She would be saying words now, maybe sentences, exploring the dangerous world with only my pot-smoking boy magnet of a runaway daughter to keep her safe from cliff edges and mean dogs and traffic-heavy roadways.

Almost two years. I thought I'd gotten a handle on it: the never knowing, at all, at all, where my child was, where her child was, if they were safe or warm or fed. But that morning, when I should have been baking a pink cake and blowing up balloons, it reared up and bit me hard in both my eyes and deep down in my gut. I'd been downright foul at work. At closing, Doris, my branch manager, told me to get my crap together and come back sweeter tomorrow, or else I might not be coming back at all. Then she'd shoved an enormous pile of three-ring binders full of loan data at me and told me she needed me to drive all the way to Pascagoula and drop them off at the regional manager's office there. It felt like a punishment because it was one.

I muttered cusses the whole way there and dropped the things off. As soon as I got back into my car, I busted out in a riot of crying. I headed home anyway, sobbing and dripping snot. I was thinking that at least the day could not get worse, and of course right then the flashing lights of Lawrence's cop car came on behind me. I looked at the speedometer and saw I was speeding by exactly fifteen miles an hour—that God-cursed number, wrecking me again—and that made me cry harder.

I pulled over and then dropped my face down on the wheel with my chest heaving and tried to put a stopper in it before he tapped on my window. A quick glance in the rearview showed me piggy-puff eyes, a swollen nose, and splotchy red cheeks streaked with chocolate brown mascara. I wasn't even having a good hair day.

I rolled the window down, hitching and streaming, and wordlessly held my driver's license and insurance card up to him. I saw a broad, craggy-faced fellow, about my age. His mouth was set into the standard trooper slash, but he had kind eyes, deep-set and hound-dog brown. His eyebrows lifted a fraction when he saw me.

As he took my ID, I said, "I was going to try and flirt my way out of the ticket, but... well, you see the problem." I waved a hand at my ruined face.

His lips twitched into a surprised smile, and he dipped his head to hide it. He looked down at my license for a good five seconds. He turned it around to face me right quick. "This is you?"

"Yes, but that's a terrible picture. I'm cuter than that, I swear," I said. I wiped at my nose with my sleeve.

"Really?" he said. He looked at the license again. "It's a shame, then. Flirting probably would have worked."

He'd almost made me smile back. I pressed my hands against my swollen eyes and sniffed hard and swallowed. I was finally drying up. "I'm not crying because you pulled me over, by the way. I'm not a crazy ticket weeper. I had a bad day."

Still, he didn't head over to his car to write me up. He hesitated by the window and finally said, "Since the flirting is out, did you want to try another tactic?"

A *huh* noise that might have been the start of a laugh got out of me, and then I *was* actually smiling. I shook my head. "I got nothing. I think it's bad karma to pretend I have a dying mother or that I'm rushing to unendanger some whales. Especially since I was speeding because I'm purely desperate to get home and take these pinchy shoes off and pour myself a huge Jack and ginger."

He looked down at me for another twenty seconds, and then he said, "This is an official warning. Don't drive when you're that upset. It's not safe." He held my license and my card out to me.

"That's it? Really?" I blinked at my things, surprised, then reached out and took them. "Why?"

He spread his hands, as if letting me off the hook had puzzled him, too. "My shoes pinch, too. Go home." He touched the brim of his hat to me, and this simple gesture undid me. It was so kind and unexpected.

I burst into a fresh squall.

He rocked a half step back, and I saw a flash of that hopeless look that nice men get around bawling women.

He said, "Now, don't do that. If you drive and cry, you won't pay attention to how fast you're going. I'll be pulling you right back over." He leaned in toward the window and handed me a real cloth handkerchief, soft with age but very clean. I gulped against the tears and got myself tamped down. I mopped at myself, streaking his white hankie with makeup and worse. I folded the ugly side in and tried to hand the hankie back through the window, but he didn't take it. He looked down at me, very grave, and then he bent at the waist and added, quickly, almost embarrassed, "In completely unrelated news, I finish work at eight. I plan to get some dinner at the Panda Garden off Exit 69. Really good moo shu. You could swing by, if you felt like it. Not because I didn't give you a ticket. Nothing like that. It's good moo shu, is all. Maybe good company." He shrugged. I opened my mouth, and he held one hand up and said, "No worries. You can just show up. Or not."

"Good Lord, why would you want me to?" I checked the rearview again, and I looked as bad as I'd thought.

"Damsel, distress, the whole thing makes me want to buy you MSG. Common cop problem." He hesitated, then added, "Also, if that's a bad photo, I'd like to see you on a good day." He straightened up, and off he went.

It was so impossibly cute and awkward that I wondered if it was a backroad route into smooth. If it was, I was willing to bet it worked. A lot. He had a kind of craggy, long-faced attractiveness, like a younger version of Briscoe on *Law & Order*. But I wasn't in the mood.

I drove home, a careful four miles above the limit, with no intention of showing up at Panda Garden. I kicked my shoes across the room the second I got the door shut behind me. I poured my drink and plopped onto my sofa. Then I sat there and watched the ice melting, my throat too swollen up to swallow. The very air felt bloated with all the absent Liza-and-baby sounds that should have been breaking it. Not ten minutes later, I was hopping in the shower. I washed the weeping off my face and went rummaging in my closet for the brown-and-gold wrap dress that brought out the red in my dark hair. I didn't have any damn thing better to do, I told myself as I headed right back down the highway to meet him.

I was driving down that same highway now, toward Lawrence's house. Liza was strapped in the passenger seat beside me with her face tilted toward the window. She'd seemed tucked way down deep inside herself all morning. She hadn't even seemed curious about why I'd put a swimsuit on her under her dress or why I'd packed all her water weights and floaties up in my old beach bag. The woman with war in her eyes had disappeared again. I hoped she was only resting.

"You want to get back to working in a pool again?" I asked her. She didn't look my way or respond, but the rehab doc had said it was important to keep asking her things, so her brain would search for a new pathway to answer me. Listening to myself trying to sound perky about a pool, it struck me that if Liza was whole and herself, she would have snorted and ignored that. The answer was so obvious.

Thinking back, I realized I'd been asking her for months how she wanted her eggs cooked, if she wanted to wear her white Keds or her blue ones, as if her stroke had set her back to age two. Nothing that interested her, really. Nothing that would make her brain care enough to forge new paths. Mosey and our lost girl buried in the yard—those were things she cared about. Yesterday that had woken her. I tried to think what else might call to my Liza, the Liza she'd been before. Men, I thought. Men and making trouble. Here I was, on my way to both and leaving her out of it.

"The guy who owns this pool we're going to? He's a cop." Liza's head twitched at that. She knew how deep my cop thing ran. "He used to be my cop, and I'm banking he still has some warm feelings that run my way. We're going to ask to use his pool, but really I'm going to get him to tell us what Rick Warfield and them are thinking, what directions they're investigating. See if we need to be worried." I couldn't afford to wait either. I already had a message on my answering machine from Rick, wanting to set a date when he could come by and question Mosey and Liza.

Now Liza was looking at me at least. I couldn't tell what she was thinking or even if she was thinking at all. That was the hardest part. Her face was so familiar, and I used to be able to read every blink and lip quirk. Now half of it didn't work right, and the other half seemed to have gone stiller, too, so I couldn't tell if what I was saying was getting the whole way through. But this time it seemed to me there was an energy coiling up in her, like she was listening closer.

"I called Doris this morning to ask for the day off and ended up telling her all about Tyler taking out the tree and what he found. It made me feel cheap, trading something so personal to get a stupid day off. I hope you don't think ill of me for doing that. I wouldn't have, for a pool. We'll have our own pool soon enough, anyway, if Rick will ever take the damn yellow tape out of our yard. I did it because Lawrence—that's his name—he knows things we need to know to keep Mosey safe."

I could feel Liza's interest, so I kept talking. "Doris said it was like an episode of *Cold Case* come to life in my backyard. She couldn't wait to get off the phone with me so she could call someone else and talk about me. It made me want to drive to the bank and hit her with my stapler. But she gave me the day—as a sick day, too, not a personal day, so my pay won't get docked."

We were getting close now. We'd left Immita and driven through places where very few people knew me or my history or my family. Now Immita was far behind, and we were on the far side of Moss Point, nearing Pascagoula. I didn't know any of the neighborhoods or even what grocery stores or fast-food places might be off these exits. It was like a weight lifting from me. No one would see me or care what I did here. No one would call everyone they knew to chew it over.

I was driving deep into Lawrence's territory. I felt my foot get heavy on the wheel, like I could call him to me by speeding. Lawrence wouldn't know the Malibu; I'd only had it for six years. I wondered what he would do if he did pull me over, when I rolled down the window and said, "Hey, Lawrence. How are your shoes fitting these days?"

I made myself ease up on the gas. Lawrence, never a morning person, had always worked the later shifts. Right about now his wife would be opening up her junktique store and he would likely still be dragging around in his bathrobe, drinking the bitterest black coffee alive and wishing he still smoked.

We exited the highway, and I found myself driving straight to his subdivision like a homing pigeon. I said to Liza, "Weird, isn't it? I haven't been here in more than a decade, but I didn't have to think about it. I remembered every turn." I found I was much more willing to trade Lawrence stories to connect Liza to the earth than I had been to trade the story of the willow for the day off. I peeked at Liza sideways, and sure enough both her black eyes were fixed on me. "Yes," I said, like she'd asked out loud. "He's married. You see? I have my secrets, too, Miss Little."

Lawrence had a four-bedroom ranch on a cul-de-sac. I drove directly to it as well, even though every other house in the neighborhood looked exactly like it.

I pulled in to his driveway, then sat there, engine idling. His closed front door and all the windows with the blinds down made the whole house look like it was buttoned up tight from the inside. I'd never felt quite comfortable in there, behind his wife's ugly eyelet window treatments. We'd spent most of our time at my place, where the sounds of us being happy together had broken the awful quiet of the Liza-and-baby-less air. His house felt overempty, too, but not in the same way. An absent wife makes her own kind of quiet. It's harder to break that silence with another woman. At my place he wasn't taking up anyone else's room.

The old swing set was rusting away in the side yard, and Liza lifted her good hand and pointed at it. "Yep, two boys," I said, knowing the question. "Don't blame him too bad. I knew he was married from the very start."

It was the third thing he'd said to me at Panda Garden after his surprised hello, after he'd half risen and asked me to sit down.

I'd slid into the side of the booth across from him, and we'd looked at each for five expectant seconds. Then he said, "I'm still married."

He couldn't have made me want to leave faster if he'd opened by saying he was a devout Southern Baptist. Which he was, turned out. It was only that middle word, "still," that kept me in my seat. A timer started in my head, though, like he had two minutes to explain before I was smoke.

She'd left him. Three months back. He'd come home and she was gone and both his boys were gone, off to Wisconsin to be with some asshole she'd met playing Internet bridge. She'd inched her way from online cards and typed chats to exchanging pictures to long phone conversations to the guy coming down to Mississippi and helping her bust her marriage vows on a vibrating bed at the Holiday Inn Express. Now she was calling him the love of her life.

She'd filed for divorce, but Lawrence was fighting it, trying to make her bring his kids back to Mississippi. He told me, "This thing with Sandy and the lawyers, it's sucking up my money and my time and my will to live. All I want is my boys home. I don't know what I was thinking, asking you to meet me here. You looked so pretty in your driver's-license picture, but in the car you looked on the outside how I felt on the inside, and you know what? This is the most words I think I've said all at once in five years. It's ironic, actually. Last night I called that asshole's house, and Sandy answered. I said for her to put on Harry or Max, and she said that was typical. She said if I had ever bothered to talk to *her*, she might not have kidnapped my children and dragged them to Wisconsin so she could fuck a shoe salesman. She didn't phrase it exactly like that. But anyway, I have no business being here. I'm wasting your time, and oh, look, there's the waiter. I wonder how long he's been listening to me whine like a fifth-grade girl and waiting for you to give him a drink order or storm out, because yeah. I'm still married."

I said, "He's been here for most of it," and then I turned to the stoic young man and said, "A mai tai, please. A great big one," because Lawrence'd had me the moment he said all he wanted was his boys back home. All I wanted was my girls, Liza and the new one whose name I didn't know, and there I was, sitting with a person who was lonely in exactly the same gaping, ripped-up way as me.

"We could just be friends," I'd told him. "I could use a friend myself."

He nodded, so I stayed for the mai tai and then the moo shu, which was pretty damn good, and then green-tea ice cream with a frozen banana in it. I met him for dinner the next day, and the next. I took to calling him Mr. Friend to remind myself that he did not belong to me.

I could call him that all I wanted, but I liked how his deep-set eyes kept roaming me, always moving, like they couldn't decide which pretty piece was prettiest. The first night I cooked for him at my place, I found myself pressed between his broad, hard body and the piece of wall beside my bedroom door, my legs wrapped tight around him with my jeans dangling off one ankle and only a brand-new pair of pale blue lacy panties in between us. I'd bought them earlier that day and shaved my legs, too, hoping more than knowing that this was coming. Mr. Friend was in the same frame of mind; he had a string of three brand-new condoms in his wallet.

I'd gasped into his mouth, "We're real friendly, friendly friends." He'd had one hand gripping my ass, holding me up. His other hand went roaming, and then I couldn't talk anymore. We tumbled down together and had each other right there on the floor of the hall, not able to get the last few feet into my bedroom.

Now I was sitting parked in the driveway of Lawrence's house like I still had the right to be here, and that was when Liza reached out with her good hand and poked my side.

I knew what she wanted. "It didn't work out. It never does with married guys, as I suspect you know all too well." I pushed her hand back, but inside I was grinning. After six weeks of nothing, Liza was with me in the car. This whole time Mosey and I had been calling her the wrong way.

I wondered if he would see us as we came up his sidewalk to his porch, Liza seeming more alive with every shuffling step. I could hear the radio going inside. I pushed my hair back off my face and said, "Wait here a sec, Little." I went up the three stone steps to ring the bell.

I heard footsteps coming. Before I could fully register how light and quick they sounded, the door was already swinging open.

It wasn't Lawrence. It was Sandy. I was so surprised I don't know what my face did, but hers was a slide show. She went from polite eyebrows—*May I help you?*—to confused—*Do I know you?* That held for half a second before her eyes flashed recognition, and then her eyebrows went up and her lip curled in disbelief—*Really, bitch? You dare besmirch my porch?*

I opened my mouth to speak, and she held up one hand and said, "No," before I knew what I might have said. "I know who you are. Don't you dare start this conversation off with a 'Hi, how are you?' like this is coffee hour right after church." I realized I'd never heard her voice before. It was pitched higher than I would have imagined it, or maybe she was so upset she had gone squeaky.

I was suddenly glad I'd taken such care with my hair and plucked my eyebrows. She was in sweatpants and no makeup, her dark hair back in a scraggly pony. She was holding a deep red coffee mug, and I knew if she turned it around, I'd see a pig in a football helmet on the other side.

I said, "You know who I am?"

"Oh, yes. I came by the bank where you worked to get a look at you. Years ago." Her eyes could have burned holes in me. "You're her. You're Ginger something."

"Close," I said. "Ginny. Ginny Slocumb. This is my daughter, Liza."

She'd been so focused on me she hadn't realized that Liza was there. She looked past me, down the steps, and her breath caught as she took in the walker and Liza's half-beautiful face with its right side drooping and the left side of her mouth tilted up into a lopsided version of her old reckless grin. Liza seemed to be enjoying herself immensely, but Sandy, seeing her, got about half the pissy punched out of her.

Sandy stared for twenty seconds more, then threw her hands up. "I don't even know where to start. I'm trying to imagine the thing you are here to say to me, and why you brought her, and it is impossible. Have you come to gloat, or fight me, or sell me Girl Scout cookies?" She looked me up and down, taking in my beach bag with the ends of the folded pool noodle sticking out. "You came here to go swimming?"

Of all the ways I'd seen this playing out, none of them had included Sandy and no Lawrence. I shrugged, because now I wanted nothing more than to get away from here. "Being in the water helps Liza," I said. "Lawrence is the only person I know who has a pool."

There was a blank pause, and then she started laughing. She laughed until she had to lean against the jamb. "Of course," she gasped when she could talk again. "Well, why the heck not? Come right on in."

She stayed put, though, wiping at her eyes, her body blocking the doorway, like she knew I wouldn't actually enter. She stared me down, still chuckling, waiting for me to tuck tail and flee. I took a step back, tail obediently tucking, and behind me, at exactly the same time, I heard the tines of Liza's walker click as they hit the first step. Liza was not fleeing.

I turned and hurried to help her before she took a tumble. Steadying her as she went up was all I could do, because Liza, good eye blazing, was upward bound, meeting Sandy's gaze. I couldn't have dragged her backward down the steps even if I had much wanted to. Sandy's mouth unhinged, and as we came up the last step, she walked away from us into the house, leaving the door open like a dare.

Liza and me, we took it. I closed the front door behind us.

We went through the foyer and into the den. Sandy wasn't there, but I came to a sudden halt anyway, pulling my breath in sharp. The den hadn't changed. Lawrence and I had made love on that exact blue sofa with the mallard-covered cushions and in front of the fireplace with Sandy's wooden decoy ducks watching from the mantel. Lord, but the woman liked waterfowl. The only new thing was a Mac and a lap desk, sitting on the end table. That surprised me. When Sandy came home from Wisconsin, the first thing Lawrence had done was rip out anything a person could use to get on the Internet.

Every corner of this room held memories of me and Lawrence, so I hurried on through, fast as I could with Liza. We had to go through the kitchen to get to the backyard. Sandy was tucked in the breakfast nook, sipping coffee. That pulled me up short for a second. She lifted her mug at me in an ironic salute.

I left Liza in the middle of the kitchen and went past her to open the back door. Sandy turned in her seat, tracking me. The lock was sticky. It never used to be. I struggled with it under her gaze. Finally I spoke to her over my shoulder to bust up the silence. "Are you sure we aren't putting you out?"

"Of course you are, but what the hell, eh, Ginger?" she said, her voice too mild to match her words. I finally got the door unlocked and swung it wide to make space for the walker. Behind me Sandy said, "I'm curious. Did Lawrence say this was okay?"

I turned to face her. "I didn't ask him."

Her eyes narrowed. "How'd you know I'd even be home to let you in?"

I snorted. "You think I wanted this? I thought Lawrence would let us in. I was hoping you'd be at work."

Her head tilted, and I could see that gears had started grinding inside it, meshing and whirring. She opened her mouth to speak, but right then this huge clattering smash of sound exploded to our right. We both jumped, and I whirled to see Liza standing by the sink, the rail of the walker pressed against the counter. She had a water glass clamped in the claw of her bad hand, lofting it up as if it were a trophy, and on the ground by her was the dish drainer. She'd knocked it to the floor getting the water glass, and the floor was sea of broken shards around her.

"Oh, crap!" Sandy said, jumping up.

I was already crunching through the glass to get to Liza. I tried to take the water glass out of her hand, but she clung to it, making a high, honking noise like she was one of the endless ceramic goslings Sandy had lined up on top of every cabinet. I finally wrestled the cup away from her and put it in the sink.

"I'm sorry," I said awkwardly to Sandy.

She laughed, but there wasn't any real mirth in it. "It's only broken dishes. This time anyway," she said. "I'll get the broom."

Liza made an angry, throaty noise. I pushed at the walker and forced her to turn, making an angry, throaty noise right back at her.

"I'll pay for these," I said to Sandy.

Sandy didn't answer. She watched without comment while Liza and I trooped and thumped our slow way across the glass and headed outside. I closed the back door behind us and walked Liza over to the edge of the pool, hissing, "What was that?"

When I looked back at the house, I saw that Sandy had pushed aside the eyelet drapes to watch us. I turned and stepped in front of Liza to block Sandy's view. I was furious with Liza, but I found I still I didn't want Sandy ogling her thin, wasted leg as I helped her out of her Keds and peeled her dress off over her head. She was wearing a modest one-piece I'd bought her at the Target.

I kicked off my sandals and pulled my dress off, wishing hard I'd gotten myself a modest one-piece, too, instead of a tankini splashed with silly daisies. It had high-cut legs and a built-in underwire that pushed my boobs up. I'd wanted Lawrence to see I hadn't given up fighting gravity, that bitch, not even twelve years later.

I didn't like wearing it for Sandy. I could feel her looking, and I was irked to find myself sucking in my stomach as I buckled a wide cloth belt around Liza's waist. At the rehab center, the therapist had used something like it to keep a hold on Liza in the water, so if she started to fall, they wouldn't have to grab any of her hurt pieces to keep her upright.

We waded in, making identical peep noises as the cold water hit our suits. Then Liza started shaking, and it took me a second to realize she was laughing.

"This is not funny. I bet those stupid dishes are going to cost me a mint. Most of them were her good ones, with those Italian chickens on them." But even as I said it, I started laughing, too. We stood crotch-deep in the shallow end, giggling together like vicious little girls who have played a mean prank at a sleepover. I was glad our backs were turned to the window. When I finally got it tamped down, I said, "They are some ugly-ass dishes, though, Lord, and what kind of a dreadful girl are you, only perking up when we start smashing things that belong to my ex's wife? What possessed you?"

Liza stopped laughing, instantly, when I asked that last question. Her mouth opened and closed, opened and closed, but nothing came out. She tried again, her jaw unhinging and working like a word was caught in her throat and she was trying to maneuver it on out. Finally she said something that sounded like "soup." We blinked at each other, both of us surprised. She shook her head no, then said, "Pick soup." These weren't the words she meant. I could see it in her scared eye, that she had heard herself, and whatever was inside, it wasn't coming out properly. Her shoulders tensed, and she wagged her head back and forth, close to panicking.

"Don't," I said. "This is good. You're talking, and that's good. Even if the word isn't right, it's a word." She kept wagging her head no at me, but I slapped the water, hard. I said, firm, "This will help. We will get there. Come on."

I thrust the pool noodle at her, and we walked out farther and deeper, my hand steady on her back belt. I tried to forget Sandy and turn all my attention to repeating the exercises I'd seen the PTs do with Liza, first warming her up by walking back and forth across the pool, shortways. After a couple of laps, we went a little deeper. Liza spread her feet apart to get her shoulders lower and then lifted her arms up as if she were doing the top half of a jumping jack. I held steady to the back of her belt as she repeated the movement. We'd begun a series of careful squats when the kitchen door opened and Sandy came out.

She had changed into a swimsuit, too, a Lands' End tank that held her body so rigidly it looked lined in whalebone. My eyes narrowed. It was the kind of suit I'd have to buy if Mosey got her way and started calling me her mee-maw, but Sandy didn't have a bad figure. It was like she'd picked it so that anyone watching would know at once who was the wife and who was the mistress.

Sandy came to the edge of the pool and sat down, swinging her feet in the water. I felt Liza straightening, the good side of her mouth curling irrepressibly up. Well, why not? With Sandy in the pool, she was back in the middle of an aborted catfight over an absent man. It was practically her home territory. And whether she knew it or not, she'd been in the middle of this very fight before.

I'd been seeing Sandy's husband for almost six months when Liza showed up on my doorstep, strung out six ways from Sunday and toting Mosey. I'd called Lawrence and asked him to give me some space and some time. It wasn't only because my hands were so instantly full. Lawrence was a cop, and even though Liza said she was off meth, she drank cough medicine like it was Coca-Cola, using it to wash down the brightly colored pills that lined her pockets. I didn't want to put Lawrence in the position of either arresting my kid or ignoring illegal substances. I spent my time researching rehab centers and waiting at legal aid so Liza could grant me a say in Mosey's life before I checked her in. I burned all my vacation and sick leave in those weeks, forging a bond with the baby so she wouldn't be scared while Liza was getting clean.

While I was in the middle of all that, Sandy came back home, Harry and Max in tow. I guess the sex had worn off enough for her to see that her shoe salesman was fatter and older and poorer than he'd seemed online.

"She wants to work it out," Lawrence told me on the phone.

"What do you want?" I asked.

"You," he said. But he said it soft, almost like it was an apology. I waited, holding my breath, and he said, "The boys are... they cling to me like a couple of freaked-out monkeys. Then they tear off and act like natural-born assholes, looking to see how I'll react. They are so relieved to be home, but they don't trust it, you know? Not the way they used to. I want them back. I want their lives put back together."

"But do you want *her* back?" I asked again, and in the long silence I had my answer, even before he spoke.

"The boys need us. Not me. Us," he said, like it was exactly that simple. I had Mosey and Liza home, so I knew too well that it was.

Still, I said, "How can you ever trust her?"

He sighed. "I don't trust her, but hell, I cheated, too, Ginny. That helps somehow. It's like we're even."

It took me a second to realize that by cheating he meant me. There was silence on the phone between us. I was furious, and my heart was smashed, but inside I knew, if it was him or Liza and the baby? Well, when they'd shown up, I'd cut him out immediately and thoroughly. So thoroughly I hadn't even known that his dumb-slut stupid wife had come home. So I said, "Bye, Lawrence," and I set the phone back careful on its cradle and went to read *Goodnight Moon* for the nineteenth time that day, trying not to feel anything except the magical way sleepiness made Mosey get heavier. I didn't even cry until she was a limp string of trusting weight and heat, sleeping heartbeat to heartbeat on my chest.

Now here was the same dumb-slut stupid wife easing herself down into the pool with us, saying, "You looked like you could use some help."

"How kind of you," I said, terse. "Liza, you want to try some backward walking?"

Liza made her "yes" noise, "Yarrrrr," long and growly like a pirate. I gave Sandy a nod, translating. Sandy got on Liza's other side and kept pace with us. She wasn't actually touching Liza, which seemed wise to me, but I had to admit I was glad to have a person there. The real PTs had worked in pairs in the water, with Liza between them.

As we made our slow way, Sandy asked, "What's happened to your daughter?"

"She had a stroke," I said. "She can understand you, by the way. So don't you talk around her like she's a dog or a French person."

We reached the other end of the pool in silence. Much as I appreciated how alive Liza felt with Sandy beside her, I didn't want to talk to Liza in front of her, or make Liza try to talk. I didn't want her to say "soup" to Sandy when the word she was looking for was "bitch." We were already in our swimsuits. I didn't want us to be that kind of naked, too.

"Now what?" Sandy said as we got to the end.

"Now we go sideways," I said. We shifted around so we were all facing the deep in a line, me first, then Liza, and Sandy by the wall. We crabbed our way back across the pool, step together, step together. Liza led with her bad side, something that would be impossible on land. By the end of the second lap, Liza was tiring. We'd been at it more than half an hour. I said, "I think we should stop here."

As soon as we were out of the pool, Sandy left us. I started packing up the gear and pulling our dresses on over our wet suits.

It seemed to take a long time to do everything backward. When we went back through the house, Sandy was sitting in the den, dressed in jeans and a T-shirt. She'd taken her hair down and brushed it, too, and put some color on her lips. She seemed different with her clothes on. Harder and sharper.

Liza was exhausted from the workout, and Sandy seemed to sense it. For the first time, it felt like the two of us were alone in a room.

"Thank you," I said, and she nodded, acknowledging my words but not really responding. I added, "Don't blame Lawrence. He hasn't been sneaking. He's not sneaky. He didn't know I was coming."

"I know." She smiled with a weird, sad triumph. "It's strange, but it makes me like you more. Knowing he hasn't called you. Somehow it's better for me, knowing he didn't spend the last decade pining and suffering my presence."

I said, "I don't want to get into this. I only wanted to use your pool." Liza was slumping with tired. I began helping her turn the walker, wishing I'd brought her chair.

Sandy called after me, "Max—that's our youngest—he took early admission at Georgetown last summer. Lawrence stuck it out for another year. But we both knew it wasn't any good. He moved out at the start of July."

That stopped me dead. I turned to her. "Lawrence left you?"

"Yeah," she said. "I assumed he'd gone back with you. I know my husband, and that's what I would have bet, really, if anyone had been willing to lay odds." She laughed, a bitter bark of sound. "If you want to work out in my pool again, you can. It's funny, how much I don't mind, now that I know that pool's the only thing of mine you've used in recent days."

An awful triumph shone in her eyes, and beside me, so soft only I could hear, a grumbling sound like a growl began in Liza's throat. Tired or not, she was getting this.

I said, as evenly as I could, "Thanks, but I'm having my own put in."

She nodded. "A fine idea. It's always better to get your own."

I wanted out of there, that very second, but all at once it was a battle to get Liza moving. I could smell intent all over her. Sandy was lucky my girl was caged in the walker. She would have lost an eye had Liza been herself. I felt an awful, unnamable something surging in me in a wave, but I ignored it and did what I could to get me and Liza the hell out, fast.

It wasn't until I was driving home that I understood what I was feeling. Rage. He was free, and yet he'd never called me. I would have put my money with Sandy's. I would have bet that he would call me, first thing.

"Oh, you bastard. Really?" I said out loud to him, and Liza grunted in response. To her I said, "I'm glad you broke those dishes. I wish you'd broken more stuff."

When I mentioned the dishes, Liza went dead still, and then she started looking around, like I'd stopped existing. My anger was huge enough to keep me warm company anyway. I sped home, daring any yahoo in a Lawrence-style uniform to pull me over. Liza and me, we would take his face off.

Or *I* would anyway. Liza had disconnected, but not from Earth. Just from me. She was rooting around in the car, hunting something, fingers curling into the Malibu's cup holders, one by one, and then she starting searching the center console.

My hands were wrapped around the steering wheel, squeezing like it was Sandy's skinny throat. It had never occurred to me that if he was free, he wouldn't come. Never. I'd believed he was still mine in a place so deep that I'd never so much as thought it through. It was as basic as breathing, but it must have been in my head that way only. Who knows how many nice men I'd failed to notice or respond to because I'd held them up to what was turning out to be a wholly imaginary Lawrence and found them lacking?

I roared off the highway and forced myself to ease off the gas, lest I mow down some neighborhood children. Beside me Liza was still twisting around hunting through the car. She bent at the waist, pressing her face almost to her knees, her good hand sweeping the floorboards in front of her.

"What?" I snapped.

She stayed in that position, digging in all the crap that seemed to pile up in my car, junk mail, crumpled Taco Bell bags, three or four paperback thrillers, a pair of Mosey's socks.

As I pulled in to our own driveway, Liza sat up, making a rooster crow of triumph. She had an old, empty to-go cup from Starbucks, lid still on, clutched in one hand. She held it toward me.

"Okay..." I tried to take it, but she wouldn't let it go. Her gaze met mine, her one eye so alive and fierce, in spite of how the pool work had tired her. Her jaw worked again, the way it had at Sandy's when she'd lofted that water glass. When I'd talked about the broken dishes and she had told me to pick soup. Now she had a Starbucks cup.

"Liza, what?" My long-silent child was trying to tell me something, something important, her first real attempt at complicated communication since she'd come home from the hospital. "Something about a cup?"

The half of her face that worked burst into sunshine.

I said, "Cup?" and all the breath came out of Liza in a joyful whoop. "So yes, a cup, a cup, something with a cup? Is this about Sandy? Rehab? Mosey?" The second I said Mosey's name, Liza began making her "yes" noise, so sharp and hard it was like a bark. Three times, yes yes yes.

I looked from her face to the cup, my anger leaving in a flood of relief or hope, something, because if she was trying so hard, then there were things inside her head to say. That meant she was remembering. Not just listening and understanding but responding and making connections to her past, to the Liza that she used to be. I reached past the cup and grabbed her wrist and clung to it, tight.

My girl was talking in the only way she could, and with an urgency that told me this was a thing I needed to know. Now. "I'll figure it out," I said.

I took the cup from her and clutched it tight. It was a letter from the real Liza mailed to me from somewhere far away, but written in a language I did not speak.

CHAPTER NINE

Liza

LIZA IS SO tired that the now is a great gray wash around her. The now is Liza alone in her room, alone with her damn leg and her half a face, swaying in her walker. She pulls pictures from the vast sea of memory that washes inside her, whole and huge, the only piece of her that feels unbroken. She finds that row of girls from the TV Christmas. Radio City girls, beautiful long legs made of shapely muscle clicking open and shut like scissors. Charlie Brown at Thanksgiving, driving a mighty kick toward a football that Lucy has already pulled away. The Karate Kid, dangling his broken foot in space and then lifting straight up like a weird bird to knock someone's teeth out with his other leg.

She shoves at her own dead leg with these pictures, straining for high and mighty and bold. Her right foot twitches, shuffles forward. Then the left one goes, thoughtless, perfect, unfairly easy. She's sore and tired from the pool, but she won't stop. She gathers them again: high-kicking Rockettes, determined Charlie Brown, unstoppable Karate Kid. She thrusts these things in a roaring wash of power down into her body. But they diffuse as they go, easing to a stream and then a dribble. By the time they reach the leg, they are nothing but an old man's painful shuffle.

She accepts. Breathes in. Goes again.

Big has washed the chlorine out, and she feels her wet hair as a weight, dampening the back of her pajamas. This last step has brought her to the bed, and she wants nothing more than to ease herself down into it. Big has the cup. She got the cup to Big, and doesn't this earn her a rest? The answer is no, and it comes to her in salt smell of her own effort-filled sweat. Salt air. The beach. That baby. Melissa. The second-worst day of Liza's whole and bloody history has resurrected itself. The past is alive, and it's coming to eat Mosey.

The cup is not enough. Big needs more, and she begins the long, inching process of turning the walker, readying it to go back across her room. Rockettes. Charlie Brown. Karate Kid. She creeps forward, lost inside herself now, kept company by the babies, all the babies that she didn't steal.

The first at a grocery store in Alabama, two days after crib death took her own child in the night, and she put her keepsake trunk deep in the earth near the willow. She's come in to steal fruit or maybe crackers, not a baby, but she hears it crying three aisles away, and instantly her breasts gush milk. It cries and cries, and its mother should fix it. Liza would fix it, if only it were hers. She should go and get it now and put it to her aching breast and hush it, walk away with it into the black night.

She leaves the grocery at a run, leaves whatever town she's in, crosses another state line.

There has to be a place far enough from the willow. A desert place. Not like home. A place where the air is so dry it will suck the milk out and parch her eyes and bake her slick sweat off her skin as fast as she can loose it. She heads west, hoping Nevada can cook her until she is as light as a leaf blown along the road.

The carnival she joins has excellent pot. In the day she sleeps without dreaming, and at night she stares into a crystal ball and tells lies. She looks good in the Gypsy clothes, saying futures when she can't see any future at all.

Then a bearded lady joins. She has a baby. Fat legs, a shock of dark hair. Her very first night after the midway closes, the sword swallower gets the lady on her back. The baby sleeps in an empty dresser drawer in the front room of his trailer. Liza stares at it through the window. "Oh, oh, oh!" the lady hollers through her beard. She would never hear the creak of the door if Liza slipped inside and lifted up that drowsy bundle.

Liza turns away as the bearded lady finishes and walks until she finds an on-ramp. She climbs up into the first big rig that stops for her.

She likes the truckers. Some have pot, and they all have speed. She sleeps in the day, so she can tell more lies and help them stay awake at night. The headlights wash the black road, and if she swallows enough Christmas Trees, it feels like flying, high up in the cab. The truckers seem uncomplicated, or at least unkinky. She has sex and conversation, they have drugs and forward movement, and this trade is the closest thing to love that she can stand.

The seasons change, and she keeps moving. It's very simple; no one brings babies to truck stops, so Liza doesn't steal any.

Then she meets Buck. He's closer to fifty than forty, and she calls him Sugardads. Buck is sweet, likes holding her hand, and the two of them take runs all the way back and across the country, California to Vermont, Vermont to California. She's with him six months. It's good until he thinks that he's in love. He wants to buy her a little fat steak wrapped in bacon from a place he knows off the highway in the smack-ass middle of the country. At the table next to them, there's a family. Mommy, Daddy, Susie, Tommy, baby, and it's all Liza can do not to put her steak knife in the mother and grab the infant, so desperately do her empty arms want filling.

She smiles and excuses herself to go pee, and once she's out of his sight, she goes out the front door instead. Her red backpack is in the truck, and it's locked, so she leaves it. She runs to the highway and then puts out her thumb. Liza has a halter top and long red-gold dirty curls and no visible baggage—what's not to stop for? The second truck she sees pulls over. The driver is a bald white guy, maybe forty, with kind, tired eyes. Kind and tired, but not fatherly.

"Hey," Liza says, smiling. "You got anything? I want to stay awake. I can be pretty good company." He has a little something, and the truck rolls off into the black.

Two months later she's back in Alabama, the closest she has come to home in however long it's been. She's wearing nothing but a filthy sundress, sitting by the washing machine with every other article of clothing that she's collected spinning inside it, when a twitchy little momma comes in wearing sweatpants. She's got a crying baby in footie pajamas stuffed in a sling, and she's dragging her laundry in a basket. She has brown circles under her eyes, and she sniffles and picks at her skin as she loads the clothes in. The baby whimpers. She doesn't seem to notice it's close to crying. Maybe she doesn't even like it.

Her name is Janelle, and she can't be much older than Liza. They talk some while the laundry swishes. They both like Björk. They both like Mustangs. They both like Pixie Stix.

"Listen," Janelle says, "can you maybe watch the baby for a sec? Make sure no one takes my clothes? I have a errand."

The baby is loaded into Liza's arms, filling them. Liza looks at the baby. The baby looks back, solemn. It smells like cigarettes and old milk, and under that it smells like perfect baby.

"Do you want to come with me?" Liza asks. The baby doesn't seem to have any objections.

Still, she stays in the chair. She has no underpants; they are all in the washer. A mother shouldn't be sitting in a laundry in nothing but a sundress. If her panties were dry, she'd have walked with the baby already.

She looks at the baby, and the baby looks back.

"Thanks," Janelle says when she returns. The twitch is gone; she obviously scored.

Fucking junkie. Liza should have taken it.

Liza moves her clothes to a dryer, goes to the bathroom. She leans on the sink, trying not to cry. Handing the baby back felt about as easy as pulling out her own lung, passing that over. She gave it to a fucking junkie mother who likes Björk and Mustangs and Pixie Stix.

She should go out there, offer to watch it again when her panties are dry. Steal it this time. But she meets her own eyes in the mirror. She has no diapers, no bassinet, no little cotton sleepers from Kidworks, and it strikes her that these are greater obstacles than a simple lack of underthings. In the mirror she is looking at another fucking junkie who likes Björk and Mustangs and Pixie Stix.

Babies need a Big, and she's a Little whose own baby stopped breathing in the night and turned quietly blue and died for no reason other than karma and Melissa. No reason except that Liza deserved it.

Back in the laundry, Janelle has some Jolly Ranchers. She gives Liza a cherry one. It's both their favorite.

"Liza," Big says. "What on earth? You have to rest. You have to stop."

Liza blinks. Rockettes. The leg shuffles forward.

Then Big is by her being Big. Being the thing that babies need. Putting Liza to bed.

CHAPTER TEN

Mosey

WHEN ROGER GOT TO The Real Pit to pick me up, it was pouring rain, but he still pulled in to his regular place instead of driving up to the door. His car was a jet-black Volvo station wagon, like ten years old, because his mom had Googled around till she found out that this make and year had never had a driver's-side fatality in the whole history of Earth. Safety first, or whatev, but it didn't have a port for his iPod. He'd had to burn his playlist to CD. I could hear Cage the Elephant, and he was headbanging all oblivious while I ran across the lot to his car, getting soaked. When I pulled open the door, the front seat was full of crap, and I couldn't even get in.

I hurled a pile of blankets and two pairs of his mom's gardening gloves into the back. Under all that I found some big-ass wire clippers with wicked-looking blades, thick and curved like Toucan Sam's face if he went serial killer.

I slammed the door and dripped at him, glaring and holding up the clippers I'd almost sat on, giving him "WTH?" eyebrows.

He totally missed the point, saying, "In case we have to go through one of those fences." He was so excited about this spy-vs.-Duckins outing he was practically vibrating as he drove out of The Real Pit lot.

I put the wire clippers down on the floorboards, rolling my

eyes. It was true that big pieces of Ducktown had chain-link fencing as high as my chest, some even with lines of barbed wire over the top, but we weren't going to crouch in the weeds and try to hack through the links at three in the afternoon on a school day.

"We're not ninjas," I said, sour.

He laughed and said, "I swear, Mosey, you could suck the fun out of a puppy."

"Anyway, we don't need to be ninjas. I have a plan," I said. I rummaged in my backpack and unearthed a textbook covered by a homemade grocery-store-bag cover. "Behold. Patti Duckins's remedial math book. She *misplaced* it today. You and I are so very sweetly going to return it to her."

"How convenient. For us," Roger said. He gave me a sideways smile. "Did she *misplace* it down your pants?"

"Something like that," I said. I'd spent half my day ghosting around behind Patti, waiting for her to take her eyes off her army-surplus duffel. Finally, at lunch, she dropped it by an empty table in the cafeteria and went to pee. When I'd unzipped it, this weird, dry smell had puffed out at me, like if a bear used to live inside there a long time ago. A bear who liked pimento cheese. I'd grabbed the top book, my heart booming in my chest like it was made of a thousand firecrackers, but not scared. It was more like when I was little and used to run everywhere for the sheer fun of fast moving.

Roger said, "She's a bus kid, right? We might as well go get a Blizzard. She won't be home for half an hour."

I said, "Nah, I have no idea where she lives in Ducktown anyway. Let's head on over, so we can see where she goes when she gets off the bus."

"Hey, if we beat her home, we'll have to ask the other Duckinses where she lives. Duckinses? Is that right? How do you pluralize a Duckins?"

I said, "I think they're like moose: one Duckins, two Duckins, a thousand Duckins."

Roger nodded, and then his eyes lit. "We can pound on doors and ask them all about Noveen, too."

"You are insane," I told him. "I heard last year one of them shot a Jehovah's Witness in the butt with a .22."

Roger seemed to think that was hilarious. "Oh, come on, Mose, that's a completely reasonable response. Would you like a copy of the *Watchtower*? Blam! Cap in the ass!"

Just then Snow Patrol came on, and he leaned in and jacked the volume.

"Very stealthy!" I yelled, but he grinned and cranked it even higher.

We got outside Immita in about ten minutes, and then Roger banged his foot down on the gas, wailing along with the CD. He had a good voice, pitched so deep it didn't even sound to me like it really belonged to him. We both cracked our windows, and soon I was singing, too. I couldn't stay mad with us both singing good and loud and the rainy wind zooming through the car, making my hair be one big, wet tangle. I didn't care. We were hunting Noveen Duckins, not headed for prom. I looked good enough for Ducktown, and Noveen had known my mom when she was my age.

Back then the other Mosey Slocumb had been a teeny, secret shrimp, something Liza toted around from geometry to English and no one knew. That was weird, to think that baby hadn't been me. If it had been, I'd be sitting through Mrs. Bload's world-history class for the second time now. I guess that was too much for the universe to ask of any human being.

We turned on Nickerjack, a two-lane road so old that even wet and darkened down by rain the asphalt was ash gray. For a couple of miles, Nickerjack went straight through some woods. It would have no doubt been a kegger hot spot if it wasn't for all the illegal traps and the very real chance of getting totally shot, even off season. The Duckins didn't own all of it, but they sure hunted it, and they didn't much care about seasons and licenses; word at school was they'd eat roadkill.

After a couple of miles, the woods ended on my side in a fenced field with ratty bald patches all through it. Right in the front corner was a rusted-out Dodge Dart with no doors or tires or even wheels. It rested on its belly. Inside it, three damp nanny goats were huddled up out of the rain. There was a wheelless truck next to it with a skinny boy goat hanging his head out of the driver's-side window, trying to drink raindrops. Toward the back I saw a fleet of rusting old sedans, all different colors, all with the wheels and doors gone, chock-full of jostling sheep. We were in Ducktown for reals now. Roger turned the music down and slowed to a crawl, looking around.

The woods ended in another meadow on his side, dotted with ten or twelve trailers. On the far side, the scrubby meadow backed right up to a mess of bushes and loblolly pines and old, spreading oak trees. There was a double-wide mobile home in the corner closest to us. Cars were parked all around here, too. These ones still had all their pieces, although one of the Buicks looked like its back door was held on with duct tape. As soon as it died, some Duckins would no doubt strip it down and fill it up with chickens.

Roger pulled the car over across the street from that first double-wide.

"We gotta start somewhere," he said. There were some ranch houses farther up that faced the road, also full of Duckins, and if we turned off onto the next two crossroads, we'd find more mobile-home meadows in between the fields and more little pieces of woods. There were a lot of Duckins.

This meadow was fenced, too, as if the people Duckins were as likely to wander into traffic as their leathery old goats were. He shut the car off, and the music stopped, and we could hear this high-pitched beeping noise coming through the open window. It was too breathy and hooty-sounding to be a machine. It was more like if a really sad monkey tried to imitate a truck backing up. It was loud enough for us to both hear it over the sound of rain beating hard on the Volvo's metal roof.

"What is that?" I asked. "Is someone crying?"

Roger shrugged, mystified as me. "Let's go see."

"Freakin' pouring," I said. I grabbed one of the blankets out of the backseat and flopped it around to unfold it. I draped it over my head like a little kid playing Mary in a Christmas pageant. Roger pulled his hoodie up, and we got out.

The weird beeping was coming from the double-wide, it seemed like, but the gate was all the way down in the middle of the fence, fifty feet past it.

The sorrowful hooting got louder as we dashed across the street, then quieter as we ran down the fence. The gate was wide enough to let the cars in and out, held shut by a loop of wire around a post. Roger reached for it, his hoodie already soaked. I was doing better under the blanket, so I tried to hold a piece of it over him as he got the gate open and we went through.

The double-wide was a white rectangle of cheap siding, sticking up on poles about a foot off the ground. There were three handmade wooden steps leading up to the front door, all saggy and half rotten. There wasn't anything like a porch, only a strip of awning over the steps. We ran under it, crowded together on the middle step.

The noise was driving me crazy. It came about once every five seconds, but not completely regular. There were all these wind socks and pinwheels stuck in the ground on either side of the stairs, where normal people might plant flowers. The socks hung limp in the rain, but most of the pinwheels spun madly, flinging droplets.

"WTH? Is it a person? Inside? Do the pinwheels make that noise?" I shifted from foot to foot, all nerved up. We were on Duckins property, off the county road, and at their creepy mercy.

"I dunno." Roger's eyes glowed out of his hoodie like he was some kind of lunatic Jawa and being killed and eaten by a Duckins was the very most fun he could imagine. "You should let me do the talking. I'm a hella better liar."

I nodded, although I wasn't all that sure if that was true. Maybe last week it had been. But now? I hadn't used a single pee stick, and I'd been giving Big all kinds of backchat and following Patti Duckins around, being stealthy and intrepid and stealing things. I probably could pick up lying, too, easy as Big picked up eggs and milk.

He banged the door three times with his fist. While we waited, I kept looking around to find who was making that breathy beep. It sounded like it was coming from really close, like right under my feet, but it was hard to track the sound with the rain drumming so hard on the plastic awning. I finally thought to look straight down, between the slats of the steps. Eyes stared up at me from under the stairs. I let out a little scream and went leaping backward, right into the rain.

Roger hollered, "Hey!" and turned his back on the door.

I stayed out in the rain and bent to peer under the steps.

"There's a dog up under here," I called to him. The poor thing was wet through, with its hair plastered down so I could see how skinny it was.

"What kind?" he asked.

I shrugged. It wasn't any kind of dog in particular. I took a step closer, and Roger also bent to peer between the stairs at it. It had a boxy head that was too big for its body. It was mostly honey brown with bits of white and black on it. It looked like a beagle had done a genetic drive-by shooting on a mixed-up terrier. The dog's mouth hung open a little, and I realized the sad noise was coming out of it. It was so skinny and ragged, and it looked at me like it didn't even really see me, beeping mournfully to itself. I hadn't seen a dog in this bad a shape since Bunnies.

"Oh, man, poor thing!" Roger yelled over the rain, and I straightened up just as the door swung open. He stood up then, too, turning fast to face it.

A woman Duckins stood framed in the doorway, glaring at us. It was hard to tell her age, like with all of them, because she was so leathery and scrabbly-looking. Her hair hung in strings around her face, and her long, droopy boobs were almost falling out of an honest-to-God tube top.

"What?" she hollered in Roger's face. The rain was even louder now, because with the door open I could hear it pounding on the mobile home's flat roof.

I edged back under the awning, standing behind Roger on the bottom step. I couldn't stop looking up and down between her and the dog, his eyes peering up from between the steps. He sounded like Road Runner under there, *meep-meep*, if Road Runner really needed to be on antidepressants.

"What d'you want?" When she opened her mouth, I saw that her front two teeth had been broken out, kind of on the bias, so they looked like isosceles triangles. Or fangs.

Roger answered her, but I couldn't hear exactly what he said with his back to me and over the rain sounds and the sad dog.

The Duckins lady yelled, "She lives down Nickerjack a piece, in a green ranch house! And what you shitty babies think you're doin', knocking for Patti on *my* door, I'd like to know!"

Roger was hollering back something about the textbook.

I boosted myself up onto the second step, crowding in behind Roger, and asked, "Is that your dog?"

The Duckins lady blew her breath out at me. It stank of drinking so bad I went back down a step.

"He's up under my got'damn porch, so what do you think, Miss Smarty?"

I said, "He's real wet," and she took a threatening step toward me, right to the edge of her doorway. She had on saggy old jeans that looked like they were about to slide off her skanky hips, and her bare feet had long troll toenails, half-moons of pure black dirt under the nail like the filth version of a French pedicure.

"Patti don't live here. Now, get your asses off my stairs and leave my got'damn dog alone. He likes it there."

The dog made that miserable *meep* again, like it was calling her a liar.

Roger shot me an irked look over his shoulder and hollered, loud enough for me to hear this time, "I'm not sure what green ranch house you mean! Does Patti maybe live anyplace near Noveen Duckins?"

The second he said that name, Noveen, the women took her threatening, pointy gaze off me and put it hard on him. Her eyes went all slitty, and she made this hawky mucous noise down in her throat. She spit a big globby wad of spit so thick and yellow I could see it shoot through the rain past Roger's ear.

"Get your shitty baby asses offa my steps!" She slammed her door.

Roger turned around, mouthing, *Wow*. He grabbed my arm as he went by me and dragged me back across the meadow to the gate. I could hear that poor dog beeping after us, fading as we ran to the gate and then coming back louder as we came down the other side of the fence to the car. We jumped in and sat there dripping all over the leather seats.

"We can't leave that dog there," I said.

Roger was already starting the car up, saying, "You can't put a dog down your pants, and anyway, that woman had a shotgun. I saw it in the room right behind her. But, Mosey, did you clock the look on her face when I said Noveen's name?"

"God, that poor dog," I said. "No more random Duckins doors, please. I will throw up."

"I know, right?" But he didn't look ready to throw up. He looked like he'd just come off the Rock 'n' Roller Coaster and was hot to go again. He started up the car, saying, "Let's go up the street and see if we can find the house. Green, she said. If Noveen is Duckins non grata, maybe Patti knows why."

We drove between a row of brick cube houses and another meadow with animal cars before we saw a ranch house facing the street with enough peely paint still clinging to the siding to qualify as green. We pulled off across the road from it and waited for Patti Duckins's stupid bus to get all the way out here and drop her off.

Apparently the bus didn't come this far, because when we finally saw her, she was walking along the shoulder of the road. The rain was still falling out of the sky in sheets, but she trudged along with her head down, taking it. Her faded blue T-shirt stuck to her bony frame, and the weight of the rain made her draggy floral skirt hang so low the hem almost touched her feet. She wasn't wearing a skirt for any holy reason, like how the girls at Cal can't wear pants and even the cheerleader skirts come to four inches above the knee. I'd seen Patti at school in overalls and torn pants and even a jean mini so short that her butt almost hung out from under. Like most Duckins, she wore whatever crap they had in her size in the "Clothes by the Pound" bin at Goodwill.

Roger and I both slumped down low in our seats. She stomped past us without so much as glancing in our direction, heading straight to the green ranch house and going inside.

I said, "Dude, look at her. I'm so not a Duckins." It came out sounding really fervent, almost like a prayer.

Roger didn't notice. "Let's go ask her about Noveen." He was still jazzed.

We were too wet by now to bother even trying, so we dashed across the street and up onto the porch, me kinda hunched over Patti's textbook to protect it. Roger pressed the doorbell, but we didn't hear it chime inside. After a minute, Roger knocked.

A fadey-looking lady with grayed-out hair and big pooches under her eyes opened the door. She had a cigarette clamped between two of her side teeth. The eye on the Marlboro side was squinched half shut against the smoke. If she was surprised to see us on her porch, she didn't react. Just blinked at us, dumb as a lizard, and said, "What."

I looked nervously at Roger, and he was looking back at me, jerking his head encouragingly at the textbook I had clutched. I held it up and said, "I go to school with your... um, with the girl who lives here?"

The woman blinked at me. Now I had surprised her. "You here to see Patti-Cakes?"

"Yes, ma'am?" I said. "She left her book at school."

The woman stared at me, real hard, and then said, "You brung her book back to her?" I nodded, and she swung the door wide. "Come on in."

She shut it hard behind us with a raspy clang that sounded final and awful. Roger started peering around, unabashedly curious. We were standing in a room like a den, but with no sofa or TV, just a bunch of armchairs in a circle. Against the far wall, I saw a big pile of blankets dumped onto a recliner, and it wasn't until the blanket pile rasped out, "Who the hell is that then?" that I realized an old man with a bald head and stumpy, gappy teeth was swaddled up in it like a baby. His head stuck out the top with his hair tufting up like it was more of the rumpled blankets.

"Shush, Daddy," the woman said. "It's friends of Patti's from school." Then the two of them stared at us like we were space aliens, like no friends had ever come for Patti from school before. I guess they hadn't.

"Is Patti home?" Roger asked.

The woman smoked at him for a second, like still wondering at our existence, and then hollered "Patti!" without turning her head. A good minute passed, and then Patti came up from the hall and stood in the doorway staring at us, hostile and suspicious. She had changed into dry clothes, a faded shirt, and a pair of striped men's pajama pants.

"What do you want?" she said to me.

I said, "Hey. I'm Mo—"

"I know who you are. What do you want?"

"Now, don't be a little bitch," the woman said, real mild, though. "Your friends come alla way out here, doin' you a favor. You offer them a drank of something." She said it perfectly like that, "drank," as if it was something that had already happened instead of a noun.

I held the book up in front of myself with both hands, like a shield. "You left this at school," I said.

"Naw I din't." Patti's eyes went slitty in the exact same shape as the tube-top woman's had. I didn't think my eyes went into that shape, even when I narrowed them. Patti took one step toward me, peering at the book through the smoky haze, and then her lower lip pooched out and her eyebrows came down. She took a quick step in and snatched it out of my hands. "How'd you git my book?"

I blinked at her with no good answer ready. Her mom, or whatever the smoking woman was to her, saved me. "Patti! You quit being nasty." She said to me, "You want some lemonade or something?"

"That would be lovely," Roger said, super polite, very Calvary kid, but he couldn't stop jiggling his leg and looking around, taking it in like an anthropologist who's had too much Red Bull. He peered at what looked like a heap of trash in one corner and a pile of what was maybe laundry or rags in another. It was like it was the set of some vile movie about squalid people to him, not real.

It was realer to me.

Even though I'd lived in Big's clean nice house for as far back as I could remember, Liza and me, we used to live in places like this. Liza'd told me. I knew if Liza hadn't brought me back to Immita, she and I would probably be living in a place a lot like this now. Roger had his own phone in his bedroom and drove the safest Volvo in the known universe. He hadn't been inside a house like this, not in his whole life.

Roger ignored how mad she was and said, "Hey, Patti, guess what we found?"

Patti said, "My book," in this awful dark voice.

"No, I mean, yes, but also we found an old yearbook. It had a pic of one of your relations hanging out with Mosey's mom. Noveen, her name is. They used to be really close. Isn't that cool?"

At the name Noveen, Patti's momlike object stopped walking to wherever the lemonade was. From the recliner the heap of rags with the old man inside made that same hawky-phlegm throat noise the other Duckins woman had made, but he didn't spit.

Patti's mommishy thing said, "Noveen don't come around here no more."

She went on out of the room and left us there staring at Patti and Patti staring back, really hostile.

I wasn't sure if the woman was coming back with lemonade or if saying Noveen's name had already gotten us kicked out.

The heap of blankets rustled, like they were so filthy they'd gone crackly, and the old man said, "You Liza's kid? Liza Slocumb?" Patti shot him a dirty look for speaking to us just as she was about to glare us out the door, but he ignored her. "You look like a white kid to me. Your daddy a white man?"

"I guess," I said, and he actually cackled, almost exactly like Big used to do when she read me *Baba Yaga*.

"Don't know for sure, heh? Well, that does make you Liza Slocumb's kid, don't it?"

I took an angry step toward him, but Roger put a hand on my arm, eyes alight and interested to have this ancient Duckins relic talking to us. "Liza and Noveen were really tight, huh?" he asked.

"Pah, thick as thieves, we thought. Noveen tooken her sleeping bag over there about ever' weekend. Said she was camping out with Liza in her tree house. Camping. Shit. Up in that tree whoring, more like."

Patti said, "Maybe you better git. He's gonna get all worked up."

The heap of rags seemed to straighten itself up in the recliner. "Shut that piehole, little girl!" he said. "You don't boss and sass your elders. You can take a good lesson from Noveen. She got her whore self flat cut off, din't she?" Being cut off from this family seemed to me like it might be a super plan, but Patti frowned and looked down at her bare feet. Now the old guy was upset, I could see it. Spittle flecks had foamed up in his mouth corners, and the whites were showing all the way around his eyes.

"You see! You riled him," Patti said to her feet. They were pale and clean, and I was surprised to see that her toenails were neatly painted pink.

He was fussing on, not hearing her, looking me up and down with his eyes all shiny. "I thought sure Liza would fetch up a nigger baby, since Noveen found the only Chink in Mississippi and laid claim to him."

The mom lady came back in time to hear this. She was carrying a plastic pitcher and some Dixie cups, but she took one look at the old guy and set them down, just bent and plopped them right on the floor by the doorway.

"All right then, Daddy," she said. To us she said, "Maybe you best come back another time."

"Or not," Patti added.

Roger and I started moving toward the door.

"Why ain't you a little half nigger? Your momma was even whorier than Noveen!" the old man called after me.

The mom lady was following us. She glanced over her shoulder at the old man, and then she herded us all the way out onto the porch and pulled the door shut behind her. Outside, the sky was very gray, but the rain had slowed down to a drizzle.

I said, "I'm really sorry."

"Naw," she said. "I think Noveen is doin' real good, you ask me. She married that boy what knocked her up, and she's got a good job working for a dentist in Biloxi."

"What happened to the baby?" Roger asked, on mission.

"Oh, he's fine. Must be about your age now. He got her eyes, so that's good. Though he's a little brown, you ask me."

"She had a boy, then," Roger said, disappointed, and even though I had never believed I was a Duckins, of all things, I couldn't help but be relieved.

"A half-Chinese boy, sounds like," I said.

"Daddy don't really mind coloreds, as long as they keep to theirselves and don't go mixing blood," she said, like this was totally reasonable. "Now, me, I don't hold it against Noveen." Then she added, "Don't you mind what he said about your momma. Liza was a real sweet girl to Noveen, and anyway, you sure do look like your daddy was a white man."

"Oh, yes, I'm relieved to hear you think so, too," Roger said, in the same Captain of the Boy Scouts voice he used on teachers to explain all his absences. "A white guy for sure. Probably. We hope."

She beamed at him, all benevolent, and I stepped down hard on his foot, grinding it while I tried to smile at her.

The door opened, and Patti slipped out. In the moment it was open, I could hear the old guy still yelling the very bad N-word, over and over. Patti said, "I think he's gonna need some Tylenol PM and a shot of Jack."

"Well, shitbirds," the mother said, still real mild. She went inside.

Roger said to Patti, "So Noveen still lives—"

"Who are you? You don't even go to my school," she interrupted. "So you can shut up. My cousin just called and said you was at her mom's house before, asking about Noveen and pretending to hunt me like we's friends."

I swole up, trying to look indignant as best I could, which was not a lot because she had us dead to rights. "See if I come all the way out here next time you lose your book."

"Don't do me no favors," Patti said. "I think you tooken it on purpose, to come here and make fun and see my house. Asking about Noveen like some butter-eatin' asshole, getting Grampa all foamed up." I tried to answer, but she got louder, overriding me, saying, "You better get on off my porch before I kick your skinny, book-thieving whore ass, and that's all."

"Come on, Mosey," Roger said. I didn't move. For the first time in my life, I was aching to actually hit someone. I could see me just popping Patti right on her mad mouth. I thought, *I can steal and lie pretty good—I bet I can fight, too*, but Roger grabbed my arm and started pulling me backward.

"Yeah, that's right, you *better* go," Patti called after us as Roger yanked me down the stairs. "And at least my mom ain't a whore." I tried to go back up the stairs then, which surprised me. People had said much worse about Liza, and it had never made me this mad before. Patti took a stampy step toward me, like she'd be happy enough to meet me halfway and get into it. Roger had to grab me with both hands and drag me down the cracked-up walkway.

"Are you kidding me?" he hissed. I got a hold of myself. He was right. In sixth grade, one of the Duckins girls grabbed another girl's hoop earrings and yanked them out, tearing through her lobes. Patti looked mad enough to scratch my eyes out, and who would have thought a Duckins would be so smart and see right through us?

I turned with Roger, and we jogged off in the drizzle of remaining rain to the car, Patti glaring after us the whole way.

"Oh, man, I feel kind of shitty now," Roger said, shutting his door and rolling up the window. "She thinks we came to make fun of her being so poor."

"She can go to hell," I said. I was still mad about how they had talked about Liza, and used the N-word, and been altogether vile about Noveen's mixed-race baby. Roger just thought it was funny, because no one would ever think of the Knotwoods, with their car dealership and their yearly Disney World cruise vacations, as poor white trash. My family lived in a crappish house with no money or husbands, and people like the Richardsons snooted down on us, comfortable believing that poor and having babies out of wedlock was the same thing as hateful and racist. They could do that because of folks like the Duckins, who were happy to live up to every cracker stereotype in the handbook and invent a few of their own, even worse.

"She's in hell already, Mose." Roger started up the Volvo and did a three-point turn, heading back up Nickerjack toward home. "Maybe at school you can apologize and tell her we weren't there spying on her."

"But I'm not sorry, and we were too spying," I said.

"But not to make fun. We were making sure you weren't Noveen's kid."

"As if," I said, still fuming. I turned away and stared out the side window.

We were almost back to the first meadow we'd come to, where the auntie who had called Patti to rat us out lived drunk and mean as whole crowds of snakes in her double-wide.

"Stop the car," I said.

"No way," Roger said.

"Stop," I insisted.

"So you can go back and get your ass kicked?"

"Roger, do not be stupid, and please can you stop the damn car?"

Roger shrugged and pulled over. We'd already overshot the double-wide, and we came to rest on the shoulder by the woods. I unbuckled and bent down to get those wicked-looking wire clippers from the floorboards. I pushed my door open, and immediately I could hear that the dog was still *meep*-ing. Roger started to turn the car off.

I said, "You stay here."

"Oh, hellz no!"

"Seriously. I need you to keep the car running."

He shook his head. "This bad idea is bad." Still, he didn't turn the engine off.

"Five minutes," I said, and got out.

I snuck up on the mobile home from behind, creeping through the woods that went all the way up to the wire fence. My heart had jacked itself up into my throat, pounding so hard it was like it was thumping at my gag reflex, but the sad *meep-meep* kept me moving forward. Screened by the trees, I took the wire clippers and I flat went after that fence with them, like *it* was the thing that called my mom a whore. I had to work hard to clamp through the links, but it felt good to tear it open. Once I got the hang of how to work the leverage, it got easier. I was sweating into my damp clothes and breathing hard by the time I'd cut an opening big enough to slip through.

I ran right up to the back of the double-wide to get out of sight of the windows. They didn't have curtains or even cheap blinds. The mobile home itself hid me from all the trailers. I bent low and peered down under. The dog had crept from the steps to under the double-wide, in the middle. He'd come to see what I was doing, but he was tied up to the stairs and couldn't get closer. His beep had stopped. He looked at me, head tilted, curious.

I said, "Hey, buddy," really soft and sweet. At the sound of my voice, the poor thing wagged his tail. He didn't look like any human alive had ever been anything but a complete douche to him, but he still wagged.

I got on my belly and wriggled under to him. He could have bit my face off, but instead he watched with his tail swishing back and forth. I used the wire cutters to nip through the clothesline tied to his collar, then wrapped him in the blanket. He let me. He probably should have weighed thirty pounds or so, for his size, but he wasn't much more than skin and bones. I shimmied backward. He was mostly wrapped in the blanket, so I had to drag him. He let out a startled bark as I pulled him off his feet.

From inside, I heard that woman yell, "Shut the fuck up, Pogo!"

The dog barked again, like he was answering her.

I panicked and pushed his head down in the blanket, wrapping him up like it was a bag, and he started barking for real then, really mad or scared or both.

I jumped to my feet and threw the blanket full of struggling dog over my shoulder like I was Santa and he was a squirmy bag of upset toys. I ran for the fence, whispering, "Shut up, I'm helping you." Pogo clearly did not speak English, because he kept on barking and struggling and pawing at my back. I got to the fence and scraped my arm open pretty good trying to get through the slit toting the blanket full of panicking dog and the clippers.

Behind me I heard the mobile home's front door bang open, and the woman started calling, "Pogo? Damn it, Pogo?" I took off through the woods with her yelling, "Pogo? Hey, Pogo?" behind me. She must have heard his barks fading off and away.

"Shut up, shut up," I hissed as I reached the car and leaped in, yelling, "Go go go!"

"Tell me you did not," Roger said. But he threw the car into drive and jammed his foot down.

I set the angry blanket on the floorboards and dug in the folds until Pogo got his head out.

"I couldn't leave him," I said. "Liza never would have."

Pogo shut up once his head was free. He sneezed twice, then flopped in a misery heap still half in the blanket, like he didn't much care about whatever might happen next. I reached to give him a reassuring pat and saw that his thin fur was crawling with so many fleas they were practically a mat. "Oh, vile."

Roger looked where I was looking and said, "Awesome. Those things will be all over my car in thirty seconds. Should I go by the pound or what?"

I said, "No! Maybe a vet? His name is Pogo. I'm totally keeping him."

Roger snorted. "Seriously? Well, roll the windows back down. He smells like someone ate him and then pooped him out."

I nodded, turning the crank. "Or puked him up."

Roger eased off the gas as we got closer to Immita. "Big is going to kill you."

I shrugged. "Big doesn't really have a say. She and I aren't even really, like, related."

Roger shook his head and kept driving, but he also kept stealing little peeks at me. He said, "Man, Mosey. Who are you?"

I laughed and put one hand outside the window, pushing at the wind and feeling the wind push back. "Not a Duckins," I said.

That made him smile, and I smiled, too, even bigger, because who I was still and probably forever was a thing that only Liza knew.

CHAPTER ELEVEN

Big

A YEAR AFTER Liza and Mosey came home, I caught sight of Lawrence when I was stocking up at the Sam's Club in Gulfport. He was pushing a cart piled high with juice boxes and family-size frozen lasagnas. My feet stopped dead, but at the same time I felt my inside self leap forward, sweeping toward him like I was made of wind. Then I saw Sandy. She was ahead of him, letting the boys get sample sherbet at the end of a frozen-food aisle. She looked tired, and I hated her because the tired didn't stop her being pretty.

I barreled backward into Liza, practically giving poor little Mosey whiplash as I jerked the cart out of sight, back into the cereal aisle.

"Big, what the hell?" Liza said as I shoved the cart past her.

I didn't even correct her for cussing in front of our preschooler. I trotted halfway down the aisle and started hurling box after box of Honey Nut Cheerios into the cart.

"Wannit," Mosey said, reaching. Shades of baby Liza asking for the Gulf of Mexico, but then she smiled her sunny Mosey smile and said, "Please!" while she opened and closed her starfish hands at me. The box had a maze on it that Buzz the Honey Bee had to navigate to get to a picture of a healthy breakfast. I handed her a box and dumped another in the cart.

Liza stayed at the mouth of the aisle, scanning, and then she turned toward me with the ghost of her old up-to-no-good smile growing. I owed the dentist a chunk, but it was worth it to see that smile again. She was close to getting her first-year pin from NA, and she'd bounced a long way back from the hard living she'd done on the road. The glow was returning to her pale gold skin, and her hair was thick and bright as new pennies. She came sauntering down the aisle to join me, hips swaying.

Mosey was absorbed in tracing Buzz's route with her finger, and Liza leaned in close to me and murmured, "Yum. Two thumbs up. Who is he?" in a conspirator's tone.

"Did you see the price on this?" I said, too loud, putting two more boxes in.

Liza's lip quirked, and she whispered, mock pitiful and wheedling, "Talking about boys makes me want the meth less."

My cheeks were so hot that I knew I must be glowing like cranberry glass. I fixed Liza with my sternest mother gaze and put two more boxes in. "A lot of things make you want the meth less. Borrowing my shoes, holding the remote, not doing the dishes."

Liza laughed and nodded. "Yup. Is that his wife, and do you really want all this bee cereal?"

"Yes," I said, and began wheeling the cart away.

"Yes to wife or yes to bee cereal?"

"Yes to bee!" Mosey said, triumphantly lofting her box, and that, at last, shut Liza up. At least until we got home and Mosey was playing dolls in the den. Then Liza came into the kitchen where I was trying to figure out where to store fourteen boxes of Cheerios and leaned on the counter, ankles crossed.

When she spoke, it was like she was picking up in the middle of an old conversation, but it wasn't one she'd had with me. "Couple weeks back I did some stuff with Denny Wilkerson."

I stopped putting things away and wheeled to face her. Denny

Wilkerson was over thirty years old, not to mention married. "What do you mean, 'did some stuff'? How much stuff?"

"Not *all* the stuff," Liza said. "But a lot of stuff. I needed something, you know? There's all these things I'm not allowed to have."

"Yes, and he is one of them," I said, fierce.

"Exactly. Something I can't have. But not the worst thing on the list." She was meeting my eyes dead-on, confessional but not all that sorry. She looked so young, and I wanted to take her by her still-frail shoulders and shake her until some sense got in. Her honesty was a mother trap, catching me wanting her to be able to talk to me, and yet, Lordy, never wanting to hear about her climbing on Denny Wilkerson looking for something to fill up the hole she had inside of her. I counted ten in my head, reminding myself that I'd helped to make that hole. She'd grown up with no father, no grandparents or cousins or kindly aunties, no community of wacky, warm, closer-than-family friends that people on TV seem to find so easily. No church, and in small-town Mississippi that had surely limited her social life. All she'd had was me, too young and dumb to know how to discipline her. I didn't even know where to look for support. Not that I would have. I'd been too busy proving to my parents I could do it all on my own, so busy I hadn't even noticed they weren't watching.

When I thought I could answer in a quiet, calm way, I said, "If you need something, go to a meeting. Call me, or call your sponsor."

She shot me an impatient look, like I'd completely missed the point. "I'm telling you that whatever you did with Mr. Sam's Club, it happened. You could talk to me. I'd get it. I'm the last person who would judge you."

All at once I could feel a headache coming on. "Are you trying to have girl talk? About Denny and—Liza. No. That man in the Sam's Club, it was not like that."

"So you're saying that wasn't Mrs. Sam's Club and her cubs?" she scoffed.

"It's too much to get into, but trust me, it was not the same thing as you canoodling with Denny Wilkerson."

She bounced away from the counter and planted her feet, her jaw set. "It never is, if you do it. Stop treating me like I'm some kid having sandbox adultery, while you have a complicated, grown-up kind I wouldn't understand," she said, and while her words were hideously convicting, her voice was pouty as any thwarted child's.

"I'll stop treating you like a kid when you grow up, Little," I said, gentle as I could.

Her lip curled. "God. Do you ever get a day off from all this Big shit? This constant mommism? Do you ever get to be a human?"

"No, sweetheart. No, and you don't get to either. Not anymore. You want Mosey running around 'doing stuff' with guys your age in a few years, daddy hunting? I'm telling you, Liza, if it takes a village, we are screwed, because we don't have one. We have us. We have to do better for her than I did for you." Liza started stomping away, and I called after her, "That means staying out of Denny Wilkerson's truck, Little."

She paused long enough to say, "No worries. I have plans to run around the house with a stick in my mouth all day, so I won't have time for screwing any father figures." Then she was gone.

We had to eat that stupid cereal for a month, but good kept growing out of that bad day; back then, Liza had taken my words to heart. I don't know what-all trouble she got up to with the fellows. Plenty, I'm sure. But she kept it down low and away from Mosey. Now the memory of that day was paying off again. It made me understand I had to take her with me to see Lawrence.

I planned to go on Saturday. Most of Lawrence's Sundays were eaten up by church things, and on Monday, at the latest, I'd have to call Rick Warfield back and schedule a time when he could come by and question Liza. He'd left another message, still sounding friendly and patient, but if I didn't call him back soon, he'd start to wonder if I wasn't avoiding him on purpose. Which of course I was. I had to talk to Lawrence before Rick came, had to know what Rick was thinking. The only problem was, Mosey had invited her friend Raymond Knotwood over on Saturday.

Mosey wasn't allowed to have boys over without either me or Liza home, but I'd decided to bend the rule. Just for this one day, and for this particular boy. Sure, Raymond had grown up a lot in the last year—the top of his head almost reached Mosey's eyeballs now—but he was still pale and gangly and about as seductive as a teenage Spock. The Leonard Nimoy one, not the new hot Spock they'd sexed up for the movie reboot.

I knew I'd made the right call when I looked at myself in the mirror that morning. I hadn't dressed myself so careful in a decade, and I felt a breathless press on my chest, like I was heading toward Christmas or kissing or both. My eyes were overbright. I said to the pink-cheeked woman in the mirror, "You are an idiot." I was going there to use him, not to get myself good and used. I'd been telling myself I was bringing Liza because an afternoon in the pool with Sandy had lit up all the darkened corners of her brain, and so it followed that a morning with my ex-man himself ought to flash even brighter. That was true. However, it was also true that today I needed a chaperone more than Mosey did.

I poked my head in the den where Mosey was watching *Mythbusters*.

"Mosey? You and Raymond stay in the den or the kitchen, you hear me? He is not allowed to hang back in your room."

Mosey rolled her eyes like that was the stupidest thing any stupid person on the planet had ever said out loud. Her gaze slid right over me, full of snit, and she didn't even notice I'd put on mascara and blown out my hair to supposedly go to the grocery. I got out the door with Liza while the getting was good.

Liza was moving faster in that walker. She inched her way to the car, internally bright and interested. As soon as she was buckled in, I popped open my old flip phone. I'd waited to the last second, but I had to call now. I didn't want to find myself living the sequel to *A Nightmare on Sandy Street*. I imagined what it would be like to show up at his place and find it empty. Or worse, what if he wasn't alone? I pictured a sleepy, hot thirty-something in underpants and one of his T-shirts peeking through the door to tell me he was in the shower, asking did I want her to pass on a message.

I'd put Lawrence's number in my phone when I'd looked up his new address on the bank's computer yesterday at work. It rang four times before he picked up. I could tell he'd been sleeping by the way he answered, his voice a cracky, deep rumble in his chest. The sound of him made my stomach drop as if gravity had suddenly decided to stop working.

"Are you by yourself?" I asked. It came out a little too husky for my liking.

I heard him breathe in sharp, and it sounded like he'd sat up in the bed. When he spoke next, he sounded like he'd gone from zero to wide awake in less than a second. "Ginny?"

"I said, are you home by yourself?"

"Yes. What—"

I interrupted him. "Well. Stay put. I'll be there in twenty minutes."

I flipped my phone closed before he could answer. It had been so long. Almost twelve years since we had so much as exchanged hellos, and yet my hands were shaking. I'd dated a few men after him, but no one that could get him out of my head enough for me to take them serious. If hearing his voice hit me this hard, then bringing Liza was an act of pure genius.

As I got in my car and backed out of our driveway, Raymond Knotwood's dowdy black wagon was pulling up to the curb. I lifted my hand in a wave, and he gave me that egg-sucking dog smile of his.

"I'm pretty sure that kid is evil," I said to Liza.

She muttered something that sounded a lot like "gladiola" back.

"What?" I said. Whatever it was, it was responsive, and yet another new word. I asked again, more eagerly, "What did you say?"

She waved her good hand at the road, impatient to be going. So was I, truth be told, and so I took gladiola as a good sign and drove.

Lawrence's new apartment was on our side of Moss Point instead of the Pascagoula side, so it didn't take long to get there. He was living in a large complex, very depressing, I thought, a host of rectangular buildings painted the same split-pea-soup color, with fake shutters glued beside the windows. Lawrence lived near the back, on the first floor right near the Dumpsters.

His door opened while we were coming up the walk, like he'd been watching for me, and he must have gotten off the phone and jumped straight in the shower—his hair was wet and slicked back off his face. His hairline had moved an inch or so higher than where it used to sit. His eyes had gone creasier around the corners, too, but the lines around his mouth looked the same, as if he hadn't been smiling very much. He was a little thicker in the middle, but his shoulders had that broad, easy set I remembered.

I was wondering what he thought about the miles I'd put on me. I'd dug out my old chocolate-and-gold wrap dress from the back of my closet. He'd always liked me in it, and I'd been pleased at how well it still fit me.

"Hey, Ginny," he said, stepping out to meet us.

"Hey, yourself," I said.

"You must be Liza," he said, and he said it right to her, looking into her half-lovely face. He rested his hand over hers on the walker for a moment, not at all awkward, like it was a regular way to do a handshake. He'd always been smooth, but this was too smooth, unless he already knew about the stroke. Moss Point and Immita were different worlds. It wasn't like he and I ran in any of the same circles. If he knew, then he'd been keeping up with me from afar, on purpose.

Liza was eating him up with her eyes, and she leaned in toward him and said, "Yes." Not her old noise that meant yes, but a slurry-*s*'d version of the real, actual word. Yes and a word like gladiola; every little step forward like this felt to me like the pointy tip of a miracle.

"Come on in," he said, and swung his door wide for us.

His front room was big, but it had only a stripe of a kitchen, open to his living room with a breakfast bar running in between. There was a little TV on the bar, tuned to CNN with the volume on low. The back wall had two doors, one open to show a half bath and the other closed. The walls were plain white, and he hadn't hung anything on them. There were only a few pieces of furniture: a couch, a coffee table, a bookshelf, the bar stools. It all looked like the cheap stuff they have for dorm rooms in the IKEA catalog. I didn't recognize a single thing from his old house except some of the books lining his pinewood shelves. He liked the same kind of reads I did, full of lawyers and cops and private detectives.

"You want coffee? I'm having coffee." He walked away past us and picked his mug up off the counter. It was plain and white, probably from IKEA, too.

"You didn't take anything from the... your..." I petered out, uncertain how to say it. The room was so full of elephants I didn't even know a single word I could say that wouldn't jostle us into one of them. Finally I said, "Sandy's house."

He nodded. "Seemed easier. So you heard we busted up?"

"Yeah," I said. I pointed at his plain mug. "You didn't even bring your pig mugs."

"Razorback," he said automatically. It was the echo of an old play fight we used to have, mostly when we were naked, drinking coffee in bed the morning after a night of tumbling all the sheets around. I felt my whole body flush.

His throat had to work to swallow; he remembered, too.

"Sandy doesn't even like football," I said, and I could hear an edge of mad in my voice. How could he remember and still not have come for me? If he knew about Liza's stroke, he must also know I was still single. He should have been on my doorstep thirty seconds after he walked out on his wife.

He shrugged, his eyes on me gone wary. "I wanted out. Wanted something fresh."

"I guess so," I said. I couldn't help adding, "What's the something fresh's name?"

His eyebrow cocked. "I meant the place. I wanted a fresh— Stop it."

"I didn't start anything," I said, and that was a lie. I most certainly was trying to start something. Maybe something ugly. My vision had pinholed down to only him, standing there being not Sandy's anymore, and still not mine. I was all pent up, wanting to hit him or throw things, make him angry enough to forget everything and put his damn hands on me.

This was exactly wrong. I needed to finesse him. I had to get him to tell me what suspicions Rick Warfield had pinned on Liza, if he was wondering about Mosey.

I took a breath and turned away from him. Liza was standing still and quiet in her walker, taking us in. I went to her, put my hands over hers, and said, "You need anything?"

She met my eyes. She smiled, like she was bucking me up, and it seemed to me that it was a pretty good smile. Her right side, the bad side, was pulling up a little, not just twisting as the left-side muscles worked. But then I saw how her good eye gleamed, filled to the brim with devilment. An old Liza look. A Liza-up-to-something look.

I cocked a warning eyebrow at her, though I wasn't sure what I was warning her off of, and Lawrence said, behind me, "I was going to call you." Smooth. Like he meant it.

"When you got around to it," I said. I couldn't seem to get on topic, not at all. I wanted to smack him. Smack him and leave. "I don't think I can do this right now." I turned toward Liza, to tell her we should go, just in time to see that her eyes were slipping shut and she was sliding down her walker to her knees.

"Liza!" I yelled, and stepped in to catch her.

Instantly Lawrence was beside me. Together we got her wrestled over onto the pinewood sofa and sat her down. She made the most pitiful noise, like a sad kitten.

"Oh, baby, are you okay?" I said, furious with myself and her for pushing too hard and with Lawrence for everything, even breathing. The worst part was, Liza had all but fainted, I was worried nigh to death, and yet a teeny piece of me wanted to lean a little closer to Lawrence as he settled Liza on the sofa. Lean in and smell the skin on the back of his neck.

"I'll get her some water," Lawrence said, and left us.

I found Liza's pulse, and my anxiety went down a notch. It was steady and even. Then I looked at her face, and she was grinning at me, her good eye wide and full of mischief. I heard Lawrence coming back, and Liza's eyes sank to half-mast and her smile vanished.

I gave her good arm a tug, but Liza made a *hmmm* noise and snuggled herself low into the sofa. My jaw dropped. She was playing possum.

"Is she okay?" Lawrence said, holding a water glass.

"She's just... tired," I said, not sure what she was doing. I had no way of knowing if she understood our mission, knew we hadn't accomplished it yet, or if she was simply basking in the hormones thickening the air and the man drama piling up in heaps around the room.

Lawrence took over, setting the water on the coffee table nearby. He grabbed a folded blanket from the back of the sofa and started tucking it around her. I shifted and stood, wanting to get away from him, as he put a couch cushion under her head. I almost ran the three steps across the bare room to the breakfast bar. Lawrence picked her feet up, like he'd been doing this all his life. He stretched Liza out on the sofa, fixing her blanket, and in less than a minute she was tucked in and her eyes were closed, like she was sleeping peaceful. But I knew better. I could see she was smiling, faint, but enough to make the start of the dimple on her good side.

"This was a bad idea," I muttered, not sure if I meant mine, coming here, or whatever the hell the idea driving Liza was.

Lawrence stood up and turned to face me. His hound-dog eyes had gone all sorrowful. I looked back at him, and there was nothing to be said. I was furious and Liza was faking, but neither of these facts could stop the mother in me from noting how gently he'd handled my hurt kid. I had never questioned the choices of Lawrence-the-daddy. What I couldn't understand were his choices now, after the boys were raised and gone to college and his marriage was over. I understood that my idea about slipping questions at him sideways through a casual conversation was not going to work. I couldn't chitchat, couldn't ask how his momma was or say, *How 'bout them Bulldogs?* Every avenue of conversation led right to me throwing his plain white coffee mug at his head; his sweetness with Liza made me not want to do that, exactly, either.

We stood looking at each other, and there wasn't anyplace to go from here. So I simply asked him direct, "What's Rick Warfield thinking about those bones in our yard?"

Lawrence regarded me with unreadable eyes. "That's why you came to see me?"

"Yes," I said, trying for staunch, but I could feel my lower lip trembling. His gaze dropped to my mouth, and I knew he'd seen. I said, very sharp and too loud to sound truthful, "That's the only reason."

Liza made a snorty noise, like my raised voice had disturbed her. He watched her until she subsided, and then he said, quiet and calm, "Let's go back where we can talk."

He crossed the room to the closed door, and I followed. It led to a short hallway open to a couple of bedrooms. He closed the door to the den behind us and started down the hall. I could hear a radio playing soft.

"I can't say much about an open investigation, Ginny," Lawrence said. "Ask me what you want to know, specifically. I'll tell you what I can."

I said, blunt, "I'm worried he'll think Liza had something to do with it simply because it's our yard. She didn't, of course, but she can't tell him so."

Lawrence opened the door at the end of the hall, and as we went in, he said, "I wouldn't worry about that. That's not the direction the investigation is going. Not at all."

He was saying exactly what I'd hoped, but I couldn't answer. I'd gone speechless. He'd brought me to his bedroom, so small that the act of going inside had fetched us up against the side of a queen-size bed. The walls were stark and white here, too, and the dresser and the bedside table were more pasteboard IKEA dorm stuff, but the bed...I knew this bed. It was Lawrence's old cherry four-poster, and I knew the butter-yellow sheets with the cranberry pinstripe, too, thin and cottony soft from a thousand washings. It was unmade, the sheets in a stir. A faint scent rose up from them, familiar. Tide detergent and, under that, the warm, oaky smell of Lawrence, clean and sleeping.

He was being tight-lipped, but he'd said enough to reassure me, and here we were, alone with the bed we'd made love in half a hundred times. I couldn't swallow. He was still him, and I knew him, and I knew this bed.

Everything I'd thought was anger blazed up in me, higher and hotter than any rage could go. Almost unable to help myself, I went up on tiptoe and I put my mouth right on his still-talking mouth. My arms wound themselves around his neck, feeling the cool, summer-grass spring of his short hair against my forearm and the warm skin at his nape. It was the same, all the same, and my body remembered perfectly the shape of him and melted to it.

His body remembered, too. His mouth opened against mine, opened to the taste of Lawrence and Crest toothpaste. His hands went right where they belonged, cupping my ass and pulling me into him, lifting me so I was almost off my feet and we were hip to hip.

"Goddamn it," he said into my mouth, but it sounded more like a prayer than cussing. His breath mingled with mine. All the days that had passed with the sun coming up and going down with him not touching me, they had all been wrongful and off-kilter, and now, with his hands on me, at last the world spun right. I slid a hand between us, cupped him, felt the hard, familiar weight of him wanting me; he folded at the knee, pulling me with him. We tumbled sideways onto the mattress, spilled together into the sunshine splashed across it. And there we were.

It was me and Mr. Friend; I'd brought a chaperone and come to weasel information, but that hadn't stopped me from choosing my prettiest panties, hopeful pink and lacy. Panties for company, a few years old but looking brand-new from lack of wear. Lawrence's clever fingers were already seeking things inside of them, and I arched and clung and I let myself forget, for a little while. He took everything—my hurt child, the chance we could lose Mosey, how scared I was, how sad I was for Liza's lost baby. I gave it all up, and I gave myself up, too, opening to all the things he was doing to me in the sunshine, and it was like coming home.

After, we lay together in a tangle. My company panties were hanging from his plain IKEA floor lamp like a cheery pink flag. The top sheet was a twist at the foot of the bed. I pulled it up over us and then put my head on his chest, listening to the thump of his big heart, trying to tell myself this hadn't solved damn-all. But I couldn't help feeling good.

He said, quiet, "So much for doing it right this time."

I laughed. "Trust me. You did it exactly right." I lifted my head and rested the point of my chin on his chest. "This is your real bed."

"Yeah," he said. I raised my eyebrows, asking, and he said, "When Sandy came home, she wanted us to get a new one. She said this one wasn't hers anymore, and she was right. We got a sleigh bed, and I put this one up in the attic. It's the only thing I moved over here from the house."

I nodded, digging my chin into his chest, and he blinked a long, slow blink. I remembered this, how he got so slow, lolling around like a sleepy zoo tiger after, while I always wanted to get up and bake bread or garden or go dancing.

Panties aside, I hadn't planned this. But my chaperone had apparently had another agenda, and so had my body, and I'd landed here. My jumbled feelings were one thing, but I'd come for a reason. I found myself still willing to use him and this glowy aftermood, both.

"So what direction *is* the investigation going?" I asked, as if our conversation had never been interrupted at all. Meanwhile my finger was tracing a pattern in his chest hair.

He smiled and said, "I told you I can't share details, Ginny. How many commandments do you want me to break today?"

I realized that the pattern I was drawing on his chest was a little heart, over and over, like a teenage girl doodling in her notebook. I stopped myself and sat up. "You know I'm not asking so I have the best gossip when the PTA meets. I'm asking because I'm worried about my kid."

His smile went down a notch, and he propped himself up on an elbow. "If I thought Liza was in trouble, I'd tell you. I'd have told you myself, before this, if I thought you had reason to be worried."

All at once I didn't like being naked. I reached over and snapped my happy panty flag down. I turned away from him to put them on.

"Is that a fact," I said, but not like a question. I got up and started struggling back into my dress. "I have to get home. Mosey has a friend over, and I don't like to leave her."

His eyes had reset to wary. "Want me to help you get Liza to the car?"

"I think Liza probably feels really quite rested now." My voice was hard and sharp.

I checked the mirror, frowning helplessly at the dark riot of auburn curls my carefully blown-out hair had become. I started for the door, but his voice stopped me.

"Ginny," he said. "I'm serious. I would have been on your doorstep long before this if I thought Rick Warfield was barking up your tree."

I paused. I found I believed him. After all, the day Tyler had taken out the willow, Lawrence had come by to chase the looky-loos from the yard. But he hadn't rung the bell. I said, "I don't want to dig all this up, but, Lawrence, you left your wife months ago. I haven't noticed you showing up on my doorstep, no matter what trouble came my way or didn't."

"I was going to," he said, earnest, sitting all the way up in the bed so the sheet fell from his chest and puddled in his lap. "I was going to call you. November fifteenth."

My eyes narrowed. The whiteness of his bare walls was bothering me. His words sounded truthful, but who could tell in such a stark, bare place? The room seemed too wholly unfinished to have corners and nooks to hide things in, as if anything he said must be plain speaking. I asked, "What's so all-fired special about November fifteenth?"

"It's my court date. I'll be divorced."

That hit me in exactly the wrong way. I took a step toward him, and my words came out so forceful it was like I hissed them. "You were waiting on *the paperwork*?"

"Not the paperwork," he said, terse. "Waiting to be free."

"*Seriously?*" I said, like Mosey in a snit. "That didn't stop you last time."

"Yeah. See how well that turned out?" he said, his own voice rising now.

"If you really wanted—" Then, all at once, I got it, and even my knowing that Liza was a few feet down the hall couldn't keep my voice from going louder and higher with every word. "Oh, holy shit, it's because of God. No, not even God. That I could maybe see. But you were worried what that stick-in-ass whispery pack of vicious Baptists down at your church would think of you if—"

He swung his legs around, out of the bed, this time sitting up for real and talking over me. "Wait a second, now—"

I didn't so much as pause. "—if you took up with the other woman again right after leaving your wife. But I was never the other woman, never." He didn't want to be naked then either, and he hunted up his boxers while I kept on, snappy as a harpy. "Sandy was gone off busting her marriage vows sixty ways from Sunday before I ever laid eyes on you, and I never so much as kissed you good-bye when she came back and you had made your choice."

He was holding up his hands, pushing the air at me like this could shush me. The second I finished, he was talking back, low but intense, and just as angry. "I know that your parents and their church were awful to you when you got pregnant, but don't you judge my friends, my church, by them. This has been so hard on Max and Harry. It's not a cakewalk when your parents split, no matter how grown up you are. My church has been nothing but good to me and them, and Sandy, too." He jerked his pants on, one leg at a time, as he spoke. "Yes, I wanted to wait until I was divorced. I wanted to do it right this time. I deserve it to be right, and you do, too. Believe it or not, being Baptist can sometimes mean only that you try your damnedest to do right by people. 'Baptist' isn't a word that means 'out to screw Ginny Slocumb.'"

"Even so," I said, cold, "you managed."

"Wasn't that hard," he shot back, and I wheeled out of the room, stomping along the hallway. I found Liza sitting up, alert and clearly listening to us yell over the buzz of CNN. She looked as pleased as any dozen cream-eating cats.

"You are still you, and I should have paddled you more when you were little," I said to her, fierce and soft. "Let's get out of here. Warfield isn't looking too hard at us, so that's one good thing." I grabbed her walker and brought it over, and she pulled herself up into it with very little help from me. She had this smug look on her face, like mission accomplished, but I wasn't sure whose mission she was so happy over, hers or mine.

We were headed toward the door when Lawrence came in. He'd taken the time to stuff his feet into Top-Siders and pull his shirt back on, but the buttons were done up wrong.

"Don't," I said to him, and we kept going for the door, much too slow to be at all satisfying.

"I am going to call you, Ginny," he said, firm and mostly calm, though he'd been at least as angry as I'd been. "November fifteenth."

"You do that," I snapped over my shoulder. "I think I'm busy that day, dating every single man who asked me out this whole last stupid decade."

"Ginny..." he said.

I stopped and wheeled on him. "Don't you 'Ginny' me, Mr. Rules. November fifteenth and wait and patience and you'll do it with me but you won't even talk to me, Lordy—" I let my voice go all officious and deep, mocking him. "'I can't discuss an ongoing investigation.'"

He spread his hands wide and said, "All right, all right, look. There are good reasons for that."

"Mmm-hmm," I said, snotty.

"There are. Things are going strangely. Rick doesn't have the budget for all the things that need doing to solve a case this cold, especially since he isn't sure there's a crime there, past an improper burial. But a top-notch private lab is running DNA from the teeth that were left"—I flinched at that phrase—"and when I asked Rick how the department could afford it, he said... Ginny, someone else is paying for this. Which is ethically gray. Rick is only allowing it because the couple paying came in and asked to be tested. They think the bones belong to their lost baby. I don't want this getting out— Is she okay?"

Liza had her back to him, braced in her walker, so he couldn't see how her jaw swung open and then pulsed, like a landed fish gulping and drowning in air. But he'd heard her sharp intake of breath, saw her sway. He ran and caught her as she started to slide down her walker for the second time today, and this time she wasn't faking.

She didn't collapse, though. I saw her will rise, saw her rally, and her hands reached again for the front bar of her walker, shoving at it, trying to move to the door.

"I need to get her home," I said to Lawrence.

He nodded, all business, and said, "I shouldn't have been yelling...."

But I didn't think our fight had upset her. In fact, she'd enjoyed that part, if I knew my girl. It was what he'd said about the investigation, even though the news that Rick was so off track should have reassured her.

Lawrence was still talking to Liza. "Let me help you." She let go of the bar, and he swung her easily up into his arms. I grabbed the walker and followed him to my car. He got Liza settled in the passenger seat, and I took over from there, buckling her in. I checked her pulse while I leaned over her, and it was strong and not fast enough to be truly worrisome. But she seemed torpid. Shut down and gone.

I closed her door and headed around to the driver's side. Lawrence stepped away and let me.

"Thank you for your help with . . ." I gestured at Liza, sounding so stiff and formal that it was like I was a mee-maw after all, thanking a Boy Scout for helping me across the street.

His gaze was level and grave, and he said quietly, "November fifteenth," and that pissed me off all over again. My body felt like it had whiplash, still glowing with the aftermath of sex that had been such a long time coming and yet awash in anger with him and fear for my kid. I was in a swamp of feeling things, and I gave up on sorting any damn bit of it out and got in my car without so much as a nod and started driving.

"Liza," I said. "Liza," but she was staring out the window. Every trace of the woman who had played possum and tricked me into Lawrence's bedroom was gone. I decided we could do without a grocery run. I had to get her home and let her recover, try to find a way to understand what Lawrence could have said that disturbed her so deeply. She'd disappeared all the way to the deep downs inside herself.

When I finally pulled in to our gravel drive, Raymond Knotwood's car was still parked in front of our house.

"Oh, just damn," I said to Liza. She stayed slumped, staring unseeing out the window.

I got the wheelchair out of the trunk instead of trying to make her walk more. She'd had enough today. It was all I could do to rouse her to where I could get her into it. I pushed her up the walk and inside, but Mosey wasn't in the den. I assumed they must be out in the tree house, and that made me flat tired. I didn't feel like going out back to rout that big-headed little booger so I could have a quiet house. But as I wheeled Liza into the den, I heard a strange sound, and I felt my eyebrows come together.

It was splashing. Shower sounds, coming from the bathroom.

Liza was oblivious, but my mouth dried up.

I took off running for the hall, which was useless, because I already knew what I would find. There was only one reason for a boy and a girl to be in a bath together. I'd been so stupid. I'd left her here, thoughtlessly, even while Lawrence was reminding me exactly how powerful a thing sex could be. So maybe Raymond Knotwood wasn't my idea of a heartthrob; that kid carried a torch for Mosey so big and bright it was a wonder he didn't set his own hair on fire.

I ran, already too late, my heart cracking open inside me, because she was too young to be doing this, way too baby young, and how could she not know the damn consequences? She *was* the consequences. She was living the consequences. And that big-eyed, blinking, overinnocent evil fetus of a boy! By the time I reached the bathroom hallway, I was charging, my hands reaching out like claws for the door, ready to tear open Raymond Knotwood's skinny throat.

I jerked the door open, and Mosey screamed.

I stopped there in the doorway, shocked to stillness. Mosey was fully dressed. So was Raymond. They were on their knees, side by side, bent over the tub, where all four of their hands were on a slippery wad of soap and pure, living ugly. I had a heartbeat, maybe less, to take in its wrinkled skin, its scant tufts of splotchy fur. It looked like an enormous, leprous rat.

Mosey and the boy were so surprised they lost their hold on the awful little creature. It came leaping over the tub edge, trailing soap and splashing dirty water, black eyes rolling. It barreled right at me.

I jumped back and screamed louder than Mosey. The thing tore past me, howling like the tiny, wet damned.

"Oh, my God, Big!" Mosey shrieked, and she jumped up and shoved past me, too, arms foamy to her elbows. Raymond knelt there, gaping at me, his whole front soaked by the passing of whatever the hell it was.

I left him there and ran after Mosey.

I caught up to her in my living room, where the animal was shaking filthy water all over my sofa, yammering in a panic.

"Hush, Pogo! Hush," Mosey said, panting and trying to sound soothing at the same time.

"What is that thing?" I asked. It still looked like a wet, awful rat to me, mostly bald, with big red sores on pasty pink skin.

"It's a dog, what do you think? I rescued it."

"You rescued it?" I said, incredulous. "From where? Dog hell?"

"Yes," Mosey answered, loud but quite sincerely. "Roger and me rescued him from dog hell. He's been at the vet. He had ticks and needed shots and stuff. We went and picked him up after you left, and we were trying to get him cleaned up good before you came home. We wanted him to look nice when you met him."

I blinked, thinking that would take more than a bath. So much more. Like a ton of plastic surgery and a miracle.

"You rescued it," I repeated, and my head started shaking side to side, shades of Liza filling up the room. "Not just no, Mosey. Hell no. You think this is what we need right now?"

The dog thing was running back and forth across the sofa, still panicking, its black eyes rolling. I expected it to start spewing rabies foam any second. I've always thought of myself as a dog person, but this looked more like an animatronic mini-monster that might appear in a scary movie, living in the sewers and popping out to eat up people's reasonable-looking pets.

Raymond Knotwood appeared in the doorway, saying, "Mosey? Maybe we could—"

"We are *so* not taking him back," Mosey said, talking over him.

The dog caught her mood, and its worried yammer changed to barking, an unending string of shrill yaps.

I yelled to be heard over all of them, saying, "Then I will, because there is no way we can handle that thing on top of—"

I was flat-out yelling, but somehow, underneath my own yelling, I heard Liza say, "Bunnies."

I stopped like my vocal cords had been neatly snipped in two. It was the wrong word—she was calling a singular dog a whole bunch of rabbits—but it shut me up anyway. She was back, head up and alert in the chair. The *s* blurred, but I could hear how hard she'd worked to shape this word, "Bunnies," in her broken mouth.

Mosey had heard it, too. She was staring at her mother with her eyes gone wide and hopeful.

"Bunnies," Liza said again, loud, over the dog's barking.

I understood then. It wasn't the wrong word. Not at all. She'd had a foster once named Bunnies, the only dog I'd ever seen who looked as bad off as this one.

Liza braced her good hand against the chair's armrest and put her feet on the floor, moving down to the carpet in a controlled slide. Her eyes, both of them, were all lit up from the inside.

The dog stopped tearing back and forth once the room was quiet. Liza's good hand patted the floor, and I stood there with my mouth hanging open and my eyes filling up with tears at how dumb I'd been and how wise my Mosey was turning out to be. I'd been pleased with myself for using Liza's favorite sins to call her, but here was Mosey using Liza's own best goodness. My attempt had ended with Liza locked up tight in that dark place inside herself, but here was Mosey lighting up the pathway to that door.

"His name is Pogo," Mosey said, whisper-soft. The dog's ears cocked at the word.

"Bunnies, come," Liza said again. Slurred, but it was still perfect. A whole perfect sentence that made sense, with a noun and a verb. "Bunnies, come," she said again, and patted the carpet with her good hand. Pat, pat, pat, rhythmic and gentle, and that awful little ruined dog, just as broken as she was, did what every damaged dog I'd ever seen always did. He went right to her, belly low and tail down. Scared and hopeful he went, all the way to her, and he put his sorry head into her hand.

CHAPTER TWELVE

Liza

LIZA WALKS. SHE lifts and clicks her walker forward, then her good foot, then a desperate mental shoving to make the bad foot go. Rockettes.

She knows the way. She's been this route a thousand times in the swelling, ebbing past that washes all around her, a past that is so much larger and realer than the now. This is the way to Melissa Richardson's house.

That man, Lawrence, the one Big loves, he tried to tell Big. Big didn't hear or understand.

This is Liza's fault. Big couldn't understand because she only has the cup. Noun. Subject. Big has the cup, and it is up to Liza to give Big the verb. The verb is at Melissa's house, and Liza knows the way. She must lead Big there.

The words are coming back, and she has tried to tell Big, but everything that must be said is a swirl in her mind that boils away to word pairs when she tries to say it out loud: This does that. Bunnies comes. Liza walks.

Big must come down this road, come with Liza, until Big knows the word that goes with "cup." Bunnies comes. Liza walks. Big must learn what "cup" does.

Liza lifts and clicks her walker forward, and the wind that blows her is a resistance, a current that sweeps her back even as she moves forward. Her good, strong, young legs push against the pedals. She is Liza-then, biking to her best friend's house, and Liza-now, creeping the same route in her walker, one foot after another. She travels, caught in the ebb and wash of memory.

Liza-then is faster. The bike soars through the six miles and fifteen years that separate her from Melissa's house. She is nearing the end of her first trimester. Standing on the pedals to coast down the last hill, she can feel the slight shift the baby is making in her center of gravity. No one knows except Melissa, who has been perfect. Melissa has said and done every right and good thing a girl should say and do when her best friend is pregnant. Until today. This afternoon, at school, Melissa stopped speaking to her. In the hallway after fifth period, Liza was made of air and Melissa puffed right through her, unseeing, unhearing. Liza had stopped existing. She is going to see if Melissa will speak to her now.

Liza-now stumps another three inches forward, less than a block from her own house. She knows that when Liza-then arrives, Melissa *will* speak. This is the first of their three final meetings, each a monkey-paw wish of an encounter, with fallout that will set the troubled courses of her life.

She pushes herself, trying to catch up, but Liza-then's bike is already sailing up the wide white drive. Poured concrete, not gravel. The house is white, too, with columns and a wraparound porch, stuffed full of all kinds of things that don't belong to Liza: a canopy bed, cable TV, cashmere sweaters. Melissa has her own clunky computer, where they troll the message boards, the only girls online, it feels like sometimes. Even Liza's e-mail can be accessed by Melissa: flirtybits@HoTMaiL.com. Melissa owns brothers, three of them, and a bitch of a mother who is at least the right age and the right kind of adult stylish. Not like Big, who wears the same brand of jeans Liza wears and who will take Liza in her arms and then put her head on Liza's shoulder and cry and cry when Liza tells her she is pregnant. Melissa's mom would kill Melissa first and properly cry alone into a pillow, later.

This house, the correct mother, and the pack of brothers—these things are only Melissa's, but Liza is allowed in like a favored pet, no need to knock. Melissa owns her daddy, too, in some ways. He knows how to carve a chicken. He sits at the head of the table, and he has a barrel chest and a swoop of blond hair like a lion mane and a big laugh that Liza feels as a reverb in the floor when he unleashes it.

She lets herself in, and Mrs. Richardson gives Liza her "I smell poo" smile, the usual, as Liza flies by on her way up the staircase to Melissa's room. Taking the stairs two at a time is still easy, but once again she is aware of the shift at her core. She thinks, *It won't be so easy next time, to go up these stairs*, with no idea that there will never be a next time. This is the last time she will ever set foot in this house.

Melissa is on her stomach on her big four-poster bed, reading, legs bent at the knees and bare feet waving in the air. As Liza comes in, Melissa looks up from her book and stares, and for the first time Liza can see that Mrs. Richardson is Melissa's mother. It's in the ice-blue eyes, the haughty chin lift, the mouth tilting up to a wry and vicious angle at one corner.

"What happened?" Liza says. "What did I do?"

Melissa smiles, but it isn't nice. "I know," she says. "I heard you talking to him."

Liza is about to ask what Melissa knows, but she chokes on the words. She sees that Melissa does know. Melissa knows who the baby's father is. The world pauses under her feet for a lurching heartbeat, but then it keeps on turning.

"Does it help to know I love him? I really, really love him," Liza says.

Melissa laughs, but there's no mirth in it. "I love him, too," she says, and it is simple and nakedly true.

Liza says, "So this is nothing new." She's trying to make Melissa laugh, but it's still true. They've loved the same boys before, and it never mattered between them. They could pass Carter Mac back and forth, take turns owning all three of the Davidson brothers. They made out with a boy named Pete at the same time, one on either side of him, his head turning back and forth, his hands roaming, too gobsmacked by his own great luck to be too pushy. Neither girl would let him get any of her clothes off. Too weird. But this is different.

"He's my dad," Melissa says simply.

Liza, who has never had a dad, understands anyway. Liza owns Melissa's father in a way Melissa never would, never will, never can. Liza thinks it is the reversal that upsets her most, Melissa on the outside, empty-handed, this time.

"You'll have to accept it at some point. When it all comes out," Liza says, easing closer, coming all the way to the bed so Melissa can see her face, see how sincerely Liza means it.

Now Melissa is laughing. "God, you are so stupid. You think my dad is going to let any of this 'get out'? You're my age. It's a freakin' felony."

"You don't understand," Liza says. Liza knows she's young, and that worried him, too. He doesn't fool around with high-school girls, as a rule. *But you aren't like them*, he told her that first time, in his study on a Thursday afternoon when no one else was home. *You're such a grown-up kind of pretty.*

"Do you have any idea how much money my mother has?" Melissa looks back down at her book, like this conversation is over, but her eyes don't shift back and forth the way they would if she was truly reading. She says, casually, to the pages, "I so fucking hate you."

"It's not about money."

"Yes it is," Melissa jets back fast. "He won't leave us, and he'll kill you dead if you say anything. To anyone. If he doesn't kill you,

I will." She sounds almost firm and matter-of-fact, but Liza can hear how her voice trembles under that.

"He loves me," Liza says, chin lifting. "We're so in love."

Melissa snorts. "Tell that to my old piano teacher. Tell that to our ex-maid and our stupid neighbor's fake-titty second wife."

For a second, Liza doesn't get what Melissa means, and then she does. "I don't believe you. He hasn't been with anyone but me since we started. Not *anyone*."

Melissa drops all pretense of reading and boosts herself up, curling her legs under her and sitting. She's still laughing while she does it—a mean, hard sound. Now she is laughing so hard that tears come out her eyes. "You total dumb-ass. You moron. You think my mom is getting fat? You ever seen my mom get fat? She's pregnant again. Like, due a month or so before you. You dumb-slut moron."

That shuts Liza up. Of course Liza noticed; she's woman grown enough to check her body against the body of her rival. And she has thought it, that Claire is finally getting fat. But she's loved Coach so long now. And finally, oh, finally, he was miracled into loving her back. She imagined them living in this very house, feeling his boomy laugh shake the floor as he carves chicken and she watches from a permanent place at the table.

Coach is downstairs. She wheels to go to him, demand he reassure her, and all at once Melissa is up, grabbing her arm so hard she feels the grip like a grind against her bone.

"Don't you dare," Melissa says. "You will not say a word with my mother in this house."

"I have to," Liza says, and tears her arm away, runs for the door.

Melissa shrieks, loud as an air-raid siren, and something white flashes in Liza's peripheral vision. It passes her and smashes into the door Liza is reaching to open. It is the white lamp with its lace shade from beside Melissa's bed. Melissa keeps screaming. Throwing more things. Screaming like snakes are eating her from the inside out.

Mrs. Richardson comes running. Coach comes running. The one brother who is home comes running, too.

Mrs. Richardson shoves past Liza. She grabs Melissa, who is flailing and screaming, tries to hold her, croons, "Oh, no, honey, what? What did she do?"

Melissa's scream is words now, over and over. "She took my boyfriend! She took my boyfriend!" And her voice is hysterical, and her face is flushed, but her eyes are icy-cold and doing math.

"Get her out of here," Claire Richardson says to her husband.

Coach puts his hands on Liza's arms and jerks her away, past the brother who Liza sees now is Davis, with his eyes wide and his mouth swinging open. Coach propels her past his middle son and down the stairs, hands hard on her, pushing her ahead in a way that somehow feels like dragging. Her feet hardly touch the ground.

He's had his hands on her plenty, but not like this. Never like this. These hands ruffled her hair a thousand times when she started coming home with Melissa most days after school in sixth grade. This year, for the first time, they've been all over her, teaching her the difference between having a boy and having a man. Now they are cold and press hard into her skin like she is a bag of garbage being taken out.

They reach the foyer, and Liza, through her weeping, manages to say, "There is no boyfriend. She means you.... There is only you."

"You told my goddamn daughter?" he hisses, and instead of throwing her out the door, he reverses, then turns right and shoves her ahead of him into his study.

In six minutes he will leave this room. He will go upstairs to soothe his daughter and unruffle the feathers of his suspicious wife.

By the time Liza leaves, two minutes after he does, a lot of things will have changed.

She will go in weeping and come out dry-eyed.

She will go in empty-handed, but she will emerge carrying the case torn off a throw pillow, stuffed with everything in the study that both belongs to him and looks valuable enough to pawn.

When she closes the study door behind her, she will no longer be in love.

She will bike home, weighed down inside by the growing baby, outside by the pillowcase. She'll stop at the tree house to dump the stolen things into the chest there, a thing she used to call her hope chest. Now it's a fuck-you chest.

"We'll be fine," she will say to the baby, and feel, for the first time, an inner flutter. Moth wings against the inside walls of her. She will take it is as a sign.

She bikes toward home, leaving Melissa's house for the last time. She travels in reverse, flies through Liza-now and past her and back home, while Liza-now is still creeping forward, still trying to lead Big to the word that goes with "cup."

Liza doesn't even make it out of the neighborhood before a panicked Big finds her. Big doesn't listen, doesn't ask the right questions, only cries and yells and then bundles her into the car. At once Liza understands how little she accomplished. In less than a minute of easy driving, Big wipes away all of Liza's hard-won steps. Fifty effortless, thoughtless seconds, and Liza is back at the start.

There has to be another way, but it's more than a week and six more thwarted attempts to walk to Melissa's house before Liza realizes that all the words she needs can be found in her own room, boxed up with Bunnies, under her bed.

CHAPTER THIRTEEN

Mosey

THE WHOLE NEXT week was a festival of creepy stalking. Roger was the stalkmaster, all up in Liza and Melissa Richardson's ancient business, barely even answering my texts. He was supposed to help me study math on Tuesday, but he never showed at my house. I texted him, and he was still at Cal, hanging around the PTA–Student Coalition meeting so he could pounce on Claire Richardson when she came out.

He blinked his big eyes at her all lamblike and told her he was doing a story on genealogy for the school paper. Claire jumped right at that bait. She invited him to her house on Friday to gaze with reverence at her side of the family tree, which apparently went all the way back to Adam, or at least to the world's first rich, important, white person. Wednesday he ditched me again, so he could actually join the Cal paper and get permission to do the stupid story. I blew my Algebra II quiz, but hey, I understood. He was very busy, what with all the rummaging around in my mom's history like it was a garage-sale bin and leaving me out.

Thursday was Gray Meat Stew day in the Cal caf, and we always met at The Real Pit after school so he could get a late lunch made out of food. He didn't show. I texted him four times before I gave up and called.

"You didn't say to meet you," was his excuse, which was complete BS, because asking if Thursday was Real Pit day would have been like asking him if he planned on breathing oxygen tomorrow. I held the phone to my ear, stony quiet, until he broke and said, "Oh, come on, Mose. We can Real Pit tomorrow, before we go out to the Richardson house for the interview. Okay? Oh, and bring your mom's digicam. We can say you're taking the pics for the story."

I ignored that and said, "Where are you now anyway?"

He said, "I'm heading over to the big library in Pascagoula. They have all the old city papers on microfiche. It's an ass pain, but they've never been scanned in, can you believe? I guess they think if they clot up the Internet with the *Moss Point Register* and the *Immita Citizen Times*, there won't be room left for porn."

"The *Times*, are you kidding me?" I said. The *Register* was almost like an actual paper, but the *Immita Citizen Times* was a four-page flyer that came out every other week. Its front page had stories about church jumble sales and high-school football, and no one would ever even pick it up if it didn't sometimes have coupons for a dollar off Blizzards at DQ.

There was a pause, and then he said, "I want to read up on Melissa Richardson, read all the stories about when she baked her baby sister and blew town."

"Drowned," I said, irked all over again. "And who cares where she went, after?"

"You know your mom's old friends are our best shot at finding out where Liza got you. Maybe the papers will have some guesses about where Melissa went."

I snorted. "You mean where the Richardsons stashed her."

He ignored that, and his voice got all wheedly. "If you want me to have time for Real Pitting, you could get in on this stalktastic action. Cut my workload."

"No way," I said. All week, when he'd bothered to answer

my texts at all, he'd been after me to cozy up to Coach Creepy McCreeperson. I'd rather be drowned or baked myself.

"It's not even out of your way," Roger protested. "Just hang back after class, like you need to ask him something about Life Skills."

"No one has questions about Life Skills," I said. That class was mostly driver's ed; we watched 1970s films about reckless-driver teenagers who died wearing the most embarrassing pants: *Blood on the Highway*, *Anytime Is Train Time*. Right at the start, we'd had a two-week section on "Personal Health," which . . . ew, I was sure not asking Coach anything about that. He spent the whole vile unit pacing back and forth like he was on the sidelines, hollering about abstinence and teen pregnancy, which was when everyone turned and looked at me for a second. Meanwhile he was staring at Briony Hutchins's miracle rack like he wanted to teach *her* about teen pregnancy up close and naked-style personal. He really got off showing all the slides of the vile diseases every one of us would absolutely get if we did it, even once. Then on the last day, he showed us how to put a condom on a banana. Just in case.

"So ask about track. It will be easy to get him to talk to you," Roger coaxed, and then he added, all awkward, "You're cute."

I flat lost my temper. "You stood me up at The Real Pit, and now you want me to get into some kind of lure-the-pedo boob competition with Briony Hutchins, who will completely win, by the way. How humiliating will that be, considering I hate her forever? Worse, you want me making snuggy bunnies with a gross old guy so you can hunt his attics for letters my mom never sent to his baby-drowning, psycho daughter. The one who ditched Liza just as hard as Briony ditched me. Seriously, Roger? Fricken seriously?"

He got kind of self-righteous and said, "I'm doing this for you, Mosey."

"Well, who asked you?" I said, and hung up. He didn't even call me back. I sat by myself in our usual booth, my thighs sticking to the vinyl, and after a minute I felt the buzz of a text landing in my phone.

I am, tho, it said, which was hardly an apology. I shut my phone off.

It didn't help that I was starving and so flat broke that I had to dig change out of my backpack to pay for the Coke I'd already ordered. I'd missed the school bus, thinking Roger would drive me. I had to walk, and I got home all sweaty, and it was a half a million degrees inside, because Big shut the A/C off in September whether it was cold or hot or both, back and forth, running the fans and keeping the windows open to save money.

I had my own stalk-related problems at home; Big was making dinner for Liza, wanting me to sit at the table and tell her all about my day while she cooked. All week she'd been after me, tracking me room to room, trying to make me have talks. She'd turned into this smothering Biggety blanket monster that wanted to wrap around me every second, and it was all fake. That's the part I couldn't stand. She had no idea I wasn't hers.

The only reason I hadn't gone flat crazy was Bogo, which was what Liza and me were calling the dog now. I thought I should change his name, since I had kidnapped him and put him in Dog Witness Protection. Bogo was close enough to his old name for him to know we meant him, and it had the B from Bunnies, so Liza liked it, too. When Big heard it, though, she made a skeptical face and muttered that no sane person would buy that dog in the hopes of getting another one free. I told her I would, and then I took Liza and Bogo out into the backyard with one of her old dog-training books. I did what the book said, pushing his butt down while Liza made approving clicky noises at him. I wasn't sure how teaching him to sit was supposed to get him to stop crapping in the house and hiding all the time and eating up Big's shoes, but it was a start. Anyway, Liza was calling him Bogo now, clear as anything, and saying more things real clear, like "Bogo, stay" and "Bogo, sit."

I had plenty of stalkers at school, too. Most kids still hadn't given up on getting the grisly scoop out of Boneyard Girl. Worse, every time I turned around, Patti Duckins was peeking out at me from behind a bank of lockers or around a corner with her eyes all slitted up and glarey. I figured she knew I'd stolen the dog and was plotting some awful Duckinsy revenge involving a switchblade and my face.

By lunchtime Friday I was flat paranoid. I went skulking into the cafeteria, sticking close to the wall like a sewer rat. Janie Pestre and her friend Deb tried to flag me over to their table, but I didn't feel like being mysterious for them that second. I saw Briony watching me, too, but I looked away before she could so much as wave. I sat down at an empty, square table.

I was brown-bagging, like I did every day now. Big pretended it had to do with nutrition, but I wasn't stupid; she'd gone all Food Revolution because home-packed lunches were cheaper. Big did her main grocery shopping on Saturdays, and these days when we ran out of something, we stayed out until the next week. Today she'd packed me a dregs lunch: bologna sandwich with no cheese, a yogurt, and a bag of tired-looking baby carrots. She'd put in my old Ninja Turtles thermos from grade school, too, probably full of whatever was left of the orange juice.

As I stared down, distracted by the pure awfulness of my Friday lunch, Patti Duckins slid into the chair right across from me. I jumped, and this humiliating, squeaky noise came out of me. Patti snickered, then peered at me from under her shaggy Duckins bangs.

I said, "Bogo is ours, now," and my voice came out all high and pathetic.

Patti looked puzzled for a second, but then she shrugged, as if she didn't know who Bogo was or didn't care, one. She didn't talk, just kept staring at me with this weird look on her face, part crafty and part suspicious. Like I'd come over and flopped down at her table instead of the other way around. Finally I gave her a WTH glare, and she said, "I thought sure you'd be sitting with your friends." She jerked her thumb over to where Briony Hutchins and Barbie Macloud were watching us, whispering behind their hands.

I snorted. "Briony Hutchins is so not my friend."

"Well, them ones, then," Patti said, nodding toward Janie Pestre's table. "Whatever ones. I watched you all week, sure you'd be pointing your fingers at me, laughing with some bunch of crappy assholes about how my house was and my old grampa."

"I told you, we weren't there to spy on you," I said.

"Maybe that's so," she said. She sat there. If she didn't care I'd taken Bogo, then what was she doing?

"Twelve minutes to the bell. You should go get your lunch," I said.

Duckins kids got free-lunch cards, so she could be lording it up with a corn dog if she wanted, but she shook her head, flushing. Maybe she'd left her card at home and was too embarrassed to say. Maybe she'd sold it. I wanted to eat, but it seemed rude since she didn't have anything, so I pushed half my sandwich toward her. It was cut on the corners the way Big always did. "Want half? It's super gross."

She scowled at the sandwich and then at me, her mouth scrunching up like she was trying to figure if I was looking down on her or trying to poison her. She left the sandwich half where it was, not picking it up but not pushing it away either. "I called my cousin. Noveen. The one who's married to that Chinese fellow. I asked her about you." I must have looked surprised, because her frowny mouth turned down even more fiercely, and she added, "What? I go see Noveen a lot. You think because my old grampa's prejudice, I must be just as ass-backward?"

"Oh, my God, you are so freakin' touchy," I said. "Did you specifically sit down here to be all weird and yell at me for stuff you make up and say I'm thinking?" I could feel half the cafeteria staring at us now, like we were zoo animals and they were hoping to see a fight, or at least some poo getting flung. Patti didn't even notice them—she was focused so hard on me. Or maybe she was used to people staring.

"I'm not ignorant," she said. "Or a racist."

"Okay already," I said.

"I'm not," she said, like I'd argued with her. She tilted her chin up so she could look down her nose at me and added, real sly, "I gave a black guy a BJ once. His dick tasted just like a white boy's." Then she busted out laughing at the expression on my face. "You never did that, huh? For your boyfriend?"

I had no idea what she meant for a second, and then I said, "Roger? He's not my boyfriend."

"Why not?"

"Because he's *Roger*," I said. She was looking all speculative, like trying to decide if Roger was available, which was plain vile. She didn't even know him a bit, but the boy had all his teeth, so that must make him a catch by Duckins standards. I said, "He's not gonna be your boyfriend either," so fierce it surprised me. She shrugged like it was no skin off her nose and changed the subject.

"Noveen, she says your mom was the coolest person she ever knew," Patti said. "She said Liza Slocumb's kid wouldn't have come out to my place just to make fun."

I felt my cheeks flush, but not embarrassed. It was a hot rush of pink pride filling me. "I *am* Liza Slocumb's kid," I said.

"Your mom, she still cool?"

I wasn't sure how to answer that.

"You know my mom is sick, now," I said. "She got hurt. She... my mom's real sick."

Patti said, "Naw, I didn't know. I'm real sorry. Noveen, she told me some wild-ass stories about Liza. You anything like her?"

"Some ways I'm like." Patti's weird country way of talking was rubbing off on me.

"Not so wild," Patti said, "I know because of you jumped when I said I sucked off a black boy. Which I was kidding, but look, you jumped again."

I wasn't sure if she was kidding or not, but I said, real stubborn, "I'm a lot like Liza, though."

After a second she nodded and picked up her half of my sandwich and started eating it in quick, small nips that told me plain she was hungry. She talked right through the food. "So what do you do with that guy who ain't your boyfriend?" I felt myself straightening up, and she grinned with her mouth full. "Or mine neither."

"I'm his best friend." I said, thinking, *Or I used to be.* This week it was more like I was his science-fair project.

She nodded, very serious, and said, "He don't go *here*, though." She said it like she was making me an offer. It took me a second to get it. Finally here was someone at my school trying to make friends with me, and it was a Duckins. So surreal. But then Liza had been friends with a Duckins, so it must be doable. The fact that Patti was trying at all made me sorry that I'd stolen her book instead of being straight with her.

"Yeah. I don't have a friend here," I said.

She looked at me, not saying the obvious, but I heard her all the same. I pushed the bag of baby carrots to the center of the table, so we could both reach. We each grabbed a handful and crunched at them, not talking.

Finally I said, "You want to maybe go see a movie Saturday?" I was supposed to go with Roger, but it might do him some good to see how it felt to get stood up. She didn't answer, though, and I felt a blush rising. Because seriously? Rejected by a Duckins? Roger would bust something laughing. I sounded huffy when I said, "Or not. Maybe that sounds dull, since I don't go around, like, doing multicultural wiener taste tests."

She grinned, getting the joke, which kinda surprised me, and not taking it mean, which surprised me more. "Noveen said she and your mom used to hang out in her tree house, listen to music, look at trashy magazines."

"Yeah," I said, and it occurred to me maybe she'd hesitated because she didn't have money for a movie. That kinda put my dregs lunch into focus. With my mom's medical bills and the paying for the pool we didn't even have yet, I thought things were tight at home. But it was nothing like what tight meant at hers. I said, "That'd be cool. You could come over after lunch on Saturday if you want."

She nodded and gave me a quick smile, a little shy, and then said, "PE," just as the bell rang. She got up and slouched off, leaving me sitting there wondering what Big would think. Maybe she'd be happy to see me hanging with a person who didn't have the right equipment to impregnate me. More likely she'd crap herself, because Liza had made friends with a Duckins and they'd both had babies that same year. It was out of my hands, though, and all I could do was hope to God that when she came over, Patti would wear clothes that had been dropped at Goodwill by some long-skirt Pentecostal instead of a charity-minded hooker.

When school let out, I saw Roger waiting in his Volvo across the street. I stopped dead at the curb, thinking I should zig out of sight behind the bus, but he'd already spotted me. He waved, and I glared back, half tempted to breeze right onto the bus anyway. Before I could decide, he held up a greasy paper sack and waggled it in the window. He'd already gone by The Real Pit, and my lunch had sucked. I decided that forgiveness was the better part of valor, especially if he was going to ask for it with pulled-pork sandwiches.

I grudgingly crossed, using Patti Duckins's resentful-style slouch so he knew plain he wasn't completely back in my green graces, and got into the car.

Roger pulled out of the school lot as I dug in the bag and saw he'd also gotten me baked beans and a spork. I opened that up first and dug into it.

I said, "You've been a total douche all week," with my mouth full, then added, "You're lucky Patti Duckins ate half my lunch today, or I probably wouldn't even be speaking to you." I kept my voice super casual, but I was watching him in my side eyes to catch his reaction.

There wasn't one, though. It was like he didn't even compute that I'd eaten with a Duckins. His were all bright, like he had a fever, and his cheeks had two pink spots in them.

He said, "Can you read while you eat?" He had a manila folder stuffed full of copy paper in his lap, and he grabbed it and thrust it at me. "Everything came clear when I was reading the old city papers."

I ignored the folder until he set it on the seat between us so he could get his hand back on the wheel. I took a huge bite of the sandwich and said around it, real crabby, "Blahblahblah. You're a douche, and P.S., Patti Duckins is making BFF noises at me. Hey, wait, where are we going?"

He'd turned the wrong way for my house.

"Try to keep up, Tardina Tardmore. We are going to the Richardsons' house to interview Claire. You have to keep Claire busy taking pictures so I can sneak off and search Melissa's old room. Did you forget to bring your mom's camera?"

"I didn't 'forget.' I just didn't bring it."

"Damn it, Mosey! Okay, you'll have to take the pics with my iPhone, then. It's even more important to get into Melissa's room now. Like, vital. Which you would know if you would look in the fricken folder."

When I didn't bother to answer or reach for the folder, he blew air out his nose and stomped down on the gas, saying, "I'm trying to ease into this here, but you aren't helping. I know where Liza stole you from, Mosey. I know who you are."

I stopped chewing. I looked at his face, his eyes lit up, his cheeks burning, and I believed him. The hunk of sandwich in my mouth turned into a big glob of wet cardboard. He glanced at me, and then he put his blinker on and turned in to the first gas-station parking lot we came to. I spit the sandwich lump into a napkin while he shoved the car into park and flipped the folder open. He started pulling out these printouts of old stories from the *Moss Point Register*, setting them down in a line on the dashboard. He had circled all these lines and highlighted others.

"Look at this, you were mostly right. Melissa did take the little sister to the beach. And she got high and the tide came in and sucked the baby away in the car seat. But she didn't drop acid. She just smoked it up. No big, right? I'm sure she'd babysat plenty stoned before. Except this time the pot was laced with PCP. That's some seriously bad shit. It's amazing she didn't pluck her own eyes out or pick up her car and start throwing it around."

I didn't see where he was going. "Who would do PCP while babysitting?"

"Nobody," he said. "Nobody, right? Not on purpose. I bet she had no idea the pot was laced. Here's where it gets weirder." He pushed a printout at me. "Look here, this is an interview with the last people to see that baby. This couple, the Grants, were walking on the beach. It had been storming on and off all day. No one was there except Melissa, standing in the surf, barefoot, jeans rolled up, holding the baby. It was asleep, and Melissa smiled at them and then set the baby in the car seat. She had a beach chair and umbrella set up for herself, real close to the surf.

"The Grants headed back to get their car, like an hour later, because it looked like another storm was going to roll through. They saw the umbrella getting sucked back and forth in the waves. The beach chair was gone. Then Mrs. Grant saw this thing, like a bright pink hump bobbing up and down way out in the water. All at once she remembered that the baby seat had been pink, and this hump, it looked the right shape to be the car seat, if it was floating away out there, upside down. It doesn't really say, but if you read between the lines, it's pretty clear the Grants kinda lost their crap about then.

"The man Grant wanted to swim out and get the baby chair, but it was a red-flag day, with a wicked undertow because of the storms. Not even any surfers. His wife started crying and wouldn't let him. She figured there's no chance the kid was alive by then. The car seat was upside down and way out there. Also, she thought maybe Melissa had the baby on a walk and the tide only got their stuff, and if her husband went out there, he could drown for no reason. She lost her shit and went tearing to the beach highway to flag down a car."

"But where was Melissa? Who got the baby?" I said.

"There was no baby. That's my whole point. Are you following me? The cops find Melissa naked in the dunes, wonked out on PCP, shivering and crying and not making any kind of sense. They take her to the hospital, and the coast guard goes out and finds the car seat, and there's no baby in it. The straps aren't even buckled."

"Wait a minute," I said, and now he had every bit of my attention. "You're saying they never found the baby's body? Like, not ever, ever?"

"Not ever, ever. The Grants only saw Melissa, alone on the beach that day. So everyone thinks the tide grabbed the car seat and the undertow sucked that baby way out to get eaten or wash up in—I don't know, Cuba. But come on, that kid was only a month and change older than you. They never found a body, and then here you are? Come on."

I blinked at Roger's earnest face, because I understood what he was saying, in my brain. My brain got it, but it didn't make any sense anywhere else. It was like he was telling me about some movie he saw a long time ago, one full of actors I didn't like. Nothing to do with me. Nothing I'd even pay to see. But I heard myself say, from really far off, "Right, because if I'm not a misplaced, inbred Duckins, I *must* be the royal Richardsons' missing princess."

I thought my try at sarcasm came out pretty hollow, but he laughed and said, mock solemn, "Oh, yes, Anastasia. How freaky would that be? You could make Claire buy you a car."

I shook my head, because it was too unpossibly unpossible and also vile, to think that I could be a Richardson. I exhaled and said, "No way, Roger, because how did I end up with Liza?"

All at once Roger looked shifty. "This is the part you won't like." His eyes went so wide that I could see whites all the way around, and his voice dropped low, and he talked really fast. "We know Melissa and Liza hated each other after Liza got knocked up. And I bet lacing pot was one of your mom's best life skills by then. What if Liza gave Melissa that pot and took the ba—"

I interrupted, "Bullshit." My voice sounded really loud in the Volvo. "Liza's not evil. And why would she take Melissa's sister? She was still pregnant then."

"I'm not saying she's evil, but come on. They never found a body. And here you are."

I knuckle-punched his arm, hard as I could.

"Ouch," he said. "You done?" I wasn't. I hit him again, same spot. "Ouch! Okay, I get it. You don't like it. But how can we at least not check it out? How can you not want to know?" He waited, but I didn't hit him again. I stared at him, panting, and finally my head moved itself in a little bob like half a nod. Instantly he put the car back in drive and pulled out, heading for the Richardsons'. I sat beside him, feeling like every breath of air I pulled in was made of cold shards of glass. It couldn't be true. Liza would never. I would not let it be true.

"This is why you've avoided me the whole week," I said, and my voice sounded hollow and really far away. "Because you were finding all this out, and you thought I'd freak."

"Well, yeah," he said, eyes forward. "And here you are, freaking."

"I'm not freaking, because it's total bullshit and my mom isn't like that," I said, too quavery for even me to believe myself.

I blinked this really long blink, it seemed like, and then we were pulling up in front of Claire Richardson's square, white house with its Tara'd-out slaveholder-style pillars. I thought it looked like pure ass, but it was the biggest house in Immita, right near the downtown on a short street lined with willows.

Roger turned the car off and rummaged in the glove box for his iPhone and handed it to me. "While you take the shots, I'll pretend I need to pee and then try to find Melissa's old room."

"Oh, my God," I said. Roger was already getting out of the car. I followed, unable to help myself, but my legs felt thick and heavy. Still, my blocky feet moved forward, and there we were, on the porch.

Roger pressed the doorbell. It made this long, fancy ringing in that same tune Big Ben plays right before it bongs the hour. A breath later, Claire Richardson swung the door wide, a huge smile already plastered over her face. She had it aimed at Roger, and then she caught sight of me and it curdled up and all but disappeared.

One eyebrow twitched, and her nostrils flared. She said, "I thought this was for the *Calvary High Herald*?" She was looking at me, but it was pretty obvious she was talking to Roger.

Roger said, "It is. Mosey came along to take some pictures."

Roger nudged me and I held up the iPhone, but I couldn't speak. I couldn't stop thinking about this book Big used to read me all the time when I was little. This baby bird falls out of the nest and he goes all over, asking things if they are his mother. He asks a dog and a cow and a dump truck, Are you my mother? Are you my mother? Standing here looking at Claire's flared nostrils and cold eyes, that book made perfect sense to me, in a way it hadn't since I was three.

Right then, if a dump truck had pulled up, I'd have asked it if it was my mother and cried with relief if it had nodded.

Roger stepped forward, crowding her, but she stood firm. "Don't you think a Calvary student should take the pictures." It wasn't a question. Not really. It didn't curl up on the end. "It counts as extra credit for the kids who have journalism as their elective."

"I didn't think of that," Roger said, all guileless, pressing forward. "And Mosey's here now."

If he nudged up toward her again, he'd be standing on her feet, because she wasn't budging. Not an inch. "No need to waste her afternoon. You can send someone to take the pictures another day."

The message was flat clear: No Slocumb trash was coming over her doorstep, which really ought to have put paid to Roger's crazy theory right then. Because if I was Claire Richardson's kid, wouldn't she somehow know it? Wouldn't she sense it, if only a little bit in her scaly, Sleestak heart, and not be such an enormous bitch to me?

Watching her lip trembling with the effort it took not to let her mouth twist into a more truthful shape with all her teeth bared, I could tell she felt no twinge of doubt or hope when she looked down at me. To her I was just only Liza's, and she blamed Liza for getting Melissa into drugs, and drugs had killed her baby and made Melissa run away. Easier to blame Liza and drugs than Melissa, I guess, and now here I stood on her porch, feebly waving an iPhone like I wanted her to say cheese for me.

Roger said, "Okay. But I'm Mosey's ride, so she's kinda stuck here...."

Claire Richardson finally looked away from me to him. She made a tut noise. "Well, that's too bad. Maybe you can come back and do the interview another time." She started to close the door.

Then I heard my own voice talking. "It's fine. Go ahead in and get your story." Roger kicked my foot, because if he went in alone, he wouldn't get a chance to escape Claire. Too bad on him. "I have things I need to do at home anyway, and it's not that bad a walk."

"All righty, then," Claire said, brisk, like everything was settled and everyone was pleased. She swung the door wide, and Roger shot me a furious look and walked through it to spend the next three hundred years listening to Claire warble and coo about her prime genes and all the Glorious Dead in her lineage. She wheeled to follow Roger, pushing hard at the door as she spun. She meant to slam it in my face.

I watched the door swinging hard toward me, and my arm shot out like it was someone else's arm. Chuck Norris's, maybe, flying through the air in slo-mo. The door banged into its frame at the exact second that Claire's outsize crystal knob smacked into my hand like a baseball. I caught it perfect. The door was a hair away from closed, but the lock hadn't caught. I could feel it hanging in its frame, unlatched, my elbow and shoulder flashing pain at the impact.

I realized I'd been holding my breath. Oh, my God, that woman hated me. I finally breathed out, and if my exhale sounded a little bit like saying, *Bitch*...oh, well. I meant it, too, even if I was her kid. Genetically. Because inside I was totally Liza's. Big was only tricked into having me. Liza had taken me on purpose, so I was hers no matter what. And right now I was damn well doing exactly what Liza would do. I'd caught the door, and that was way too cool a move for me. Liza-level cool, for sure. I gave them two minutes to get out of the foyer, and then I swung that door wide open.

If I'd been trying to bust into Big's house, the hinges would have creaked and squealed on me. Claire's ritzy-ass door glided open all polite and silent. Sometimes it sucks to be rich. I stepped inside and eased it shut behind me, my heart hammering so loud I was surprised that Claire didn't come running back to see who was pounding nails into her gleaming hardwood floor.

There was a fancy chandelier hanging over my head and one of those vomity-looking rugs with the fringe and all the colors on the floor. The air conditioner was really cranking. It felt like you could take your time eating ice cream with no danger of it melting and plopping off the cone.

I'd never been in this house before, but I could hear Claire talking somewhere off to my left, so I went right, into a hallway. The walls looked like leaf skeletons had been ironed one by one into pale gold paint and then glossed over with some kind of shiny top coat. I came to a closed door and tiptoed past with my mouth full of spit. My throat had closed up so tight I couldn't swallow. I kept picturing Coach, home already and right behind that door, flipping through his secret stash of old *CosmoGirl* magazines and touching himself.

The first open door showed me a home office that looked completely fake. No bills or papers piled on the desk, and all the books were leather-bound and the same height, with the titles gleaming gold down the sides. They were for looking good, not for reading. I hurried on and came to a gilt powder room, all fake-French-looking and smelling so strong of roses that the stink of it leaped out at me.

I thought, *Claire must have taken her usual flower-scented shit in here*, and that made me grin and feel proud. It was a Liza line, and I had come up with it in the middle of breaking and entering and feeling so nervous I thought any second I might puke up everything inside me, first the Real Pit food, then everything else all the way back to the pizza I ate a week ago. Then I'd puke up my own guts.

I had to make my legs keep going. At the end of the hall, I peeked through a half-open door and saw I'd struck pay dirt. It had to be the master bedroom, the exact room that I wanted. I wasn't Roger, hunting mythological postcards to Melissa, trying to dig up Liza's past. I was me, and interested in right now, in this woman I might belong to in a truly awful way. The light was off, but the sunlight peeking around the edges of the pale blue drapes showed me it was empty. I slipped inside and closed the door silently behind me.

Just like the office, the bedroom barely looked lived in. It was all icy pale colors, except for these round crimson throw pillows that looked like blood spatter on the big white bed. I found myself drawn over toward that bed. It was so big and crisp-looking, like a hotel bed. I wanted to roll on it, leave my old school dust, spit between the sheets, and then wipe my feet on the pillows.

I figured Coach must sleep on the far side, because two remotes sat on that bedside table and Liza always said she'd never marry, because the first thing a guy did was take the remote. He had the alarm clock, too. I went on tiptoe to Claire's bedside table. It was made of a frosty, pale wood that was "distressed." All our furniture had knock holes and pits, because it was mostly hand-me-downs and just plain old, but someone had done this to this table on purpose. Nothing on top but a coaster, a lamp, and a couple of books. *The Help* and *Water for Elephants*. Calvary Mom Book Club picks, but the spines didn't look like she'd so much as cracked them.

Her table had three drawers, a flat one at the top and then two deeper ones. I pulled the top one open and found a sleep mask and a battered paperback. The cover showed a big-boobied lady pushing away from this bare-chested muscle goon in a kilt. This book looked read to practical tatters. There was a squeeze bottle of K-Y right next to it, and I shut the drawer right quick, making a quiet gag noise.

The next drawer had a little sewing kit and a box of expensive-looking buttons, some scented candles, and a spray bottle of lavender pillow spray. Nothing interesting.

The only thing in the third drawer was a large velvet pouch. My mouth dropped open. It was a deep blue velvet, and Liza's had been purple, but I knew exactly what this was. I touched it, and sure enough I could feel the hard outline of the wooden box inside. I thought, *I bet Noveen Duckins has one just like this in green*, and a silly little giggle tried to rise up in my throat at the idea that every possible mom-o-mine would turn out to own this same-style box-o-perv.

I was about to close the drawer, but then I didn't. I had that weird feeling rising in me again, a little like when I'd slipped Coach's framed picture off his desk and down into my pants or stalked Patti Duckins and lifted her book. But more than that. I didn't only want to do a thing that Mosey Slocumb wouldn't do. It wasn't even that it was such a Liza-like idea; I wanted to get at Claire fucking Richardson.

The box in its velvet pouch was already in my hands, like it had leaped there. I was already rising, running light-footed and quiet as I could back to the door. Maybe I could write her name on the box in Sharpie and have Roger slip it into Calvary's lost and found. She deserved it.

As I tiptoe-sprinted down the leafy-walled hallway, I could hear Claire droning on to Roger. I grinned a mean grin; he must be ready to put a knife in his eye. I let myself out the front door and went to wait in his car. I put the box on the floorboards and grabbed Roger's manila folder, pulling out all those run-off articles and layering them facedown over the box like shingles until it was buried. Just in case Claire walked him out.

It was about a thousand degrees in the black Volvo, so I rolled the windows down and sat sweating to death in the faint cross-breeze. I got bored after a little and picked up my backpack, doing my homework like a model kid until Roger finally came out about four hundred years later.

He sagged out to the car empty-handed and grumpy. He opened the door and slumped into his seat.

"Oh, my God, but that woman can talk about her family. Which you aren't part of, by the way. I was wrong," he said. He started up the car, and at once the blessed A/C kicked in, pouring frosty air out in a mist. I wanted to lean into it, but I was watching his face too close. I was breathless with hope.

"Are you sure?"

"Pretty damn sure. After the family tree, she got out family photos. She has about seventy billion, starting with her kids and going all the way back to those weird, grim-faced old-timey things where it took hours for the thing to expose so no one could smile. It's all *her* ancestors, though. She made it clear that Coach's family isn't relevant. But anyway, she had to go answer the phone, and I poked around in the recent books. She had pictures of the drowned baby. You are so not that baby."

"You mean it didn't look like me?" I asked.

"It mostly looked like a potato. But it was a blond, blue-eyed potato. Not that muddy gray baby blue that can get brown like yours later either. Real icy blue, and it was super white-skinned to boot. You aren't half that pale even in the middle of winter. So."

"So I'm not a Richardson," I said, giddy with relief and now almost sorry I'd taken her vibrators, but only almost, because she was still a monstrous bitch. "It's too bad, really. I'd sure like a shiny red Coronado and some Prozac for my birthday."

But Roger barely smiled. He was shaking his head as he drove off toward my house. "It's been such a waste. Like, all this time in Ducktown, and the library, and here. We still don't know anything. Claire hardly talked about Melissa or your mom, and I gave her twenty openings."

"I'm surprised she talked about them at all."

Roger blew a big raspberry. "It was just for a second after she slammed the door on you. She didn't apologize for leaving you in the yard like a dog or anything, but I guess she felt like she owed me some kind of explanation. So while we walked to the room where she scrapbooks—she seriously has a whole room for that—she talked sideways about y'all's bad history, said how Liza got Melissa all mixed up in selling drugs out of her tree house. Once we got to Scrapbook Central, mostly she talked about the Civil War, and did you know she had ancestors on both sides playing key roles? A Confederate plantation owner and a Union guy who was a big deal in Boston, and really the only thing those ancestors had in common was that they were both super, super boring."

He was still bitching, but I'd stopped listening. Two words Roger had said had banged in my ear like fireworks. Tree house. Liza used to sell drugs out of her tree house. She hung out with Melissa in the tree house. That old Grampa Duckins, wrapped in his blanket heap, and Patti both had talked about Liza and Noveen taking boys up to the tree house.

Maybe we hadn't been wasting our time. Because if it hadn't kept coming up, over and over, from all those different people, I might never have realized.

Tyler Baines built my tree house in our backyard. He'd gotten the kit at Home Depot and built it when I was little. When Liza was a kid, my backyard tree house hadn't even existed. Even if it had, Liza couldn't have been selling drugs and hosting orgies in a tree house thirty feet from Big's bedroom window.

I felt my heart speed up. Somewhere Liza had a secret tree house. My brain leaped to another connection, remembering all those times Liza'd headed off into the woods with just a bedroll and a foster dog. No tent. I'd assumed she was sleeping in the nettles. Then I had followed her one day and seen her being a full-on druid, and after that I had tried super hard to never think about her camping trips at all.

But no tent meant she still had her secret tree house. She'd still been using it, up until the stroke. No wonder I hadn't found a single personal thing when I searched her room. If Liza had journals or old letters or any secret things, that was where she would keep them. Not at my house. Not with her old friends from high school, where Roger was looking. In an old hidden place that was all her own.

For the first time, I was glad I'd practically burned my eyes out of my head when I followed her into the woods last year, because now I knew exactly where to go looking.

I breathed in sharp and opened my mouth to tell Roger, but in the next second I clamped it shut again so hard my teeth banged together. This was between Liza and me.

Roger had caught my intake of breath. "What?" he said. I shook my head, like it was nothing, but he knew me better than that. "Mosey, what?"

All at once I had another reason to be glad I'd stolen that box. Roger would get a kick out of it, for sure, and since it wasn't Liza's, I felt like I could show him without it being weird. I said, "In the sadness of learning I wasn't the lost heiress of two boring-ass Civil War colonels and a pack of current assholes, I forgot to show you. Pull over, pull over."

We were back in downtown, so Roger swung the car into the DQ lot and looked at me expectantly.

"While you were talking to Claire, I totally broke into her house," I said, scrabbling through the paper to find the velvet pouch at my feet.

"Holy shit! You did not," Roger said.

"Hellzya, I did. I may have accidentally taken a little souvenir," I said as I lifted the wooden box off the floorboards.

I think I knew even as I handed it to him. For sure I knew before he opened it. I hadn't noticed when I was stealing it, because I'd been so freaked and in such a hurry, but as he took it, it finally hit me that it that it felt too heavy. A lot heavier than Liza's box.

Roger was already sliding the box out of the velvet pouch, saying, "You're my hero. What balls! I mean, girl balls. Whatever girls have like that." He creaked it open, and then we both went still and speechless, staring down into the case.

It was sleek and dull black and long and horrible. But my stomach popped a little, like it does in the movies when the guy finally kisses the girl and it's exactly right.

Roger touched the trigger with one reverent finger.

"I think it's a SIG," he said, which shouldn't have surprised me. Boys knew things about guns.

All I knew was, I had taken it. So it was mine.

CHAPTER FOURTEEN

Big

I GOT PREGNANT before I'd ever had a real boyfriend. It wasn't until after Liza and I moved to Immita that I took a good run at figuring men out. There was the guy who turned out to be married and the guy who turned out to be gay. There was a good-looking fellow with a college degree, but it was in English literature; he could quote the most beautiful poetry, but he wasn't going to ever get a job. He mostly sat on his sofa smoking hash through a water pipe and watching British television.

When Liza was nine, we met Davey at the park. He was walking a golden dust mop of a dog with a manicure and a pink hair bow. Davey and I talked easy on a bench while Liza played fetch with Priss, who turned out to be his sister's dog. He was perfect on paper: good job, good hair, good sense of humor, good kisser. He took me nice places, and he didn't pressure me to fall right into bed. I liked it that he was doing the gentleman thing. I liked it even more when he told me he thought he should get to know Liza, since he hoped to become a constant in her life. We decided to go for a beach day, all three of us, that weekend.

I was packing up a picnic in my kitchen with a guy I was falling for, and then Liza came in the room to meet him. For a second, maybe less, his eyes slid sideways off me. He took a darting, sip-like look at my gorgeous kid, her red-gold corkscrew hair, her little girl's knob-kneed legs, preening in her pink bikini. I caught the faintest whiff of dark electricity, an ozone smell, sharp and unwholesome.

It was gone faster than a silent streak of lightning, but I thought, *I met him in a kiddy park. He borrowed a dog to explain his presence, and it was tarted up to be the perfect little-girl bait.* Liza put her hand, eager and trusting, directly into his as he leaned down and introduced himself. She smiled up at him, hoping he would like her, daddy-hungry and eager to please.

All at once the gentlemanly pace of his courting bothered me. Getting pregnant at fifteen had made me cautious about sex, but still, a girl likes to be asked with a certain amount of fervor. I'm not saying he definitely was what my gut said he was; I'm saying in that single second of doubt I knew I wouldn't gamble. Not if I had to ante up my kid. I sent Liza to pack towels and sunscreen and broke up with him, then and there. She and I went to the beach that day on our own.

I didn't have that falling-for feeling again, not about anyone I dated before Liza ran away. Then came Lawrence, and long after Liza was home and he was back with Sandy he was the stick I measured every other man against. Lordy, but they all came up so short. I sat through bad dates remembering how he made me laugh, how easy we felt being quiet together, how safe he made me feel.

I didn't remember the sex.

When Liza came home, I'd packed sex in a box and put it deep away, then stacked a thousand other boxes on top of it to wedge the lid on. I'd thrown myself whole into being what Mosey called a mommishy mom, being nothing but a Big. But now? I'd done all those things with Lawrence in the sunshine spilled across his bed, and sex had ripped its way up through all the boxes, leaving my insides in a wanton disarray. Now I couldn't stop remembering.

This was my trouble year; every fifteen, like clockwork, God came after me. This was the worst one yet. The last thing I needed was sex rearing up, huge and alive and messy. It wasn't a single rooted object, like a weed I could pull out and toss away either. It was a thick layer of wanting, padding every bone I had.

I'd pass my potted plant in the kitchen and remember the green smell of a potted plant in the kitchen at Lawrence's old house, how I'd smelled leaves once when he'd laid me out on the counter and put his mouth on me. A man with square hands and tidy nails came into the bank with his kid's birthday checks, and I lost count of the cash three times, because Lawrence had hands shaped like that. I kept flashing to how hard those hands gripped mine when he was moving deep and slow in me, when we'd been face-to-face in his bed, eyes open, our gazes eating each other up. A scrap of familiar song, one we'd made love to, or that sounded like one we may have made love to once, long ago, was enough to stutter my feet and stop me in my tracks, bent a little at the waist, gut-punched and swamped with sudden, awful longing.

And the bastard didn't call me.

At home Mosey glared at me like she'd caught me eating kittens if I so much as asked how her day went, and she always had Raymond Knotwood or her new little friend over. She'd introduced her as Patti, no last name, but I'd lived in Immita long enough to know a Duckins when I saw one. Patti was so wan and lanky an object that my first thought was, *Why, this child has a tapeworm.* I liked her, though. She had a sweet smile, and she leaned hard into any casual pat I gave her like a touch-starved orphan. Lord only knew what her home life was like, but I reminded myself that Noveen Duckins had been a better friend to Liza than Melissa Richardson had, and Melissa was from the wealthiest family in town.

On Thursday, Rick Warfield came over to question Liza. She stared into space, so unresponsive she was practically drooling.

He got nothing, but having him in my den, leaning toward her, asking her question after question about those bones, made me a wreck. Then he asked to talk to Mosey, and I couldn't see a way to stop him.

She came sulking in when I called and sat in the chair opposite him, spine slumped, mouth turned down.

He started by saying, "You have a pretty good view of the woods from that tree house of yours, don't you? Have you ever noticed anyone hanging out behind your house?" Maybe he was thinking whoever buried those bones might be sneaking back for visits.

"What, like a perv?" Mosey asked, deliberately obtuse.

"Anyone."

Mosey shrugged, then said, "Once I saw Jack Olsen and Larry Dart out there, smoking pot."

Warfield started. Larry Dart was his nephew. I could tell by the challenging tilt of Mosey's head that she knew it, too. He wrapped it up pretty quick then and left, distracted and probably heading for his sister's house. I felt sick down deep in the pit of my stomach. I suspected that Mosey had made up the pot smoking, but I couldn't tell. That was a first; Mosey usually lied like a toddler, eyes too wide, toe scrubbing the dirt, chewing her bottom lip like it was bubble gum. The thought that she might've learned such a perfect poker face in this short span chilled me to my marrows. What else was this trouble year teaching her?

Day after day went by, Liza withdrawn, Mosey unreadable, the pool stalled, the cops still working this cold case, and me out of ideas.

Then I came home after the longest Tuesday in the history of time to find Liza's room looking like storm clouds had formed near the ceiling and rained down a thousand glossy photographs. She'd dragged every one of the bins out from under her bed, and then she'd tumped them over and scrabbled and tossed and flung pictures in all directions. Now she sat flat on her bottom in the middle of a sea of photos. The bins themselves were lying empty, on their sides and upside down like capsized boats. The photos were mostly face-up, scattered in heaps and drifts. It was such a jumble that I found myself looking helplessly from picture to picture: a cicada husk on bright grass, a stack of red checkers, a single neon rain boot abandoned in a puddle.

I was still in my bank clothes, my eyes grainy with tired from the long day of recounting greasy cash. All I wanted was to throw a frozen lasagna in the oven and pour myself an enormous glass of wine to dull my insides, but I was looking at a good two hours on my knees instead. I'd have to restack all those scattered photos, or they'd never fit back in the boxes. Liza smiled up at me, so pleased with herself she was practically alight. Bogo peered out from behind her. The little wretch had visible rays of twitchy guilt shooting out his ears, and his worry-soaked face said, plain as if he spoke English, that he'd hidden a turd or two somewhere in the mess.

"Big, come," Liza said, like I was her dog, too, beckoning at me with her good arm.

I held up a "wait a sec" finger and turned away, hollering, "Mosey Willow Jane Grace Slocumb!" in a dire tone that would have brought her to me on the run a month ago. Today she and Raymond Knotwood and Patti were in the den, playing Texas hold 'em for Skittles, and I got no response.

I yelled her whole name again, my voice rising so full of temper it cracked in the middle. After another thirty seconds, she came sauntering down the hall, speaking in this overdramatic theatrical whisper. "Big! I have friends here."

"Have you checked on your mom at all?" I asked.

Mosey came even with me, and her eyes widened when she saw the room. "Wow! Lookit that!"

"I am looking. When you send Mrs. Lynch home, you are supposed to be taking care of Liza."

"She was lying down." Mosey spoke in a defensive, aggrieved whine that she'd invented when she'd entered adolescence. It used to be she only used that voice on Liza. These days she whispered sweet in Liza's ear and saved that tone for me.

I said, "We all have to pitch in here. If you can't take care of your mom and have your friends over, guess which one of these things we'll stop doing?"

Mosey puffed herself full of air like a mad toad. "Well, I'm not the one who let Liza escape and go running down the road."

I looked back over my shoulder at Liza, impatiently sitting in her stew of photos. She waved me in again and repeated, "Big! Come!"

I said, "Sec, baby," then stepped out of the doorway, pulling Mosey a step down the hall with me. "I am one breath from grounding you. I did not let her esca—"

"I meant Mrs. Lynch," Mosey said, eyes rolling. "God."

That derailed my lecture, all right. "Wait, Liza left the house again?"

"Yah. Today. We saw her when we were driving home from school. She was halfway to Woodland Street."

That paused me. Liza had been heading in that direction, toward Woodland, the time she escaped on my watch, too. "Why didn't you tell me?"

"You *just* got home. But, Big, I think it's happened more than once," Mosey said. She leaned toward me, and suddenly we were on the same team. It had been a while. We'd been at odds every second since the day I let Tyler Baines take the willow out. Now I so wished I'd listened to Mosey and let that tree alone. I should have fenced the front yard and plopped a pool down out there. "When we brought Liza in, Mrs. Lynch was asleep in front of the TV, and she woke up all snorty and blamey. She was like, 'I can't help it your mom's so tricky. I can't hardly turn my back or have a pee without her heading out the front door.' It sounded to me like Liza's done it a bunch and she didn't tell us."

"That woman . . ." I said. We were sure getting what we paid for with our three-dollar-an-hour sitter.

"I know, right?" Mosey said. "Total B-word."

"I'll talk to her tomorrow morning." I paused there, not wanting to break the moment.

She did, though. She dropped her eyes, as if she were uncomfortable agreeing with me on anything, even this. "Is that all? We're in the middle of a hand." She'd quit my team as fast as she'd joined it. She didn't wait for my nod either, before she turned and trotted off back to her friends.

I stepped back to Liza's room, and when I reappeared in the doorway, Bogo let out a startled yip. He ducked behind Liza.

"Oh, stop it," I told him, but in a soft voice. The silly animal twitched and shivered if I spoke in anything above a gentle coo, but I had to admit he did love him some Liza. The way he pressed against her, the way she worked to move her bad arm to give him a reassuring touch, that made me fond of the ratty object in spite of myself. She hadn't been able to pat him like that when he first came.

Her room was a wreck, but cleaning would have to wait. I wanted to put my feet up and drink enough wine to stop thinking about all the sex with Lawrence that I damn-it-all wasn't having, and I needed to get Mosey alone and try to bust through the coldness that was threatening to make a permanent home between us, but those things had to wait, too. Liza was acting with purpose, like she had at Sandy's house and again at Lawrence's apartment. The walks toward Woodland, getting out all the pictures—this was Liza trying to surface and tell me something.

I squatted down beside her and asked, "Where are you trying to lead me?"

Instead of answering she thrust a slim stack of photos at me, clutched hard in her good hand. I cleared a place by her and sat on the floor, then took the stack and flipped through: A teacup. A shot glass sitting on an orange barstool at The Crow. A wineglass full of milk. A coffee mug. I stopped looking and said to her, "I know. Cup."

"Cup!" Liza repeated, almost a crow of relief. "Cup! Cup!"

I set the pictures down and laid a soothing hand on her arm. "I know you want to tell me something about cups. What about the cup?"

She was already pulling another stack of pictures out from under her good leg. I shifted through them: A brightly colored tree frog. An abandoned snake skin in the dunes. A pirate's eye patch with a skull and crossbones on it from one of Mosey's old Halloween costumes. A spray of pale flowers. Lastly a picture of the back of Liza's own hand, her nails painted with a clear gloss, which was unusual. She'd always kept her feet pumiced and painted her toes in summer colors, but she never gave herself a manicure. In this shot her hand was tilted toward the camera, like she wanted the lens to admire the ring she was wearing, even though it was broken; the blue gem was tipped up on its side, half out of the setting.

"These pictures, they mean a word?" I said, puzzled.

She swatted at the photos in my hand, impatient. "Cup," she said.

I looked through again. Frog cup. Plant cup. Pirate eye patch Halloween cup. They didn't tell me anything.

"Big?" Mosey said in the doorway. "Can Patti stay for eats?"

I looked up, distracted. "I don't know. It's getting dark earlier and earlier." But that wasn't exactly a firm no. I'd never had trouble telling Raymond Knotwood to go to his cozy house and eat his own mother's supper, but when Patti stood in her ratty hand-me-downs, snuffing the air like baked-potato soup or my meat loaf was French perfume, I had an almost primal urge to feed her. Still,

I worried about sending her off afterward on her rickety bicycle, heading all the way out to Ducktown after sundown. She wouldn't take a ride.

Mosey wanted it bad enough to wheedle me. "Well, if Roger stayed, too, he could drive her...."

"Mosey, I am doing something here."

"Not cleaning up," Mosey said, eyeing the chaos. "Please can they stay?" She lowered her voice and added, "I think Patti's really hungry."

That registered with me. I said, "It's just Stouffer's and a salad."

Mosey grinned. She knew that meant yes. She was happy with me for this one second, so I took advantage of it.

"While I've got you, turn the hall light on and help me with this right quick." I brought Liza's stack of pictures out into the hall and laid them out in a row on the floor. "Look at these. Can you see how they might go together?"

"What do you mean? Did Liza pick these out?" I nodded, and she knelt down to see, intrigued. "Why is Liza picking out pictures?"

I thought up a lie so fast I felt like the Grinch tricking Cindy Lou Who out of Christmas. "It's a new kind of therapy for stroke victims who've lost speech." Mosey was beetling her brows at me suspiciously, and I said, "Well, who knows when we'll get the pool done? I've been asking Google for alternate treatments on my lunch hour. I saw this on the YouTube today."

"It's not *the* YouTube, it's just— Never mind. I wonder if the order matters," Mosey said, touching the frog with one finger. "Frog...maybe that's the subject? Like a sentence diagram or something?" She raised her voice so suddenly I jumped, and Bogo, who had come to the doorway to see what we were doing, skittered backward and disappeared. "Roger! C'mere!" She sounded like Liza, demanding, *Big, come.* So exactly like that I couldn't help smiling; she was ours, no matter what her genes might say. She went on, talking softer to me. "Roger is supremely awesome at any kind of puzzle."

Raymond Knotwood came down the hall with Patti following hesitantly behind, like she wasn't sure if she was wanted.

"Lookit," Mosey said. "Big says these mean something. Liza picked them out." I glanced into the room to check on Liza. She sat flat on her butt, quiet, good hand soothing the ratty dog.

"Hi, Big," Patti said. She'd picked up Mosey's name for me.

"Dude!" Raymond Knotwood said, dropping to his knees, his oversize eyes going even wider with interest. "Like a secret message?"

"No," I said, instantly and a hair too loud. I forced a smile and tried to sound casual. "She's supposed to pick out pictures that relate in some way. It's to help her brain. But I can't see how these have anything to do with one another."

"Oh, well, that's cool, too," Raymond said. Patti drifted past him, coming to stand by me. Raymond dealt the photos back out in a row, like he was laying down a hand of solitaire. "Oh, man! A Machiavelli ring!" He touched the picture of Liza's hand.

"A what?" I asked.

"Mom never paints her nails," Mosey said, crowding closer.

"That's what struck me, too, but what's a Machiavelli ring?"

Raymond Knotwood said, "See how the gem is tipped up? There's a secret compartment under it. Like, the Medicis and all those murdery people in the Renaissance would put poison in there, and then they'd flip it open and dump it all casual into someone's wine. Like at court."

"Secret compartment. I don't see another picture that could mean a secret place, though," I said. I looked back at Liza, sitting on the floor with Bogo in her lap now. She didn't react, but maybe she hadn't heard me?

Mosey's cheeks washed a faint pink. "Why would Mom be showing you pictures about having a secret place? She doesn't have a secret place."

I said, soothing, "I'm sure she's not saying that at all." It was a mistake to ask for help. What if we did figure out Liza's message and it wasn't something I could pass off as therapy?

Raymond was looking at Mosey with his head cocked, making a thinking face. He saw me watching him watch Mosey, and he flushed and turned his attention back to the pictures. He rearranged the order, twice, and then he tapped the photo of the ring and chuckled.

"Got it." He shot a show-off's grin to Mosey, peacocking his big brain like tail feathers. "In the ring pic, it's not nail polish or the secret compartment that matters. See this frog? It's poison frogs that are jewel-colored, so birds know not to eat them. I saw it on Discovery Channel. Snake skin, snake, poison, that's obvious, right? And this"—he waved the eye patch photo—"forget pirates. It's the skull and crossbones. They put that on cleaning products so people who can't read don't drink bleach." He was so proud he was vibrating, and Mosey rewarded him with an admiring smile. He held up the picture of the tiny flowers. "I don't know what these flowers are, but I'd bet they are toxic enough to flat kill you."

"Naw," said Patti softly.

"You know this plant?" Raymond said. "Are you sure it won't kill you? Because everything else here will."

Patti's eyes were bright beneath her shaggy bangs, and it was sweet to see how pleased she was to be helping. I gave her nearby calf an encouraging squeeze, and she flushed red and said, triumphantly, "You won't die or nothing, but you sure dun wanna get in it. That's the flower part of...*poison* ivy."

"Shazam!" Raymond Knotwood said. He reared up for a high five with Mosey. "Poison. These pictures all show poison."

He'd said it loud, and Liza banged the floor with her hand, calling, "Yes, yes, yes!" Bogo barked along with her pounding.

"I told you he was great at this," Mosey said, beaming at Raymond like she had invented him.

"Great job," I said, smiling, trying not to seem impatient to get them gone. "Mosey, I want to keep working with Liza some, since it's going so well. Can you kids throw the lasagna in the oven and go ahead with supper?"

"Sure," Mosey said. She headed for the kitchen.

Raymond Knotwood stood and went after her, saying over his shoulder, "Call me if you get stumped again."

Patti stayed a second longer. I smiled up at her and said, "Good for you! I didn't even know poison ivy had a flower." She flushed even darker and ran after her friends. I shook my head. Bogo wasn't the only stray that Mosey had adopted for us all recently.

As soon as she was gone, I walked fast on my knees to Liza. "Someone put poison in a cup? A cup of poison?"

"Cup poison," Liza repeated, slurry but firm. Her good eye blazed with a bright and fervent triumph.

I lowered my voice to a bare whisper. "Is this something to do with Mosey? You poisoned someone to get Mosey?"

Liza's mouth worked, silent, and I knew there were a thousand other thoughts washing around in her brain, but all she could do was say it again. "Cup poison!"

I shook my head, and she pushed all the air out of herself in a frustrated gobble of sound.

"No, no. I can get this. You were trying to lead me someplace, weren't you? When you left the house. A place that has something to do with a cup and poison..."

"Cup poison," Liza said, still slurry, but she had those words now, and she wanted me on point.

"Who?" I said. "Who did the cup poison?"

Her eyes filled up with tears, the good one faster, and I wasn't sure if it was relief or sorrow, if I was asking the right question or the exact wrong one. Her good hand lifted off Bogo's head and opened, and she placed her palm flat on her chest, patting at herself. She patted three times, tears spilling over now and running in two thin rivulets down her cheeks. One plopped onto Bogo, and he looked up and whined, worried and sorrowful.

"You?" I said. "You?" She kept patting. "Someone poisoned you?"

I had a thousand more questions then. Where and when and how and what did this have to do with Mosey, but then, like an audible click in my head, part of it came clear for me. A cup, poison, and the walk toward Woodland. Woodland was the first turn Mosey used to take back when she was walking to Calvary every day.

"The night you got sick. That godforsaken Calvary End-of-School Luau. Are you telling me...?" My hand went to her weak hand, ran up her wasted arm to touch the sagging side of her lovely face. "You can't be saying someone did this to you? On purpose?"

Tears spilled down Liza's face. Her relief was confirmation. "Cup poison," she said, weeping, but triumphant. She owned these two words in this moment, whether she would keep them or not.

"Who?" I said. "Who?"

I grabbed the tops of her arms, watched her face close as she went inside herself, trying to find her way to the name. My mind was racing now, my heartbeat speeding up to match it. That night, at Calvary, she'd been going to meet someone, I'd felt certain. She'd been so dolled up, not saying exactly that she had the money for Mosey's tuition but implying that she was about to have it. Liza always played her man cards close, usually because she was with the wrong man. Sneaking and sex were welded in her head, and I'd worried she was suckering some married man into paying.

But maybe "suckering" was too nice a word? If Liza was seeing a married fellow on the sly, she could have asked him to pay Mosey's tuition. That was more like blackmail than suckering.

I read mysteries and thrillers, and I'd read my share of true crime, too; this was the exact kind of thing that drove the quiet, never-hurt-a-fly guy next door to murder. A married fellow, a pillar of the community, he might trade Liza's life to keep his own on course.

"Was it Steve Mason?" I asked. She'd been climbing him like he was her own personal oak tree when she collapsed.

Liza blinked at me. Made her "no" noise. She closed her eyes, sinking down into herself, maybe seeking the right name, maybe too exhausted to keep going.

Every second of the next part of that awful night was seared into my brain. I remembered her dropping her cup, the dregs of one of those Virgin Coladas splashing the legs of the woman in metallic sandals. That foamy drink looked so much more sinister in my memory now. I'd shoved my way through the crowd toward her and picked up that cup. I'd smelled it, thinking Liza had been drinking, but I'd smelled only the suntan-oil stink of coconut and pineapple. All that sugar, had it masked the taste of something bitter and unwholesome? What had happened to the cup?

After Liza collapsed, my memory decayed into a blur of panic. The ambulance ride. The hospital. Had I thrown the cup away? Dropped it on the ground?

I remembered those cheerleaders in their hula-girl costumes, weird fleshy leotards under the coconut bras. I guess Claire Richardson thought it was better to look deformed than slutty. They had passed around the drinks and macadamia-nut cookies and big wicker bags full of fruit-snack samples and coupons for 10 percent off backpacks for next year at Target. I'd been carrying my good clutch, and I'd put it down inside that wicker bag. I remembered holding the wicker bag in my lap like it was a baby, unthinking, all the time we waited at the hospital. I was pretty sure I'd taken it home. Then what? Had

I thrown out a bag full of free samples and coupons? It didn't seem like me.

"Stay here," I said to Liza, which was crazy. It wasn't as if she was about to leap up, trit-trot out of the house, maybe go dancing.

I could hear Mosey and her friends laughing in the kitchen as I tore down the hall. I ran into my bedroom and threw open the door to my closet, which was a cataclysmic mess. My good clutch was back on the high shelf, gathering dust, waiting for me to have someplace special to go. So much crap was piled on the floor. I started digging through it, hurling shoe boxes and laundry out until my room looked near as bad as Liza's.

Then I saw it. The gift bag from the luau. It was in the bottom back corner, so crumpled that the cheap wicker had sprung into twigs down one whole side.

All the air came out of me in a rush. I hoped. I hoped so hard it almost stooped to praying. I pulled the bag open, peering down. I saw the cup at once. It was crushed in on itself but present, nestled between a sample-size fruit roll-up and a brochure about the Jump Rope for Heart program.

I'd read enough cop books to know not to touch it. There was a pencil in the bag with an ad for the Knotwoods' car dealership on it, and I grabbed it and threaded it into the crumpled opening of the cup.

I lifted it out, holding it up high, and inside I could see a faint crust of dried white along the seam at the bottom. I carried the cup to my dresser and set it down, still careful not to touch it with my hand. Then my knees got weak and I had to sit.

Hope warred for room with an equal share of leg-shaking rage. Hope because, if she'd been poisoned, maybe there could be a better kind of help for Liza, and at the same time some bastard had tried to kill my kid. Under all of that, I was shaking with strange relief; I'd always thought the stroke was a late gift from

Liza's drug abuse, and the drugs were mostly my fault. If I'd been tougher, more diligent, less naïve . . . But this cup could hold proof that Liza was hurt for a reason other than my failures as a mother.

I sat trembling on the bed, wishing that hope and rage and weird relief were all I felt.

But there was more. I couldn't help it. Inside me, under all my skin, sex was lighting me up. It flexed and pulled in a shivery, whole-body clench. The cup, the dried white seam of Virgin Colada, these things were physical evidence. A cop problem, and I knew only one cop who would help me on the quiet. My blood sped up, zinging through my body, heart pounding to the rhythm of his stupid name.

I left the cup where it was for now. I needed to get a ziplock bag from the kitchen and seal it up, but first I went back to Liza's room to get her off the floor. She was slumped there, exactly where I'd left her, and no Bogo. He'd been seduced away by the smell of Stouffer's drifting from the kitchen.

Liza didn't react when I came in. I had to lift her mostly on my own steam. As I settled her into her wheelchair, I tried to get her to focus on me. "Liza, I need to know who did this. I need a name."

Liza's eyes widened, but she wasn't looking at me. She was staring past me, at something so far away it must be through the wall, outside the house, maybe on the other side of the world.

Her breath sounded shaped. I put my ear close to her mouth and said, "Please, baby, say it. Say a name."

She inhaled, and when the air came back out, it had a name on it. A name from long ago. The last word in the world I expected to hear.

"Melissa."

My own breath stopped. I grabbed her shoulders. "When did you see Melissa Richardson? Liza? Liza?"

She didn't answer me.

I gave her a little shake, asked again, "Who poisoned you?"

Her eyes closed, but her good hand came up and clenched my forearm.

She said it again, louder, clearer. "Melissa."

No mistake.

CHAPTER FIFTEEN

Liza

LIZA'S ROOM IS a sea of photographs, and they rise and fall around her, wavering as she sways and sinks. Her memory is an ocean, but there is only one tide, one current, one place to wash up. Liza finds herself again being driven to those white sands. Melissa Richardson waits there, on a sunless day too gusty and cold for September in Mississippi.

Noveen is driving. They are both so pregnant that they barely have room for breathing. She herself is stretched to a thin shell. The eyes of boys, something she has always owned, slide away from her now, fearful or sniggery. She can't sneak a beer, or six beers, or light up, or drop 'cid, because there isn't enough of her. She is a husk, and anything she puts in will go straight to her chewy center. She wonders if after the baby is out she will ever be Liza again, or only someone's mother, like Big.

Noveen has driven them in loops, through town and then up to the Ducktown woods, back through town, and now down the beach road. They are happy simply to be in motion, driving away from place after place but not toward anything in particular.

At least until she sees Melissa's red Eclipse pulled over on the sandy shoulder.

"Stop," she tells Noveen, pointing. Noveen obeys. The primer-painted Chevy, pulled up close to the Eclipse's shiny bumper, looks like something that the nicer car has crapped out. "I need a sec." Noveen shrugs, her best quality her ability to roll with it, but she leaves the engine running. Liza jacks her unwieldy body up and out, lumbers down the path between the dunes.

She hasn't been alone with Melissa since that awful day at the Richardson house. The day Liza fell out of love. Melissa is constantly surrounded by the cadre of followers who used to be Liza's, too. They whisper and point and glare, and whatever story Melissa has invented for them, it's clear that Liza is the bitch in it. She supposes that's fair.

The ocean is a dark army green, no sun to spark its colors. If it were ten degrees warmer, if the charcoal humps of clouds weren't rolling toward them, this place would be packed. But now it is only Liza and Melissa and Melissa's baby sister in a pink bucket seat. Melissa sits in a beach chair, close to the water. This is the second-to-the-last time they will ever speak.

The coming storm sends wind that cuts through Liza's T-shirt, but she is only the thin, chilled outside wall. She is built around a furnace, and the cold can't touch her. Nothing can touch her.

Melissa watches the waves roll in, barely glancing up when Liza comes to stand beside her. She lifts two fingers in a lazy salute, like this was old days. With no witnesses, Melissa accepts Liza in her old place as if it were normal, or at least inevitable. They watch the waves together as the baby in the bucket sleeps, and the baby inside Liza is still and sleeping, too. It is as if both little girls are pretending not to be here, giving Liza and Melissa this moment alone.

Liza remembers being Liza. She remembers being Melissa-and-Liza.

From the outside it may have looked like Liza was charity. Melissa had the clothes, the money, the big house, the concert tickets, all the good drugs. But they both know it was a potluck friendship. Stone soup. Liza had the body, the face, the confidence, all the good pick-me-up lines. Liza brought the boys. It was almost equal.

"I miss you," Liza says.

Melissa answers instantly. "Then why did you fuck everything up." She speaks calmly, not playing to an audience. It's not even a question. It is a flat statement of blame that acknowledges her own loss.

Liza squats by her ex-friend, trailing her fingers in the glass-hard grains of sand. The rain has packed down its usual powdery softness. "Big thinks the dad is that carny guy."

"My carny guy? That would have been a cute baby." After a pause Melissa peeps slyly at Liza and adds, "I told everyone at school you screwed some old pervo you met at the arcade for five hundred dollars."

Liza nods with more than a little admiration. It's a good story. It accomplishes a lot, really. "Thanks for at least making me expensive."

Melissa looks straight at Liza. "Just because I'm not scratching your eyes out, like, right this second, it doesn't mean that I still don't fucking hate you."

Liza absorbs that, then says, "Just because of your dad and all, it doesn't mean that I still don't fucking love you."

It's a very grown-up line. Liza's kind of proud of it. Before the baby she wouldn't have even thought of it. It's close to an apology, and that's what Big says adults have to do when they righteously screw everything up. Be sorry, and do better next time. In this case the being sorry is the best Liza's got. It's not like Melissa has another dad that Liza can choose not to fuck.

Melissa's face twists, as if she is fighting the idea of crying. Liza feels like crying, too, but she isn't sure how much that means. She cries at AT&T commercials these days. Melissa gets it tamped down, and they stay there quiet beside each other. The waves roll in. Liza should go. Noveen will be getting impatient.

Then Melissa pulls a joint out from behind her ear, her favorite hiding place. At school most days, she had one tucked there, masked by the fall of her long hair. She holds it up and says, "From a guy at the Phish concert. He handed it to me, said, 'Christmas gift for the pretty girl.'" She smiles a tight-eyed smile, because Liza used to be the pretty girl. Her dart hits home, and as Liza flinches, as Liza's hand goes to her swollen belly, Melissa's expression softens. "Oh, well. Whatever." She offers the unlit joint.

It is more than a simple tube of herbs in paper. What Melissa is holding toward her is an invitation to once again be Melissa-and-Liza. To visit the Liza that she used to be. If they smoke it up, they will start talking. They will laugh. Old threads will reach and spin together.

The waves are hypnotic, and the baby inside is sleeping and still. Liza's out of love with Coach. He made sure of that. All she has left of that imagined life is the baby, and here is Melissa, cracking open a door that leads back into her old one. What's to stop her, really? This baby inside her has finished making all its pieces. What's one joint going to hurt, at this point?

Melissa's little sister wakes and starts to fuss.

Liza stands and goes to the bucket seat. Rocks it. The baby's eyes are open, a pale ice blue like Melissa's. Like Coach's. Her own baby might have eyes like that.

It strikes Liza that this child in the bucket and the baby sleeping so still inside her are half sisters. They will be in the same grade. They may look alike. They might one day be friends. Melissa's little sister screws her eyes shut and truly wails. Liza unclips the buckle and lifts her out. She holds the squirming baby against herself, shushing, and inside, like an answer, her own girl wakes. Liza feels something connecting their movements like a guitar string, plucked and vibrating, running from the baby in her arms to the baby in her womb.

In that moment she understands that what Big says is right. It is time—too early, but whose fault is that?—it is time to put away childish things.

Liza waves off the joint. "You can't be smoking that shit," she tells Melissa. "You have to look out for your sister." She soothes the squirming outside baby, and inside, her baby spins and kicks an answer.

Melissa snorts. "Jesus Christ, Liza, how many times have we baby-sat stoned?"

Plenty, is the answer, but the difference is, now Liza knows they shouldn't have. She has a real person in her, alive and whole, thumping its feet upward. The baby sister is a real person, too, thumping back, so that Liza is a talking drum, inside and out.

Liza says, "Really, don't. You have to drive the baby home."

Melissa rolls the joint back and forth between her fingers, holds it under her nose, and sniffs with relish. The door slams shut between them. "I'm not stupid. I'll wait till I'm okay. Run along, now, Liza. I'm very busy and important."

Liza knows what she should do. She should pick up the bucket and walk away. She can move the car seat's base out of the Eclipse, into the Chevy. This is her own baby's sister. She shouldn't leave it here. She should drive it home to its bitch of a mother, say, *Your other daughter is smoking pot down at the beach, and I didn't think I should let her drive the baby*. That part will be fun, and, more important, it's what Big would do. It's what anyone's mother would do.

Liza is almost someone's mother.

"Don't make me call Claire," Liza says.

Melissa's face twists into a sneer, but her tone stays mild. "You're pretty holy for a girl who fucked my daddy. You think my mother is going to take your call? Go away now, Liza. And next time I see you? When you aren't pregnant? Rest assured I'm going to kick your big fat postpartum ass."

Liza hesitates. She should take the baby. She knows it. But instead she kneels and settles her back in the pink bucket. She tucks the blanket around the fat legs.

Liza starts walking away.

The year she met Melissa, at Rich People VBS, Claire Richardson used the felt board to tell the story of that wise king, the two mothers, the baby who died in the night. Solomon offers to cut the remaining baby into halves. One mother says, *No, no, let her have it. Just leave that baby whole.* The king gives the baby to that woman. He doesn't actually care who gave birth to it. He gives it to the one who will lose everything to save it.

That's what real mothers do. They save the baby.

Liza can stand to lose her friendship with Melissa. It's already soured in her mouth. She can give up the remains of her childhood, too. She never much wanted it. What she can't release is the thin shell that is *her*. The un-mother. The cool girl everyone watches, wants, the rebel girl who gets away with everything. That's the thing that she decides to keep.

Every time she washes up here, she has to watch herself walk away. Every time, she knows that when she leaves that baby behind, she ceases to deserve her own.

Then Big's hands grab her, pull her away, yanking her out of the waves of photographs, off the beach, settling her into her own chair in her room. Big's mouth moves. She is asking something, but all Liza hears is the sound of waves rolling in. Over Big's shoulder she can still see Melissa, putting the joint to her lips now. She doesn't know the "present for the pretty girl" is laced with PCP.

"Melissa!" Liza says, calling to her, trying to stop her. But Liza is in Noveen's car now, they are leaving. Melissa is lighting the joint that will take her brain away, steal hours, send her careening into the dunes with no idea of time and tides and little sisters.

Liza calls again, "Melissa," but Noveen is turning up the radio and Big is grabbing at her shoulders, pulling Liza toward the now. She won't see Melissa again, not for years.

Not until the day they have their final conversation.

On the beach Melissa breathes deep. Holds the smoke.

The ocean takes the one baby. God takes the other. Melissa and Liza have nothing left to divide between them.

CHAPTER SIXTEEN

Mosey

I WAS PRETTY sure I could find Liza's tree house in my sleep, because I already was finding it there. Almost every night I dreamed about the day last year when I'd followed my mom down that crooked path. I'd wake up motion sick, like my bed had been sloshing me back and forth while I was sleeping.

When I was awake, I didn't go there, not even in my thinking. It was like I was scared that Roger would read the words "Secret Tree House" off the worry creases in my forehead. Having Patti around made it less likely that Roger would smell the stink of me keeping something from him, so I invited her along all the time now. She always said yes, and she never even had to call home and check if she could. I knew she didn't have much money, so mostly we hung at me or Roger's house. On Thursday, instead of Real Pitting, I got Roger to pick up a huge bag of Taco Bell, and the three of us took it back to my house and let Mrs. Lynch go early. We sat in the den watching court shows with Liza, eating Meximelts, and passing around a two-liter of Big's gross generic soda that Roger called Diet Brown.

Patti got me and Roger's weirdo humor, and she had a high-pitched cackly laugh I liked. She fit with us fine, but seemed more comfortable when it was only her and me. Like, in Life Skills, Patti talked my ear off. We literally did not stop talking, because

Coach was out Friday, and he didn't come back at all the whole next week either. The Life Skills sub put on films and then sat studying for the MCAT, ignoring us as long as we didn't yell.

The only time Patti shut up was when Briony Hutchins found out Coach wasn't coming back at all, and she came mooping into class all pink-eyed. Patti and I eavesdropped while Briony wailed to her whole entourage.

"His wife is making him take early retirement! Both *her* kids who were any good at sports have graduated, so I guess she's going to screw over our whole football team. And right here at the start of the season! Cheer is so going to suck now."

When Roger was around, though, Patti got sidekick quiet, especially at his house.

I understood it. At Roger's house the cushions on the sofa matched the print of the easy chair. His dad was his real dad and lived with them. They had a cat with white feet named Socks. If me and Patti went over, his mom kept coming at us with snacks, asking, "What are you kids up to?" with this big, white smile. It was like she thought if she left us alone too long, Patti and I would leap at him and ravish him or stuff him full of drugs. Between the matchy cushions and his helicopter parents, Roger's life freaked Patti right the hell out.

That next weekend Roger had to go to Biloxi and watch his bulimic cousin finally get married. Patti and me biked to the Great Clips, and I klepto'd like a total pro from all my practice, lifting a whole stack of ancient gossip magazines while Patti distracted the girl at the front. Then we holed up in my tree house to look at pictures of the hottest celebrity couples from three years ago. Roger texted us every fifteen minutes to tell us wedding stuff, like how the bride was spitting all the chewed bites of her lunch into a napkin and how the old people were bombed by 2:00 P.M. and doing the most embarrassing dancing in the history of time to "Louie Louie."

I read the texts out loud to Patti, and then she started telling me about the last wedding party she'd been to, in Ducktown, after her uncle took his common-law lady to the justice of the peace. It was hard to follow, because everyone was related to everyone else in all these weird ways, but the gist was, Patti's diabetic second cousin got super drunk and passed out in the yard. Her uncle stole her cousin's prosthetic leg and drove down the highway to a roadhouse bar and beat this guy half to death with it, because the guy used to sleep with the bride. Then the uncle came back to his reception and stuck the leg back on the passed-out cousin to try and frame him. It didn't work, for one because Rick Warfield was too smart to buy that the guy who actually needed the leg to walk would pull it off and hop around a bar parking lot, banging someone's head in. Also, her uncle left bloody fingerprints all over the ankle.

She told it all casual, lying on her belly and swinging her feet back and forth, flipping through a tattered *People* magazine. For her that wedding reception was normal. I'd never had a friend I could play "Whose Family Is Weirder?" with and not win before.

I think that's why I told her about how the bones in our yard had belonged to the other Mosey Slocumb. Once I started, I couldn't stop. I told her about Liza's years on the road, where she stole me as some kind of baby replacement, and how Roger figured it out with Occam's razor and then turned into the Unstoppable Supersleuth. When I got to the part where we came out to Ducktown, to her house, Patti closed the magazine and sat up to really listen, but not like shocked or freaking the way Briony Hutchins would have. I even confessed that Bogo was a stolen Duckins dog, and all she said was, "I knew that was him. It's okay. She's a mean bitch, that one you stole him from, anyway."

So then I told her about how I broke into Claire Richardson's place. The only thing I didn't mention was the gun. It was still boxed up in my backpack, nestled between my history and math books. I took it with me everywhere, spooky heavy in my backpack, still not sure what I should do with it.

When I was done, we sat there looking at each other, and I asked, "I have a whole 'nother mom and maybe even a dad wandering around out in the world. How weird is that?"

"Not that weird," she said. She scooted a little closer, her voice gone soft, like she was worried the blue jays yelling in the yard next door might overhear. "That lady you met? That I live with? That's my auntie. I never knew my dad, and my real mom fell in love with a drummer and went 'total Yoko.'"

"What's that mean?" I asked.

"I dunno," Patti said. "They kicked him out of the band for it, though. Him and my mom made a suicide pact. He jumped off the Bryer Street overpass and smashed his legs and almost got run over. My mom wussed out. She stayed clunged up to the railing. So, soon as he got out of traction, he left town, going after his band. My mom asked my auntie to watch me for a couple days, and she went after him. I was, like, five? But my auntie still says shit like I need to get my math grade up before my mom comes back."

I scooched a little closer and asked, "Do you remember her?"

"Kinda," Patti said. "She smoked these long, long, skinny cigarettes, and she had really soft hair that went in curls, like Big has."

This wasn't a funny story to her, like the uncle and the leg. This was her really telling me a true thing, same as I had about the bones. So I took a deep breath and told her the thing that was eating me up. The thing I couldn't tell Roger.

"My mom? She has a secret tree house in the woods behind our house. She was a druid, or she said she was anyway, so she'd go off alone on these camping trips to be one with trees or whatever." I paused, gulping. "I followed her one time. Last year. I wanted to see what druids did." I'd never told anyone. I'd tried not to even tell myself.

Patti said, sort of encouraging me, "Real druids, back in olden times, they did human sacrifice. They pulled out people's hearts and baked them and ate them."

"I think that was Aztecs," I said, but at the same time I didn't feel so squeezed and worried. It was like she was saying that even if I'd seen my mom doing cannibalism, it was okay. And really, what I saw wasn't as evil as cannibalism, just maybe a little grosser.

"What did it turn out to be? What druids do?" Patti asked.

But I started talking just after she did, before she could finish asking. "You want to come help me find her tree house?"

Patti said, "Shah!" which was a weird Ducktown word I'd learned meant "hellzya." I was willing to bet that no matter what we found—nothing, or a journal, or letters from my real mom, or baby pictures of me before I got stolen—Patti would have seen weirder. Also, she wouldn't follow leads like a crazed bloodhound, dragging me to places I might not want to go. She'd let me decide.

We shimmied down out of the oak tree. Patti wanted me to go tell Big we were going for a walk, so Big wouldn't worry if she called for us. Patti could walk out of her house at 1:00 A.M. and bike to the mini-mart for Pop Rocks without anyone even asking where she was heading, so she thought the totally enraging way Big had to know where I was every second was sweet.

"Let's just hurry," I said. "Big knows we're outside, and we aren't actually going anyplace but *deeper* into outside."

Once Patti and me were in the woods, it took barely two minutes to find the start of that twisty trail I'd followed Liza down last year. If I hadn't known it was there, we wouldn't have found it. It petered out and picked up again fifteen times, winding back on itself. It was so slight a trail, the woods so thick, it had been easy to follow Liza without her seeing me. Now I went along it so fast, remembering it perfectly, that Patti started puffing. She was real skinny but not in great shape.

"It's not that far," I told her.

"Are you going to tell me what druids do, though?" Patti asked. "I told you my worst thing."

I said, defensive, "You don't think the bones and being stolen is my worst thing?"

She shook her head. "Roger knew all that already. I mean a secret for us, like you have on me now."

I chewed at my lip, because I'd wanted to tell someone. Not Roger, because that was unpossible, and Big would have crapped herself and then killed Liza. But Patti, I thought I could tell. I said, "Okay. But keep moving," because it was easier with no one looking at me. I grabbed her hand and towed her along, but slower.

"I followed Liza to this clearing where we're going now. Where I think the tree house is. I could hear her rustling around, starting a fire, I guess. I was about to go home when Liza started talking, I thought maybe to the foster dog she'd brought along, or even starting some kind of mystical chant. But a man's voice answered. He must have come in another way."

I heard Liza laughing, too, loud and throaty-sounding, but I didn't say that.

"I crept closer, not on the trail. Through the brush. I peeked into the clearing. Liza'd made a bonfire under a big oak at the back of the clearing. She was in front of it with a guy."

I could see the scene perfect in my head, like it was yesterday instead of months ago. She had one bare leg poked out of her sheet sari and wrapped around this big, shirtless guy with a hairy chest, her spine bent back and both his hands kneading her ass. She had an apple jammed in her mouth, and he wolfed and gnawed at the other side, like he was trying to eat his way right through the core and get at her.

He had apple juices running down his chin. His throat was slick with it. He shifted his hands off my mom's butt, trying to unwind her from her homemade sari, and I saw his face.

I said, "It was Celia Mason's dad, from Calvary, and he is still totally married to Celia Mason's mom. My mom had her hands on his belt buckle, and I realized I could never, never, never sit through world history with Celia, not ever again, if I saw her dad's junk."

But then I did. My mom pulled his pants down to just under his ass, and this big purple-headed thing bounced out, all probey-looking and angry. I'd never seen one, and then I did see, and it was attached to someone's gross old father. My mom reached up under him, her hand going down in his pants in a digging way, and she lifted more out as the pants slid farther down. His balls, I guess, but not how I thought balls would look or even how they were in the drawings I'd seen. It looked like a hairy sack of plums she was hefting in her palm, like she was checking the weight.

"That's where I was hiding," I told Patti as we came around the trail's last little twist. I pointed to a thatch of bushes, just off the trail. I stopped walking, and now I could look at her, and she wasn't shocked or even much surprised. "She got down on... He had this... She put... Anyway. I turned and ran, crashing and banging as loud as I could." I'd wanted them to hear me. Wanted to interrupt them and ruin them and make them quit and be sorry. I wanted Liza to come after me and apologize for being vile, and also an enormous hypocrite. I'd felt this huge, ragey scream building in me, and I had to hold my breath to keep it in. I sprinted off, airless, until I was so dizzy that I had to stop and puke.

"Did they hear you?" Patti asked.

I shook my head. "I guess she was too distracted. I was so mad, because she acts like if I so much as French a guy it'll be like getting a Gremlin wet. Fifty babies will come popping out of me. And yet there *she* is... Oh, never mind. It made me puke, is the point. No it isn't. The point is, this is the clearing. That's the oak tree. See that fire pit? The dog was lying right by it, watching them with his eyebrows twitching, one up, one down, then swapping, like he didn't know what was going on but he hoped he'd get some apple. That was Rufus, and he was a weird dog. He would eat anything he saw a person eating. Which just made me feel worried."

Patti said, "My auntie's cousin's ex-boyfriend used to press his junk against the front picture window of her house every time I walked past coming home from the bus. Like, here's my wiener, hello, all squashed. First time I was so surprised I had to stop walking and just ogle at it."

"Ew!" I said, but inside I felt all washed out with clean relief, because she knew. She got it without me saying clear that I hadn't been able to make myself leave. Not immediately. Not quick enough. "Anyway, this is the tree." It was the right kind, a good, big oak, older than mine at home, even.

We walked directly under it and looked up. The leaves were starting to color but still mostly on. Hidden in them I could make out the bottom of Liza's tree house perched way high above us. It looked very old, so old it had gone gray, like beach wood.

"Holy crap," I said, surprised to be right, to find it so real.

"How do we get up there?" Patti asked.

We circled the trunk. There was a creeping vine running up one side of it. I made a face; vines like that always look roachy to me. But I made myself feel around in it, and once I touched it, I stopped worrying. The vine was made of plastic. I found a board nailed to the trunk, hidden in the leaves, the first in a series that acted as a ladder.

"Smart!" I said, and started to climb. Patti followed me. The ladder ended when the branches began, and after that we had to go up the old-fashioned way, clambering branch to branch and wedging our feet in the forks.

"Shit, we're up tall," Patti said, nervous.

I could see a hatch in the tree house's underside. I shoved it open, and it moved easy and quiet. I clambered into it, then got out of the way so Patti could follow me. Inside, Liza's tree house was made of pale, varnished hardwood. Sometime pretty recent, someone had built a solid Home Depot kit house with a roof and cutout windows over the bones of the gray wood platform we'd seen from the ground. Patti whistled, low and impressed.

I said, "This is new, and Liza can't hardly change a lightbulb. Someone helped her rebuild her old tree house." A man, for sure. Maybe more than one. I started crawling around, looking for a way to make it brighter. Near the front I saw an aquarium with three big scented candles inside. There were cigarette lighters in the aquarium, too, but I didn't like the idea of live fire up here, even inside the glass. I turned back and saw Patti holding my old Girl Scouts camp lantern. It was shaped like a kerosene lamp, but really it ran on batteries. She found the switch at the bottom and flipped it on.

We saw a couple of rolled sleeping bags and some big throw pillows by the trunk, far from the cutout windows. They were up against a couple of cheap plywood bookcases. I crept over to read the titles. It was mostly the dark, twisty kind of novels my mom liked, but Liza also had all my old Moomin books up here, too, which was kind of sweet. I saw the snowflakes I'd drawn in Magic Marker down the spine of *Moominland in Midwinter*. If I had doubted for a second that this place was Liza's, I didn't doubt now. I realized I'd been holding my breath, and I blew it all out and whooped in new air, just as Patti pulled *The Joy of Sex* right out of the middle shelf. I turned away, but Patti started flipping through, studying the pictures.

I began digging gingerly in the bedding, picking up the throw pillows with two fingers and setting them aside. Under the big one, I found a chest. It was built into the floor and wall of the tree house, so even if someone found this hiding place, they couldn't steal it. It had one of those super-heavy, expensive combo locks on it where you turn the individual wheels to get it open.

Behind me Patti said, "There's a whole gross chapter on toes. Who wants to have sex with toes?" I heard the book smack shut.

"Look at this," I said, and she crawled over, her eyebrows rising.

"There must be something good in there, huh? How are we gonna get that open?"

I wasn't worried about that. I knew that my mom's bank-card number was 7676. Her voice-mail password was 767676. I turned the dials to 7-6-7, and the lock opened up in my hands.

"Ta-da," I said. I shoved the lock in my back pocket but hesitated before opening the lid. The pillows and candles and *The Joy of Sex* were reminding me exactly what druiding meant.

My mom's brain event had taken most of her away, but before I came out here, I'd been feeling closer to her than I ever had. Now, digging through the artifacts of Liza's secret life like some kind of pervy sex archaeologist, I was seeing plain how little I was like her. The only thing I'd let get in my pants, ever, was Coach Richardson's framed newspaper story. I'd snuck through the Richardsons' house, rescued a dog and maybe a girl from Ducktown, and I was even toting a gun that would get me insta-expelled if anyone had a single clue I was packing. I thought these things made me bold, like her. But I'd willfully forgotten that Liza was a whole different kind of bold.

"Open it!" Patti said.

Still, I paused. Before the stroke my mom seemed to drip sex off her fingertips. Everyplace we went, men looked at her like she was made of fudge brownies. I'd always felt like a gangly she-beast looming and lurching along by her. Now I'd stopped peeing on pregnancy sticks and instead become some kind of crazy klepto, but that didn't make me Liza. The only thing she stole, really, was other people's husbands. Nothing I'd done had really made me more her kid.

Meanwhile Big was clueless. I mean, hello, I was taking a huge-ass gun to school every freaking day. She didn't even suspect, because gun toting wasn't a thing Mosey Slocumb would ever do.

I didn't belong to either of them, and somehow that thought put a sad, burned taste in my mouth, like I'd licked ashes.

There was nothing to make this chest mine. I said to Patti, "If Liza stole me, if I don't belong to her and Big in any real way, what gives me the right to bust into this chest?"

Patti snorted. "There could be something telling where she stole you from. Who's got more right to that than you?"

She was Roger-style right. Which meant she sounded right enough for me to throw the lid open.

"Well, shit," Patti said.

We were looking down at a netbook. It rested by a sleeve and a power cord and a wireless mouse. It was a nice machine, newish-looking. Probably expensive. I was positive that Liza couldn't have afforded it, like she couldn't have built this tree house on her own. Celia Mason's dad—or someone else's dad, or a whole slew of dads—had helped her out, in all kinds of ways, because that's who she was. If who I was was anywhere, it would be in her files and e-mails. I could feel the truth, buzzing under my fingers as I booted up the machine.

"She got plugs here?" Patti asked.

"No, but the battery must still be charged. These little netbooks, they can last hours. Briony had one." It finished booting, but the only thing it showed us was a log-in screen with a picture of a beehive and slots for a user name and a password. All these stupid barriers, each one a place I had to pause and ask myself how much I really wanted to know.

I tried the user name "Liza" and put "7676" in the password slot but got rejected. Her password was probably a string of sevens and sixes, but I didn't know how many. Her user name could be anything.

Patti voiced what I was already thinking. "We need Roger."

"I know, right? But I can't tell him. He will be so killed I took you here and not him."

"No, it's good. You can't show a boy your mom's secret sex place. That's not cool." Then she shrugged, real practical, and said, "Tell him we found the computer hidden at your house?"

I thought about it, then nodded. "Let's pack this stuff up and go. I don't have cell signal out here, and I want to text him. I can't lie to his face. I get all red, and he'll so bust me."

My cell phone didn't get bars until we were almost at my house. Patti and I sat down on the ground and leaned against the back side of the privacy fence that ran around my yard. Liza's woods looked deep green and closed. I couldn't even see the start of the winding trail from here. While Patti got the netbook out of the sleeve and booted it up again, I flipped my phone open and thumb-typed, OMG. Liza had secret laptop under her floor. How do I bust in???!!!111.

I read it over. He'd buy that. He knew I kept my stash of pregnancy tests in a similar place in my room. I'd practically forgotten they were there, expiring and getting all dusty. I hit Send.

He texted back almost immediately, before the laptop was even done grinding its way to the log-in page. He was back at his cousin's house, down in the basement rec room while upstairs the adults rehashed the wedding and drank more. After he got done freaking that we had found a super clue without him, he wanted to know all kinds of technology boy crap about the machine. Patti and me, bent over the phone, rolled our eyes at each other. I texted, Like we know, dufus. It's a Gateway and we need a login and PW. PS low bat and we are hiding from Big in yard pls hurry.

So he got down to business. Type the letter A into the login name slot.

I did it. Now what?

He texted, If nothing filled in, try B. Then C.

All at once I got what he was doing. OMG autofill! GENIUS = U!

I only had to go to D before the word "Druidess" filled itself in in the log-in name space, and the password slot filled itself in, too, in a row of unreadable asterisks. I hit Enter, and while Liza's desktop loaded, I texted to Roger, U R FULL OF WIN!

The desktop wasn't cluttered. There were a few icons for Spider Solitaire and Minesweeper, basic Microsoft Office stuff, Paint, and a program that downloaded and stored photos from her digital camera. I popped that open just as my cell phone rang. It was the theme song from *Underdog*, Roger's ringtone.

I passed it to Patti and said, "Put him on speaker." I hauled the netbook onto my lap.

"Hey," Patti said into the phone. "Sec." She turned it on speaker and held it up so we could both hear.

Roger sounded small and very far away. "I can't tell you how hard this sucks. This sucks goats. How am I missing this? Patti, tell her to open the browser. Tell her she has to go on the Interwebs and check Liza's browser history."

Patti said, "She can hear. We both can."

I said, "I'm looking at her stored pics, and this is so weird. There's lots of her weird-ass shots of leaf piles and cocoons. But there's also a crap ton of pictures of me that I had no idea she took. Some of them are two or three years old. Like here I am on the old bike Big took to Goodwill."

Patti leaned in to look, but Roger was practically yelling now.

"Look at pictures later! You need to check her browser history. I'm telling you."

"Fine." I pirated onto our left-side neighbor's wireless; Roger had learned a long time ago they hadn't passworded it, when he was skipping school up in my tree house with only his Mac for company. As soon as I connected, I opened up Explorer, while Roger foamed impatiently and Patti bounced on her knees all big-eyed, just as bad a solve-monster as Roger, now that we were so close. Liza's home page was Google, and she had bookmarked a bunch of sites, but nothing interesting, mostly stuff like eBay and Etsy and Netflix.

"Hello," I said. "Liza bookmarked Hotmail."

"Shazam!" Roger said. I hit the link and used Roger's autofill trick to get past the log-in. This time I had to go all the way to F before flirtybits@hotmail.com appeared, and the password sweetly followed in a row of unreadable bullets.

"We're in!" Patti said.

I could hear Roger crowing. "I love dumb-ass PC users. They all do this. Why have a password if you are going to let your browser put it in for you?"

Liza hadn't checked her e-mail since she'd had her stroke. I said, "Oh, my God, her in-box has almost three hundred new mails in it."

Roger said, "It has to be mostly spam, because people who know she had a stroke wouldn't e-mail her. Just scan the titles."

Sure enough, the first titles were all Cheap Canadian Pharmacy. Be her Drillosaur! COUPON CODES. And then The Boosterthon Needs You! Apparently no one had ever taken her off the Calvary PTA mailing list.

My breath caught. The title under the PTA e-mail was u goddam whor I am going 2 find u and kill u.

I pointed at it and was surprised to see how hard my finger was shaking. Patti read it off to Roger. It was from someone called halfcocked57@gmail.com. Roger started hollering, "Open it! Open it!"—so loud that I shushed him, worried the wedding drunks would hear him caterwauling.

I clicked it open, Patti and me crowding close, pressing our faces forward toward the screen.

I read it aloud. "'U better call me or at least e me the pictures. Sick here from freaking. Freaking the fuck out. You better be dead. She better not be. You bitch. U better.'"

Patti and I exchanged mystified glances.

Roger said, "That's it? Not even signed? Damn it, go back to the in-box. Does Hotmail let you sort by sender?"

It did. We found twenty-four more unread e-mails from half-cocked57, starting a couple of weeks after Liza had her stroke. The earliest one had a different tone, but all of them wanted to know where Liza was, when Liza would send the pictures. As the days passed, halfcocked57 got angrier and more abusive. The e-mails didn't come regular, though. There were three furious ones that came the same day, same hour, one after another, then nothing for ten days, when the worst one of all came. Halfcocked57 called Liza words I had never heard said out loud in my whole life.

"Sent file!" Roger said. "Go back and see what pics Liza was forwarding?" But I think all three of us already knew it would be the candids of me.

I clicked into Sent and searched for the last thing Liza had mailed to halfcocked57. It was the top thing, titled, Our girl, May 17th.

Inside, the text said, We did our summer shopping, and she only wanted shorts. She's tired of skirts, wants to go all rebel soldier next year with her school's dress code, demand jeans. It's cute to see her so righteously indignant, like a school with a dress code is communism. No boyfriend on the horizon, thank God. She may run track this fall, she says. She's built for it—look at those long legs. Little beauty, she is.

It took me a second, but I remembered going to the mall with Liza last spring and bitching about how at Cal all the girls had to wear skirts, like women haven't had the vote for a thousand years now. The attached picture showed me in shorts I was about to outgrow, standing in the backyard by the willow that wasn't there anymore. I was looking to the side, so I was almost in profile. I didn't look like a beauty on any planet except maybe planet Liza, which we all knew was one crazy-ass place.

Liza had taken this picture, though. I was sure of it; she was always good at composition, and she understood lighting. I could see how she had set me a little off center and included enough of the willow to balance me. She must have been lying in the grass pretending to photograph ants, because the camera had been angled up at me, and I could see I really did have long legs. I had never noticed them, because in the mirror I always ended up staring at how I had no butt and squat-all to train with my trainer bra, but Liza's photo showed off pretty legs I never knew I had and caught the sunlight that glowed off my skin and made it look olive and nice.

I closed out and kept going back in her Sent file. Every month Liza had attached pictures of me and zinged them off to halfcocked57.

"This person, this halfcocked57, do you think that's who Liza got me from?" I asked. My voice sounded as tinny and distant as Roger's did. Patti shrugged, but her face looked like she was thinking, *Well, duh*. Roger said nothing. I opened the next attachment and saw that Liza had even sent halfcocked57 last year's goony school pic.

"Look at that," Patti said, pointing. The school logo was missing from my Calvary shirt.

Roger said, "What? What?"

I explained, "Liza Photoshopped my school picture. Or edited it in Paint anyway. She took my Cal logo off. And all these pics, it's me in the plain grass or by trees or inside the house. Never by a building. No signs or street names." Which meant Liza really, completely, absolutely, totally stole me. Weirder still, she had been e-mailing updates, but nothing that would let halfcocked57 find me. That meant whoever halfcocked57 was hadn't handed me to Liza like a present. Maybe they'd been looking for me, hunting Liza this whole time, desperate to get me back. I had this crazy picture in my head, some nice daddy-looking guy with an embarrassing mustache, a plain, smiley lady with eyes like mine wearing ugly mom sandals and baking a nice pie.

"This is roadkill-humpin' crazy," Patti said, and that made me laugh in a short, near-hysterical burst.

Liza had done something awful enough to impress even a Duckins. The imaginary perfect family washed away. People like that, they didn't even know the words halfcocked57 had called Liza.

"It's all true," I said when I was done laughing. "It's all really real."

"Write back!" Roger said.

I nodded, which he couldn't see, but Patti said, "She hit Reply already." I looked at the screen and was surprised to see she was right. I had.

"I don't know what to say."

"Be Liza," Roger said. "Say, like, 'Chill, bitch. My comp died. Gimme your snail addy, I'll print the latest pics out and throw 'em in the mail.' Then we'll know where halfcocked57 lives."

My hands typed it as he spoke. Even though I felt muffled and distant from this, like I'd been wound around in a thousand layers of cotton fluff, I was impressed at how he could make it so real-Liza-sounding, totally off the cuff.

I sat there with the cursor hovering over Send.

Patti said, "Are you sure? What would Big say to do?"

"Leave Big out of it," I said, sharp. Still, I moved the cursor up to X the message away.

"Send it," Roger said. "It doesn't mean we have to do anything. Just, we'll know."

I hovered the cursor back over the Send as Patti covered the mouthpiece of the phone with her hand and whispered, "You really think he won't do anything if an address comes? Just because you say?"

I stuck there, not doing anything, and then I heard Big yelling from the house—"Mosey! Mosey!"—and my finger jerked, accidentally, but not all the way an accident.

The e-mail sent.

"Oh, my God," Patti said.

"Did you send it?" Roger hollered.

"I did," I said, and we both heard him whooping. "Big is calling, text you later." I grabbed the phone from Patti and flipped it closed. "Can you pack the netbook up and bring it to the house? I'll get Big in the kitchen, and you come in the front and run this back to my room. There's a plug under my bed. You can hide it there while it's recharging."

Patti nodded, and Big hollered again, sounding real mad, "Mosey!"

Her voice was coming from the back door. I didn't want her to see me hopping the fence and know Patti and me had been out in the woods. I ran around the outside of the fence to the front door. She'd quit calling by the time I got there, so I went into the den yelling, "Big? Big?"

Almost immediately, she poked her head out from the swinging door to the kitchen and said, "Mosey Willow Jane Grace Slocumb, do not yowl at me like I'm your maid. Come in here."

Her head disappeared back into the kitchen, but I stood there blinking for a second before I followed, because she'd been wearing lip gloss. Not ChapStick either, but shiny cranberry-colored stuff.

Liza was sitting in her usual place at the table, and Big was pulling a pan out of the oven. She had on her favorite navy cotton skirt with the silvery threads shot through. She'd blown her hair out straight as it would go, though it was already springing into waves on the ends.

I asked, "Where are you going?" I couldn't think of a place Big could go where she would need her lips to be so glossy.

"Errands," she said, but she'd already gotten the groceries and stuff this morning. "Can you please stay with Liza? If I run late, I'll need you to help her to bed."

My eyes narrowed, and I stepped closer. Sometimes Big got set up on blindies or had a dinner invite, but she always met the guy out. She said she didn't want me getting attached if it wasn't going to be serious, which she acted like meant she was thinking marriage, but I thought it was code for sex. Either way, with Big it never turned out to be serious.

I said, "Big, when you say 'errands' like that, all weird, does that mean there's a guy?"

Big pushed her hair behind her ears, nervous like. "When I say 'errands' all weird like that, I mean errands."

I snapped, "God, you can just say if you have a date, you know."

Big startled like a horse and said, really loud, "It's not a date." Then she flushed so hard that of course I knew it had to be.

"Whatever." I couldn't believe she was going off to eat at Applebee's with some balding accountant and talk about whatever boring crap old people talked about on dates, like everything was normal. Like Liza was still Liza and I was still me.

Patti came through the swinging doors. She glanced at me, then did a double take and said, "You look like you ate bees."

I rolled my eyes at her. "You talk so weird."

"Oh, she does not," Big said. "You do not," she told Patti. "You want to stay for supper? Just Tuna Surprise and a pot of green beans, but I made plenty."

"Sure," Patti said.

"I have to run," Big said. "I'm late."

"For your *errands*," I said.

"For my none-of-your-beeswax," Big answered, tart. As she passed by us on her way out the swinging door, she gave Patti's hair a quick rumple. Patti leaned into it and looked up at Big in that same starvey way Bogo looked at Liza. Big breezed out past, not even noticing.

All at once I was sick, so sick in the pit of my stomach. I couldn't imagine putting a single bite of that casserole in my mouth, even though it was the good kind I liked, with the chips on top.

Because what was I to Big, really? Just another little stray like Patti, and if she knew, maybe that's how she would touch me, too.

A quick head rub and a smile, like I was a broken-y dirty dog and she was setting out to be kind to me. Not like I belonged to her. I didn't belong to anyone, except maybe whoever halfcocked57 was.

After Big left, I did all the right things. I made plates for us and Liza, and we ate them in front of the TV so I didn't have to talk much. I especially didn't want to talk to Liza, so when Patti left, around nine, I went ahead and helped her to bed early. Big still wasn't home. She was off on her none-of-my-beeswax, and I guess nothing she did was my beeswax, really. That meant nothing I did was her damn beeswax either.

I looked under the bed, and sure enough there was the netbook, charging. I pulled it out and sat down with my back braced against the door so Big couldn't come in and surprise me, if she even bothered to come home. I pirated onto our neighbor's wireless and jumped right to Hotmail.

Liza had a new e-mail.

I gulped. I couldn't breathe well. I went to the in-box, and sure enough it was from halfcocked57.

The message was short. How do you forget my address, asshole? And then under that, 91 Fox Street. No city or state, so halfcocked57 must think Liza would remember those things, but there was a chain of five numbers that had to be the zip code.

I put the zip code into Google and came up with Montgomery, Alabama. That meant halfcocked57 was only about four hours away.

I was trembling so hard I couldn't hardly get my phone open. I texted Roger the address, just that, and then sat there, waiting for him to text back. It took him about thirty seconds, like he'd done nothing but sit in the basement holding his breath and the phone until this moment.

Whoop, there it is. So. Mosey. We going to check it out?

I swallowed, unsure. But my thumbs decided to click and send words back to him all on their own, while I sat there shaking.

O. Hellz. Yah.

CHAPTER SEVENTEEN

Big

MELISSA RICHARDSON. THAT girl was poison from day one. She was blond and so tall that she always looked older than she was, with the kind of model's body that was made to show off clothes. She had the clothes to show off, too, and she was quite pretty, though not half the beauty her mother was. Her eyes were set too close together, and the things that made Claire's face so elegant—razor-blade cheekbones and that long, thin Meryl Streep nose she loved to look down—were blunted on Melissa.

Liza and Melissa were the very devil in middle school, but that was just the start. By ninth grade the only person with any control or influence over either of those girls was the other. I remembered Melissa standing in a slouch on my front porch wearing her signature bright blue eyeliner. She put it on so thick it was like she hoped her icy pale eyes would leach color from it. Or maybe she wanted to distract me from noticing how red the whites were. Either way, it wasn't working.

Liza answered the door, but I'd followed her. I stood right behind her with my hand on her shoulder, like that could hold her with me.

"Hey, Liza. Ms. Slocumb." Melissa gave me the insincere smile of a dog who has already been down to the henhouse to suck every egg you've got. She was wearing leggings and a baby-doll dress that probably cost more than my whole week's paycheck, yet she looked like second place beside Liza in her tatty jeans. Her pale gaze stared right through me. "I wanted Liza to go down to DQ with me for a cone." She wasn't really asking for permission, or even informing me as a courtesy. She was speaking in code to Liza.

I said, "Melissa, you know she's grounded. Quite frankly, I'm surprised you're not grounded, too."

"Oh, I am," Melissa said. She tossed her hundred-dollar haircut. "I think it means something different at my house than it does here."

"Well, here it means you're actually grounded." Melissa gave me a quick-flash grin, like I'd scored a point in some game I wasn't playing. I stepped up, practically between them, and started swinging the front door closed. "Good-bye, Melissa."

Through the narrowing crack, Melissa called, "Check ya flip side," to Liza. They exchanged a speaking glance that lasted barely half a second, but it held a thousand cues.

Liza and I went back to doing laundry. I sorted darks and lights, and Liza carried the basket of socks and underthings to the nook in the kitchen. I heard the washer start, but a minute passed and Liza didn't come back. I ran to the kitchen. The back door was hanging open, and Liza was already gone.

When she got home, I'd scream and cajole in turns. I'd ground her again. I'd try a thousand different ways to get her to open up and talk to me. She'd look hangdog sorry when I shrieked at her. She'd promise to be better when I wept. She'd accept whatever punishment I handed out. But when it came down to it, yelling meant nothing. Crying meant nothing. Punishment meant nothing. The second my eyes were off her, she was gone, doing whatever Melissa wanted.

I tried taking away her favorite clothes and items, but any beloved object I took away, Melissa replaced. Claire Richardson kept her kid well funded. And still Claire blamed Liza for the drugs. It never seemed to occur to her that she, Claire, was paying the tabs that let our kids get high. Liza was too constantly on restriction to get even her meager allowance. Granted, Liza was so pretty and Melissa was so stylish that I bet they rarely paid for drugs, but Melissa paid for taxi rides and concert tickets, cover charges and fake IDs, a new one every time I ferreted out Liza's and destroyed it.

Not that Liza was a blameless lambkin. They egged each other farther down every bad path than either girl would have gone alone. They'd been a bonded pair, right up until Liza got pregnant and Melissa had decided that meant she wasn't fun or useful anymore.

Now Liza had said her name, twice, but she'd been looking through me with a thousand-year stare. It wasn't easy to believe that Melissa Richardson had risen out of whatever hidey-hole she'd been stashed in all these years. Would she risk exposure, maybe arrest, to come back to Immita and poison Liza for some ancient slight?

But the name sure had made me rethink. At that Calvary luau, Liza had worn her best white silk blouse, lined her eyes, and put on lipstick. She knew damn well the fellows liked her plenty in an old T-shirt with her hair wild, bare skin glowing, maybe some Burt's Bees to make her mouth shine. In the past she'd fluffed herself up for female rivals in a way she never needed to for men. She'd been meeting someone, all right, but not a man, and not the long-gone Melissa either, though that was closer.

Liza had gone to meet Melissa's mother, Claire. It had to be.

Liza had been standing by Claire Richardson when I first arrived at the luau. When Liza collapsed, Claire had ignored my seizing kid and gone to help the woman with the splashed sandals. That would have struck me as odd if I hadn't been panicking. It would have been more in character had she snapped her fingers and called for janitorial. Now I thought she'd bent to help that woman clean up her shoes for cover, so she could grab the Dixie cup and dispose of it. I'd swooped in and snatched it up first.

I was hoping the cup would give me some answers, but when I called Lawrence, I got his machine. The beep came and went, and I stood there breathing into the phone like a pervert, not sure where to begin.

Finally I said, "I need to see you. Can you meet me at Panda Garden?" and hung up.

On Friday he left a terse voice mail for me, saying he was up visiting Harry at his college and he thought we'd agreed that he would call me *after*, in November. Ten minutes later he'd called back and left another voice mail. This one he talked sweeter. *"I keep listening to your message. Your voice sounds... something. Are you in trouble? I get back Saturday evening."*

Maybe I shouldn't have picked Panda Garden, considering the history. It was the place where he'd blurted out, "I'm still married," and the way he'd said "still" had kept me sitting there with him. On the other hand, there wasn't a memory-soaked queen-size bed set up by the fish pond or the big gold Buddha statue, so it wasn't the worst place I could have chosen.

Even so, when I walked in and saw him sitting in the exact same booth that we'd started in, with his hair brushed back and his big, square hands folded on the table in front of him, sex reared up inside me and started battering at my insides like a homeless animal. It wanted to run at him, eat him up, then lay its head down, tame and sweet, in his warm lap. It didn't care how much I had on my mind. It only cared that Lawrence had come when I'd called, just because my voice had sounded "something."

Our booth's window faced the parking lot, and Lawrence had his face close to the glass, peering into the lot like he was watching for me. It wasn't dark out yet, but the sun was going down. He must have missed me coming in.

I slid in across from him. He glanced up and said, "Hey," but then went right back to looking out the window.

"Are you on some kind of Panda Garden stakeout?" I asked, a little irky to see he hadn't been watching for me after all.

He shook his head and turned to face me, settling back into the booth. "No, this guy out here— Ah, probably nothing. I'm off duty. What's going on?"

"Straight to business, Lawrence?" My voice stayed tart for no good reason. I wanted to get to business myself. I just didn't want him to want to.

"Yes," he said. "There's a lot I want to say to you, Ginny, that doesn't have damn-all to do with any kind of business. You know that. But what else can I say right now?"

I thought he could try, *I can't keep breathing with you this close and me not touching you. Let's go out to my cop car and climb in the cage and break some public-decency laws, and I will never let you go, and if it turns out the Richardsons are truly coming after your family, I will take my big cop fists and beat them until they stop.* That seemed to me like a great start, but he didn't say any of those things.

"Business, then," I said. I took out the Dixie cup in its plastic bag and set it on the table.

"I think someone poisoned Liza, and that's why she had that stroke. There's some dried Virgin Colada in the bottom of this cup, and I need to know if that's all that's in there. I figured someone at some lab somewhere might owe you a favor?"

Lawrence said, "Wait, what? Why do you think someone poisoned Liza?"—the very second the waiter dashed up to our table. He was a pudgy kid with dark hair and eyes that were shaped round already. They went rounder when he heard Lawrence. He looked back and forth between us, twice, while I tried, and failed, to look bland.

"Hi, John," Lawrence said.

"Hey, Officer Rawley. What's going on?"

"Just hungry," Lawrence said. His bland look was better than mine.

The kid nodded and asked for our drink orders. We both said water and hot tea, and then Lawrence went ahead and ordered food, too: steamed dumplings and moo shu pork and General Tso's chicken. All our old favorites. He looked to me to see if I wanted anything else, but I didn't. The kid wrote the order down, but then he lingered, staring at us like we were zoo monkeys, I guess to see if we were going to talk any more about poisoning people.

Lawrence leveled a patient cop gaze on the kid, and he got fidgety under it and went scurrying.

When he was good and gone, Lawrence asked, "Why would you think that?"

I said, "Liza said so. She's been working hard for weeks to tell me."

His mouth thinned down. It was his thinking face. "What are you not telling me?"

"A lot," I said.

The hostess, a high-school-age blonde in a fake-silk kimono, came close to us then, leading a lone man past the goldfish pond to the booth across from ours. Lawrence watched, his brow crumpling, and we both shut up until she'd seated him and walked away. The man put his face in the menu. I leaned in closer to Lawrence to talk, but he shook his head, barely, in a faint no. He glanced at the guy in the booth beside us, a speaking glance. I looked, but all I saw was a regular-looking fellow, maybe fifty, balding, in a blue suit and wire-rim glasses.

While I was looking, Lawrence stood up, and in one smooth move he stepped across the aisle and pushed himself into the booth by the man. He shoved the guy over with his hip.

"Hi," Lawrence said to him, fake and bright.

"Lawrence?" I said, but he kept his eyes on the guy, who was starting to sputter, very indignant. I stood up and stepped across the aisle, sliding into the seat across from the two of them. "What are you doing?"

The guy said, "Yes, what *are* you doing?"

Lawrence crowded in even closer to him, smiling easy. "Don't bother. Your car followed hers into the lot, and then you sat tight till she was all the way in. I saw you peering in her car windows. What were you looking for, buddy?"

The guy edged farther into the booth, trying to get some room. "I don't know what you're talking about." Now his affronted sputtering sounded so fake even I wasn't buying it.

"This is a four-top booth, and there's plenty of two-seaters open down the other wall. So you asked to sit here. By us." Lawrence stretched his arm over the back of the booth and leaned in closer to the guy. Really close. Now the guy's head was pressed against the back wall. Lawrence showed the guy his teeth, but it didn't look like smiling. "You're so interested in my friend here, I figured we better join you. See if we could satisfy your curiosity."

The guy's righteous indignation dropped from his face like a hat he was removing. "Back off," he said, hard, and all at once he didn't look so regular. Lawrence eased back a few inches, giving the guy the room he asked for.

Immediately the guy swelled up like a puffer fish, leaning into the space Lawrence had made like he'd won a round. He said, "Now, get out of my way," as Lawrence's free hand disappeared under the table. His last word, "way," came out an octave higher than the rest of the sentence. He sucked his breath in, and his face went white, and his mouth twisted. His spine went very stiff, jacking him up straight. His hands jumped up off the table and hovered in the air, almost as high as his shoulders.

"That better?" Lawrence said, fake friendly and conversational.

"No," the guy said in a strangled voice.

"Lawrence?" My voice sounded thready and scared, even to my own ears.

The guy's shoulders flexed, bracing, and Lawrence leaned a little closer, talking low. "Try it. I'd love for you to try it. But I'm fast. And I've got freakishly strong hands. See?" The guy gasped. "You won't get these back. Not whole." Then Lawrence said, louder but very calm, "It's okay. Set the tea down on our table and go." I saw that our waiter, John, had come back. His mouth was frozen in a silent O shape.

"Call the cops," the guy managed to say to John. His eyes were bulging in their sockets.

John blinked and stuttered, "But...but he is the cops." His voice was wobbling. I couldn't blame him. I felt wobbly, too, all over. I stuffed my hands under my thighs to make them stop trembling, or at least so I couldn't feel them doing it.

"Set the drinks down, John. It's fine," Lawrence said, unworried and almost soothing, but his eyes never moved off the guy in the booth, and his expression didn't match his voice. Not at all. John set the whole tray down on our table and abandoned it, scuttling back toward the kitchen. "Now, I could just call you 'asshole,' but I'd like to know your name, I think. Show me some ID."

A fine sweat had sprung up on the guy's forehead. He reached into his inside jacket pocket, gingerly, got his wallet out, and flipped it open. Lawrence glanced at the ID and read, "Mitchell Morissey. Nice to meet you. You're a PI? Interesting. Why don't you put your hands flat on the table for me. Nice and slow." The guy did what Lawrence said, his wallet under one palm. "Good dog. Ginny, why would a private investigator be following you?"

"Following me?" I said. My throat had gone too dry to swallow, and a panicky spit was building up in my mouth. "I don't know."

"You want to tell me why?" Lawrence asked Mitchell Morissey.

"No." It was more like a gasp then a real word.

I couldn't quite take it in. Lawrence, my straight-arrow Baptist, was doing something very bad, and not coppish, and probably illegal, under the table.

Lawrence smiled, but it wasn't a pleasant one. His arm twisted a little. Tears sprang up in Morissey's eyes. "You sure? Because this woman you're shadowing, she's important to me."

"I don't think so," the guy said, his voice going higher still.

"Shame," Lawrence said. "Hope you've already had your kids."

Morissey's only answer was a squeak.

It was awful, and wrong, and the worst part was, in a deep and primal place down in my belly, a dreadful, girlie piece of me liked it. I had to stop it, though. I had to stop him doing it before he got into trouble.

"Last chance," Lawrence said, leaning in close. "Who hired you? Whisper me a name and we're done here."

Morissey was as white as paper napkins now. He said nothing, but he didn't have to, because I realized then that I knew the answer. I said it for him, to make Lawrence stop. To make me stop liking it.

"Claire Richardson."

I saw surprise, a clear confirmation, cross Morissey's face. He wiped it away fast, but we'd both seen it. Lawrence had better control over his own features, but one eyebrow twitched and he flashed a glance at me. I'd surprised him, too.

Lawrence let Morissey go, and Morissey immediately slumped forward, his spine curving, facedown. His breath came out in a soft, gobbling burble. Both his own hands went under the table, into his lap, to cradle himself.

Lawrence leaned in close to his ear and said, so quiet I had to strain to hear, "I think you're not hungry. You're going to get in your car and go. Next time I see you around my girl here? You won't get them back." Morissey made a gulping noise. "We understand each other?"

"I understand you fine," he said, rolling his forehead back and forth across the cool tabletop.

Lawrence gave a short nod, satisfied, but my eyes narrowed. I'd been Liza's mother for a long time; I'd learned there was often a big fat gap between understanding and agreement.

Lawrence stood up, and I hastily followed suit. I moved back to our booth, but Lawrence stayed standing as Morissey clambered painfully to his feet. He dropped a five on his table and turned, still hunched over, and limped out. Lawrence watched him go, his eyes so cold and hard that it occurred to me he must know the difference between understanding and agreement, too.

I said, "I don't want you to get in trouble, but should we let him go? What if he heads to my house? Liza and Mosey are there alone."

Lawrence was shaking his head. "The guy is a licensed PI. He's a digger, not a heavy. If he does stake out your house? Call me. I'll handle it."

"What does that mean, you'll handle it?" I said, not liking the sound of it.

Lawrence said, "I warned him. He keeps following you, then he gets what he gets. Forget him."

He sat back down across from me. Neither one of us spoke, watching out the window as Morissey hobbled across the lot. He got into a tan Saturn and drove away.

Once he was gone, Lawrence asked, calm, direct, "What kind of trouble are you in, Ginny?" I said nothing. "Okay, let's start simple. How did you know that Claire had hired him?"

I wasn't ready to answer that. I reached for the empty cups on John's abandoned tray and set one down in front of each of us. My hands were shaking so hard the lid chattered against the pot as I poured us both some tea. I stirred half a packet of sugar into mine while Lawrence watched and waited.

I took a bracing sip and said, "That was the least Baptist thing I've ever seen you do." I sounded too breathy, even to my own ears, but it made him chuckle.

"Oh, really? Maybe not the least." He quirked an eyebrow at

me, and I found myself flushing at the memory of the two of us, twined together on his sunshine-covered bed. I smiled back, a shaky smile, but present. He went on. "I don't think you're all that angry with Baptists anyway. You're plain old mad at God. We Baptists are easier to yell at, though."

I puffed air out and said, "Maybe so. He does seem to have it in for me some years. But to be fair, very few of the Baptists that I've known have made me feel any kindlier toward God. You're the exception, and look what you did to that PI. Not exactly Christian."

That made Lawrence flash his quick grin. "Nothing unbiblical about a little righteous fury." Then his face got serious again. "How did you know it was Claire Richardson?"

"Who's asking? A cop? Or a guy who loves me?" It came blurting out. We hadn't talked love. Not for years. It was pretty bold, but I was too wrung out for bullshit.

"Ginny," he said, and the way he said my name was almost an answer. His voice was so sweet and low and deep, like a honey drip. And it stayed sweet, even as his words got spiky. "I grabbed another man's testicles at the damn Panda Garden. It's pretty clear that I'm all in. It's me who should be asking. You came to my apartment pretending to be curious about my marriage, then slipped me a bunch of questions about an ongoing police investigation. I'm so tied around your pinkie finger I didn't spend nearly enough time wondering why you were asking." His eyes on me were so warm. "It's me who needs to know, are you here because you love me or are you deep in some bad shit and playing me?"

I didn't have a good answer, because all those things were true. I loved him, and I *was* in deep shit, and I had been playing him. I thought of my girls, and I gave him the simplest truth I had. "There's only two things on this earth I love more than I love you, Lawrence."

He breathed in, then out. If anyone could understand my choices, it was this man, who had stayed with Sandy until his kids were grown and gone. Who had tried for more than a year to stick it out, even after his youngest was in college. "It all comes back to Liza and Mosey somehow, doesn't it? Tell me. Let me help you."

I thought about it. Hard. But I'd jumped into a huge heap of felonies, headfirst and eyes wide open. It was wrong to pull him in, too, blind. I shook my head.

He swallowed and said, still toothache-sweet, "Dumb-ass. I am telling you, I'll break every stupid law I'm sworn to uphold and go to hell on top of it, if that's what you need. Tell me."

I was crying then, because I believed him. I believed him. And that meant I had to settle this myself, so I could start with him clean, in November. I understood then his wanting to wait until his divorce, in a way I hadn't before. I didn't want anything wrong or underhanded touching us. We deserved better.

I said, "If that's true, then the best thing you can do for me is look away. Don't think too hard about it. Don't try to know. Let me fix it, and I'll call you in November."

He had to stop looking, because he was too smart. If he looked close, he would figure it out. No one had yet, because of Mosey. She was the perfect blind. It was like one of those old riddles, like the one where the emergency-room doctor is a woman and that's how the patient is her son. Or how the guy who only takes the elevator when it's raining is a midget and needs an umbrella to reach the buttons. The answer was so obvious, but no one could see it: The lost baby in the yard couldn't be ours, because Mosey made all our babies look accounted for.

He said, "You don't even want to tell me why Claire is having you followed. Did you... You never had anything going with her husband?"

"God no," I said. "Why would you think that?"

He shook his head. "She's following you. So she must think it."

I felt my eyes narrowing. "What aren't *you* telling *me*?"

He shook his head. "All right, Ginny. You're playing your cards close, but I'm going to show you my whole hand. The investigation stalled because the state coroner didn't find any trauma on the bones. Nothing to indicate shaken baby or any kind of violence. He said the most likely cause of death was SIDS. Meanwhile it's football season, so Rick is up to his ass in new DUIs. The investigation was back-burnered. Indefinitely. But then the married couple I told you about approached him. They thought the bones in your yard might be their missing infant. They paid for more testing."

"No," I said. Not because I didn't remember, but because I didn't want him to say what I was afraid he would say next. He said it anyway.

"It was the Richardsons."

All at once I was back in the yard, recognizing that little pink dress. Recognizing my lost grandchild. Claire and her husband had never accepted that Melissa had let their baby drown. They must have thought those bones in our yard belonged to their baby, and that gave Claire even more blame to lay on Liza's doorstep. The world spun out from under me and dropped away, exactly as it had that day. My vision pinholed and grayed for a moment, and I had to grab the table.

"It came back negative," I said. I sounded so very far away. "It wasn't Claire's baby in that yard." I stated it as fact, because I knew it.

"Right. The child's DNA proved it wasn't Claire's," Lawrence agreed. "Here's the thing: The husband was a match. The child buried in your yard was definitely Coach Richardson's. It was a hard way for Claire to find out that her husband cheated. Rick told her in the bluntest terms, too, hoping she'd turn on Coach and help Rick find out who the mother was. But that is one cool-blooded lady. She didn't make a scene. Rick said she went so still it was like the news had turned her to stone. Then she said, 'Come,' at Coach, like he was a dog, and they got up and walked out." He was still talking, but it came from so far away. "Rick tried to question Coach, but Claire lawyered up for both of them. So he went back— Ginny? Ginny, what's wrong?"

I shook my head at him. Then I was up and moving so fast I didn't even feel myself go. I was out of the booth and running. I bolted directly into John with a huge tray of Chinese food. I staggered back, and I heard the same sound outside of me that I was hearing inside, everything cracking and shattering and falling into pieces. Lawrence had his arms around me as I stood in a sea of broken glass and spilled food, the General's chicken looking like the bloody chunks of something dead and in pieces, and my stomach heaved, and I fought and twisted in Lawrence's arms.

John said, "Oh, no! Oh, no!" over and over, and I was saying it, too: "Oh, no!"

"Ginny!" Lawrence yelled, loud, like he was calling me back into my body. "Where are you going?"

I had to bite my lips to keep from saying the answer, because the answer was very simple. I was going to shoot Coach Richardson in his face until he was dead. Because Liza was fourteen when she fetched up pregnant, and she'd told me the daddy was some kid she met at the carny. I tried to break out of his arms again, because I had to go find myself a gun and shoot a man, and only Lawrence bulling me down into the booth and wedging himself in beside me and putting his hands on me made me be still. He waited until he felt my legs stop straining to rise again, until my fists stopped shoving at him. He waited until I was limp, and then he stood up, the backs of his legs against the edge of the booth seat to block me in.

I heard his voice talking, making soothing noises, and I heard him opening his wallet and passing money or a credit card to John, but I sat there dumb as a cow. I stared at our ruined food, splashed like roadkill on the navy carpet. I'd been so stupid. That's why Melissa had ditched Liza. Not because pregnancy spoiled the parties. Liza had stolen her father. I thought I might throw up. Liza had a woman's body then, but she'd only been fourteen. I had to go shoot him. I should go shoot him. There should be no law against shooting a grown man who goes after your little girl. I tried to get up to go shoot him, but Lawrence pushed in beside me again, trapping me in the booth. John was gone.

"Ginny," Lawrence said, his voice low and urgent. "Promise me. If I ran your DNA against that child's, tell me it wouldn't match."

I stared at him, and I felt myself gathering together. So many things were making sense now, but I could hardly process it. Liza had claimed that Coach was *Mosey's* father; that's how Liza had blackmailed Claire into paying Mosey's tuition, by threatening to expose her husband. Claire may not have wholly believed it, or else she wouldn't have let her husband stay on at the school. Denial was powerful, but she must have been worried enough that it was true to fork over the money. Maybe she'd told herself she was paying to keep her good name clear of gossip, not because she believed it.

That's why Claire had poisoned Liza, in part to stop the blackmail, but mostly so she wouldn't have to ponder if her husband was truly keeping such a filthy secret.

Then, when the bones were found, Claire believed they were her own child's bones, that the ocean hadn't taken her baby. That Liza had. Now Claire knew that her husband truly had fathered Liza's baby, and that the baby had died. There was no way to stay in denial. And that meant she had to be asking herself who on earth our Mosey was.

It wasn't possible to pull myself together, but I had to, for my girls, so I did. Possible or not, I packed everything I was feeling away in that deep-down box where I'd kept sex for so long, then piled everything I owned on top of it. I met Lawrence's worried gaze, and I breathed in and out.

"Ginny. Talk to me," he said.

It was too many felonies. I believed him when he said he'd break the law for me, but I loved him too much to ask it of him. I took a deep breath and made myself be still inside. Once I was calm, I gathered some truths up into words. Truth, and only truth. This was Lawrence, with a cop's good nose for liars. I made sure everything I planned to say was gospel, and then I spoke.

"That is not my baby in the yard, Lawrence. I never, never had anything going with that woman's husband. I'd sooner lie down with a snake. My only child is Liza. Liza has only ever had one child. Mosey is my granddaughter."

I watched relief start in his shoulders and rise up to his eyes and spill down into all his limbs.

"Okay, then. But then why would...?" He trailed away, thinking again. I had to nip that in the bud.

I said, still scrupulously truthful, "Claire blames my family, mostly Liza, for everything that happened with Melissa and the baby, down at the beach. She has had it in for us for years. As for my yard, there was no fence back then. It was all woods behind my house. Liza and every wild child in Immita were back there all the time, having sex and smoking dope and worse. Lawrence, think about the time line. If Claire did poison Liza, she did it before those bones were ever found."

"That's true," Lawrence said. "So then why poison her? Why hire Morissey to follow you?"

I said, "I think Liza had something on Claire. I think she was blackmailing Claire to pay Mosey's tuition to Calvary. Maybe Claire is trying to find out how much I know?" I had to fight to keep my face still, because all at once I understood Liza's insistence that Mosey go to private school. She'd never send Mosey to the school where Coach taught. Either because Coach thought Mosey was his or because Liza knew that young girls weren't safe around him, or both. "I think any number of women have had ample opportunity to get pregnant by Claire Richardson's husband. I don't care about that. I only care about what Claire tried to do to Liza. Please, please, can you get someone to test this cup?"

He measured that, then reached out and picked up the ziplock bag and put the cup in his jacket pocket. "If that's what you need, you can have it. I have a guy at the lab who owes me. Owes me huge. I'll get it done fast. But if you need more, call me. November be damned."

"Just the cup," I said. Then I sat looking at him, like I was trying to memorize his laugh lines and the exact pattern of brown and gold in his deep-set eyes. Because I wouldn't see him again until we were free. Both of us.

He looked back in that same kind of memorizing way, and then he said, real quiet, one word: "November."

I said it back because it was easier to say that word than it was to try and say good-bye.

As we left, John and the young hostess were standing by the greeting station in front of the fish pond, whispering and watching us with big, interested eyes.

Lawrence lifted a hand and said, "Sorry about that," as we passed.

He walked me straight to my car, but before I could get in, his arms came around me. I tipped my face up, and he put his mouth on mine. It was more comfort than anything, and I leaned in, soaking in the smell of him. I still wanted to go shoot Coach in the face, but I was so damn wrung-out tired. Truth be told, I wished I had the energy to go higher, and shoot God in the face as well.

As if he'd read my mind, Lawrence said, "There are good things coming, Ginny. I promise. I promise you, there's a balance."

I wanted to believe him, but there'd never been a trouble year like this one before. It almost made me hope I would die before I saw sixty and God came at me again. Every fifteen years I won a cosmic lotto for an Old Testament–style shit storm. Never the good stuff.

What I thought then, strangely enough, was something like a prayer. A whiny child's self-pitying, miserable prayer, but a prayer all the same, though God and I, we had not been on speaking terms for years. It was a "why me?," but it was more than that. In some deep, wordless piece of me, I found myself asking God if I would ever win one of the good things, if I would ever beat the odds the other way and stumble into huge, undeserved, and unexpected joy.

I had no expectations of any kind of answer. I wasn't even sure the God I was so angry with was there. But at that moment Lawrence buried his face into my hair, like he was breathing me, like I was oxygen and he needed me to live. I tilted my face up again, and he kissed me again, and I wanted nothing more than to lie down with him then. To let him touch me and make everything else go away, if only for a little piece of time.

He pulled back to smile at me, and I realized I ought not to be feeling this low-down coil of building heat. The dates had gotten away from me, but today I should be curled up in my ugly sweatpants drinking tea, smack in the middle of my clockwork period. I stared up at Lawrence, not even seeing him, doing math in my head.

I was three days late.

I thought, *Well, at my age I* should *start being late.* But I never had been before. It would be too much even for God, even this year, to throw me headlong into early menopause the same month I had sex for the first time in, literally, years. I started laughing then.

"I'm forty-five years old," I said to Lawrence. I fell back a step and leaned on the car. I was laughing so hard now I could barely choke the words out.

He looked puzzled, smiled and shrugged. "I'm forty-six."

"Once!" I choked out, howling now, with tears streaming down my cheeks. My insides hurt with it, I laughed so hard. "Once!"

"What?" he said. It was catching. He was chuckling now, too, helplessly, with no idea why, and that made me laugh harder.

I'd that moment asked when my turn to win against the odds would come, and now this? There had never been a worse time in my life to be pregnant, not ever, not even when I was fifteen. There couldn't be a worse time for any one woman to be pregnant in the history of Immita, Mississippi. I laughed and laughed, because Claire had tried to kill my daughter, I was being followed, I'd just learned that Coach had molested my child, Claire had probably guessed that Mosey was stolen, my other grandbaby was forever lost, I was an accessory after the fact in about a thousand felonies, and I was even now planning new ones to add to my tally.

Even so, even so, I leaned on the car, my arms looped around a man I loved so fierce and true it was like a living light in me, laughing, with him grinning down at me and shaking his head, and all I could feel in that moment was a bright gold wash of shining, shining hope.

CHAPTER EIGHTEEN

Liza

MOSEY IS FLOATING away from them. She's going under; Liza is losing her.

Liza thrusts her walker forward, following it as fast as she can, reckless and willful. She has to rescue Mosey. She stops dead in the doorway of Big's green-tiled bathroom, puzzled. There are no Grateful Dead bear stickers on the mirror, no peeling white lino, no ancient claw-foot tub. Liza is not in Montgomery, and Mosey needs a different kind of saving. She's desperate for it.

It's in her taut voice, the hunched shoulders as she turns away from them and keeps on turning. If Liza, fighting her own leg forward down the hall, can see this, then how can Big not see? Why is there no black angel to grab Big's eyes, shake them like dice, roll them toward Mosey? Big needs a harbinger, like Liza had.

Liza pushes the walker into the bathroom, but her good foot lands on the gray carpet of the Boulevard Branch Library. She pulls the bad foot into the library after her, and it is more than a dead piece she must drag. The leg feels stronger, or at least more eager, as she steps into her past.

Liza's lived with Janelle in Montgomery for more than a year now. They started partying after their loads of clothes were dry, and Liza crashed at Janelle's house. She's never left. Janelle likes how she helps with the baby. Even more, she likes how Liza always seems to know who's holding. They share the falling-down bungalow that belongs to Janelle's partially dead mother. The mother is dead enough that Liza has never seen her, but not quite enough for Janelle to stop getting her Social Security checks. There's an old-school fifties bomb shelter under the back where Janelle's sometimes boyfriend cooks up meth when they can get the stuff for it. That's why Liza's here. To meet the pockmarked stock boy from the pharmacy.

He's late. He's too ugly to be late, but she isn't what she goddamn used to be, now, is she? She's so skinny she can balance the salt shaker on her hipbone. She has to smile closemouthed to hide her teeth. She's off it now. She quit. Again. But if the pocky guy still feels okay about making her wait, what the hell good is being off it doing her?

Liza's sick with the shakes, and there's a hacking in her lungs she can't get rid of, even on days like today, when she's washed a Percocet down with half a bottle of Robitussin. The bookshelves and the furniture look like they've been constructed from plops of gray wallpaper paste. The very air is lukewarm sludge. Meth is not her problem. Life sucking is her problem. The only reason she's on a break right now is that Janelle has been tweaking bad for days and can't remember to give Jane Grace a bath. Or dinner. Or the time of fucking day.

The pocky guy will have something, though, maybe some Dilaudid. Liza finds herself cracking her knuckles. She's been quit more than a week, when she came home from an overnight at some guy's trailer and found Jane Grace crying in a diaper filled with two days' worth of her own leaking waste. Liza doesn't let that happen. Not usually.

But the pocky guy, he'll have something. Maybe meth, which she's off because Janelle is tweaking and so Liza can't forget Jane Grace. But Liza could write herself a note, maybe? Then she will remember. A note is all she needs.

"Dear Liza, pick up fruit and diapers, be home by six, and don't blow the pocky guy in the stacks again, no matter how many boxes of expired Sudafed he's got for you."

She goes to the bank of computers and logs in to her e-mail. It's the old flirtybits e-mail address, the one she set up on Melissa's home computer back when Hotmail was brand-new and they felt like the only real girls on the Internet. She hasn't used it in the last couple of years, but she could start again. She logs on, waiting for the slow-grinding library computer to bring up her in-box. She could write herself notes every day. Never forget again.

When the screen loads, there is a letter for her already waiting. It was sent more than three months ago.

I need to see you. I will come to you. Just say.

No signature, but Liza knows damn well who bitsyflirt@mcbob.net is. Who it has to be. She feels a mix of things, all in a jumble, but the loudest of the things sounds a lot like yes.

She sees the pocky guy's Honda turning in to the lot, and so she quickly types, Montgomery, Alabama. Friday. 4 PM. Krispy Kreme donuts on the corner of Alabaster and Pine. She hits Send before she can talk herself out of it.

She doesn't change her mind. Come Friday she's still quit, maybe a Vicodin and some Xanax here and there. She arrives at Krispy Kreme early, sitting at the counter facing the big plate-glass window. The machine glazes an army of doughnuts as they slide by in formation. She pours cream into her coffee, watching it bloom into surreal whipped cloud shapes in the oily black liquid. Melissa called that "Dalí in my coffee," back in the day.

As if thinking her name can conjure her, Melissa is there. She slides onto the stool by Liza. She's wearing crisp linen slacks and a white blouse. Immaculate. She's barely got on any makeup, and her hair is long, so straight it looks ironed. She smiles, and her eyes are warm, but surprised, too. Not to see Liza, but at the Liza she is seeing. Liza can suddenly smell herself, a dank, unpleasant thing, and Melissa smells like clean trees and lemon peel. Liza smiles back with her lips closed.

Melissa says, "We're glad you came."

The "we" tips Liza that the square-jawed guy is with her. He's a couple of years older than them. Blond hair. Big shoulders. This must be Mcbob, and he's Captain fucking America. He takes the stool by Melissa and smiles, too, very wide and white. "This is Liza?" It's clear from his tone that Liza is not the girl that Melissa described.

Liza stares down into Dalí blooming in her coffee, not stirring. Melissa is talking and talking. She is—of all damn things—apologizing. But she uses a warm, pity-filled voice to do it. She's catching Liza up, filling her in on what came after that bad day on the beach. She got to go straight home after the hospital. Her family lawyer had the cops at bay, for the moment. That night she paced her room, wanting to pull off sheets of her itching skin, wanting to bang her head into the wall until the thinking stopped. Just before dawn she left. Stepped out of her life as it if were a pair of too-tight shoes.

She ran off, just like Liza. Except first. She makes that very clear in her Melissa way.

"I was very self-destructive," she says. "Drugs." She lays her hand on Liza's shoulder in such moist and cloying sympathy that Liza is dizzy with the urge to lean down and bite a chunk out of her forearm.

Captain F. America is the guy who has remade her life. Helped her get clean. Helped her change her name and start fresh.

"I'm here to make amends," Melissa says. "My therapist says it was my dad who had the power in the relationship. Not you. For sure not me. It was easier to blame you. . . ."

Her buzzwords run together: Toxic environment. Atonement. Process.

Even so, Liza hears the message: Melissa landed on her feet. She killed that baby, same as Liza, maybe more than Liza, but she's clean and blond and shiny and forgiven. She's finishing her steps. She's rehabbed and reborn, the girl with everything, version 2.0. There's a modest diamond winking on her finger.

Captain America says, "Liza. Let us help. There's a center where Melissa went..."

Liza smiles with her lips closed and her eyes dead. She rises. It is time to walk away. Melissa grabs her hand, and Liza would yank her own away, but she realizes that Melissa's hand is pressing money into hers. The money and Melissa's pity-soaked smile, they are nothing more than ways to say, *I Win.* The *I Win* is there, under every therapy-soaked platitude and patronizing kindness.

The worst part is, it's true. Melissa is winning. Liza's hand closes around the bills, like she's having a muscle spasm in her fingers. She wants to throw them in Melissa's face, followed by a volley of her own slick spit, but she needs the bills, needs what they will buy, too much.

She walks out, with Melissa calling after, "Our door is always open. You know my e-mail!"

Liza does not look back. She hasn't seen Melissa Richardson since.

She heads to Reg's place. Reg is always holding. Half an hour later, Melissa doesn't matter. She is Liza and beautiful and good, striding into Reg's bedroom, confident, riding him and blind with the brightness of being happy.

She's happy until she isn't anymore. Until Reg and the money are all used up. She dozes, but Reg's bed feels like it is made of cold oatmeal. She's half submerged in it. Melissa won. She should hitch down to Mobile, walk into the bay, and keep walking until it closes cool and blue over her and Melissa will realize she has caused this, yes, sent a girl into the ocean once a-fucking-gain. It seems like a good idea until she remembers Jane Grace. She almost never forgets Jane Grace, but this is the third time now. No, fourth. Only the fourth, which isn't so bad, not really. Only the fourth time she forgot the baby.

She finds herself outside, and it is nighttime, and she doesn't even know what night. She's running for home, fast as she can, with the street feeling tacky and sticky under her feet. The road wants her to lie down and sink into the tar.

She pushes on, though. Janelle is worthless. She's forgotten Jane Grace a thousand times. Liza has only forgotten her three. No, four. Liza is the one who remembers, who cuddles and cleans and makes jam sandwiches and who knows the words to Big's old country lullabies. Liza has been in love with Jane Grace ever since the day in the laundry, when she got herself invited into Jane Grace's life instead of stealing her; Liza doesn't much like the rare days Janelle remembers that she has a kid and tries to reclaim territory, but now she desperately hopes Janelle is home. She tries to believe in a Janelle who is making mac-a-chee and running the fuzzy *Dora the Explorer* tapes over and over so Jane Grace won't bug her.

The house is ablaze with light, but Janelle has gone out. Liza runs from room to empty room. Den, galley kitchen, Janelle's bedroom, her own room, the walk-in closet where Jane Grace sleeps. Most nights Jane Grace gets up off her mattress and creeps past her mother's bed to come climb in with Liza. It's Liza she looks for every morning. Liza she calls when her knee is skinned or the bad dreams come. Now Liza forgot her, and every room is empty.

The last place she looks is the bathroom, and her heart stops. The tub is full of water, and Jane Grace is in the tub. A listing rubber ducky and three little black baby turds bob on the surface. The tub is an old-fashioned claw-foot kind, with walls too high and slippy for Jane Grace to scale. Jane Grace's limbs are still and pale, and the skin around her closed eyes looks swollen. The ends of her flossy hair float. Her face is half under the water. Her mouth is under. She is so still.

A bad black is washing over Liza, the fast feel of her own heart bursting, when she sees a ripple on the water's surface. Jane Grace's snub nose is above the waterline, and the ripple is her breathing, in and out.

Liza runs to the tub. She snatches a dirty towel up off the floor as she goes, and as she bends and reaches, she is remembering a yellow blanket, the baby who stopped breathing in the night. She kissed that little face a thousand times, her lips pushing warm air, two fingers pressing the tiny chest, but she couldn't call back the breath, couldn't make the heart beat. At last Liza wrapped that baby tight and lowered her into the earth. Her arms have been so empty, she's been so black and empty since that night. Now her arms fill as she is lifting Jane Grace out of the water, wrapping her chilled body in the towel. Jane Grace moans and turns in her arms.

"This isn't a place for babies," Liza tells her, and Jane Grace mutters and buries her wet, tear-swollen face into Liza's chest. Jane Grace smells faintly of urine, and her skin is clammy and wrinkled into prunes on every tip, but she is breathing and her hands fist themselves in Liza's long, dirty hair. As she wakes, she smells the bad smell that is Liza and she smiles.

Liza stands up, Jane Grace in her arms. She's loved Jane Grace from the day she almost stole her at the laundry, but it isn't love that comes now to save them. When she works the baby's socks on, she's thinking of Melissa, not love. She remembers how they met at Rich People VBS, when there were only two pairs of pink scissors and Melissa and Liza got them every day. She remembers Claire Richardson smacking the smiling Bible-times people onto the felt board, telling their black, violent stories in a perky voice.

Now Liza says to the sleepy-faced baby, "I'm going to name you Moses, because I pulled you from the water. Only you." She slots the baby's arms into her outgrown jacket, thinking of a rattle-bellied stuffed duck, how she and Melissa let the ocean take the one baby and so God took the other. She is taking this one. "I'm going to name you Willow, because a willow is a special tree."

The baby says, "I Jane Grace!"

Liza says, "Yes. You are. You're my Mosey Willow and everybody's Jane Grace, too. But I have to go away now. You want to come home with your Liza?"

Mosey Willow Jane Grace clenches herself, arms and legs wrapping so tight around Liza that it's a choke hold and an answer.

Love alone doesn't make Liza head for the highway with Jane Grace stuffed in her old baby sling, looking for a ride out of town. It hasn't been enough, not once, this whole damn year. Today love has Liza's history, pushing her forward like a loaded gun pressed hard into her spine; she is Liza Slocumb. She is Big's girl, and she'll be damned and dead before she'll let Melissa Richardson beat her.

Liza stares down into the empty tub in Big's green-tiled bathroom. Today Liza cannot do the thing Melissa failed to do. There is no baby to pull from the water. Mosey is mostly grown now, and it isn't so simple to stop her from sinking. Mosey is going under, and Liza doesn't know how to stop it.

She turns her walker, and her feet follow, the good one, then the bad one, too. She turns the walker again, but the bathroom is so narrow. The walker's legs knock hard against the bathroom trash can. The can dumps over, its contents spilling out across the floor.

The stick rolls out last. It must have been buried down deep, hidden under crumpled tissue and mini–Dixie cups and dental flossers. It lands faceup.

Two pink lines. Liza knows what that means.

Liza's mouth opens, and a loud and angry vowel comes out. A long *O* that rises up high in pitch and volume until it is an endless wail. Too late. Too late. She saw Mosey drifting but was helpless, and Big saw nothing, and it is all too late. Now Mosey and Big come, crowding the doorway as Liza howls and howls, and then they see it.

"Oh, my God!" Mosey says. "But I didn't even...I haven't... They're all under the floor!"

Big rushes forward, passing Mosey to take Liza in her arms. She presses awkwardly against the walker, leaning over it to squeeze Liza tight and shush her. "It isn't Mosey. Mosey is not pregnant. It's me. It's me. It's me."

Liza's voice cuts out. She looks over Big's shoulder at Mosey. At Mosey's stricken face. She stares from the stick to Big and back again.

Two pink lines.

"It's a good thing, it's the best thing," Big croons, so happy.

But Mosey is rolling away from them, away from Liza's fear and Big's accidental joy. Mosey turns and keeps on turning, turning away. Then she's gone.

CHAPTER NINETEEN

Mosey

IT WAS ONLY me and Roger. Patti wouldn't go. At lunch Monday she said skipping school and driving to Montgomery to find halfcocked57 was the dumb-assest idea she had ever heard in her whole life.

I said, "'Dumb-assest' isn't a word, and if you knew where your mom was, would you go to there or sit through world history?"

Patti muttered, "Well, but I have at least met my damn mom before. You don't even know who you're going to see."

"You don't have to come, but you do need to cover my butt," I said. "Can you tomorrow go by the front office and drop off my out-sick note?" I had a good one, courtesy of Roger.

She dumped her head down so her bang strings covered almost all her face and then glared at me through them. I thought she was going to say no, but in the end she snatched the note out of my hand.

"I'm telling anyone who asks that you're puking and pooping everywhere."

The drive took four hours and seventeen minutes, which was a long time. We could have stopped and turned around ninety million different places. I guess I had more than four hours and seventeen minutes' worth of pissed-off at Big, because I never even suggested it. We listened to all Roger's mix CDs, and Roger did steering-wheel drum solos while I played mean-ass, angry air guitar. We ate Hardee's lard biscuits, and every minute felt completely fake, like a movie of a road trip we'd seen before and were redoing.

It got realer as we got closer, though. Maybe I thought about turning back a couple of times. But I kept seeing Big's pee stick lying on the bathroom floor. She tried to talk to me about it, but I so was not having that conversation. Her face was all worry forehead and serious sorry mouth, but little burbles of happy kept squooshing out around the edges. Good for her. If she ever did figure out that Liza had brought home an impostor baby, she'd have a really-hers replacement already cooking.

Meantimes I didn't want to know about whoever Lawrence was or listen to her apply her "Everyone makes mistakes, it's what you do after that shows your true character" speech to her having gross, old-people sex while I sat all nunned up through Algebra I, right behind Beautiful Jack Owens and never once even sneak-touched the back of his floppy blond hair. I put my fingers in my ears and sang, "Lar lar lar!" super loud until she hollered, "Okay, Mosey! I get it. But we have to talk sometime."

About what? How the queen of Mosey-Keep-Your-Pants-On hadn't managed it? About how sex was a battlefield and anyone who decided to go on the battlefield could get shot? Especially Slocumbs, apparently. Big didn't know I wasn't one.

I finally told her I needed her to crawl down out of my butt for five seconds, give me a minute to breathe. She agreed, but she wanted to know when we could talk. I instantly said, "Tuesday night." Of course, I already had plans with Roger to skip school and head for Montgomery on Tuesday morning, so either I wouldn't make the appointment or we'd have hella more to talk about.

By the time we took our exit off I-65, Roger was vibrating like that weird fork that Mr. Bell bings at assembly before the chorus dorks out on a madrigal. MapQuest said the Fox Street address was less than two miles away. I knew we weren't in a good place the second I saw the greasy-looking Krispy Kreme with the fritzed-out neon sign flashing H T D NUTS NO .

"That's my new deejay name," Roger said, pointing. "Hot D Nuts No."

"There's no *o* in the 'hot,'" I said, and my voice sounded small and shaky.

Roger shot me a glance and said, all bucking-up like and hearty, "Well, I'm adding it. 'H T D Nuts No' sounds like VD medication."

I didn't answer. My stomach was starting to feel all puffy and sour, like a pillow stuffed full of diseased feathers. The neighborhood only got worse. We passed a liquor store and TitleMax, which Big called ThiefleMax, then a pawnshop with heavy-duty jail bars over a window full of guns and car-stereo parts. A check-cashing place shared a dirty building with something called the Gas-N-Gro, which told me we were in a place where people were too crimey to get a checking account and too stupid to know that "Gro" was not a true abbreviation for "groceries." Not good.

There was a mean-eyed drunk guy swaying on the curb. Roger ogled him the way Yellowstone tourists look at bears, so fascinated that he was ready to throw marshmallows and bologna with no idea he would for sure get his arm pulled off and chewed. He said, "If some Duckins lived in the city, this would be the part of the city they lived in."

I looked at the MapQuest directions he had printed and said, "Take a right at the Gas-N-Gro." As we swung around the store, I added, "Whoever Liza stole me from, they probably buy their Twinkies and forties there."

"To eat together?" Roger said, aghast but totally missing the point.

This street was full of trashed, squatty houses, and the next street was Fox, which meant Fox was a real street. I was seeing it. Then I was sitting in a car that was driving down it. There would be a real house with the number 91 on it, and inside, halfcocked57 was listening to music or cooking eggs, maybe petting the cat. I couldn't make halfcocked57 be my bio mom or dad or, best of all, be somehow in a magic lucky way no relation of mine at all. The person in the house was already who they were, real and separate from me, and I couldn't change it. All I got to do was decide if I wanted to see or not.

I was almost out of time to decide, and the air thicked up into Jell-O. It felt to me like the Volvo had to shove and rev through it. I was trying to say something, but it took a long time.

What I said was, "Never mind."

Roger stopped the car. I blinked. I couldn't believe he stopped so instantly, like it was that easy. Except not, because there was a rusty mailbox right by my window. It had a nine on it and the shiny shape of a one, like the metal had been protected but recently the one had fallen off. He'd stopped because we were already here.

The mailbox belonged to a square, pink bungalow made of rotty siding. The paint was peeling away all over, and the house was gray underneath. The yard was part overgrown and part dead. It was no different from any other rotty, sag-roofed house on the street. Maybe a little worse off, but not by much. There was a dead azalea and another mostly dead one framing the porch steps, the dead one's naked branches stretching toward the railing like long, brown, knobby fingers.

I grabbed my backpack before I got out of the car, carrying it by one strap, like a purse. I had taken all my books out and left them in my locker yesterday, but the pack didn't feel light. The gun's box hung low in it, making it feel all weighty and serious.

Roger got out, too, and came up even with me, jingling his keys. For first time since he'd sliced my freakin' life open with

Occam's razor, he looked uncertain. It was past eleven in the morning, but the whole narrow street was dead, as if the people who lived here were nocturnal or had all been body-snatched away.

"Come on," I said. Me, not him. Part because I was too close now to stop and part because Roger was in his crisp school uniform. I'd put on this flowered skirt and my nicest peach T-shirt. I felt too colory and shining, like we looked as eatable as Hansel and Gretel on a street full of falling-down candy houses.

I hurried us up to the porch. The steps sagged and squeaked under my feet. I put my hand on the railing, but it wobbled. I let go and went up all five steps with no help, one leg after another.

I shot Roger's jingle-jangling keys a glance and said, "You are on my last nerve with that."

He gave me a sickly, almost green-faced grin and put them in his pocket.

We stood in front of the door with our feet together, side by side like we were lining up for preassembly at Cal. It was a plain wooden door, no screen. No peephole. Someone had painted it charcoal gray a million years ago. I started to shake my head, and Roger put a thumb out and ground it into the doorbell. I heard his thumb clicketing against the button, but it didn't bong inside.

"It's broken," he said, and then stood there like that was his whole big plan all along, to push a doorbell, and now that it hadn't worked out, he was flat stumped.

I made a *hmf* noise at him and pushed it myself. The button rattled in the socket, feeling like whatever it used to press had fallen away into the space between the walls. I reached out with one hand to knock, soft, and the door swung away from me a couple of inches. My eyes widened. I looked at Roger, and he was looking back at me. It wasn't latched, even, much less locked.

Roger got a little less green, and he cocked his head sideways, interested. He put both hands on the door and pushed harder.

It swung wide, making a *scraw*ing noise like a sleepy crow. We froze.

Nothing happened. No one came.

We were looking into a den with a ratty sofa running along the back wall. A squatty seventies-style coffee table sat in front of the sofa, every bit of it covered with dirty plates and coffee mugs and fast-food bags and a bong and junk mail stacked three deep. Outside, it was this gorgeous, sunny day, but it was like the blue sky and the crispy clean air couldn't cross the threshold. A dim slice of sunlight made an arc on the carpet through the open door, but it looked faded and it didn't seem to have any, like, conviction.

"Hello," I said. I meant to call it, but it came out scratchy and soft. I found my hand reaching for Roger's hand, and he took it, and we held on tight with clammy sweat springing up between our palms. I stepped gingerly inside, towing him with me onto that slice of fadey sunlight.

"Hello?" I tried again. Still soft. We stepped farther into the dark of the house. I could see what looked like a kitchen through a doorway on one side and a hallway on my right.

We took two or three more steps in, angling toward the hallway.

That was when we heard that sleepy-crow sound again, but louder and harsher, like the crow had woken up pissed. We whirled as the door banged shut behind us. I heard a short, high scream, almost a bark. I wasn't sure if it was Roger or me that made it. We'd lost each other's hands. A man was sitting in this gutted recliner. It pressed against the wall next to the door, and we had walked in right past him. He was huge. He filled up the chair and then some. He'd put one saucepan hand on the door and banged it shut, and now he sat with his hand still on it, like he was holding it closed.

He smiled at us, a big smile, but not nice. His teeth looked like weird gray moss, growing in spongy squares out of his red gums. He had Riff Raff hair, bald on top and then long side scrabbles.

"Hey, kittens," he said.

"It was open!" I said, and it came out so high and squeaky I sounded like a cartoon mouse. I tried to pull it down as I said, "I'm looking for someone?"

"I know what you looking for, sugar," he said. He said it all oiled, like fake nice. His eyes shone and gleamed in a way that was so, so, so not right. He stood up, and he was even huger than I thought. His chest was like a slab, and his arms looked thick and meaty. I backed up one step, not able to help it, and Roger did, too. He said to Roger, "Let's see the green."

"What?" Roger said.

Then the guy's face clicked over to anger. It happened so fast. "Cash, asshole," he said. "I look like I take fuckin' Visa?"

Roger blinked, and when he spoke, it was all stutter and not like him, and that scared me more than anything. "No, we were... um, l-looking for a person? From an e-mail address. Half-cocked57. We came to see—"

In two big strides, the guy's long legs ate up every bit of good space that had been between us. He stood over us, all loomy and huge, and I was scared most by that shine in his eyes, like that was all the soul he had shining on the surface there, and under his skin it was all worms and black holes. He flicked the logo on Roger's shirt, and Roger flinched.

"Dumb-ass little slumming richy kids, can even you be stupid enough to not bring cash?"

Roger said, "We can go get some. I have my mom's bank card." His voice was high, too, like he'd sucked helium, but so not funny.

That made the guy chuckle, low and mean.

"Your mom's bank card," he repeated, like it had been a punch line in a joke he wanted to remember.

Then he turned those shiny, weird eyes on me. I'd seen kids

stoned at school before, but this wasn't that. I hadn't ever seen a person look like this in the eyes. Now, with his face pointed at me, I saw a bunch of scab-spackled sore spots on his face, like he'd picked himself open. He was looking at me, but he was talking to Roger still, I could tell.

"Yeah, buddy, you run on out to the AT-fuckin'-M. I'll keep your little friend here company."

He smiled at me, and the dim light of the lamp behind me gleamed off his weird gray teeth. I took a step back. He crowded in after, and I took another step and found myself squashed in between the floor lamp and the arm of the sofa, my back against the wall. All at once I wanted the gun so bad. I couldn't understand why I had left it inside a box inside a pouch in a zipped-closed backpack. I wanted it free, in my hand, and then I remembered I had never even looked to see if it was loaded. I didn't know how to check, even.

The big guy's hand came at me, and I flinched, but all he did was give the side of my hair a tug, almost friendly, like my hair was a horse's mane. His hand smelled like that after-match smell. My breath caught.

I knocked his arm away and said, "Stop it."

His shiny eyes stayed on me, but he was still talking to Roger. "She's feisty, huh? You like 'em all sassy, yeah?"

"Stop it," Roger said, like an echo.

The gun hung like a huge weight in my backpack. It would take so long to get to it. I should trick him, say I had money in my pack in my pouch in my cash box. But his hand was coming up again, reaching toward me, that burned-match smell, and I couldn't stand to have it on me. I swung the backpack at him, using the gun's weight in the bottom, swung as hard as I could.

He caught it in one massive hand, and he grinned. He ripped the whole bag away from me and tossed it behind him, toward Roger, grinning at me with a weird, shiny confidence, not scared of anything. He stepped closer, and now I couldn't even see Roger, but I hoped to God he knew to get the gun out, now. The big man blocked out everything.

I thought, *This is drugs. This is what Liza was like. This is what I am not supposed to do or be.*

Part of me was all calm and stepping away out of myself, noticing how all the obvious, boring things Big and Liza said to me a thousand times were so much truer and realer than I ever thought. Drugs *were* bad. I *shouldn't* go to dark places all alone with boys. I wanted to holler that I had learned all these super-valuable lessons now, and so please someone needed to come and get me and say, *See, Mosey? Now you know it is all all so very true, and let's go home.*

But no one came, and his big hand was coming at me again.

I ducked under his arm, and I ran. It was the wrong way, toward the hall instead of the front door, but anywhere away from him was good. I heard Roger yelling, "Stop it, stop it!" but I didn't know where Roger was.

I didn't even make it out of the den. The guy's long ape arm snagged me and picked me right up off the ground, so my arms were pinned. I kicked and flailed my feet at the air. I could hear myself screaming and Roger screaming, too, behind us. The guy put his other hand over my mouth and nose to stop me, and I couldn't hardly breathe, and I was too scared of him to bite him.

Roger hollered words then. "I will call the cops!"

The guy laughed. He didn't even turn around, just started walking toward the hall with me kicking helpless at the air.

"And I will snap your fuckin' neck. Shut up and be glad I'll take a piece of this instead of cash."

My whole body started jackknifing in his arms like a fish, trying to get away from him. I thought I might be peeing, and I almost laughed because it seemed not real, except his crazy, shiny eyes had already told me he would rape me anyway, pee or no, and

I could feel what I thought might be his dick, hard and pressed against my butt. I whipped my whole body with all my strength, fighting so hard, but he held me like all my mightiness was nothing. I was too breathless now to scream, and he shifted his hand from off my mouth, moved it down to rumple at my boob.

He called to Roger, real casual over his shoulder as he walked away with me, "She ain't got tits for squat," like he was complaining. Like Roger could have brought him something better.

I kicked backward, hard, trying for his shin, but I got nothing, and this was really happening, and I couldn't stop it.

Then I heard Roger say, "You put her down, or I am going to shoot you. I am going to shoot you a lot in your back."

That made him stop. He still had his hand on my boob, like he forgot it was there, though it was burning me like acid eating through my clothes. He turned around, so I was a shield hanging between him and the gun. The SIG twitched and wobbled in Roger's hands, and I was staring into the weaving black hole at the front of it. I got still then, too.

There was an endless pause. I looked down that black hole, and everything in me and the room and the world went deadly quiet. Then the guy threw me. He tossed me toward Roger like I was weightless paper. I landed on my hands and knees, and I scrambled away from him, wedging myself against the wall by the lamp again, pressed up against the sofa's side. He walked slow to Roger, and I could see his crazy drug face and it was fearless. Roger's hands had gone white on the gun, he was squeezing so hard, and nothing happened and nothing happened. Then the guy reached him, and he ripped the SIG out of Roger's hands and tossed it away, back behind him near the hallway. He was between both of us and it.

"Safety, numbnuts," he said to Roger, and grinned this ugly grin. "Oh, how I love me some dumb-ass rich kids."

His big hand swung out hard, and it caught Roger in the

face. Roger tumped over backward. I found my voice and started screaming for real. I grabbed the first thing I found in my hand, and it was the floor lamp. I picked it up like a bat, and I ran at him swinging it and screaming and screaming. I hit him with it twice before he caught it and wrenched at it so hard he tore me off my feet. I went down still screaming, and I saw something zinging through the air past me. Roger had pulled himself up on the coffee table and was throwing the plates. The guy ducked, and the first plate shattered into the wall like a bomb going off. The second thunked into the guy's arm with a meat-slapped sound. Roger was screaming, too, words, but I couldn't understand them. The guy laughed this awful raging laugh and wading toward me through the glasses that Roger was throwing now, batting them away. I tried to crawl backward away, but he dropped down to all fours and grabbed my ankle and pulled me across the floor toward him.

That was when the world blew up. It exploded into this most loudest bang that rang the air and kept on ringing after. It was a noise like the end of the world, and we all just stopped.

It was the SIG.

A woman had come up the hallway in all the loudness and gotten the SIG and pointed it up and made it shiver the world with its huge, booming voice.

No one moved, except the woman. She scrubbed at her eyes with her free hand, all sleepy, and plaster came sifting down from the ceiling in a powdery hail where she'd shot it.

"Mother*fuck*, Janelle," the guy said, letting go of my ankle and pushing himself into a squat. My heart had stuttered, and every hair I had was standing straight up, but the guy, he rose to his feet and turned to her, like, *exasperated*.

She took her hand down away from her face, and then he didn't matter anymore. I could only look at her. I heard Roger, behind me, breathe the words "Holy shit," and I knew he was looking at her, too.

She was me. She was me if I was old and awful and a monster. Her thin hair was my color hair, her scabbed-up nose was my shape nose. She wore my own wide mouth pulled down into my exact mad frown. She was a gray skin sack stretched too tight over my very own shape of bones. She was me.

I glanced at Roger, standing frozen with the bong lifted up in one arm, ready to hurl it like a round, glass javelin. He was staring at her, and his arm slowly lowered. I stared at her, too, but she was only looking at the big scary guy.

She had a scratchy voice, clogged up with sleepy, and she croaked, "What is going on in my goddamn house? Huh? Huh? Now you made me shoot a gun, and my whore neighbor will call the cops if she is goddamn home. Chuck, you need to get the product and go out the back door." She glanced at me and Roger, then said, "And who—"

She saw me. Her creaky voice got stuck in her throat. She looked and looked at me with my own eyes. Her voice tried to make more words, but they petered out into panting. The gun wobbled, and her hands dropped so it was pointing at the floor. Finally she got words out. Two.

She said, "Jane Grace?"

I answered so fast, so loud. "No."

"Jane Grace," she said again, but this time, there wasn't a question sound to it.

"No," I said again. "No. I am just some girl."

"What's up, Janelle?" the scary guy said.

The woman didn't take her eyes off me, not at all. She said, "Chuck, get the goddamn product out the back. And this, too." She held out the SIG.

"Oh, right," he said, and he took it and headed down the hallway like this whole day with the attempted rape and the shooting and the plates coming at his head was a normal day in his life. I sat on my ass on the carpet with my boob burning from where he had touched it with his grossness, and I was looking at my mother.

"You're so pretty," my mother said. "You're so prettier than pictures."

I think I was crying. "I'm not her," I said.

We looked at each other for a long time, me crying and her standing there. She looked at me like she was drinking me. She looked at my nice skirt and my hair and my face, her eyes going place to place, and they were my shape, my color, except the whites were the color of dirty snow and her lids looked stretched out so far they'd gone saggy. She took one step toward me, and I scrabbled backward, and I would die and burn up into an ash pile if she touched me.

I said so loud I was yelling, "I'm just some girl! I'm just some girl!"

She stopped. She didn't step toward me again. She twisted her hands together in a worrying way. She looked at me for what seemed like a long time, with my ragged breathing the only sound in the room. In the pause I could see her deciding something, because she made my very own deciding face. Then she blinked and swallowed, and finally she spoke. "My neighbor really might call the cops. You kids better scoot." It started out very plain and matter-of-fact, like she was talking to a mailman, but her voice cracked near the end, and I could tell she was close to crying.

I felt a hand on me, and I almost came out of my skin, but it was Roger, helping me up. He'd dropped the bong on the floor, and we could hear the water gurgling out onto the carpet.

That woman watched me with her ruined eyes still all huge, like eating eyes, and Roger and I backed up and backed up. He got his hand on the door, and I heard that beautiful sound like a crow scraw. Sunlight came in behind us, so unkind, and lit up the gray-faced ghost that was my mother.

She let us go. And I was crying still, because it was so plain that this was mercy. She let me go.

Roger slammed the door shut behind us, and we ran for his Volvo. We got inside and locked it, and his hands were shaking so hard he couldn't get the key to go in. He laughed, kind of hysterical sounding, and said, "Do you see this?" nodding at how the keys wouldn't go.

I hadn't stopped crying in a thousand years, but all at once it really amped up. I was letting out these awful whooping cries.

He said, "Mosey..." and he stopped trying to get the key in. "I think she..."

But I couldn't even think of her yet. I couldn't stand to hear him say anything about her. She was too big and for later. I whooped out another huge sob, and I hollered over him, "He touched me on my boob!" Roger shut up and looked at me all helpless, not sure what to do with that. "I didn't want him to, and he did anyway, and then he complained about it! Like my boob wasn't good enough!"

This was the only place I could get to now; that big guy's hand on me and how it shouldn't be that way. It should be my first boyfriend, whoever that would be, and I should just like him so much. We should be in his car, in the dark, maybe behind the DQ with our mouths all cold from ice cream, but warming as we went on kissing and kissing for a long time, and I should be wondering if I was falling in love with him, and his hand should creep sweet up my waist all careful, waiting to see if I would stop him, and I wouldn't. It should matter, and it should be like a present we would give each other, me and a boy I liked just so very much. I didn't know how to say all that, but it was in my head, and all I could say was, "Like, seriously, he gets to *complain*?"

Somehow Roger got it. I know he got it, because he put his keys down in his lap and he turned to me and his face was very serious. He reached out slow with his hand, and I knew what he would do, and I sat there, and he did it. He put his hand right over my boob, the one the scary guy had grabbed. He took it like he was meeting it, formally, shaking hands. His pinkie was a little under, so his hand cupped it. I went still, and his face washed into a blush, this bright tide of red coming up his neck and flushing his whole face. His breath changed, going short.

He said, "Well. It's my first boob. And I think it's goddamn perfect."

He never said "goddamn" because of being Baptist. But he said it now and meant it, and he sounded all strangled about it. Then I smiled at him, and it was like I felt myself going all clean under his hand. He was taking it away, what that scary guy did, because he so, so very meant it, and he was my best friend. It wasn't at all romantic or anything like that. I didn't want to kiss him now and be all, oh, yay, a boyfriend. He was only my best friend Roger, fixing my tit for me.

Then someone banged the window with a fist, and he jerked his hand away. I screamed because I thought it was the cops or, worse, that the zombie mother who was me had changed her mind and come out after us. It was even worse than all that, though.

Roger jerked his hand off my boob too slow, and I was outside my secret corpse-mother's house, and glaring in the window at me, banging at it with her fist, was Big. Big in Montgomery. Big losing her total shit.

It was the worst possible thing, but I was so glad to see her. I tore the door open, almost knocking her down with it. She came around it, and I spilled out into her arms, already crying more.

She clamped me to her, hard and said over my head to Roger, "You! Start your damn car and follow me. I want to see you in my rearview every second all the way home. I am going to get you safe back to your parents before I decide if I have to murder you. And if I ever see you with your hand where it just was? You will be drawing back a nub. You hear me, mister?"

My face was pressed hard into Big, the warm brown-sugar-and-vanilla smell of her. I heard Roger say, "Yes, ma'am." Then the car door slammed.

Big hauled me along the street to her Malibu, parked right behind us, and I hadn't even noticed her coming. She pushed me against the side of the car and grabbed me by the shoulders, her eyes going up and down me. All at once I felt how dirty and crumpled I was, my clothes all twisted up and filthy from the fight.

"Are you hurt?" I didn't answer, and she rattled me around by my shoulders. "Mosey. Are you hurt? Did anyone hurt you?"

I shook my head. She dug her hands into me harder and stared into my eyes until I said, "No, really. We got out okay. I'm okay."

Then her eyes sprang up full of tears. She dashed them away, mad. She put me in the passenger seat like I was this limp little rag, and I was. I sat there snuffling as she came around and got in the car. She peeled away from the curb and drove toward the highway. I sat there thinking how the cops still hadn't come, which was the scariest part of all. I had screamed and screamed, and a shot was fired, and that man could have done anything to me and taken the gun and shot us and buried us under the almost-dead azalea for plant food, and who would have ever known?

That started me up again. I cried like a dork all the way to the interstate and for a few miles down it, until my eyes were so grainy and dry they couldn't make tears.

Big was so mad her lips were white, and her one hand was white on the wheel, too, like she was strangling it, but she put her other hand on me, soft on my leg. She squeezed me gentle and sweet, her palm warm through the thin material of my crumply skirt.

When I could talk, I said, "How did you find me?"

"Patti called this morning while I was getting ready for work. And don't you be mad," she said. "That girl is a good friend to you. Tattling was the smartest thing any of the three of you has ever done in your whole lives."

I wasn't even a speck mad at Patti. I wanted to kiss Patti on the face, because it was so good to be in the car with Big driving away from that place with that woman in it saying, "Jane Grace?" like a question and then, worse, "Jane Grace." Like she knew. When she said those last two of all my names, there was a sound to her voice, and a bell tolled in me like an answer. The way she said that part of my name stirred a pot full of memories I couldn't get to, old ones, alive in my underbrain, and they knew that name and answered to it.

We went fast down 65, and I could see Roger's Volvo in the rearview, obediently staying right behind us. We were quiet for a long time. I was thinking about that woman now, that house, the scary guy's gray teeth and how my mom-monster was missing a bunch. Her mouth slacked open in the sunlight had been full of gaps so that her lips crunched in like an old lady's lips.

Big drove, intense and quiet, her hand warm on me. I mostly didn't want to think. I mostly wanted to go home and climb into Liza's bed and press up beside her and sleep for a week with Big sitting in the chair beside to keep us safe.

But Big didn't leave it alone. "What was it like there? What were they like?"

I didn't know quite how to answer that. That man's hand on me. Her eating-me-alive yellowy eyes. When I finally did answer, my voice was all trembly and high. "It's not a good place. They were very bad."

Big breathed out, like relieved. Like this was a good answer.

"I knew that Liza wouldn't hook you from some happy little mommy at a McDonald's. I mostly knew. But it's Liza, and she doesn't have the world's best judgment, and she couldn't tell me.... A tiny piece of me worried I was keeping you from something you deserved to have. That I was helping some good souls someplace stay broken."

My heart went bang in my chest. She was talking like she knew I wasn't Liza's real kid, like she knew that the real Mosey Slocumb had been under the willow all these years. I gulped and asked, "Did Patti tell you *everything*?"

Big cocked an eyebrow. "Patti is a teenage girl, so I seriously doubt that. But she told me where you'd gone." She took her hand off my leg long enough to poke an angry thumb back at the Volvo. "I should have known that kid would clue in. I watched him look at those pictures of Liza's and come up with the word 'poison' in eleven seconds." Her nostrils flared, and she shook her head.

So she knew. She knew now. An awful thing reared up in me, an awful thing I had to ask, but I couldn't say it out loud to her. So I asked instead, "Are you upset Liza stole me?"

Big shook her head, immediately, but she kept her eyes on the road. "It's done. Looking at that place, looking at you now, I can guess enough to understand why she did it. How long were you inside?"

"Hardly any time at all," I said, and that was true. It seemed like we were in there forever and I came out the door fifty years old, but really we hadn't been in there more than five minutes. I couldn't ask still, not the only thing that mattered, but I sidled up a little closer to it.

"Were you upset when Patti told you?"

She snorted again, even louder. "'Upset' does not cover it. I was so scared and furious all at once. I drove here like a crazy woman. I called your cell phone a thousand times."

I said, "Patti had it. So me and Roger could text her what happened."

"Oh, dear God," Big said, on a long exhale. "You all three need to be spanked and then grounded until you are past thirty and have some sense. I might let Patti off the hook at twenty-five."

I peeped sideways at her. She was mad, but not all the way at me, I didn't think. More mad at us as a group and just, like, everything. That was why I could finally say the hard thing I wasn't sure I even wanted her to answer.

"Don't you care?"

She shot me a glance. "Of course. I mean, what? About what?"

My voice was all small. "About what Patti told you. About I have another mom."

Big's eyebrows came down, and she didn't answer. She started scanning the road ahead. She pressed her foot on the gas to speed up, and then she took the next exit we came to. She turned and cruised into the parking lot of the closest gas station. Roger followed us in and then sat behind us idling, I guess too terrified of Big to get out and come see what was up. Probably a good call.

She shut off the engine and turned toward me. I was looking down at my hands, twisting them together in my lap, but she said, "Hey," and then she said it again, twice more, until I looked at her. Her eyes were burning at me, all deadly serious. "Patti told me *where* you were, Mosey, and why. That's all. She didn't have to tell me anything more. I already knew who you were. I mean, who you weren't. I already knew for a long time that the baby Liza gave birth to was under the willow."

That couldn't be so. I said, "No, but how?" because Big didn't have a Roger.

Big said, "It was just one of those senseless, awful things, Mosey. Crib death, they call it. Liza was so young, I think she panicked, and her heart was broken. She made some bad decisions. She buried that child, and she ran."

I shook my head. I was glad to know for sure, about my mom and the little bones, but she'd misunderstood me. "Not how did it happen. How did you know?"

Big's eyes softened, going all kinds of misty. "Liza's silver box. The pink dress. The duck. I knew who owned those things."

I said, sounding really slow and dumb, "So but then... but if you knew the whole time? Why didn't you say?"

"I was trying to keep you from knowing," Big said, smiling a ghosty version of her own real smile. She shot an ire glance at the Volvo.

But it still couldn't be so. Because nothing had changed. She had stayed her same Bigly self like always, no matter how awful I got at her after, as if I truly belonged to her. Nothing in her had changed. Not the way she kept her eyes on me, or her rules, or the way she talked to me or made my eggs. She had stayed all the same. So it couldn't be true, and yet—I looked at her in her earnest eyes, and she was still my Big. She had been, every minute, while I ran around learning kleptomania and ravaging Ducktown and toting guns in my Hello Kitty backpack.

I lay down across the hump between the seats then, and I was bawling my forty-millionth tears of the day with my head in her lap, and she put her soft hands on my head, saying, "Hush, hush, baby," smoothing my hair like she used to back when I was little and had stomach flu a lot. "It's all going to be okay."

Liza had stolen me, and a monster man had touched my boob, and we had found my real mother, and she was a nightmare, and now she'd seen me, and maybe she would try to find me, and Big was pregnant with some baby that could totally replace me and be her own true baby, and any bad thing could happen any second. Any bad thing was possible, and I knew that now, because I'd been in that house and so many bad things had been real and happened.

But Big was still exactly Big.

She kept saying, over and over, "It will all be okay, it will all be okay."

I kept my head in her lap, her hands soothing my hair. I stayed there, being Mosey, my ear pressed up against this new baby she was making, too tiny for it to even have ears and hear me or know me. All at once I had this weird connecting feeling, unspooling like a thread between us. A nice thing. A good thing. That baby, I felt like it was all pressing toward me from inside while Big pressed me close to it from out, and both of us were so very, very Big's.

I was smart enough to understand that this was only a pause.

This was a heartbeat in between a shit storm passed over and a thousand more coming. But it didn't matter. Because this thing she kept saying? That it would all be okay? I knew as long as I had her and she had me, no matter what came next, her words would stay completely true.

CHAPTER TWENTY

Big

I PUT A BRICK through the big stained-glass window at my parents' church once. Not my finest moment, but it seemed like a good idea at the time. I was sixteen, and I'd deposited my settlement check and gotten a secondhand Civic so Liza and I could move the required hundred miles away from her bright-futured father.

I hadn't slept well, and so we'd crept out to my packed-up car and left in the dark hour before the sun came up. The route to the highway took me past Faith First Baptist. I'd grown up in that church, been baptized in its font. My Girl Scout troop had met there, and Mrs. Finch, the organist, had given me piano lessons in the choir room. On the little playground behind the Sunday-school rooms, I'd shared my first dry-lipped, middle-school kiss with Bobby Bossi. I'd thought I would get married there someday and have a fellowship-hall reception with a shrimp tree and a poufy white cake and my mother's sea-foam punch made of ginger ale and sherbet.

After I was showing, I couldn't stand the eyes there, peeking at me sideways with smug pity or staring me down with open outrage. They had an elder meeting to discuss limiting my "influence" on the other youth group girls, though at least three I knew were only baby-free because they knew their way around a condom better than I had. I quit going to services, and they blamed me for that, too. I was clearly lost, they told each other, and it was easier to let me stay like that. Not one church member so much as dropped by to present Liza with an unwrapped pack of diapers or a used receiving blanket. They didn't want to receive her.

As I drove past, I found myself staring at the gigantic stained-glass window that loomed up over the sanctuary. It was a huge, barefoot Jesus with a flowing white robe and long, honey-brown hair. He was stepping through a grapevine arbor, treading on curling leaves and flowers. His pale hands were spread wide, palms open and welcoming. I'd seen him reach toward me a thousand Sunday mornings, as the sun shone through and pushed his colors at me.

But from this side, in the night, he was dark. It occurred to me that even when the sun came up, he would brighten and glow only for the people who were inside that building. The feeble electric bulbs inside could never light him up for the people out here. The ones who had been put out like bad cats. Outside, all Liza and I could hope for was the dark, ass end of Jesus.

I got angry in my hands first. They turned the car in to the church parking lot before the rest of me was feeling anything. Then my head caught up, and I drove to the edge of the lot, as close as I could get to that big window. Liza was sleeping, and I left the engine running so the rumble would keep her that way. I got out and ran across the narrow lawn until I was directly under it.

There was a brick-lined flower bed against the wall of the church, centered under that window. I pulled one of the red, weighty bricks out of the ground and hefted it. I wanted to heave it right through the center of Jesus's white robe. I imagined the tremendous smashing noise, then the glass pinging like chimes off the edge of the baptismal font. When I heard the distant rainfall sound of the pieces pattering onto the carpet, I'd jump in my car and speed away and not look back.

I didn't think about getting caught or how legal fees and repairs might eat up a good chunk of my settlement. I was a kid. I didn't think of consequences much at all. The baby asleep in my backseat was living proof of that. I backed up ten steps, then I reared my arm up and hurled the brick in a hard arc toward that window.

It hit a low, green leaf, dead center, and shattered it. It went right through the pane of glass, but the rest of the window didn't so much as shudder. The metal frame outlining the leaf protected the rest. I was already running for the flower bed, grabbing up another brick, then another, one in each hand. I danced back and hurled them, hard as I could with my skinny girl arms. One cracked Jesus's foot, one bounced harmlessly off another piece of metal frame. Both rebounded, reversing down toward me. I ducked and covered and barely scurried out of the way. I ran to the flower bed, snatched up two more bricks.

Then I stopped, panting. After a minute I set the bricks down. I walked back to my car and drove away, defeated; the thing I was throwing bricks at, it was too big for me, too protected. I couldn't truly hurt it.

I had never again felt so thoroughly outgunned in a fight. Not until I was sitting in that Shell-station parking lot in Montgomery, Alabama, anyway. Mosey, weeping and heaving, clung to me like she had when she was three and scared of under-bed monsters. We'd just come from the place where Liza had stolen her. I hadn't met Mosey's birth parents, or even gone inside the place. I wasn't sure I wanted to. I had seen Mosey's face, and that was enough, along with the neighborhood and the decaying pink house, so neglected it might as well have had a WELCOME TO MY METH LAB sign over the sagging dormers. I had her, though. I had found her and would bring her home. I thought that we were through the worst and everything would be okay.

I told her so, over and over. She'd survived worse already, and now I had her. I told her I would always have her, keep her safe, and she nodded with her face pressed hard into my belly, believing me.

Then over her, through the windshield, I saw a tan-colored Saturn coming off the interstate. I blinked, hard, willing myself to be wrong, but I wasn't. I recognized the car. Even as I patted Mosey's sweat-damp head and promised her that everything would be okay, I was watching Claire Richardson's private detective drive all casual past us on the access road. He turned into the Cracker Barrel parking lot and hid himself behind a big rig.

I sat there with my jaw working up and down like some stupid cud-chewing animal's, purely flummoxed. How could he be pulling off the interstate fifteen minutes after we did? How could he follow me all the way here? The only answer I could come up with seemed too sinister to be true: He must have put something, a kind of tracker, on my car. But that was a thing a private eye might do to folks on television, not to real people in little towns near the beach in Mississippi.

It surely isn't legal, I thought, and then realized how ridiculous that sounded. I was sitting not twenty miles away from the house where Liza had committed grand theft baby, blinking in disbelief to think someone might bug my car.

I'd known I'd have to face Claire Richardson, but I thought I'd have a little more maneuvering room. Claire didn't know who Mosey *was*, only that she wasn't Liza's child with Coach. But I'd led Claire's PI directly to the crumbling pink bungalow. He had seen the place where Mosey came from, so how much time did I have before he went to Claire Richardson and she put all the pieces together? Not a lot, I decided. Not a lot of time at all.

This woman blamed Liza for the death of her baby, for Melissa's drug use and her disappearing act, even for her perverted husband's unfaithfulness. She would have us at her nonexistent mercy, with no reason not to destroy us, not to try to get Liza and me into a world of legal trouble, no reason not to try to use her considerable money and influence to get the state to take Mosey.

That very night Mosey sat between Liza and me on the sofa. I had her snugged up into my armpit, her head on my shoulder, as we watched a *Law & Order* marathon. She was quiet and very, very tired, but she was all right.

I met Liza's eyes over her head and said, "I'm going to have a quick shower. Take care of her?"

Mosey said, "'Kay, Big," thinking I was asking her to watch her mother.

Liza knew better. She'd been stuck at home with Mrs. Lynch, sweating it out while I rushed to Alabama to bring Mosey back from a hell that Liza knew intimately. Thirteen years ago Liza had carried Mosey to me from that same pink house. Now her eyes burned bright into mine, and she nodded, a single, faint, up-and-down motion. I untucked Mosey and passed her into Liza's care. Liza's good arm came up around her, and Mosey relaxed against her, eyes on the television, untroubled.

I went and got the phone and our local directory from my bedside table, and I took them to the bathroom. I turned the shower on for noise cover. I didn't want Mosey to know I was on the phone at all, much less what my business was. I looked up Claire's number and dialed it. She picked up on the second ring, like she'd been waiting for me.

"Hello?" Her cool voice set my spine ashiver.

I felt my skin break out in a sweat from the forced heat of my sudden loathing. This woman had poisoned Liza, poisoned my child, and now she had us in her power. It was unendurable.

"Hello, Claire." I had to work to keep my voice level and quiet.

There was a pause, and then she said, "Ginny Slocumb. Really? You think I want to have a conversation with you?"

I did think so, actually, and she proved it by not hanging up.

"I'd want to talk to me if I were you," I said.

She forced a version of her musical laugh on me, but it sounded sour and flat through the phone. "You are not me. Not even close."

"I know you hired that PI to follow me. I saw him in Montgomery," I said, laying one of my cards flat slap on the table.

There was a surprised pause, and then she said, "Honestly, you can't get good help these days."

"What are you going to do?" I asked.

Another long pause. Unendurable. "I haven't quite decided, to be honest. I have a lot on my plate right now." Sure she did. Winter formal was coming up at Calvary High. She was probably on the streamer committee, trying to decide between blue and silver, and that had to be settled before she could spare a moment to decide whether she should ruin Mosey's life, just to get at what was left of Liza.

"You know if you tell anyone about Mosey, your husband's part in all this will come out, too," I said.

"I hope so. Chief Warfield has certainly been unable to break him. My husband has decided to defend himself by claiming he bedded so many ladies during our marriage he could have fifty little bastards buried all over the state and not know about a one of them. Claims he didn't know half the women's names or where they were from. It's just a tad embarrassing," Claire said, and I could hear acid dripping through the honey in her voice.

I was only half surprised. The DNA test would of course have turned Warfield away from us and onto Coach. Now even a self-blinding champion like Claire couldn't stay in denial about her husband's extramarital perversions. But it sounded like she was giving Liza the lion's share of the blame for her husband's infidelity. Yet another reason to come after us.

"Maybe you don't want to believe he ever cheated on you with anyone except Liza, but even so, Claire. Liza was a child. He could be arrested."

Claire said, brittle, "That would be lovely. At least then I could be sure that my prenup would hold."

I closed my eyes. So she was divorcing him—and blaming Liza for that, too. I said, "I know you hate my daughter, but the person you'll hurt most is a fifteen-year-old girl who never did a thing to you. This road you're on, it's leading someplace bitter. Please. Don't go down it."

I could hear my own voice shaking, but if begging this poisoning bitch was what it would take, I would beg. If she wanted crawling? I could do that, too. She didn't answer, but she didn't hang up. It was as if she were holding the connection to take a sweet little sip of what destroying my family might taste like, decide if it was a drink that she was thirsty for.

"Or what?" she finally said, bored and flat, as if I had made an idle threat instead of pleading. "Why shouldn't I tell the world what a piece of work your daughter is?"

Before I could answer, my other line beeped. I stole a quick glance at the receiver, and it was Lawrence, thank God, Lawrence calling. His friend at the lab must have come through.

On Claire's end she must have heard the beep as a click, because she asked, "Are you recording this?" with her voice gone sharp.

"No," I said.

"I think you are," she said. I said nothing. I heard her breathe in through her nose. "I'm not saying any more. If you wish to finish this conversation, you can meet me in my lawyers' office. Tomorrow, at ten."

"It was my other line," I said. I heard the click of Lawrence going to voice mail.

Her only answer was to rattle off a Pascagoula street address, and then she hung up.

I barely slept that night. I kept getting up to walk the hall, standing in Mosey's doorway, then Liza's, listening to my girls, asleep and breathing sweetly in and out in the dark.

At ten sharp I presented myself like a lamb at the law offices of Gishin, Todd, Sharp and Montblank. A secretary in a crisp linen dress led me back through a wide hallway lined with what looked like actual art. I could see the brushstrokes of oil paint on the canvases. The carpet was so thick that my feet sank into the pile with every step.

She left me at the door of the glass-fronted conference room. I stood on the outside for a minute, looking through the clear wall into the iced-over eyes of Claire Richardson, seated facing me on the far side of a cherrywood table. This was high-stakes poker, and Claire already had a pair of lawyers showing. They sat on either side of her in their black, sleek suits. Their ties alone probably cost more than my car payment.

All I had was the test results Lawrence had left on my voice mail last night and a prop Dixie cup, because the real one was safe at the lab.

It came back to me again then, the outgunned, shoulder-slumping defeat I'd learned while hurling bricks at that huge, impervious Jesus window, his colors shot through with secret steel. Claire was looking at me on the other side of a window now, and her face was as smooth as the face of that glassy Jesus. She was staring me down, her inside, me out, reading defeat in every line of my body and liking it.

Under her gaze, at what felt like the end of everything, I wished for Liza or Lawrence beside me, to take over and be strong for me. Then I thought of Mosey. Saw her in her best dress with its thousand tiny flowers cascading down the print. I thought about someone coming to take her from us, and I felt my shoulders squaring up all on their own. I felt my hands clench, and right then I sure wished I had a brick. Here was a glass wall in front of me I could take out with one blow.

It occurred to me for the first time that I had been wrong about that stained-glass window.

Wrong and foolish. I'd been a child then. I'd crept away in the night with my tail tucked, but as Claire's gaze lapped at my defeat like it was cream, I realized that I'd given up too easy. If I'd wanted it bad enough, I could have stood there throwing and throwing until the flower garden didn't have a single edging brick left, until the sun came up, until every passing driver was a witness. I could have driven into the grass and climbed up on my car roof to loft my bricks higher, to smash his honey-brown locks and break his inward-reaching arms. Before the police arrived to stop me, I could have run back and forth to other flower beds and thrown more bricks until my arms ached. If I'd been willing to take the consequences, I could have gotten every bit of that glass Jesus down.

I shoved the door open, and I walked in fast and angry. I didn't sit. No one spoke. Claire's face looked smooth as paper, and her eyes were alight with a pale blue, ugly triumph. I took a deep breath, and then I dug the Dixie cup out of my purse and slapped it down on the table between us. I'd bought a sleeve of them on the way over. It was the tropical-print pattern with palm trees and monkeys, same as they'd had at the luau. It made a soft, scuffing noise against the wood. The lawyers couldn't have looked less threatened if I'd set a fluffy kitten down in front of them, but one of Claire's eyelids twitched.

I said, "You know what's funny? I came here to beg. But then, right out there, in that hall behind me, I thought to myself, screw it. I'm not going to beg the bitch who poisoned Liza."

Claire's eyebrows shot up. "I never—" And the lawyer on the right, the older one, put his hand over hers again, stopping her.

"Fine. It wasn't poison," I acknowledged. "That's good, actually, because it would be harder to connect you to something everyone has in their garden shed to kill the mice. You slipped her your diet pills in that drink. Phentermine. You gave amphetamines to a former meth addict, Claire. It may not have been poison, but your intentions were not good."

Her face stayed carefully neutral, and the younger lawyer said, "It's a very common drug." His tone was so flat he almost sounded bored.

"Sure it is," I said to him, "but I bet anything your skinny-ass client has a prescription for it." Claire stayed carefully blank, but the younger lawyer's eyes twitched toward Claire and away in a lightning glance. I had scored with him, so I sent my next words his way. "Did you know that Liza was blackmailing your client into paying Mosey's tuition at Calvary? I bet a forensic accountant could trace that money. That's her motive. She hoped to knock Liza off the wagon and get her out of town, and it was just sauce and gravy for her that instead she almost killed her. She had the motive, the prescription gave her means, and at the luau she damn well had the opportunity. How many people in this town can hit that trifecta?"

Claire snorted. "Quite a few of the ladies, I'd imagine. The married ones. Your daughter has a taste for other people's husbands."

"And who set her mouth?" I said. "She was a child. Your pedophile husband put his hands—"

Claire sat bolt upright and went even paler, yelling over me, "Your slut daughter seduced him! She wrecked my marriage and—"

"—on a fourteen-year-old child!" I finished.

"Enough," the older lawyer said, loud and authoritative. Claire and I both stopped talking, breathing hard. He turned to me. "Oh, I didn't mean you, Ms. Slocumb. You go ahead. I'll take notes and begin building our nice civil suit for slander against you."

"Please, bring it," I snapped back. "It's not slander if it's true."

His lips flattened into a grim, closed smile. "It's not slander if you can *prove* it's true. That's an entirely different thing." He wafted a lazy hand at my prop cup. "What you have is circumstantial at best."

I turned back to Claire. "You need to stop this overinterest in my family. It was one thing when you thought the bones under the willow might be your child. Of course you had to know. But they weren't. It is all only and ever my family's private business."

Claire started to speak, but I cut her off.

"Understand me clearly here. If you go forward, I will trumpet everything I know about you from the rooftops. Everything. I will tell anyone who will stand still for half a minute that you are a murderous bitch, that you couldn't deal with the fact that you married a pervert, even though you believed it enough to shell out blackmail money. I will tell everyone how you poisoned my child to keep all your filthy secrets. If Liza and I go to jail, I don't care, and if you sue me for slander and take everything I own, I do not care. Because Mosey will stay mine. I raised her up into who she is, and nothing you can do now, all these years later, can truly take her. Call the state, scream kidnapping, see if you can get her carted off. She'll come right back to me, and the slow way the courts grind, by the time you get it done properly, she'll likely be twenty and off at college. As for me? If you start? I will go into all manner of debt, I will drag my feet and countersue and muddy the waters and haul your name through every patch of dog shit I can find. Come after us. I will ruin your life with this, and if it ruins mine, too, I do not care. All I have to do is stall you less than three years, and then we win. Do you really want to spend the next three years of your life thinking of nothing but Liza and everything you've lost, every minute, every day, and hear your vilest secret business whispered through the halls of your fine church every Sunday?"

Then I stopped talking. I was done. I spread my hands and shrugged.

Claire sank back down in her chair, looking at me like I was a stranger, someone or even something she'd never seen before. Maybe she hadn't. It was hard to read her, since the chemicals wiped a lot of whatever she was feeling from her face. Finally, though, I saw her throat shift, up and down, in a dry swallow. I let loose a long, slow exhale.

The older lawyer started to speak, but Claire held up a single hand and stopped him.

"Okay, then," I said. "You take care, now."

I left the cup where I had set it, and I simply walked away.

I came out of that office into the warm September air. The smell of fall was rising in it, making it sweet and crisp along the edges. I breathed it in, and it was like drawing my first breath. Claire Richardson would do whatever she would do. It was out of my hands. I would take whatever came, but only when it came. If not Claire, then another kind of trouble was sure to find us, one day, always, so there was no sense cowering around and worrying. Today was a good day, and I wasn't going to waste it.

While I was here, I might as well stop and get myself a membership at the Pascagoula YMCA. They had an indoor pool. Then I'd go through Moss Point on my way home, and I would stop at Lawrence's apartment. November be damned. This baby wouldn't stop knitting itself together to appease the paperwork and make it more convenient for us. Right now, today, this baby needed at least one parent who hadn't committed any felonies.

I would tell Lawrence to take a sick day and bring him home with me, fix him lunch in my kitchen. We could use the netbook Mosey had unearthed to research ways to rehab Liza. There would be time for all the big confessions later, when I had a ring on my finger and Lawrence couldn't be held liable or be compelled to testify against me. After we were married, it would be safe to hand him even my worst secrets, and I knew he would help me carry them. But today would be simpler. Today I only had to tell him I was pregnant.

He would be shocked. Scared, maybe. Probably a little disbelieving. That was okay. Men take longer to process these things. I would hold him, put his hands on me, and his shock would fade into surprise. After that, there would be joy. I would watch the joy rise in his face, and I would take him back to the people I loved best in the world, and we would all be together.

Nothing else mattered. I'd hold my family to me, all of them, as hard and as long and as close as I could. I would take today's joy, and tomorrow's. I would take it with both hands, anywhere it came.

CHAPTER TWENTY-ONE

Liza

LIZA IS WEIGHTLESS in the water, but she is no longer adrift. It is free swim at the Pascagoula YMCA, and the pool is churning with rowdy children. Liza, Big, and Mosey have a clear slice of water where they can work, though. The staff and the regulars are used to seeing them. They say, "Here's the girls," and "Go, Liza!" and make space for them each day. They are rooting for her.

"Let's try some squats!" Big says. She is on Liza's weaker side, her hand firm on the belt around her waist.

"You squat," Liza says, bitter, and Big chuckles in her ear, delighted at how clearly the muttered words come out.

"You're not tired!" Everything Big says when they work at the Y comes with a perky exclamation point.

Liza isn't fooled. Underneath her lip gloss and her rah-rah cheer, Big is rock-hard and implacable. She forces ceaseless rounds in the heated pool, unending streams of picture cards, questions and answers that go on until Liza's brain is pulsing like a tired jellyfish. Big reads therapy books and watches YouTube videos and is willing to try anything. She is never satisfied. There must be one more step, one more word, one more squeeze from her weak fingers. Liza wants to bite her, would bite her, except that her routine is working.

Liza squats, so tired that even her good knee is atremble. She dips down low into the water, sinking into it, and Mosey, already in a half squat, goes deeper to stay with her.

Mosey says, "That's great! You are so great! Keep going!" She is as fraught with hope and exclamation points as Big, as willful as Liza, and this damn sincere on her own, because she is Mosey.

Liza, tired and grumpy as she is, leans sideways into her to catch a whiff of her orange-zest shampoo. Mosey's tucked under Liza's stronger arm. She has a good four inches on Liza, so she has to bend into a slim, storky bird shape and mince along beside with her long legs folded. But she never misses an afternoon session.

"You squat," Liza says again, exhaling it quietly, like it is a curse. Mosey's presence makes her hold back several other suggestions for things, fouler than squatting, that Big should do.

She can practice those darker words on Big tomorrow morning, when Mosey is at school, along with regular ones like "soup" and "run" and "grass" and "round." The words come back slow and limping, but they come home to her all the same. Her noun-verb pairs are expanding, growing modifiers, budding into clauses.

Bogo comes... hopefully. Liza walks... farther every day. Big demands... and needs a good, hard pinch.

In a few more months, when winter gives into spring, Lawrence will fill their new backyard pool. They can work at home then, even longer sessions. For now they come to the Y every day, and when Big gets too unwieldy, Lawrence says he will take her place. He will hold Liza's belt, and Big can call instructions poolside, swishing her feet back and forth in the water with her rounded belly resting on her lap.

It's good. All these things are good. Even so, Liza hasn't forgotten that it wasn't love that saved her.

Not that Liza's putting love down. She's grateful to it, even. Love has saved Mosey a thousand times already, and Big is using it to save her more, every day. Love is saving Big, too, though she and Lawrence are still doing what Lawrence calls "negotiating" and Big calls "Jesus nagging" about where or if or how they are going to church this boy child that Big is making.

Liza understands, but she understands it outside, looking in. Love has never been her currency, while Big and Mosey, both of them, are soaked in it. They have so much it spills out and makes more. There is plenty for her, for Lawrence, for the little boy on the way, for Patti Duckins, who is there every other minute with Roger. Big's teeny house is bulging with it, and Lawrence is converting the carport to more house and adding a bathroom. There is enough love even for Bogo, who takes it as his due now. Every day that passes, in that great mercy that God affords good dogs, Bogo forgets that he once had a different life.

Liza doesn't forget. Love came for them and saved them, and they live so steeped in it that it blinds them. They don't see the truth that Liza learned in Alabama, where Janelle still sits in her rotting pink house, dying a little more every day, waiting for Liza to send the next photo of Mosey.

This is what Liza knows: People go under. They fall off the world, they go beneath and drown and die. Sometimes nothing saves you.

But fuck it, she's still here. She is a living thing, with twelve pins now pressed into the tree-house oak in the backyard and a thirteenth coming. She will earn more, and she will push them into the oak for Ann, her lost child, named at last. Ann, by the quiet act of staying nameless in the world, is doing what big sisters do: She's looking out for Mosey. Liza knows that Big hopes to someday safely claim her and give her a real funeral, but Liza remembers that first burial all too well. Never again. Liza likes to think of Ann where she is, a tiny sentinel who keeps Mosey safe as long as her name stays secret. She is clean and cared for in a bright white place, above ground, that Liza imagines stays bathed in gold light.

Liza will push the pins in for this foundling Moses girl, too, who is even now tucked close to her. And for Big and Lawrence and the new, small person who is inventing himself inside of Big. But mostly she will push the pins into the tree because she has to win. She has to rise and relearn her pleasure in the taste of apples, and swimming naked in salt water, and a man's eyes appreciating her fine ass, and blowing farty noises into the coming baby's round belly, and good books, and French kissing. Liza will reclaim the two-sided smile that Mosey remembers.

It's coming. She can feel it coming as her face wakes up along with the rest of her, slowly, bit by bit. She will push until she relearns it, and then she will keep on pushing, because Liza knows how black the world is, how fast it spins, and how you have to take the taste of apples and the smell of your little girl's orange-zest shampoo where you find them. You have to hold these things and strive, always, for one more word and one more step. You push forward and you fight, for as long as ever you can, until the black world spins and the moon pulls the tide and the water rises up and takes you.

Big says, "Super! Let's get you out and changed. Then we can go home and do some flash cards."

The three of them go forward, crossing the pool. The children part for them, splashing and yelling with the joy of indoor swimming while, outside, the air is chilled by a mild Mississippi winter. They wade out, Mosey, then Liza, then Big, in a chain. Big is on her weak side, where Big has always been, shoring her up. Mosey is tucked against her strong side, sheltered and balancing her. They come to the shallows and mount the steps together, rising from the water. Liza steps onto the land, held between them in this moment, safe and whole.

Reading Group Guide

DISCUSSION QUESTIONS

1. One of the opening scenes in *A Grown-Up Kind of Pretty* depicts Tyler Baines chopping down the Slocumb willow tree. What does this tree symbolize for Big? For Liza? For Mosey?

2. On page 70, Mosey realizes she isn't who she thought she was. At first, she feels liberated. Then she feels confused and lost. How is she like Liza and Big? What makes her different? Do you think a child takes on traits like compassion, humor, and good sense from her biological parents, or do you think that she learns these from the people who raise her?

3. Several men in this novel cheat on their spouses (Coach, Lawrence), but the women cheat on one another in a different way. What kind of emotional betrayals show up in their friendships, and in their families? Who do you think is the most loyal person in this story?

4. Though Liza and Melissa were inseparable when they were young, Big believes that Noveen was a better friend to Liza

than Melissa ever was. Patti turns out to be a wonderful friend to Mosey. What have the Duckins women given to Liza and Mosey? How was Melissa different?

5. One theme in *A Grown-Up Kind of Pretty* is belonging. On page 224, Big says, "Bogo wasn't the only stray that Mosey had adopted for us all recently." Who do you think are the "strays" in this story? When do they find a home?

6. When Mosey enters Liza's tree house and sees her old Moomin books covered in Magic Marker, she says, "If I had doubted for a second this place was Liza's, I didn't doubt now" (p. 245). Have you ever found a secret place or a secret box that belonged to someone you love? What part of this person did you find there?

7. Was Big smart to keep the details of her family crisis from Lawrence? If she had shared more with him, do you think he could have helped her, or protected Mosey?

8. Did Liza do the right thing by taking Mosey from her mother when she was small? Would you still feel that way if Mosey had been a Duckins or a Richardson instead? Why?

9. Big and Liza are determined to keep Mosey from getting too close to boys. Do you think they're overreacting? What would you do to keep your daughter from making the same mistakes you made?

10. When something bad happens, Big, Liza, and Mosey often respond with action—though sometimes their approaches aren't quite ethical. Does Liza break Lawrence's ex-wife's plates on purpose, or was it an accident? Did you enjoy it a little, since

Sandy cheated on Lawrence and lashed out at Big? Do you think Claire Richardson was at all justified in her attacks on Liza? On Big? Do you blame her less because she lost both her daughters? Though it was wrong of Big to throw bricks at the church's windows, do you think it was justified, given how she was treated by the church community? How does knowing the pain each character has been through change the way you respond to her actions?

THE SOUTH HAS CHANGED, THE SOUTH REMAINS THE SAME: AN INTERVIEW WITH JOSHILYN JACKSON

by Lydia Netzer

Lydia Netzer: I've lived in Virginia for ten years now, but I don't say "y'all," and I don't care about football. Do you think some people are more susceptible to Southernization than others?

Joshilyn Jackson: Yes. Children. The younger the better. You don't have to be born down here to be southern, but a goodly portion of your formative years have to be spent soaking in it.

Also, understand when I talk about the South—I mean *my* South. I am talking mostly about the blue-collar, small-town South. There are a lot of ways to be southern. We are rife with subculture. There is, for example, a whole 'nother Birmingham inside of Birmingham. You have to be born into it. You can't join it. If you are southern and outside of it, you can recognize it when you brush past it, but there's no getting in. I am not terribly interested in it—I do not understand its priorities—but it has a sub-subculture full of people knocking hopefully at its thick, oak doors.

It has more in common with some parts of Manhattan than anything else in Alabama, even though I doubt anyone in this secret Birmingham—or anyone in those parts of Manhattan—would see or admit to the similarities.

So, the small-town, blue-collar South. No, you can't become it. I honestly don't think of Southern-ness as a conversion experience. We save those for Jesus down here. But I do think there is some natural culture leak.

Narrative nonfiction author Karen Abbott moved south when her husband got a job here. After three or four years, she started saying "y'all"...in a Philly accent. It was extremely charming, this bizarre juxtaposition, and sort of a metaphor, I think, for what we are discussing. She may have gotten some Southern on her, but I am not convinced she got a lot all the way down in her.

LN: Let's talk about your characters in context. Big is a very southern woman, but Liza leaves her hometown to travel all around during her wild years, and Mosey is a teenager caught up with pop culture slang and behavior to an extent that makes her more "American" than "southern." Do they represent a changing southern culture?

JJ: Absolutely. There is definitely a homogenization thing going on. My third-grade quasi-rural southern daughter says, "What up, yo?" with zero irony. Zero. I boggle at this.

Big and Mosey live at either end of the book's generational spectrum. Big speaks Southern. Her sentence structure, her idioms, her word choices, the imagery she employs, her metaphors—they all reflect her heritage. Mosey's slang all comes from the Internet, from texting, from TV and movies and commercials. Her speech patterns are less southern as well.

I wanted these two voices to reflect the way regionalism is dissolving as every place becomes like every other place. Technology and big business have turned the heat up to eleven under the melting pot. You and I live several states away from each other, and yet we can go into the same restaurant and get the exact same crappy chicken sandwich. In the last ten years, my once-small town has bloomed into suburbia. We were infected by Wal-Marts (three of them), and chain restaurants erupted on every corner. Now our quirky little junk shop and weird, café-laden downtown is all but dead. Atlanta is reaching out toward us and my son, who talked like Opie when he was three, doesn't even use the contraction "y'all" now that he is fourteen.

I remember when I moved to Chicago, I could recognize a fellow ex-pat Southerner in about four seconds. It was a heartening thing. A little flash of home to a stranger in a strange land. And sure, I have a love-hate relationship with the South, This is a bloody piece of country. But it was our bloody piece of country, and we could trade glances and know we shared that weird love-shame thing for our part of the big earth. Also, moving to Chicago made the world bigger to me, and the cultural differences helped me define myself and my homeland. That process really shaped who I am as a writer.

I question if my kids will have that same experience when they go off to college. I am pretty sure my grandkids won't.

LN: Why do you think that southern fiction is attractive reading to people who don't come from the South? Even if they can't possibly "get it," what do you think draws in readers to this milieu that they can't really get elsewhere? When you read a novel set in New York City, for example, do you experience the same kind of foreignness that a Yankee would find in a novel about rural Georgia?

JJ: Well, we are a people who have held on to the oral tradition. We are storytellers. And I do think our ambivalence toward home makes for an ongoing conflict that is there as a constant backdrop.

I remember a friend who said she was going to write a true southern novel that didn't deal with race issues, Jesus, or mention Elvis. When she was done, race relations and Jesus were on every other page, and Elvis was in the title. So...

I don't think you need to be southern to love our writing. I like to read novels set in London, India, Middle Earth, and 1862. Reading across culture can even let you have a better conversation with the book.

I do feel a kind of foreignness when I read a novel about a different place. But I think that's kind of great. It's just a different setting, and I think that being someplace unfamiliar lets us look at what I think all novels are exploring on some level: the nuts-and-bolts ugly business of being human. We all have expiration dates. We can make more humans with our bodies. We can think in terms of eternity.

One of the challenging things about trying to write the South is, I can't do it in a literal way. I can't put anything real in. All the places where my editor tells me I have to pull back because I have gone "over the top" are the exact places that are most closely aligned with my real life. Truth is stranger than fiction, and southern truth is even stranger than that.

LN: How can regionalism be preserved, and should it be preserved? Is it a writer's responsibility to keep finding the specificity and "otherness" of her own region? Or is southern fiction destined to become historical fiction?

JJ: I wouldn't call it a responsibility, but it's something you can do with the work. It's a choice, and I would even argue it's a noble choice. It's one of my constant goals, to nail down the enraging, amazing South I know. Perhaps motivation is a better word? It is a large part of the why.

I write because story is how I explain the world to myself; for me, a novel is a way to examine—not answer—the questions that have shaped my life and my choices: What is home? How do you get there? How do you define motherhood? How does motherhood define you? How far away can you wander into the black and still stagger into a moment of redemption? How can grace find you? How does faith define you? Does love win?

But I set these explorations in my homeland in part because, yes, I want to capture this culture on paper before it gets away.

I think this is why I set *gods in Alabama* and *Backseat Saints* in the 1980s and 1990s. That was before the Internet happened to my blue-collar South. There were also so many interesting things going on in terms of the generational racism happening—where you had a generation of New South people growing up seeing the injustice, choosing a different way of living and raising their kids, but still deeply loving and being grateful to these older, incredibly racist relatives. How do you come to terms with loving another human being, being grateful to that human being who helped raise you, but at the same time finding huge chunks of their worldview abhorrent?

Will this South die? I don't know. Probably. Eventually. It isn't my job to preserve it or even care that it is preserved. For me, it is a lot less about preservation than it is about documenting the experience of who we are we are right now, as a people. As that changes, southern writing changes. As the South changes, how writers capture and preserve those moments will change.

I don't know what we will become and gain or what will be lost as the technology takes these huge exponential leaps. When I met you, the Internet had just happened. Only rich people had cell phones, and they were huge, unwieldy, ugly things. Technology isn't changing just southern culture. It's changing us as a species, I think. That's going to be amazing to watch.

Yes, I am interested in using the now as a backdrop to explore the themes that interest me, and catching the flavor of this world.

I'm also interested as all get-out in what comes next. I think Mosey is a reflection of that interest, and in *A Grown-Up Kind of Pretty*, she is only fifteen. I want to see the person she grows into, the New South she gets to inhabit and shape and become. And yeah, I want to tell those stories, too.